Grantley F. Berkeley

My Life and Recollections

Vol. 1

Grantley F. Berkeley

My Life and Recollections

Vol. 1

Reprint of the original, first published in 1865.

1st Edition 2022 | ISBN: 978-3-75258-914-6

Verlag (Publisher): Salzwasser Verlag GmbH, Zeilweg 44, 60439 Frankfurt, Deutschland
Vertretungsberechtigt (Authorized to represent): E. Roepke, Zeilweg 44, 60439 Frankfurt, Deutschland
Druck (Print): Books on Demand GmbH, In de Tarpen 42, 22848 Norderstedt, Deutschland

MY LIFE AND RECOLLECTIONS.

BY

THE HON. GRANTLEY F. BERKELEY.

IN TWO VOLUMES.

VOL. I.

LONDON

1865.

CONTENTS

OF

THE FIRST VOLUME.

CHAPTER I.

BERKELEY CASTLE.

The shrubbery gate at Berkeley Castle—My nurse and her husband—The Berkeley influence—Strength and antiquity of the Castle—Earl Godwin and the nunnery—The witch of Berkeley—Feuds of the Saxon Berkeleys and Danish Fitz-Hardinges—Murder of Edward II.—Royal entertainments—Queen Elizabeth's visit and Leicester's enmity—Surrender of the Castle to Sir Thomas Fairfax—Customs of the Berkeleys, their duties and privileges—Feudal laws for the preservation of Game—Domestic expenses and arrangements—Dress—Fools—Value of the Berkeley estates—An extraordinary instrument—My father attacked by a deer—Canvassing at the Castle—The Duke of Sussex out shooting—The Prince of Wales and the Lady of the Old School—The Duke of Clarence and the Gloucestershire Foxhunter—Lynch law—Sir Samuel Wathen—My father's death—Colonel Berkeley's pretensions to his Estates .   .   . 1

CHAPTER II.

THE PEERAGE AND COLONEL BERKELEY.

The late Earl of Berkeley—His introduction to Miss Cole and to her sisters—His admiration of Miss Mary Cole—Their sons born before wedlock—He eventually marries her—Endeavours to es-

VOL. I.   *b*

tablish a prior marriage—Inquiry before the Committee of the House of Lords in 1795—His death, and will for the aggrandizement of the elder children, born previous to marriage, at the expense of the others—The eldest son claims the peerage—Examination of witnesses before a Committee of the House of Lords in 1810-11—Remarkable evidence—Speech of the Lord Chancellor—Unanimous decision against the claimant—"Appeal to the House of Peers"—"The B——y family narrative"—Education of Colonel Berkeley—Unjustifiable conduct—His taste for low society—His influence over his mother and Thomas Moreton, the present Earl of Berkeley—His craft and caution in disguising it, and non-appearance in any proceedings which were suggested by him to support his claim—Fondness for amateur acting 29

CHAPTER III.

BRIGHTON.

Brighthelmstone—Building the Pavilion—Mrs. Fitzherbert and her alleged marriage with the Prince of Wales—Irish friends—Colonel Hanger—Lord Barrymore—Sheridan—Colonel M'Mahon—Lady Clermont and her laced tea—My father's regiment of militia—L'enfant terrible—"I've seen the cook"—Profane swearing—The Prince of Wales and Lady Haggerstone—Lady Nagle and her heart—A colonel in a rage—Mother Shipton's prophecy—The Prince's harriers—Pugilistic encounter of his Royal Highness with the Brighton butcher, Jackson, the prizefighter—Fashionable ladies at Brighton—Changes—Decay of the Pavilion—Brighton races—A love mission . . 49

CHAPTER IV.

BERKELEY HOUSE, SPRING GARDENS.

Power of the Berkeleys, Berkeley Square, Spring Gardens—Berkeley House—Elopement of my aunt, Lady Georgiana, with Lord Forbes—My aunt, the Margravine of Anspach and Princess of Berkeley—Private theatricals—My father's friends and contemporaries—Watt Smith, brother of Mrs. Fitzherbert—Sir Philip Francis—The Duke of Clarence's account of Lord Grantley—His practical joke at my expense—Mrs. Fitzherbert—Enormous amount of jewellery presented to her by the Prince of Wales—Gillray's caricatures, in which she is represented—

CONTENTS.

vii

Quarrel of the editor of the "Keepsake" with Count D'Orsay
—I make them friends—Bernal—His tricks on Mansel Rey-
nolds—Insult offered to Lady Mary Berkeley—Demolition of
Berkeley House 78

CHAPTER V.

CRANFORD HOUSE.

Ancient residence of the Berkeleys at Cranford—My ancestors—
Colonel Berkeley after the trial—Arrival at my mother's dower
house—My brother Moreton and the dancing-master—Our
instructors and attendants—Sir Thomas Bell—An unexpected
demonstration—Pugilism, how it came into fashion—Pierce
Egan and "Tom and Jerry"—My brother Augustus—His idea
of sport, and delight in a row—My tutor, Mr. Hughes—
Riding—My first fall—Arrival of my brother Henry—His
love of boxing—Charles Wyndham—My fistic combats—Lord
Grantley—My affection for my brother Moreton—Lord Munster
and the Fitzclarences—Departure of my favourite brother for
college 96

CHAPTER VI.

SANDHURST AND THE COLDSTREAM GUARDS.

My brothers at college—Moreton plucked—Returns to the university and passes his examination—I am sent to Sandhurst—State
of that establishment—Wanting a piano—Bullying—Rough
sports—Sir Alexander Hope and Colonel Butler—Teasing the
French master—An unlucky shot—The Duke of Kent—My
unexpected answer to his inquiry—Sergeant Hutton—A boy's
affections—Love of poetry—I leave Sandhurst—Wear the Prince
of Wales's uniform—My devotion to Colonel Berkeley—The
Prince presents me with a commission in the Guards—Doing
duty at Carlton Palace—The lost drummer—Dinner to the
Duke of Gloucester—Battersea Red House—Tricks of my
brother officers—George Bentinck—Taking leave of absence—
Riding races—Beau Brummel and the Prince of Wales . 127

CHAPTER VII.

HORSES AND HOUNDS.

Skeletons at Berkeley—My first shot—Scattering the pigeons—
Grumbo—Among the blossoms—My first poacher—Officers

viii   CONTENTS.

from the cavalry barracks at Hounslow—Hammersley—A retort
discourteous—Value of a horsedealer's recommendation—Filial
affection—Mr. Frogley of Hounslow—My presentation at
Court—Getting leave of absence—My brother Moreton's signature—Counsellor Fonblanque—Serjeant Vaughan—Legal
advice—Deer hunting—My horse Brutus—Lords Alvanley
and Rokeby—Remarkable jumps—Colonel Standon of the
Guards—Earl of Cardigan—Duke of St. Albans—Hon. Charles
Tollemache—Jack O'Lantern—Hampton Court Balls—Duke
of Clarence—Cricket Club—Lord George Seymour—Receiving
a Royal Duke   153

CHAPTER VIII.

HIGHWAYMEN AND GHOSTS.

Cranford conveniently situated for tales of terror—Heroes of the
road—The flying highwayman and the Irishman—Bow Street
runners performing an artful dodge—Captain Hawkes' celebrated mare—Honour among thieves—The last Lord Coleraine
—The ghost I and my brother Moreton saw at Cranford—The
ghost seen by my father—Hounslow Heath—My father kills
a highwayman—His retort to Lord Chesterfield—Changes at
Hounslow Heath—Sleep-walking—Lord Berkeley saved from
shooting his sister, Lady Granard, by the intelligence of his
dog—Ladies' pets—Admiral Prescott and my father's pointer—
Captain Cracraft and the pheasants   196

CHAPTER IX.

SPORTING ADVENTURES.

My guests at Cranford—The Duke of St. Albans' arrangement for
saving himself trouble—Duke of York—His skill in shooting—
Lord Grantley's method of shooting partridges—Liston, the
comedian—Dowton, his stage directions—Private theatricals
at Boscombe—A large love-lock—Sir Percy Shelley—Varley,
the Astrologer—His predictions—His astonishment at beholding a hunting party—Cause of poaching—Woodland scenes
—Catching a pike—Salmon fishing—The otter and water-rat
—A midnight adventure—Stealing rushes—Practice of
poachers   227

CONTENTS.   ix

CHAPTER X.

TOWN TALK.

Forced marriages—Advantages of a young Guardsman—A man to be avoided—" Beware ! she is fooling you !"—" Kitty" and her traducer—A party at the Star and Garter, Richmond—An imaginary elopement—Almack's as it used to be—Education of a beauty—Danger from male teachers—A desirable marriage —Lady —— and the loose prints—The royal guest and his awkward question—Extravagance and dissipation—Difference between Lord Augustus and Tomkins—" O, 'tis Love !" .   247

CHAPTER XI.

RECREATIONS IN HIGH LIFE.

Imitations of stage-coachmen—Members of the old Four-in-hand Club—Lord Rokeby—Count D'Orsay at " The Ship" at Greenwich—His character and fate—Returning with an omnibus— An attempted extortion foiled—Colonel M'Kinnon and the hackney coachmen—His novel way of entering a convent— Changes in St. James's Park—Lord Malmesbury—Beau Brummel in an asylum—Defence of the Prince of Wales— Kindness of the Royal Dukes—Brummel's flunkeyism—The Kembles not knowing the difference between Shakspeare and Bernard M'Nally—Duke of Norfolk in a cockpit—Patrons of cock-fighting—Conduct of Count de Salis—Police interference —I am summoned to appear before a magistrate—My public declaration against Count de Salis—A ludicrous arrest—Committed to the treadmill—Judge Talfourd   .   .   . 267

CHAPTER XII.

HUNTING THE HARROW COUNTRY.

I determine to leave the Coldstreams—Colonel M'Kinnon offers himself as a friend—His shabby conduct—Military laws—I keep a pack of hounds at Cranford—Yates the Comedian at a dinner-party—My deer—Lord Alvanley and Gunter the pastrycook—Sir George Wombwell and the farmer—Mr. Fermor pursued for trespassing—My fracas with the farmer's men— The trial for assault and trespass—Brougham my counsel— Scarlett's remark on Cauty the auctioneer—Jeames in a diffi-

culty—The seat of honour—Excessive demands for damages—
Lord Tavistock and the Oakley Club—Negotiations for my
hunting the Oakley country—Adieu to Cranford—My deer
attacked by Eton bargemen—The scholars come to my rescue
—Taking a prisoner—Stag-hunting in Montague Place—A
deer in a boudoir—Pugnacious turnpike man—He catches a
Tartar 291

CHAPTER XIII.

THE OAKLEY HUNT.

My residence at Harrold Hall—My pack and whips—Cub-hunting
—Ill-feeling in the Club—My first season in Bedfordshire—
Mr. S. Whitbread a leader of the malcontents—A hard run—
My horse Ready—The round robin—Memorial in my favour—
The second season—Mr. Whitbread's opposition—Hostile cor-
respondence—Lord Clanricarde acts as my second—A reference
to Mr. Fysche Palmer—A Jesuitical reply from a Bishop—
Thesiger's retort—My whipper-in taken by the Duke of Grafton,
but fails to secure the sport he had with my hounds . . 320

CHAPTER XIV.

IN PARLIAMENT.

Colonel Berkeley resolves to be a peer—His secret arrangement
with the Whig Government—Induces me to enter Parliament
—I am returned for the Western Division of Gloucestershire—
Faucit corrected in costume—Lord Edward Somerset—Absurdities of canvassing—Colonel Berkeley ennobled as Baron
Segrave—Withholds my allowance—Lord William Lennox and
his tricks—Lord Segrave—Letting a box—Miss Paton—Daniel
O'Connell and his beagles—Mr. Disraeli—Mr. Charlton's
maiden speech—Sir Robert Peel's effective elocution—Mr. Cob-
bett's futile attack on the statesman—My motion to admit
ladies into the gallery—Mr. Maurice O'Connell kisses the
Dowager Duchess of Richmond by mistake—Objections to ladies
in the House—Piece of plate presented to me by them—A new
idea to insure their admission into the gallery—How defeated
—Mr. John Bright—His committee to inquire into the Game
Laws—His Quaker witness confuted—Committee on slavery—
Cobden's opinion of his friend Bright quoted by me in the
House 341

CHAPTER XV.

DOINGS AT BERKELEY CASTLE.

Lord Segrave's compact with the Whig Government—Returns four members for the county, and is created an Earl—My influence for him and with him—Miss Foote and Mrs. Bunn at Berkeley Castle—Lord Fitzhardinge at this period—Sir George Wombwell—Accident to a valuable horse—My successful interposition —My brother Admiral Berkeley's serious fall in the hunting field —Lady Charlotte sent for at my request—Reports about the goings-on at the Castle—Paul Methuen's parting with his host —Lord Fitzhardinge and the Severn Pilot—The Bristol mayor and his offensive speech—Sir Alexander Leith Hay cooking— He becomes my second and exacts an apology—Affairs of honour in which I acted as second—Lord Macdonald, Lord Albemarle, and Mr. Drax (member for Wareham)—Sir Alexander Hood— Captain Berkeley and Squire Osbaldeston .　.　.　. 370

MY LIFE AND RECOLLECTIONS.

CHAPTER I.

BERKELEY CASTLE.

The shrubbery gate at Berkeley Castle — My nurse and her
husband—The Berkeley influence—Strength and antiquity of
the Castle—Earl Godwin and the nunnery—The witch of
Berkeley—Feuds of the Saxon Berkeleys and Danish Fitz-
Hardinges—Murder of Edward II.—Royal entertainments—
Queen Elizabeth's visit and Leicester's enmity—Surrender of
the Castle to Sir Thomas Fairfax—Customs of the Berkeleys,
their duties and privileges—Feudal laws for the preservation of
Game—Domestic expenses and arrangements—Dress—Fools
—Value of the Berkeley estates—An extraordinary instrument—My father attacked by a deer—Canvassing at the Castle
—The Duke of Sussex out shooting—The Prince of Wales and
the Lady of the Old School—The Duke of Clarence and the Gloucestershire Foxhunter—Lynch law—Sir Samuel Wathen—My
father's death—Colonel Berkeley's pretensions to his Estates.

My first recollection of a date points to the year 1806,
for it was on a certain day in this year that Mary
Oldacre, my nurse, after I had brought to her the
keys of the shrubbery gate at Berkeley Castle,
reminded me that it was my birthday, and that I was
six years old. It is impossible to express the affection
with which, at this age and long subsequently, I
regarded this most faithful and attached servant. She

VOL. I.   B was afterwards married to the butler at the castle, who had raised himself to that post from the humble position of nursery boy; and they became a pair of confidential domestics such as no amount of wages, no prospect of perquisites, could secure in the present day.

Mary was quite as devoted to me as I was attached to her—indeed, the relations of foster-mother and foster-child were never more powerfully exhibited than in our case. Both these servants are indissolubly connected with my earliest and pleasantest recollections; and in the churchyard, through which they so often led me by the hand, they share the sleep of eternal peace. I do not remember what is their epitaph; but I cannot refer to them here without recording my sense of their worth and fidelity.

I regarded the opening of that shrubbery gate as a manly achievement, and whenever after we walked that way, the keys were given to me to repeat the successful operation; even now—well do I recollect the shout of childish triumph I raised as the gate opened—nor less earnest was the cry of exultation with which the dear soul who had charge of me, recognised my prowess. In reminding me of my age, she intimated her conviction that no one of my contemporaries could have done as much.

The incident is of course puerile; but it is to me a most important aid to memory. It enables me to establish with all the certainty of a parish register, that I am exactly as old as the century, and secures to me a retrospection of nearly sixty years. Haydn's Dictionary of Dates is, I have no doubt, a reliable

THE BERKELEY INFLUENCE.

authority, but for all the purposes of this work, I prefer referring to honest Mary Oldacre, and with her unquestionable statement, therefore, I commence these Recollections of my career in the great world.

At about the beginning of the present century, Berkeley Castle was still regarded as one of the most interesting structures in the county, partly on account of its historical associations, partly from its having remained in possession of an unbroken male line. Its extent necessitated the maintenance of a large establishment, and this made a considerable revenue indispensable. The estate attached to it produced a princely income—the dairy and orchard farms of the Vale of Berkeley being some of the most valuable in the county—and the hospitality and liberality of successive lords of Berkeley kept up the old feudal residence in all its pride and power.

The proprietors of the castle naturally possessed considerable political influence, which in those " good old days" had been exerted, as was the case with the other governing families, in advancing their own interests ; but, as these were connected by the closest ties with the interests of subordinate families, whose interests were as intimately connected with their dependants, the benefits thus derived became so generally diffused that the Berkeley influence was believed to be a state of things that ought to be maintained; and at every general election this impression gave the power, whether exerted or not, of returning a certain number of connexions or friends of the family as members of the House of Commons.

ANGLO-SAXON NUNNERY.

My father, the fifth earl, was not desirous of lessening the importance of the Berkeleys in their own county; indeed, my earliest recollections are full of the grandeur of the castle festivities, and of the visits made by the existing royal family. Everything attempted there seemed to be done well, and on audit days, a numerous tenantry feasted sumptuously in the "great hall." In its stupendous walls and thick oaken beams and flooring the old place is perfectly untouched by time, and between the stones on the battlements, and in the very steepest part of the walls, the wall-flower and snap-dragon grow luxuriantly—in several instances, even dwarf but thriving yew-trees.

In the Anglo-Saxon period a nunnery existed on or about the site of the castle, and it was a nun belonging to this sisterhood who was the heroine of Southey's "Witch of Berkeley." Subsequently I wrote a little poem on the same subject appended to my first novel, "Berkeley Castle." The Abbess of this religious establishment was said to be a very beautiful woman, and Earl Godwin, coveting her rich possessions, induced one of his sons to enact a fall from his horse, and, under the pretence of being severely hurt, to get himself carried into the house. When there, he was to feign a long illness, and to make himself as agreeable as possible to its fair inmates. Unfortunately for the holy edifice, the mission of the gay Lothario was too successful. After a time, he sent to his father to take him away, announcing his victory over more than one of the pious recluses, including the Lady Abbess. Upon this, Earl Godwin reported the con-

vent to Edward the Confessor as a place of ill-fame,
and as anything but a godly house of prayer. That
pious, but very weak monarch, immediately caused
the accusation to be investigated, and finding the
Earl's revelations correct, he confiscated the nunnery
and its lands, and assigned them to the unprincipled
schemer.

This tradition has a hold on the minds of the people
about the castle to this day; and when the wind is
high, and strange and hollow sounds are produced
among the battlements, and heard upon the leads, and
about the towers and the tall chimneys, superstitious
minds imagine that the demon horse and rider are in
the midnight air, bearing the writhing form of the
witch on a saddle of strange shape, and that amidst
the horrors of a tempestuous night can be heard the
shrieking of the condemned nun.

History tells us that when Earl Godwin thus possessed himself of the Nunnery of Berkeley, his wife
"Gueda" refused maintenance from the rich lands so
obtained, and, to console her, the Earl consigned to her
use the Manor of Woodchester. On this manor, in
more recent times, the father of the late Lord Ducie
had a mansion and park called Woodchester, which
his son sold, and curiously enough, it has since been
turned into a convent. The old legend declares
that on a Candlemas Eve, and as a judgment on the
wicked Earl, a terrible storm was sent by Heaven to
avenge the deed by which the destruction of the
convent was effected; when some lands at that time
belonging to him were overwhelmed by the sea,
and his estate by inheritance became what are

now the Godwin or Goodwin Sands. There are beautiful stone carvings of the devil carrying the Witch, of Berkeley pick-a-back on his shoulders; and they adorn the walls of the family vault in the old Church of Berkeley.

There is some reason to believe that there was a Roman fortress on or about the site of the present structure; but the first direct information which we have as to its erection as a feudal castle, was in the time of Henry I., in 1108. In the reign of Stephen, Roger de Berkeley of Dursley, whence the eldest son's title of Viscount, had his castle at Dursley; but my ancestors had established " a local habitation and a name" long before this. On Robert Fitzhardinge, a Dane of Royal descent, coming over with the Conqueror, and doing him good service in the war, he received the castle, manors, and lands of Berkeley as his reward. A continuous raid having been kept up between the newly-installed Dane at Berkeley Castle and the long-established Saxon at Dursley, eventually, to end the hostility of the two families, King Edward the Confessor caused the elder son of Fitzhardinge to marry the daughter and heiress of the Saxon Berkeley, and thus the names of Berkeley and Fitzhardinge became united. It is an error to pronounce the name as if spelt with an e. The word should be spoken broadly, as if written with an "a," so as to sound like Barkley, for the Saxon e had the pronunciation of our a; and we, like others of Saxon descent, are proud of the derivation.

The castle was the rendezvous of the barons in

DEATH OF EDWARD II.

rebellion against King John, who seized it and turned it into a prison, devoting its lands to the maintenance of the garrison at Bristol. In 1216 that monarch resided at the castle for four days. Soon after, in 1223, Henry III. regranted the castle and manors to Thomas de Berkeley, and in 1255 the king was sumptuously entertained for some days on his way from Oxford to Bristol, by Maurice Lord Berkeley. In this lord's time, the rent of those rich lands, the lands whereon the best double Gloucester cheese is now made, was but sixpence per acre. He was a great agriculturist, and laid out and beautified the gardens around the castle; he also created a deer park, and turned the course of the little river or brook, then called the Doverte, which ran into the vale from the Cotswold Hills in the direction of Nibley, and made various ponds for fish, though none of these are now in existence. He is reputed to have discovered the fertilizing properties of marl, and used it as manure, for which at least his memory deserves to be cherished by all succeeding generations of farmers.

Edward II. met his death, as all the world knows, at Berkeley Castle, and there is extant now, at least there was some years ago, the book of the groom of the chambers, butler, or master of the household, in which there is a charge of a few pennies for supplying "new ropes to yᵉ harness of yᵉ carriage, for conveying of yᵉ King's body for burial at yᵉ Cathedral of Gloucester, and for yᵉ purchase of some pigment to die yᵉ linen inside yᵉ carriage black." The

custody of the captive monarch was not given to
Lord Berkeley, who was ordered away to his house
at Nibley or Wotton, and the charge of king and
castle handed over to Sir Thomas Gourney and Sir
John Maltravers, who foully murdered their unhappy
prisoner.

The room shown in the present time as King
Edward's (ornamented. with a bust of Charles II.,
that is or was exhibited as a representation of the
murdered king), is not the one in which the deed
was committed. It was simply the guard-room to
the entrance of the dungeon keep. The one wherein
the king was confined is the dungeon chamber, immediately over the dungeon itself, and directly
above the gloomy hole whence issued the effluvium
of a dead horse designedly put there in the hope of
creating putrid fever, and rendering a more violent
death unnecessary. The king's constitution, however, proved to be too strong for this slow poison,
so at last his enemies were forced to put him to the
most miserable death that villany ever imagined.

Any sensible person pausing for a moment to view
the peculiar situation of these two rooms, will at once
see that the dungeon chamber, overlooked by the surrounding keep, and shut in by the massive walls of
that entire wing of the castle, was, of all places, the
one to be selected for such a purpose, whence "the
shrieks of an agonized king" were less likely to be
heard. The other room, standing as it does at the
head of the stairs leading up from the inner courtyard to the entrance to the keep, and immediately

over that common passage, was in no way enclosed by other buildings, and having windows looking out upon the inhabited portions of the castle, was the very place where any noise must have been heard, and therefore not likely to be chosen for the performance of a deed that demanded the strictest secrecy.

For some reason or other, it could not have been for gain, the patched up old oaken and modern deal-mended bedstead, with its faded red cloth needle-worked laced curtains and coverlid, were sold for about fifteen shillings by the present occupiers of the castle, subsequently bought by a personal friend of mine for five pounds, and most kindly sent to me. It was the couch that from time immemorial stood on the floor of the chamber immediately over the trap-door, by which a descent into the dungeon could be effected; and if they gave the Royal prisoner any bed at all, this must have been the oaken frame on which it rested. It is still in my possession, and I live in the hope of one day being able to restore it to its ancient historic position. This relic of a barbarous time, this memorial of a worthless Queen and her paramour, the "gentle Mortimer," ought to be retained in the dungeon with the vile sentence in Latin engraved over it, purposely left unpunctuated so as to bear a double meaning, which was written by the Bishop of Hereford to Gourney and Maltravers:—

"Edwardum occidere nolite timere bonum est."

The beautiful tomb of the Royal victim, in the Cathedral at Gloucester, affords the best translation to the Bishop's sentence, and shows how it was read by the knights in charge. The body was refused burial by all the adjacent monasteries, and with considerable pride I refer to the undoubted fact, that the dead king was carried with due respect and attention to his last resting-place in our carriage, and that, according to other traditions as well as the account of Fosbroke, he "was buried by the members of the Berkeley family, and his heart put into a silver vessel."

In the reign of Henry I. in 1108, the building of the castle was commenced, and in 1326 and 1342, in the time of Thomas, the fifth Lord of Berkeley, it went through a process of renovation. This Lord Berkeley rebuilt the flag tower, still known as "Thorpe's Tower," from the name of the retainer who furnished the guard for it, and by virtue of this guard held the lands in Wanswell. The farm of Wanswell Court still remains a portion of the castle estate. Henry IV. was entertained by the Berkeleys, for ten days, when, among other preparations to do the king honour, much of the timber and leads from the great house at Wotton was removed, to enlarge the roof of the present kitchen. Considering the entertainments given to previous crowned heads, this incident will afford sufficient proof that the reception offered to Henry IV. must have been magnificent, or that he must have travelled with a retinue upon a much greater scale than had been attempted by any of his predecessors.

In 1572 Queen Elizabeth, on a hint as was suspected given to her by her especial favourite, Leicester, who owed Lord Berkeley a grudge, and believed that a visit from his sovereign just then would be inconvenient, sent to my ancestor an expression of her "pleasure that she should be entertained at Berkeley Castle." He, knowing his inability, at that moment, to do this satisfactorily, at once started for some far-off place, and made his absence the excuse of not being able to sufficiently prepare his poor domain and so to honour himself with her majesty's reception.

Leicester, well aware of the overbearing and imperial temper of Elizabeth, conveyed to her Lord Berkeley's refusal in terms which were sure to render it offensive, and the queen, in a rage, instantly resolved to invite herself, without reference to the desires or convenience of her intended host. She therefore proceeded there, attended by her favourite and her court, in 1572, and as the family historian, Smith, in his " Lives of the Berkeleys " (of which but three copies are now in existence), describes it: " There was a stately game of red deere in the Worthy." (This was a deer park adjoining the castle, the rich meadows of which are called the Worthy and Little Park to this day.) "During the which time of her being there, such slaughter was made as 27 stagges were slayne in the toyles of one day, and many others on that and the next were stolen and havocked; whereof, when this lord being then at Callowden, was advertised, having much set his delight in this game, he sodainly and passionately disparked the ground." Lord Berkeley did this apparently because his uninvited guest had left a message for him with his vassals, promising to take an early opportunity of repeating her visit.. Leicester, who knew the fiery temper of the man subjected to this insult, hoped that it might exasperate him into the commission of some overt act that should lose him his castle and lands, the possession of which he desired. As soon as the ground had been disparked, a friend at Court contrived to let Lord Berkeley know that the queen had been covertly informed by Leicester of what he had done " on repining that she" (the queen) " had come to his castel," and, the same friend further cautioned him "to carry a wary watch over his words and actions, least the earl" (meaning Leicester), "who had drawn her to the castel, and *purposely* had caused the slaughter of his deere, might have a further plot again *his. head* and the castel to which he had taken noe small likinge." These timely hints put my ancestor on his guard, and banished from his mind the angrily, and under the peculiar circumstances, rashly conceived idea, of calling the queen's favourite to a personal account for the indignities he had had to endure.

The castle, before the invention of artillery, must have been almost impregnable to a siege, when properly victualled; for in addition to its deep moat, drawbridge, and portcullis, and its strong and exalted position on a rock, the defenders always had it in their power to flood the low grounds beneath and around the building, which are now the " Castle Meadows," and by the aid of the up-coming tide from the River Severn, and an inland down-flowing fresh-water stream, to put half a mile or more of water between the walls, or the outer moat, and the

SUITS OF ARMOUR. 13

besiegers. Sir Thomas Fairfax, the general of Cromwell, besieged it, and breached it from the side of the church across the moat; proof of this may be seen in the walls of the keep now, that look on the outer courtyard, and I remember a cannon ball being taken thence that was completely imbedded in the stone.

Berkeley Castle was, I believe, the last place that held out against the parliamentary forces, and it surrendered only on condition that the garrison might march out with their arms. They did so, man and horse, five hundred strong. Then it was that we lost all our supernumerary suits of mail, which Cromwell's general, with an eye to booty, as those hypocritical God-fearers always had, took very good care to carry off with him. I never have entered that ample hall where the mail trophies of old, as well as the antlers of the chase, ought to hang, without thinking of the deeds of Fairfax, and lamenting a want of decoration so much in keeping with its feudal associations. I may, perhaps, one day have it in my power in part to remedy this vacancy, for though the successive barons and earls have certainly attended to the walls, which indeed were strong enough to attend to themselves, they as certainly, after Cromwell's time, did nothing towards restoring the ancient and characteristic decorations of the place.

It was the custom of the Lords of Berkeley to be attended by knights and esquires, and heirs of good families. When Maurice, Lord Berkeley, in the early part of the fourteenth century, went to the wars in France, many knights and gentlemen were with him

ANCIENT CUSTOMS.

as a part of his command. In the time of Richard I., not a soul of the household was exempted from attendance at church upon solemn days, except the cook, and the attendants upon the sick. Debts to the Crown were often paid in kind. King John certified to the exchequer that " Robert, third Lord Berkeley, had paid him the bay horse he owed." The salary of the keeper of the castle in Henry the Third's reign, was twenty marks per annum. The pay of an esquire at Berkeley Castle in 1273, was an allowance of a horse and boy, meat and drink, and two robes with eight shillings annually, or two shillings and a penny a day, instead of the keep of a horse, and one shilling and a penny for the keep of a boy. Trial by battle was then resorted to. In 1250, William de Fouvel demanded of Lord Maurice de Berkeley certain lands in Devon, and the combat took place; defendant's champion was overcome, and judgment given for the Lord Maurice.

The provisions furnished for one year to the castle from the two manors of Ham and Cowley, to this day belonging to the castle, and sent to the clerk of the kitchen, were as follow :—17,000 eggs, 1008 pigeons, 91 capons, 192 hens, 288 ducks, 388 chickens, 80 hogs, 110 porkers, 84 pigs, 45 calves, 315 quarters of wheat. What was to spare was yearly sold. Every day's meal was rated to the inferior servants; and much of the wool grown and sheared on the estates was put out for spinning and making cloth.

When the lord was attending the King, safety was insured to his estates, and freedom from lawsuits as

FEUDAL LAWS.   15

well as provision secured by Royal grant for his wife
and family, during the wars in which he might be
engaged, · lest the latter should "want and beg."
Thus a grant was made to the Lady Berkeley, of the
Manor of Wendon, in Essex, and of Hercham and
Intesclive, in Kent. A summary summons was issued
to this Lord of Berkeley, to attend the King in London, with all his powers of horse and foot, at only ten
days from the receipt of the writ.

The fishery of the Severn let at Arlingham for 30*l.*
a-year. On Fridays all fish derived from the fisheries
were reserved for use at the castle. Thomas, to whom
Berkeley Castle was granted, always kept open house
for all comers at Christmas. He received thirty marks
for a horse killed while attending Henry III., at the
Castle of Evesham, and the Lord Berkeley who succeeded him was paid the large sum, in those days,
of 465*l.* for horses lent in the Royal service. The
chief amusements of this Baron were tournaments,
hawking, hunting, and agriculture.

The feudal laws for the protection of deer and game
were very severe. Lord Berkeley hung a man in
Redcliff-street, Bristol, for "shooting a hare with a
cross-bow." That execution, to the death, on account
of a hare, was the last of the kind enacted. About
the year 1300, Lord Berkeley's retainer, Richard
Wink, took one William Goyell catching hares
with a net, in the Castle Woods, and killed him
there and then with an arrow. He was outlawed for
felony, but, nevertheless, remained in his Lord's
service. Also William Harvey, an under-keeper, slew

one Clift, a poacher, with a bolt from his cross-bow, and got off any punishment through "the statute against trespassers in parks."

The wedding dress of the sister of the second Lord Berkeley, in the early part of the fourteenth century, was "a gown of cloth, of brown scarlet (*bruni scarletti*), with the cape furred with the best miniver." Her saddle, "with the furniture thereof, was brought from London, and cost five pounds."

The retinue of the third lord in the middle of the fourteenth century, usually consisted of twelve knights, often more, with each of them two servants and a page; also twenty-four esquires, or more, with a man and a page to each. The expenditure of this lord in 1354 was 1309*l.* 14*s.* 6½*d.*, and he saved 1155*l.* 18*s.* 8*d.* Total revenue in money, 2460*l.* 13*s.* 2½*d.*; in those days an enormous sum. He and his brother used to be out four days and nights at a time hunting foxes with nets and hounds. A hawk was then valued at fifteen, and a falcon at thirty-five shillings, but falconry was then the fashionable pastime.

A lively idea of the course of justice among my ancestors may be gathered from the following anecdote : A subpœna having been served on James, the sixth Lord Berkeley, he made the bearer of it, "David Woodbourne, eat it, wax, parchment, and all;" standing over him while he did so. Something very like this state of things existed in remote places in Ireland within the last half-century.

At the funeral of the Lady Isabel, consort of Maurice, the eighth Lord Berkeley, at the close of the

DOMESTIC HABITS.

fifteenth century, she had thirty women of her livery in black gowns, having kerchiefs of black on their heads, "not surreled or hemmed, because they mought be known as lately cut out of the newe cloth." "Ye body lay one whole night in ye queere " (choir) " before the altar;" "ye corporation were feasted with cakes, marmalade, red wine, and claret;" and then, very quaintly adds the historian of the day, who was one of the attendants, "I thank God noe plate ne spones wast lost; yet there was XX desyn spones." The corporation and the priests in those days, or on that occasion, were either honest men, or our friendly narrator and other retainers kept particularly good watch and ward.

The retinue of Catherine, wife of Maurice, the ninth Baron, who died in 1526, "if she only went eight miles from the castle, consisted of thirty-six horse, and on one occasion of forty of her own servants."

Horse hire from London to Stone, in Kent, was one shilling and fourpence.

The domestic habits of the second wife of Thomas, the eleventh Baron, are thus described :—

"This Lady Ann, when at her castle and country houses, would, betimes, in winter and summer mornings, take her walks to visit her stables, barnes, dairies, poultry, swine troughs, and the like; which housewifery, her daughter-in-law, the Lady Catherine Howard, wife of the last Henry, seeming to decline, and to betake herself to the delights of youthful greatness, she would sometimes say to those about

VOL. I.

18   LUXURY.

her, 'By God's blessed sacrament, this gay girl will
beggar my son Henry.'"

Lady Anne was, of course, a pattern of good housewifery, such as the wives of noblemen were in those
singularly good old days. But time not only altered
peeresses, humbler matrons followed the bad example
of their betters, till the following contrast became an
established fact :—

1625.	1825.
Man—to the plough.	Man—tally-ho.
Girl—to the sow.	Miss—piano.
Wife—to the cow.	Ma'am—silk and satin.
Boy—to the mow.	Boy—Greek and Latin.
And your rents will be netted.	And you'll be gazetted.

Luxury in dress was displayed by the Berkeleys as
extravagantly as by any of their contemporaries. One
of the suits made for the twelfth Lord Berkeley and
his lady, in which to attend the coronation of Queen
Elizabeth, is thus described:—" One doublet of crimson
satin, laid with silver lace, and with silver buttons,
lyned with crimson sarcenet: breeches of crimson
velvet, lyned with crimson sattin. His hat of crimson
silk and silver, and the scabbard for his rapier of crimson
velvet. His spurs gilt and fastened with velvet of the
same colour. His shoes crimson and white velvet. The
petticoat of my ladye was of crimson sattin, her gown
of cloth of gold, and her shoes of crimson velvet."

What will amuse the sporting reader, however,
much more than all the rest of my description of the

ANCIENT SPORT.

deeds of that day, is a reference to "the considerable sporting retinue of this lord which he kept up to hunt the country where now stands 'Gray's Inn' and which is still called its "fields." Spending much of his time with his mother at "Kentish Town," her country residence, and at her town residence in "Shoe-lane, Fleet-street" (then a fashionable quarter), he hunted regularly in "Gray's-inn-fields" and about "Islington," with 150 servants in livery. The summer livery was tawney, "which colour descended to the servants of my father and myself," and of late to the hunting establishment at Berkeley Castle; as may be seen in the "tawney" or orange plush livery of the huntsmen and whippers-in. The winter livery was white frieze cloth lined with crimson taffety, and the badge of the white Danish lion rampant embroidered on the left sleeve.

A remarkable instance is on record of the sagacity of one of this Lord Berkeley's horses, called "Brinsley," as happening on a day while hunting in the Forest of Dean. Brinsley carrying his rider at full gallop with the hounds, came suddenly on an old coal-pit completely grown over and hidden by brushwood. The rider, unaware of the danger, and having his eye on the hounds, would have gone on, but the horse discovering it, "threw himself down rather than be dashed to pieces." My modern ideas suspect that the horse slipped up in an attempt to avoid the hole.

This Lord Berkeley bought and presented to his lady "a lute inlaid with mother-of-pearl, for which Queen Elizabeth had previously offered one hundred

marks." About ten years after her death he gave it to
the Dowager Countess of Derby, and old Shrapnell,
the last janitor in the castle during my father's lifetime, declared that up to the year 1810 this lute was
in the possession of the mistress of the Duke of
Clarence, the celebrated Mrs. Jordan.

As years rolled on, and feudal retinues were no
longer maintained, the officials of the castle, who were
not menials, were " a constable, a porter, a constable's
servant, and a gaoler." To them may be added the
"jester," or "my lord's fool," who really was no fool
at all. Such persons were members of every nobleman's
household, but got out of fashion and were discon-
tinued in the seventeenth century. The last of them,
called Dickey Pierce, was kept by Lord Suffolk, but
often lent to Lord Berkeley. He died at Berkeley,
and was buried in the churchyard; and over his grave
still stands a tombstone with the following epitaph.
It bears date June 18, 1728. On one side of the
stone is the following inscription :—

> " My Lord, that's made himself
> Much sport of him."

On the other is the cynical epitaph written by Dean
Swift, who was Chaplain to Lord Berkeley :—

> " Here lies the Earl of Suffolk's fool,
> Men called him Dickey Pearce;
> His folly served to make folks laugh,
> When wit and mirth were scarce.
>
> Poor Dick, alas, is dead and gone !
> What signifies to cry ?
> Dickeys enough are left behind,
> To laugh at by and bye."

INCOME FROM THE BERKELEY ESTATE. 21

One of the jesters at Berkeley Castle, so long ago as 1620, tied the castle to a gooseberry bush in the garden with a piece of string, and when asked by his lord why he did it, replied he was afraid the building would run away to Nibley, where then lived a steward, supposed to be feathering his nest from his lord's domains.

It is curious to contrast the revenue derived from this estate during the centuries I have named, and the relative value of the precious coins, with its present income (1864). At one of the periods referred to, an income of about from two to three thousand pounds was deemed immense. If it be true that around the castle, hill and vale, there are thirty thousand acres of land, as I have heard it asserted, those acres, the fisheries on the Severn, joined to household property forming part of the estate, cannot bring in much less than sixty thousand pounds sterling a year.

Among my earliest recollections of Berkeley Castle was the constant whispering and mysterious confabulations of the heads of the family as I was apparently absorbed in my games on the carpet of the breakfast-room; and strange-looking old papers, a book and a parchment were then repeatedly under investigation. These proceedings excited a good deal more of my attention than any one suspected, and thus I remarked many things not intended to come under my observation. On one particular occasion they had been busy with an extraordinary instrument which had peculiar attractions for me, not having ever before seen anything like it, nor have I seen anything resembling it since.

It was made to hold two pens, connected, but at some distance from each other, by what seemed a light brass rod. One was dry, but the other I saw the operators charge with ink, and then holding the dry one in their hands passed it carefully over some signatures or writing, on an old paper or parchment—anxiously observing if the marks made by the inked pen, corresponded with those they traced with the dry one. While thus occupied, they were suddenly summoned from the breakfast-room, and I was left alone with Shrapnell, the surgeon of my father's regiment, and janitor of the castle, who very frequently had me in charge. I heard him say to himself with, as I thought, a sneer upon his countenance, "now let *me* try." I stood on tiptoe to get a better view of what he was doing, little knowing then, though made fully conscious since, how deeply it interested me. I saw him adjust the two pens as already described, and while he traced with the dry one, observe the effect of the other. The result failing to satisfy him, he removed his hand from the instrument, and, with a shake of his head, exclaimed to himself, "It wont do;" he then flung the marks he had made into the fire.

The whole affair in my childhood was a mystery, and as such had its charm. Often have I called to recollection these experiments, with this strange instrument, in the breakfast-room. Of course I now perfectly know their object.

The next incident impressed on my remembrance was an American deer (such as I have since hunted in the once United States) that was kept in a paddock adjoining

CONFLICT WITH A DEER.

the park, attacking my father as he entered with my brothers Henry and Moreton, the present earl. My father was a very powerful man, and caught his assailant by the horns with the intention of throwing him, but the animal proving the stronger of the two, resisted his efforts till his breath began to fail him. At last his energies became so weak that the deer threw him on his back, and then made frequent and savage attempts to gore him with his brow antlers, ripping up his waistcoat, and bruising his body severely. Though on the ground, and apparently at the mercy of his assailant, he never let go his gripe of the antlers, and never lost that presence of mind for which in danger he was famous. Finding that the encounter had become a question of life or death, he called to my brother Henry (now member for Bristol) to feel in his pocket for a knife with which to cut the deer's throat—my brother Moreton having started at speed on his pony to get assistance from the keeper's lodge. The former, with the knife in his hand, lost no time in coming to his father's assistance, but found the blade too blunt to penetrate the animal's hide; he, therefore, stabbed it repeatedly about the throat till loss of blood forced it to give in. The deer, I believe, either died there and then, or was afterwards destroyed.

About this time there was a contested election for the county. Mr. Dutton was supported by the castle interest, but his opponent, whose name I have forgotten, thought proper, by way of compliment, to come to the castle in the course of his canvass, and with him came his dog, on whose collar, unobserved,

I contrived to affix a card with "Dutton for ever" upon it. During the interview which followed, this attracted my father's attention, and never shall I forget the look of confusion of the aspirant for parliamentary honours when his host, pointing to the electioneering card, abruptly, but good-humouredly, demanded how he could think of applying for his interest when his own dog said as plainly as he could speak—VOTE FOR DUTTON!

Nearly all the royal brothers were guests at Berkeley Castle within my recollection. The visits of the Dukes of York and Clarence I do not remember so distinctly, as I do those of the Duke of Sussex; but the latter made himself noteworthy to me by a habit of pronouncing the name of the celebrated Dr. Jenner, then at Berkeley, as Dr. Yenner.

While the Prince of Wales and his royal brothers were on a visit to my father, the keepers used to be sent out through all the nearest and most accessible fields to find hares seated in their "forms," for the Duke of Sussex to shoot at. In this position, his royal highness's gun sometimes took effect, but not always, and now and then a hare in a deep seat sat out two discharges before she deemed it time to run away.

The Prince, on one occasion, having learnt that an eccentric elderly Gloucestershire lady, Mrs. Purnell, was there on a visit, his royal highness sent up to her apartments a formal wish that he desired to see her; which unexpected distinction so flurried the old dame, that she hurried downstairs forgetting an important portion of her toilette. She wore

AN ECCENTRIC OLD LADY. 25

her customary high-heeled shoes (she was the last to give them up, though they had been long out of fashion). "Her person was got up in as dignified, a manner as in her countryfied ideas conformed with the strictest etiquette; but when she made her curtsey, the Prince beheld a bald pate shining before him like a large white turnip under a little laced cap, from which two bright ribbons flew back from her colourless cheeks." She had forgotten to put on her wig, which was a youthful one, and the omission had such a ludicrous and not agreeable effect, that though his royal highness contrived to maintain his gravity, he refrained from offering the salute he invariably gave to ladies who were presented to him, and which my mother had been particularly urging him to bestow upon the lady in question. On being informed of the nudity of her pate, poor dear Mrs. Purnell, uttering a shriek of dismay, fled from the room. The Prince then could no longer restrain his mirth.

By way of amusing the royal guests, a gentleman farmer and devoted foxhunter, "Jeremiah Hawkins, Esq., of the Haw," was asked to the castle that they might see a specimen of the old English Gloucester-shire Esquire, Foxhunter and Farmer, and thereafter believe in his homely eccentricities. Jerry Hawkins, like Mrs. Purnell, spoke the broadest Gloucestershire, and after dinner the kind-hearted, jovial sailor Prince, the Duke of Clarence, put questions to him to draw him out.

"Well, my good friend," his royal highness said, "do you ever wear breeches and top boots?"

LYNCH LAW.

"Please your greece," replied Jerry, looking very red, "I seldom wars onything else."

"I hear you are not afraid of water" (Jerry had swam the Severn on his horse), continued the duke; "do you ever wash your feet?"

"Sometimes in summer, please your greece, when it's hot," was the extraordinary reply.

There was a roar of laughter, that lasted several minutes.

Poor old Jerry never could be taught the correct method of speaking to a royal duke. All his life he had been used to talk to "the duke," as he called him, the grandfather of the present Duke of Beaufort, and hence he bestowed the same rank on the son of his sovereign.

As an illustration of the readiness with which Lynch law was carried out even in those days, I recollect my father riding along a public path, and meeting a fellow carrying what looked extremely like a well-filled game bag: the former immediately slipped his right foot back out of the stirrup, and kept it in readiness on the flank of his black shooting-mare; then manœuvring so as to make the offender pass on that side, he launched the toe of his heavy boot against the pit of the man's stomach with such force that the latter went down as if shot. Before he could rise, the exasperated owner of the game had jumped out of his saddle, and begun to search the bag; but was extremely disappointed to find in it nothing but rabbits.

The preservation of game was then, as now, at times the cause of quarrel: not merely between keepers and poachers, but between neighbouring proprietors. My father had a feud of this kind with a neighbour, the late Sir Samuel Wathen, and the servants of each did their best to maintain it. Of course all our family looked on Sir Samuel as a *bête noire*, and as, what he was, an upstart in the county.

I was about ten or between ten and eleven years old when my father died after a short illness. It was the first death in the family of which I was cognizant, and so profound was the impression it made upon me, that a very long time elapsed before I recovered my usual spirits; in short, I felt as if broken-hearted. A remarkable incident occurred soon after the funeral. Among the neighbours who called to make complimentary visits of condolence, was Sir Samuel Wathen. It was a great surprise to the boyish minds of my brothers and myself; indeed, we were half disposed to consider it an insult.

Sir Samuel ascended the hill from the town to the outer or portcullis gate of the castle, where once stood the ancient draw-bridge. Through that and into the outer courtyard he passed without let or hindrance, until his foot took a first step into and under the gate that gives admission to the inner court. Suddenly down came the great escutcheon that had been placed immediately over the entrance, accompanied by mortar which had stood firm for many hundred years—down it came, crashing and tearing, just as the once mortal enemy of the man whose quarterings it bore, passed beneath it.

It was a hair-breadth escape such as very rarely

COLONEL BERKELEY.

occurs, and 'for some moments Sir Samuel stood irresolute, staggered, and confused, gazing at the broken hatchment, fallen behind him, surrounded by the retainers of the dead, looking on in anything rather than an amiable mood : but all present, including tenants, friends, the Earl *de jure*, some of my brothers and myself, regarding it as a manifestation from heaven.

Colonel Berkeley, who had been locally called Lord Dursley, till the title had been set aside by a petition against his retaining his seat so elected to the House of Commons, then came into possession of the castle and estates, and claimed to be Earl of Berkeley.

CHAPTER II.

THE PEERAGE AND COLONEL BERKELEY.

The late Earl of Berkeley—His introduction to Miss Cole and to her sisters—His admiration of Miss Mary Cole—Their sons born before wedlock—He eventually marries her—Endeavours to establish a prior marriage — Inquiry before the Committee in the House of Lords in 1795—His death, and will for the aggrandizement of the elder children, born previous to marriage, at the expense of the others — The eldest son claims' the peerage—Examination of witnesses before a Committee of the House of Lords in 1810-11—Remarkable evidence—Speech of the Lord Chancellor—Unanimous decision against the claimant—"Appeal to the House of Peers"—"The B——y family narrative"—Education of Colonel Berkeley—Unjustifiable conduct—His taste for low society—His influence over his mother and Thomas Moreton, the present Earl of Berkeley—His craft and caution in disguising it, and nonappearance in any proceedings which werè suggested by him to support his claim—Fondness for amateur acting.

It is necessary, for the reader's thorough knowledge of my life, that I should afford him information respecting certain particulars of family history that exercised a deep and lasting influence over my career. These are essentially of a private nature, but they have been, unhappily, rendered so public, that there can be no breach of confidence, no real indelicacy, in their introduction here. Painful to me they may be, but their discussion has become a duty.

It is more than half a century since an authentic account of them appeared, and they have given rise to

THE GLOUCESTER BEAUTIES.

so many exaggerations' and mis-statements, that a reliable narrative ought now to be generally acceptable; besides, the circumstances affected my own fortunes so nearly, that I could not ignore them in a work professing to be a memoir of my life. Without further preface, therefore, I shall at once relate the facts of the case in the sequence in which they occurred.

My father, Frederick Augustus, fifth Earl of Berkeley, after a long minority, and a youth and early manhood passed within the influence of several of the wildest rakes who figured most prominently in that licentious period, while in command of his regiment of militia, was attracted by the beauty of three sisters, daughters of a small tradesman who resided at Wotton-under-Edge, in the neighbourhood of the city of Gloucester, and of Berkeley Castle, who had recently died, leaving them and their mother entirely unprovided for. The eldest had married a man in the same way of business, and the windows of his house in Gloucester overlooked a thoroughfare frequented by Colonel the Earl of Berkeley and his brother officers. These girls being in the habit of standing or sitting there, were of course seen and admired; but though very attractive in person, it appears that they dressed plainly, and conducted themselves with perfect propriety.

Lord Berkeley, still a young man, saw them, and found no difficulty in gaining access to their society. The two unmarried sisters, however, Susan and Mary, shortly afterwards quitted Gloucester for London, and entered the service of Lady Talbot; subsequently to which Mary went to live with a clergyman's wife in a

MARY COLE. 31

retired part of Kent, as lady's-maid. Here she bore an irreproachable character. She had not been with this lady many months when she was sent for by Susan, who represented that she had made so excellent a marriage, that she could not allow her sister to remain in her present humble position. Mary, therefore, went to London, and resided at Susan's house; but the inducement that had brought her there proved entirely fallacious. Susan was not married, but was living under the protection of a man able to maintain her; and there is reason to believe that she, in addition, received a considerable sum of money from Lord Berkeley for placing her sister in his hands.

A mistress was then so common an appendage to a man of family or fortune, that no surprise could have been excited among his friends by Lord Berkeley's following the custom; but the regard he felt for Mary Cole differed materially from ordinary intimacies of a like nature; and he did everything in his power to render her position as comfortable as wealth and affection could make it. He treated her with the greatest possible tenderness and liberality; and after having placed her in an establishment of her own, took her to his town and country residences, where, though unmarried, she gradually assumed, and at length enjoyed, all the control of a wife.

Many excuses could be found for her accepting this false position, drawn from her friendless state and the poverty of her relations; but evidence exists that goes far to prove she had no choice in the matter, and only reconciled herself to it when avoidance was no longer in her power. When she found herself mistress of Cranford and Berkeley Castle, with unlimited sway over the domestic establishment, and the command of the entire revenue of the estate, she exhibited extraordinary natural talent for management, and unquestionably saved Lord Berkeley a good deal of trouble that he particularly disliked. Her influence increased with her usefulness, till at last her sway over him was as complete as it was over any domestic in his service.

During the concluding five years of the last century she seems to have looked her position fully in the face,—not apparently so much out of regard to her own interests, as to the interests of the elder sons who were growing up around her, notoriously illegitimate. These comprised—

William Fitzhardinge	*Baptized*	Dec. 26, 1787
Morris Fred. Fitzhardinge	„	Jan. 3, 1788
Augustus Fitzhardinge	„	Feb. 26, 1789
Francis Hen. Fitzhardinge	„	Mar. 18, 1795

She was also aware that other children were likely to be born under the same social disadvantages—it is probable that she was *enceinte* at the time ; she therefore determined to exert all her influence, which was growing absolute, to induce Lord Berkeley to marry her ; and this she effected, though not without considerable opposition and difficulty. The marriage ceremony was solemnized in the church of St. Martin's-in-the-Fields, London, on the 16th of May, 1796 ; and six months later her fifth son, Thomas Moreton, was

SUPPOSED PRIOR MARRIAGE. 33

born, according to a register in which he is entered as "Viscount Dursley."

It is scarcely possible to imagine an intention more clearly implied, and all Lord Berkeley's most intimate friends, from whom he never had any reserve, understood the arrangement in its obvious sense; but it does not appear that it was made known to them till the year 1797, when they were startled by the intelligence that a previous marriage had been performed as far back as the year 1785. It was alleged that secrecy had hitherto been designedly maintained solely because the entry of the ceremony in the parish books had purposely been destroyed by the clergyman by whom it had been performed, and that the cause of Lord Berkeley's silence on the subject was his desire to screen the reverend gentleman from punishment.

All marvelled, many doubted; but it must have been evident to every one who gave the subject a thought, that this idea of an earlier marriage was intended to legitimate the four sons previously born. To place this beyond the possibility of doubt, Lord Berkeley obtained access to the parish register in which the birth of his last son had been entered, and appended a paper to the entry in his own handwriting, notifying that the title "Lord Dursley" was employed there in error, as the boy was the fifth son born to him in wedlock. William Fitzhardinge, therefore, who had previously been known only as "Fitz," was given the title of the eldest son of the house, and his younger brother received only the second baptismal appellation that had been so strangely assigned him.

VOL. I.   D

A very little observation would show the impossibility of proving the first marriage; nevertheless, in the year 1799, Lord Berkeley brought the case under the cognizance of the House of Peers, a Committee for Privileges having been constituted to inquire into his pedigree. They commenced their labours on the 27th of May, and terminated them on the 20th of the following month, after the examination of sixteen witnesses; but the proof was so unsatisfactory, that Admiral Sir George Berkeley, his next brother, was encouraged to commence another inquiry in the House of Lords, apparently to show that all the children then born were illegitimate, and therefore that he was heir-presumptive to the title.

The Countess of Berkeley, in the year 1800, gave birth to me; and the Admiral, as if convinced that his case was now hopeless, dropped the inquiry. From this period to the next ten years, everything that could be imagined or suggested was had recourse to, to establish the position of the falsely-assumed Lord Dursley as the heir of the title and estates, and throw the rights of the children of the only real marriage, entirely overboard. With that object, a will of unprecedented length was concocted, by the provisions of which all the family property would descend to the illegitimate or eldest born, permitting the sons born in wedlock nothing but moderate younger brothers' portions; and even this, by a strangely penal and therefore illegal clause in the testament, they were to forfeit if they ventured to assert their right to the title.

There could be no doubt that Lady Berkeley was passionately attached to her eldest son, and could persuade his father to do in his behalf exactly what she pleased. She was very anxious that he should be regarded as the heir; and as he grew older, and became aware of the advantages arising from his general recognition in that character, he became as solicitous about this as herself. Even at such an early stage of the proceedings, he exerted all his influence to induce his mother to forward his interests in this direction.

In the year 1810 Lord Berkeley died, and William Fitzhardinge claimed the title and estates, as next in descent, and in accordance with the testamentary arrangements of the deceased; but on his petition to sit in the House of Peers, the claim was referred to a Committee, who commenced an inquiry on the 4th of March, 1811. This proved to be one of the most remarkable trials upon record. The claimant secured the services of the two most eminent members of the bar, Mr. Serjeant Best, afterwards Lord Wynford, and Sir Samuel Romilly. The interests of the sons born of the second marriage were looked after by the Solicitor-General and the Attorney-General, who attended as counsel for the Crown.

Though preparations must have been going on for years under the direction of the claimant and his mother, to make out a clear case, the evidence to support it was soon seen to be of a most unreliable nature, and it became evident that, not satisfied with suborning his servants and pensioners, the former had

D 2

EVIDENCE OF COLONEL JOHN WEST.

induced his mother and some members of her family to make statements on oath which were proved to be totally devoid of foundation. Trustworthy witnesses came forward not only to testify that the pretended first marriage could not have taken place, but to prove that the documentary evidence brought forward to support it had been fabricated for the purpose. Two of the witnesses in support of the claim prevaricated so grossly that they were committed to Newgate on the 7th of June, whilst the inquiry was in progress.

Among the most surprising statements was one that came out during the examination of Colonel John West, who had been present at the disastrous battle of Bunker's Hill in America. He was an intimate friend of the late Lord Berkeley. He deposed that while at Weymouth with the royal family, in the year 1797, he was at breakfast informed by Lord Berkeley, that he had been married " eleven or twelve years prior to that time," and that his eldest son was legitimate. This was, he said, so great a surprise to him, that he requested permission to communicate it to the Prince of Wales and the Duke of York, which he did very shortly afterwards—equally to their surprise and, of course, disbelief. It was here, and about this time, that my father gave a fête in honour of the Prince of Wales, with whom he had been on the most confidential terms for many years. Yet the Prince was totally unacquainted with the alleged marriage. The King—George III.—was well aware of his having had several natural children, for at an interview his Majesty asked which of them was to be called Lord

MYSTIFICATION. 37

Dursley, and the reply was, "Your Majesty shall know that at the proper time." In a subsequent portion of his evidence Colonel West affirms that he might have heard this surprising announcement a year later. It was in 1797 that the king drank tea in Lord Berkeley's tent, but as the colonel of the militia was not at Weymouth till the year following, the conversation could not have occurred till 1798, about two years after the birth of my elder brother Moreton.

The witness further stated that he, a short time afterwards, dined with Lord Berkeley and the Prince of Wales; that though the marriage was then for the first time announced, Lady Berkeley retained the name by which she had hitherto been known by the intimate friends of Lord Berkeley, "Miss Tudor,"— that she was in the habit of driving a curricle about that fashionable watering-place, and appearing at the reviews attended by servants in the livery (Pompadours) of the Berkeley family, but that the king, who must have known her by sight as well as by repute, never took the slightest notice of her.

The most singular part of these strange revelations is, that this confidential friend did not hear of the second marriage till a full year later, when Lord Uxbridge told him of it, and he went at once to the town house, in Spring Gardens, to inquire of Lord Berkeley, who confirmed the report, adding, by way of explanation, that he knew of no law against " a man marrying as often as he pleased." Of course that threw no light upon the mystery. But the mystification neither began nor ended there; the inconsistencies, nay, the absurdity of the story, became more apparent the more it was carefully inquired into, and though more witnesses were brought forward by the claimant to corroborate those whose falsehood had been exposed, it was soon made evident that they were not a bit more trustworthy than the others.

Admiral Prescott, who was also on the most confidential terms with my father, in his evidence, placed the declaration of the marriage early in 1799, or the end of the preceding year, when he was stopped in St. James's Street by Sir Godfrey Webster, to inquire whether there was any truth in a report then current of Lord Berkeley's marriage with Miss Tudor. The Admiral acknowledging that he had never heard of such a thing, Sir Godfrey asked who could know, if so intimate a friend did not. He then stated that he wrote for information to Miss Tudor, who replied that, "she had for a long time past been Maria Berkeley." Whether this satisfied him he did not say; but as he stood godfather to the first two sons, and knew them only as natural children, and was introduced to their mother, very shortly after his friend's acquaintance with her commenced, the confirmation ought to have been as great a surprise as the rumour. To use his own emphatic words, he had "no more dreamt of marriage between them than of flying over the house."

From this evidence it is quite clear that Admiral Prescott lived under the same roof with Lord Berkeley, and was made acquainted with the most private of his

MARQUIS OF BUCKINGHAM. 39

domestic affairs, yet never heard of his being married until the proceedings in the House of Lords, instituted by his lordship for the establishment of his pedigree, in the year 1799, had become the town talk. This made a strong impression against the claimant, which was greatly strengthened when another confidential friend, the Marquis of Buckingham, added testimony still more conclusive. For having been invited by Lord Berkeley to become guardian to his children about the year 1790, he asserted in his evidence he objected because they were illegitimate, and did refuse on that ground, Lord Berkeley having confessed to him that he was not married. Lord Buckingham proceeded to state that his friend confided a plan he had of marrying a daughter by Miss Tudor to a son of his brother, Admiral Berkeley ; but to this plan also he objected, though he consented to lay the proposition before the Admiral. His lordship further deposed that he did not hear of any marriage till the year 1797; and that a rumour of a design to set up a prior marriage having reached him, he had reminded Lord Berkeley of his negotiation in behalf of his natural children being totally opposed to any such event having previously taken place.

After such reliable statements. there could be no difficulty in the Committee coming to a conclusion ; and on the 28th of June, 1811, the Lord Chancellor addressed the Lords on the merits of the claim. "From the bottom of his soul," so runs the report of his. speech,[*] "he could say that he had from

---

[*] "Hansard's Parliamentary Debates," xx., 770.

SPEECH OF THE LORD CHANCELLOR

the first entertained a wish that Lady Berkeley might be enabled to show the right of the present claimant. But he requested that their lordships would keep the objects of this title abstractedly considered, and putting from their minds other feelings and sentiments which had mixed themselves with the inquiry, and which had been pressed upon their attention, that they would look to the title itself, and the evidence that had been adduced to support that title. He wished them to consider most attentively the Act of Marriage, 26 Geo. II., s. 33, by which it was required that the marriage should take place after licence obtained or banns published; and that the marriage should, after the usual solemnization, be duly registered. He had no doubt their lordships would agree with him, that, if licences were not obtained, nor banns published, according to the direction of the Act of Parliament, the marriage afterwards would be null and void. God forbid he should, in saying this, be understood to declare that for want of a precise compliance with that statute the marriage would be null. If from the conduct of the parties before and afterwards—if from their mode of living and demeanour as husband and wife, they considered themselves to be married—if from the general repute of the world, or the neighbourhood where they dwelt, they were believed to be so; and if their children, borne under such circumstances, were accounted legitimate, it was his opinion that the presumption of law would supply the irregularities of a marriage ceremony. For instance, under such circumstances, he was not prepared to say that if the clergyman had not published the banns in an audible voice, and the entry of the marriage register had afterwards been made in an irregular way, that marriage, so solemnized, would be declared void. The presumption of law would be in its favour. But if these irregularities took place under circumstances totally opposite, the presumption of law would be against the marriage."

The noble and learned lord next proceeded to comment upon the nature of the evidence, and observed that that on the claimant's side could not have been satisfactory of itself, independent of the evidence adduced so strongly against the claim by so many witnesses, and from such indisputable testimony. The case represented by Lady Berkeley herself, and her brother, was surrounded by the greatest improbabilities. The object of secrecy was ill chosen by selecting Berkeley as the place for publishing the banns and solemnizing the marriage. The fact of their publication was not satisfactorily made out by the claimant's witnesses, and it was in a great degree contradicted by the evidence of the parish-clerk at Berkeley. The register of the marriage also, under every consideration, was attended with glaring improbabilities. The conduct of Lord Berkeley in leaving his wife two days after the ceremony, and not seeing her again till the lapse of considerable time, was also very improbable. The excuse alleged for keeping the matter secret on account of the improper conduct of Lord Berkeley's sister Susannah, was open to great suspicion.

42 THE LORD CHANCELLOR'S OPINION.

His lordship next animadverted upon the directions given by the Earl of Berkeley as to the register of his eldest born son, after the second marriage. The clerk of the parish where this register was made had not only to produce the register itself, but had retained to this day the letter, giving these directions, written in Lord Berkeley's own hand. The expressions of Lady Berkeley, when circumstances should have most induced her to speak sincerely, showed she did not consider herself legally married. Such as those which she uttered to one of her children, "You little dog! though I'm not your father's wife, I'll let you know I'm your mother."

"The Marquis of Buckingham's evidence was most material," he added. "The learned Serjeant (Best), who had been counsel for the claimant, and who, under all the difficulties he had to encounter, had discharged his duty well, had been pleased to represent that Lord Berkeley's conduct to the Marquis was a mere joke. But when Lord Berkeley chooses to commission a friend to inform his brother that he considers his own children illegitimate, and proposes to unite one of them in marriage with his brother's eldest son, that proceeding would, in his opinion, not permit the interpretation of a mere joke."

The noble and learned lord then stated the purport of the evidence of the most material witnesses, and independent of the presumptions of law, and the want of probability in the testimony adduced to support the title of the claimant, there was, in his opinion, he affirmed, a much stronger body of evidence to show the non-existence of any marriage in 1785. Finally,

THE CLAIM REJECTED.

he gave his opinion that the claimant had undertaken to prove that in which their lordships would be convinced he had completely failed. The committee, therefore, without a dissentient voice, came to a like decision. This, by way of resolution, was reported, on the second of July, to a full meeting of the House of Peers, who confirmed it also *nem. dis.* After which the Lord Chancellor moved that the report, with a copy of the evidence, should be laid before the Prince Regent, accompanied by an address from the House, requesting his Royal Highness would be pleased to adopt such proceedings thereupon as he might deem most proper and expedient.

This conclusion was a severe blow to the claimant of the earldom, who thenceforth contented himself with the honorary distinction he derived from succeeding to the command of my father's regiment of militia. The address alarmed those who had most committed themselves by their testimony in support of his pretensions, and they fled the kingdom as quickly as they could; "Mr. Tudor," whom my father had got appointed assistant commissary, being obliged to throw up his post, and go abroad, hoping to become a pensioner on the bounty of the man by whom he had been suborned.

The Prince Regent, however, out of his regard for his old friend, my father, most probably, did not act upon the suggestions of the House of Peers. No one knew the real state of the case better than his Royal Highness; but his good nature apparently prevented his seeming to act harshly to persons with whom he had lived on terms of the most social intimacy, and the delinquents were not molested. So much together were Lord Berkeley and the Prince about the time of the alleged marriage in 1785, the children were made to believe that the Richard Barnes, whose name figures on the pretended register as a witness to the alleged first marriage, was his Royal Highness.

"Colonel Berkeley," as he now styled himself, notwithstanding the peril in which he had placed his nearest relatives, did not entirely abandon the game he had been playing. In the same year there was published *An Address to the Peers of the United Kingdom of Great Britain and Ireland, from Mary, Countess of Berkeley.*

This was evidently written by a clever lawyer, for a more ingenious specimen of special pleading is not to be found in all our literature. It makes the worse appear the better cause, in such a skilful review of the whole case, that persons even acquainted with the facts might have risen from its perusal with an impression that the lords had been hasty, if not unjust, in their verdict. One remarkable feature in it is, the great stress laid upon the intimacy which existed between my father and mother and the Prince of Wales.

Such a production was imperatively called for, for the publication of the evidence in the periodicals, and in more than one separate work, must have greatly damaged the reputation of the claimant as well as of his agents ; but whatever benefit he may have derived from it was set aside some ten or eleven years later by the appearance of a volume bearing the following title : "The B——y Family : a Narrative." It bore

AN EXPOSURE. 45

on the title-page the name of Mary, the wife of William Tudor, *alias* Cole, the principal witness for the alleged first marriage. His evidence completely broke down under cross-examination; indeed, his complicity in the attempted fraud became so apparent, that at the termination of the trial he had consulted his own safety by concealing himself in Lisbon, till he could secure a safe hiding-place in his own country. His wife's statement not only exposes the iniquitous scheme to which he had lent himself, but shows that he was just the sort of tool to be used for such a purpose.

On his return he threatened to betray his employer, and, after a vain attempt of the latter to get him imprisoned as a madman, Tudor contrived, so says the narrative, to frighten his wealthy connexion into providing him with a liberal income. This, it is alleged, he wasted in living extravagantly with a married woman, leaving his wife and children totally uncared for.

This exposure was a complete answer to the "Address to the House of Peers." It left nothing more to be said about the pretended first marriage, and the idea of establishing legitimacy was forthwith dropped. In the course of the narrative a letter is introduced from William Tudor, which contains this graphic description of Colonel Berkeley :—

"I have long dwelt on the character of that worthless profligate. I have ranged through most of the Christian virtues, and I cannot find one in his possession. I have conned over the list of vices, and I find most which are to be found in mankind in general, united in him."

The notices I shall give in these pages of his education and after-life will show that this estimate is not an exaggeration.

I have often heard him complain that his education had been neglected in his youth; that as to religion, he was taught nothing; while he was thrown into close intimacy with a cousin who led him into all sorts of mischief, and very nearly into gambling on the turf. Mr. Berkeley Craven, according to his account, was the most dangerous acquaintance for a young man on his first start upon the world, that could by any possibility be imagined. I can very well remember that, when the two were together, the slang of the pugilist, the pickpocket, and the highwayman, and the flash term "blowen," constantly marked their conversation, mixed with many an obscene oath. A "flash blowen" seemed to them to be the thing most coveted in the world. Indeed, so fond of the name did Colonel Berkeley become, that he gave it to one of his favourite hunters.

In my Pavilion days at Brighton, which I shall presently describe, Lord Dursley, as he was then called, had a woman of this description established in the town, for whom, when at Berkeley Castle, he used to shoot my father's game unknown to him, and conceal it under his bed, to be sent away to her early the next morning. He never seemed to have any affection for either of his parents; on the contrary, he always spoke of them slightingly. This disrespectful mode of speech increased after my father's death, particularly in reference to my mother subsequently to the trial in the House of Lords. He never concealed his contempt for those who had then so grossly perjured themselves; their fault in his mind always seeming to be that they had sworn clumsily, and not adroitly enough to secure the succession to him.

For Moreton, the present Earl of Berkeley, he always expressed the greatest contempt ; speaking of him as a mere gamekeeper, and not as he really was— a simple, good-hearted soul, the preconcerted method of whose education had induced him to be to Colonel Berkeley for his life a princely benefactor, and to himself his greatest enemy ; while to me he was, without designing it, unjust in the highest degree, for he did all in his power to destroy my succession to the family estates. He was induced to make over—for he never was a free agent—for his lifetime, to the illegitimate branches, the London property, and therefore an immense amount of ready money as the leases fell in ; and, in short, was led to do all he could against the design of Lord Berkeley of Stratton, when he left the London estates to whoever was Earl of Berkeley, in order to enrich the earldom, and one of the oldest baronies in the kingdom.

Colonel Berkeley possessed very considerable mental powers. He spoke French well, and Italian a little ; he sang in glees with a fine deep voice, and he had agreeable manners in good society, and a great fund of conversation. He danced well, and had an excellent memory, so that what he did learn was always available ; but thrown over this, and marring it all, was an inherent dislike to the best society. I have often heard him say that he hated fine ladies and gentlemen, and in their company was terribly bored.

At first, in the heyday of youth, when at Brighton, he was a good deal in the society of the Prince of Wales, and mingled much in the best assemblies and balls of the period; but in later years he retrograded, and got into so many scrapes with second-class women, who ranked as gentlewomen, but who were really the wives of snobs, that people began to be shy of him; and his friends and invitations to their houses all fell off together, till the chimney-piece in his room, that used to be full of the best invitations, scarcely had a solitary card left.

There was one case of crim. con., where, to avoid heavy damages, he used the confidential letters that had been written to him by the woman—thus endeavouring to cast all blame from himself—and in this his conduct was universally condemned. He then for a time became reckless. He travelled the country as an amateur actor, associated with his brothers, Frederick and Augustus, Messrs. John Austin, Dawkins, and others; and lived in the society of public actors and actresses, usually having one of the latter under his protection.

When Mr. Dawkins played at Cheltenham or Tewkesbury, or at any of the local theatres in Gloucestershire, in the character he represented in "Simpson and Co.," he so very closely resembled the late Lord Bathurst, that the present lord begged of my brothers not to perform that comedy within the limits of the shire.

CHAPTER III.

BRIGHTON.

Brighthelmstone—Building the Pavilion—Mrs. Fitzherbert and
her alleged marriage with the Prince of Wales—Irish friends
—Colonel Hanger — Lord Barrymore — Sheridan — Colonel
M'Mahon—Lady Clermont and her laced tea—My father's
regiment of militia—L'enfant terrible—" I've seen the cook"—
Profane swearing—The Prince of Wales and Lady Hagger-
stone—Lady Nagle and her heart—A colonel in a rage—
Mother Shipton's prophecy—The Prince's harriers—Pugilistic
encounter of his Royal Highness with the Brighton butcher,
Jackson, the prize-fighter—Fashionable ladies at Brighton—
Changes—Decay of the Pavilion—Brighton races—A love
mission.

AFTER my earliest recollections of my ancestral home
come those as intimately connected with a now well-
known watering-place on the Sussex coast, then rising
into fashion through the patronage of the Prince of
Wales. When Charles II. sought to make his escape
from England, after the decisive battle of Worcester, in
this direction, Brighthelmstone was an insignificant
fishing-hamlet, and so it remained till its compara-
tively easy access from town in the old posting days,
and its eligibility for sea-bathing, attracted a few
families of distinction. The heir to the British
crown followed in their wake, and it soon became so
favourite a resort with his Royal Highness and his
friends, that new streets and squares in the course of a

VOL. I.

few years gave the hamlet a totally different aspect; but the great feature of novelty was the construction of a Chinese palace as a residence for the Prince.

In Kew Gardens some experiments in this peculiar architectural taste had already been made, but the marvellous growth of domes and minarets that rose in the vicinity of Castle Square, threw the King's pagodas and temples completely into the shade. The interior was quite as bizarre as the exterior, but the effect was marvellous. The sight-seeing world were in raptures with the sprawling dragons, and in ecstasies with all the queer-shaped, quaintly-ornamented chambers which the skill of the builder and the architect had been able to produce.

Thus honoured by royalty, under the new name of Brighton, the hamlet rose into a town, and its Steyne and its Parade became the promenade of the *élite* of society of both sexes to an extent that promised a successful rivalry with Weymouth and Scarborough. After the completion of the far-famed Pavilion, rose terraces and squares as fast as bricks and mortar, timber and stucco could be procured for them. Then came the more ingenious structure of the chain pier; but this achievement of engineering skill had not been effected at the period of my earliest visits.

Brighton then was a watering-place of very modest proportions compared with the Brighton of the present day. Kemp Town had not been imagined, and Cliftonville was as open to the winds, as the downs in the rear of both. The Brighton I remember, however, was a very gay and lively place, its thorough-

MRS. FITZHERBERT. 51

fares thronged with equipages, and chairs—not the
three-wheeled affair now known by that name, but the
sedan, with its sturdy bearers at each extremity of the
long poles that supported it, carrying the beau or belle,
the 'fat dowager, or superannuated dandy, to the
assembly at the " Old Ship," the ball at the Pavilion,—
or the masquerade at the theatre.

A more exclusive circle, confined to the most intimate
friends of the Prince of Wales, were often to be found
at this particular period of an evening, at a small house
on the west side of Castle Square, easily distinguished
from its neighbours by the little garden before it, and
the covered balcony at the drawing-room windows.
Here came the *crême de la crême* of society, male and
female—the latter apparently not quite so particular
as to their associates as they might have been according to more modern notions, for they visited a lady who
lived, as far as I have been able to understand, exclusively under the protection of the Prince.

Everybody knows that Mrs. Fitzherbert claimed to
have been secretly married to his Royal Highness; but,
as at the time to which I refer there was a Princess of
Wales universally acknowledged to be the lawful wife
of the heir apparent, whose right to that title she, Mrs.
Fitzherbert, had never ventured to challenge, it is
quite clear, even if she made her friends entertain the
idea, that she never believed in her marriage herself.
Nevertheless, maids and matrons of spotless reputation
were glad to be classed among her intimate friends.

There was more than one sufficient reason for this.
In the first place, the Prince was regarded as the head

E 2

of a great political party, and the wives and daughters of the Opposition were content to look at his fair friend with that charity which so effectually covers all moral shortcomings. In the next, his Royal Highness was also the acknowledged head of the English world of fashion, and his countenance, indirectly obtained through her, was thought worth securing at the moderate sacrifice of rigid opinions.

Hence it was, perhaps, that the beautiful Georgiana, Duchess of Devonshire, the very influential partisan of Fox, was Mrs. Fitzherbert's staunch ally; and two other handsome Duchesses, Gordon and Rutland, were almost as frequently her guests at Brighton. But I should have to go through a list of the matrons of most of the great Whig families were I to enumerate all her fair friends.

Her male visitors included the coterie of which his Royal Highness was the presiding genius—noblemen and gentlemen in his suite, and intimate friends. Fox and Grey, and Lord Holland were among the the latter; the former, in his place in Parliament, had denied the alleged secret marriage at the special request of the Prince; to Lord Grey, I believe, she had acknowledged that she had sacrificed herself out of devotion to her royal lover. The story told about the Prince having sent for her after he had stabbed himself mortally, and then exacted a consent from her to live with him is, of course, a joke. This lady had already buried two husbands, and was of the mature age of thirty, therefore she was not at all likely to be deluded by such a transparent or theatrical imposture.

The fact is, though she exhibited at first a reluctance to accede to the Prince's wishes, she allowed herself to be persuaded into compliance, and the fashion and influence she thus secured reconciled her, perhaps, to the position. Because she happens to have been connected with two or three Catholic families, attempts have been made to establish a real marriage between her and her lover, but I cannot see that there is any trustworthy evidence of such a ceremony having been performed by a clergyman, Protestant or Roman Catholic.

It is quite true that there is in existence a paper endorsed as the certificate of such a marriage, but it is sealed up, and no one seems to have examined its contents. Whatever this document may be, there cannot be a question that in the face of the Royal Marriage Act passed expressly to prevent improper alliances, it must have been illegal when written, and never since could have possessed the slightest authority to bind the parties as man and wife.

Mrs. Fitzherbert, however, was so thoroughly amiable and good-natured, that every one who came within the circle of her influence, felt inclined to shut his or her eyes against any cognizance of her true position. I remember well her delicately fair, yet commanding features, and gentle demeanour. That exquisite complexion she maintained, almost unimpaired by time, not only long after the departure of youth, but up to the arrival of old age; and her manner unaffected by years was then equally well preserved.

One or two of the Prince's younger brothers occasionally visited her, particularly the Duke of York, who, however, in his extreme good nature, chose to recommend himself to her favour by relating observations of the king and queen respecting her, which were far more pleasant than true. Queen Charlotte would not tolerate any of her eldest son's illegitimate attachments, and George the Third was quite as averse to them. Mrs. Fitzherbert always expressed herself very grateful to the Duke of York, for bringing her these agreeable testimonials of royal condescension, and his Royal Highness, knowing that he was pleasing a pretty woman, easily reconciled his conscience to the deception.

The Duke of Clarence was so favourably impressed by her amiable conduct towards him when a young man, that on his coming to the throne, he was ready to do everything she wished. Indeed, William the Fourth's good nature was so powerfully acted upon, that he not only afforded her a handsome increase to her income, but seemed almost willing publicly to acknowledge her as the deceased king's widow. Then it was that the alleged marriage, which had not been brought forward during the life of George the Fourth, began to be seriously insisted upon; Catholic priests absolutely asserting, though no minister of their church assisted in the ceremony, that it was binding.

Caroline of Brunswick was well aware of this

liaison of the Prince; and when accused of misconduct, retorted that she had never committed adultery, except with Mrs. Fitzherbert's husband. This, mere assertion as it was, however, is no proof of the bigamy. The most reasonable explanation is the supposition published in a recent work,* that the Prince of Wales, finding that no priest, Protestant or Roman Catholic, could be induced to risk the penalty of assisting in an illegal act, performed the ceremony himself, and then graciously wrote a certificate of his marriage; but this of course is only conjecture.

In Brighton no one was so imprudent as to make a remark as to the exact position of the very fashionable lady to whom it was of so much social importance that he or she should be introduced. If the gentleman or the lady found his or her way to the pretty little house in Castle Square, all went merrily as a marriage bell; and the nuptials to which it ought to have been a sequence were kindly taken for granted. The way in which the lady clung to the name of her second husband might have suggested a doubt of a third bridegroom, even before the latter had publicly contracted a marriage with the Princess of Brunswick; but Brighton visitors never thought of doubting anything that affected the respectability of Mrs. Fitzherbert.

As for the Chinese palace, and what went on within its walls, the host and his guests seemed to be of one mind; and if report does not do them injustice, this was frequently a mind amazingly careless of public

* " Court and Cabinets of George III."

opinion. That scenes of jollity should be enacted there might have been anticipated from the Irish element which was sure to appear in them; for either Colonel Hanger, Lord Barrymore, Richard Brinsley Sheridan, General Fitzpatrick, Col. McMahon, or some other Irishman, in similar repute for his social qualification, was of the company. Deep drinking and high play were much in fashion; but such excesses were perhaps not the least blamable features in some of the symposia over which the Prince presided.

These examples of the good "ould Irish gentleman" deserve something more than a passing notice. The first on the list was one of the Prince's equerries. He had previously led the wild, harum-scarum life, placed at the option of young Irishmen with pretensions to fortune or birth. In one of his early rambles he joined a gang of gipsies, fell in love with one of their dark-eyed beauties, and married her according to the rites of the tribe.

He then held a commission in one of the King's regiments, and used to introduce his brother officers to his dusky bride, boasting his confidence in her fidelity. His married life went on pleasantly among the ragged tents for about a fortnight, at the end of which his confidence and his bliss were destroyed together, on ascertaining to his intense disgust that his gipsy innamorata had eloped with a bandy-legged tinker.

The young captain very quickly quitted the vagabonds with whom he had so foolishly condescended to associate, and shortly afterwards was sent with his

LORD COLERAINE. 57

regiment to our revolted colony in America, but does
not appear to have distinguished himself there. He
returned after a year or two, got placed on the Prince
of Wales's establishment, and continued to make himself generally useful as well as generally entertaining,
till obliged to give up his post. His extravagance
made him more than once a prisoner for debt; but
his elder brother, Lord Coleraine, dying in the year
1814, he succeeded to the title, with what little
property could go with it, and lived out the rest
of his days quite unostentatiously. He survived
till 1824, and having no heirs, the title became
extinct.

Colonel Hanger was mixed up in most of his royal
master's early escapades, bought horses for him,
attended to his racing engagements, and is supposed
to have had something to do with the transactions
for which the Prince's jockey was punished. He
attended him to a certain prize fight; but the Prince's
presence there excited such general censure that his
Royal Highness was, if I remember the story rightly,
induced to publish a promise not to go to another.

Lord Barrymore had similar tastes, and gratified
them with as little regard to expense as to propriety. He was a special patron of the prize-ring;
one of the boxers he maintained in his service as a
footman—indeed, for any employment for which his
fighting qualifications were available; and the questionable retainer was always ready to do what was
required of him. On one occasion he got rather
roughly handled, for he was sent into Vauxhall Gardens

disguised as a clergyman, and having been recognised, was expelled without the slightest ceremony.

His lordship was frequently at Brighton, where he contrived to sow his wild oats as broadcast as in town. He went through a rapid career of reckless extravagance, which was brought to a sudden close whilst marching with a detachment towards Dover: the musket of one of his men went off, eventually causing his death. But this was a little before my time.

My readers will be so good as to understand, that in these reminiscences of my earliest years I give some of the facts alluded to from conversations that were held in my presence, and others from a dim recollection of some of the persons to whom I refer.

Sheridan was also often to be seen at the now fashionable watering-place, particularly during his reign of favour with the somewhat capricious lord of the Pavilion. In talent, he was far the superior of either of the two preceding; but this did not maintain the influence it ought to have done, for the splendid orator, the unrivalled writer of genteel comedy, was as unceremoniously thrust aside, when his day of royal patronage was over, as Hanger or Barrymore. Moore has told the story of his career with a fulness that leaves little to be added of biographical value; but even he, with so many qualifications for the task, has failed to convey anything approaching a portrait of his distinguished countryman, as he shone with his brilliant social qualifications, at the Prince's Brighton *réunions.*

LADY CLERMONT.   59

At this time the effects of hard drinking began to tell on Colonel McMahon, whom I very well recollect; his hand shook so that he could scarcely carry to his lips a glass of our old port wine, of which, when my father died, besides what was in use, there were five pipes in the cellar, mellowing by age.

Prominent among my earliest Brighton reminiscences are those of old Lady Clermont, who was a frequent guest at the Pavilion. Her physician had recommended a moderate use of stimulants to supply that energy which was deficient in her system, and brandy had been suggested in a prescribed quantity, to be mixed with her tea. I remember well having my curiosity excited by this, to me, novel form of taking medicine, and holding on by the back of a chair to watch the *modus operandi*. Very much to my astonishment the patient held a liqueur bottle over a cup of tea, and began to pour out its contents, with a peculiar purblind look, upon the *back* of a teaspoon. Presently she seemed suddenly to become aware of what she was about, turned up the spoon the right way, and carefully measured and added the quantity to which she had been restricted. The tea so strongly "laced" she then drank with great apparent gusto.

Of course it was no longer "the cup that cheers but not inebriates;" but what seemed inexplicable to my ingenuous mind was the unvarying recurrence of the same mistake of presenting the back of the spoon instead of the front. I was aware that it did not arise from defect of sight. Lady Clermont could see almost as distinctly as myself. Nevertheless, the cordial was

THE GLOUCESTER MILITIA.

permitted to accumulate in the tea, till the old lady chose to adopt a better measurer, and then she most conscientiously took care not to exceed the number of teaspoonsful the obliging doctor had prescribed.

I was not then aware that this was a case in which the remedy was the reverse of worse than the disease. Lady Clermont liked brandy as a medicine, and made this bungle in measuring it by way of innocent device for securing a much larger dose than she had been ordered. The gravity with which she noticed her apparent mistake, without attempting to correct it, and her little exclamation of surprise, so invariably uttered, amused me so much, that when she quitted the Pavilion the best part of my day's entertainment seemed to have departed with her.

My father's regiment of militia, the South Gloucester, in the efficiency of which he felt the greatest pride, was quartered at Brighton, and the stir and pomp of military parade were thus added to the showy elements that constituted life at a fashionable watering-place in the olden time. The officers were constantly at our house, and dinners, balls, and other social enjoyments were frequent. Lord Berkeley then lived in a mansion known as "the Yellow House," on or near the site of which now stands the Royal York Hotel. Before this the band used to play, under the direction of its efficient master—to the best of my recollection he was called "Worth"—to the special gratification of the visitors, who were sure to group themselves about within good hearing distance, to listen to the martial strains.

CHANGE IN DRESS.

I was invariably one of the audience, but no air, however inspiring, had any charms for me, unless it possessed an emphatic and liberal accompaniment of the big drum; being as satisfied as Othello that this instrument helped materially, not only to " the pomp and circumstance of glorious war," but to "make ambition virtue." The advancement made in regimental bands, and the striking change that has taken place in costume, would render such an entertainment on the Parade now more curious than interesting. The clang of the cymbals, and the flourishing sticks and reverberations of the big drum, might be repeated, but, alas! we may listen in vain for the touching pathos of " Nancy Dawson," or the inspiring strain of "Darby Kelly." Gone with them are the blessed pigtails that used to adorn the heads of civilians and soldiers, officers and privates—vanished the hair-powder, or, with the men, the tallow candle and the flour, the stiff uniform, and the long black gaiters of our South Gloucestershire heroes; and the only remains of the fashionable dress of the *élite* of both sexes, generally grouped around them, are to be looked for in the caricatures of the period. A bonnet of those days, kangaroo-like, might have held in its stomach a couple of dozens of the present day; but the ramlike freaks of existing enormities may be considered equally extravagant.

The French appellation, " l'enfant terrible," sufficiently expresses the popular idea of a listening child; but it is scarcely possible to convey an adequate conception of the effect that may be produced by his revelations or remarks on what he has seen and heard, which frequently come quite as malapropos. Notwithstanding daily experience of such awkward things, mammas and nurses continue to indulge in private communications, heedless that a small pair of ears, if they do not realize the proverb that permits them to hear no good of themselves, may become acquainted with facts which are far from creditable or pleasant to other people; and their proprietors, on some future occasion, are pretty sure to display their information in a fearfully mischievous manner.

Paterfamilias also is often equally indiscreet, not only before children, but in the presence of servants, whose use of family secrets is equally to be dreaded. The folly, however, of overlooking very young auditors is not more to be reprehended than that of ridiculing them when they utter a remark peculiarly characteristic of their limited experience, or deficiency of knowledge in the usages of the world.

I remember an observation of mine exciting a roar of laughter that left an impression on my young mind anything but agreeable. I had been sent for a walk on the Parade, had seen the regiment march past, had returned the friendly nods of Captains Cross, Pyrke, and " Wait," or, as he was called by his brother officers, " Dulken ;" but my attention was specially directed to one of the ensigns, the son of Shrapnell, the regimental surgeon, because he was not only very young and very small of his age, but seemed in danger of splitting up like a willow wand in his strenuous

DUKE OF NORFOLK.   63

endeavours to maintain the stride of his men, or, in military phrase, to " keep step."

In the crowd of lookers-on I recognised one of 'the old familiar faces of my childhood, and he was as remarkable in his way as the diamond edition of an officer .I have just named, moreover was a source of unfailing amusement to me.

I returned home to 'find the reception-room full of gay company, apparently half the rank and fashion in Brighton having looked in.

" Well, my little man," said one of the most distinguished of our visitors, as I sat, shy and quiet, coiled up in one of the capacious arm-chairs of the well-remembered drawing-room of the Yellow House; " who did you see on the Parade to-day ?"

There was immediately a hush of expectation for - the answer of the child. The buzz of gossip and laughter ceased, and every eye was directed towards me, as if waiting to hear the revelations of an oracle. Of course such public notice did not remove my shyness, and I remained silent.

" Did you see the Duke of Norfolk ?" his Grace was singular from his sky-blue dress and his ruffles.

Jockey of Norfolk might have been bought and sold a hundred times, for all I cared at that moment. I had not noticed his Grace, but I felt a little ashamed to confess my inattention ; so looked at my fingers, instead of answering.

" Did you see the Duke of York ?" was the next question.

64 A REMARKABLE CHARACTER.

I had not observed his Royal Highness; but under the impression that my having failed to do so would be regarded as a serious error by all that (to me) brilliant company, I still continued the very careful examination of each finger in turn.

"Did you see Mrs. Fitzherbert?" again asked that inquiring spirit.

Some people have their answers at their fingers' ends, but that was not the case with me. It was plain I ought to have seen the lady, and not having done so, I felt humiliated and remained mute.

"Did you see the Prince?" was next demanded.

"No," I replied, suddenly plucking up a spirit, and looking full of exultation; "but I saw *the cook !*"

Every one knew the *chef de cuisine* of the Berkeley establishment—a fat Frenchman of the genuine Gallic type—and my reference to him was accepted as an anticlimax of the most ridiculous kind. The anxious, curious crowd burst into a shout of laughter, which broke out again and again as they observed my expression of wonder and mystification as to the cause of such uproarious mirth.

This, however, was not the last of my mortification; for long afterwards young ladies of rank, superannuated dowagers, official dignitaries, grave members of the government, in short, almost every person of consequence in Brighton, used to stop me in my walks with my nurse or servant, and with an assumption of seriousness that evidently had a severe struggle with an irrepressible

ENGLISH OATHS.

tendency to mirth, inquired, "Have you seen the cook?"

Such experiments on the temper of a child would not be tolerated, or scarce indulged in, at the present day. It was also very bad taste; but strange ideas of good breeding were then adopted. This was strikingly apparent in the coarseness of ordinary forms of speech. Oaths were employed in conversation by men of the highest rank, even in the presence of ladies. The Prince of Wales and his brothers adopted it; the Duke of Clarence not much more sparingly than the rest. An imprecation commonly commenced every sentence, the Lord's name was taken in vain, and the speaker's own soul sometimes consigned to perdition. It was this foolish and disgusting habit that our lively neighbours over the water seized upon as characteristic of *perfide Albion*, and the "god-dam Englishman" has flourished in the French drama ever since.

Indeed, when long subsequently I traversed France to hunt its forests, all the gentlemen I met between Havre and Paris, and between the capital and Navarre, including the sons of my host and hostess at the Château Sauvages, in the Department of the Nieve (le Vicomte and Vicomtesse D'Anchald), considered that such vulgar phrases were still fashionable in England. The eldest son, to please their visitor, employed them in discourse. "D— my eyes, what a fine prospect!" cried a fellow-traveller, the only English sentence he knew, as he courteously, as he thought, directed my attention to the landscape by

VOL. I.

the side of the line of railway; while at a large dinner
party at the Château Sauvages, Jules D'Anchald
directed the attention of all the guests towards me by
hospitably exclaiming, as he offered to help me to a
favourite dish, " D— my eyes, sud you have some
of dis ?"

I remember a day at Brighton, when the scents of
the mignonette and wallflower were filling the air
with their fragrance, just as they did but the other
day, a fête champêtre was announced to come off at
the Spa, as a chalybeate spring at Brighton was then
called, where the beautiful Lady Haggerstone had a
pretty little villa. She was a member of the brilliant
coterie that surrounded the Prince of Wales, by whom
she was very much admired. Indeed, she was the
object of general admiration. This, however, did not
satisfy her. She was ambitious of further captivating
the heir apparent, and took extraordinary pains to
effect her purpose.

On this occasion, to which I more immediately
refer, she attempted to charm his Royal Highness by
assuming a rustic dress that would have satisfied the
taste of a Watteau in the rural picturesque. At her
residence she had a miniature farmyard, and three
pretty little Alderneys. When the Prince and his
friends and attendants had arrived, her ladyship came
forward from a side wicket as a milkmaid, for the
purpose of making a syllabub for the Prince. She
had a silver pail in one hand and an ornamental stool
in the other. Lady Haggerstone tripped along, with
ribbons flying from her dainty little milking-hat

that hung on one side her graceful head, and the smallest little apron tied below her laced stomacher, till she came opposite his Royal Highness, to whom she dropped a rurally-graceful curtsey. Then passing lightly over the beautifully-plaited straw, her tucked-up gown showing her neat ankle as well as her coloured stockings, she placed her stool and pail conveniently for use. Leaning against the flank of one of the crossest-looking of the Alderneys, she was attempting to commence her rustic labours; but not having selected the right sex, the offended animal did not seem to fancy such masquerade, for he first kicked out and then trotted away, nearly upsetting stool, pail, and Lady Haggerstone, who then, covered with confusion, made a hasty retreat back into her little dairy, whence she did not appear again.

Notwithstanding the impossible-to-be-restrained bursts of laughter around him, the Prince of Wales never moved a muscle of his face, but graciously directing the attention of his fair companions to the beauty of the day, praised the neatness of the farm-yard. His Royal Highness then led the way back into the villa, and shortly after to the carriages, as the good breeding, at least what in those days was called so, of "the best bred gentleman in England," and his own good sense told him, that after such signal discomfiture to her prettily imagined purpose, Lady H. would be more pleased with his absence than with his presence, surrounded as she was by smiling witnesses.

Among my Brighton reminiscences, of what may

F 2

be called the court of George Prince of Wales, I must not forget Lady Nagle. Her husband was dead, and she invariably wore a very long chain around her neck to which was attached a miniature portrait of him, of rather an unusual size for such a position. She was an Irishwoman; I am certain that in these days she would have been called vulgar, and she had a considerable brogue. From the length of the gold chain, the picture of her regretted partner when she stood up swung about, descending very low, and when she sat down it reposed comfortably in her lap. The length of the chain, and the size of the minia-ture, were always a standing joke at the Pavilion, particularly with the Prince, who never failed to take some opportunity or other to draw attention to it, and to elicit the well-known reply that Lady Nagle was certain to make.

"Ah, my Lady Nagle," the Prince would say, "you are never without that miniature."

"No, plaise your Royal Highness, I always wear Sir Edmond next my heart."

This excited my boyish curiosity greatly, for I used to wonder where her heart could be.

Ladies very often made up the whist-table for the Prince, when society at the Pavilion affected a homely character, and Lady Clermont, Lady Haggerstone, and Mrs. Jones, were frequently of that quiet party.

In those days, and on the opposite side of the Steyne from the Pavilion, about the centre, stood the chief library and toy-shop, kept by a tradesman named Wigley. It was at this shop where the late

THE PRINCE OF WALES. 69

Lord Bloomfield, who had been introduced by my
father to the Prince, as well as the late Sir Mathew
Tierney, the latter (afterwards the confidential physician to the Prince) bought for me my first little
drum and pewter sword, with which I deafened and
menaced attending nursery maids.

When the South Gloucester were at Brighton, my
father in command, an order was promulgated from
the Horse Guards that the regiment was to be permitted to volunteer for the Line, and for foreign
service; and the permission for the men to do so was
read in his presence on parade.

The very first to avail himself of this permission
was the right-hand man of the splendid grenadier
company. The colonel prided himself on their size,
and on this man stepping forth from the ranks, he
brought his cane to bear across his head, and knocked
him down.

Such an outrageous act as this would, even then,
have cashiered any other Colonel in the service, but
through the aid of powerful friends at the Pavilion,
the matter was hushed up, a large and fine contingent
volunteered from the regiment for foreign service in the
war, and the affair went no further.

It was my fortune very frequently to hear the
Prince tell the most extraordinary stories, which,
according to the prevailing customs of the good
manners of the day, he larded, at almost every sentence, with what would now be considered very impious oaths. The example set me by my father and
brothers had the effect too of particularly turning my

earliest notions to field sports and to the prize ring; anything regarding those two recreations, therefore, was sure to attract me beyond measure. The Prince was very fond of talking of his harriers with which he used to hunt upon the Downs, making them the theme of conversation to his guests of both sexes, at the Pavilion, and to his companions in other places. The story that most impressed itself on my mind was the following :—

"I was out one day, ma'am," his Royal Highness said to a lady, " with my harriers; we found a hare, but the scent was catching and uncertain, so that we could go no continuous pace at all. There was a butcher out, G—d d— me, ma'am, a great big fellow, fifteen stone, six feet two inches without his shoes, and the bully of all Brighton. He over-rode my hounds several times, and I had spoken to him to hold hard in vain. At last, G—d d— me, ma'am, he rode slap over my favourite bitch, ' Ruby.' I could stand it no longer, but jumping off my horse said, ' Get down, you d— rascal, pull off your coat, none shall interfere with us, but you or I shall go back to Brighton more dead than alive.' G—d d— me, ma'am, I threw off my coat, and the big ruffian, nothing loth, did the same by his. By G—d, ma'am, we fought for an hour and twenty minutes, my hunting field forming a ring around us, no one interfering, and at the end of it the big bully butcher of Brighton was carried away senseless, while I had hardly a scratch."

The Prince would then turn to some courtier present, and say, "G—d d— me, you remember it." I

MOTHER SHIPTON.

71

perfectly recollect his saying this to a foreigner, high
in the Prince's estimation, who was often there, but
whose name, at this length of time, I cannot recollect.
He invariably replied to these demands for his testimony in his foreign accent, "By G—d, your Royal
Highness, I do forget."

This tale was believed in France, and set down as
one of the common acts of the "G—d d— John Bull
Prince." It was dramatized, and all the French
people made to believe, while witnessing the performance, that from the king, prince, and peer, down to
the lowest costermonger, the English nation not only
boxed individually among themselves, but had certain
seasons set apart for the gentle pastime, Christmas
being the principal one for the general round of fisti-
cuffs.

There was another story the Prince was fond of
telling. Riding, in company with Sir John Lade, of
four-in-hand celebrity, over the Downs above Brighton,
he had proceeded a considerable distance when a heavy
thunderstorm burst over their heads. They took the
shortest cut to the nearest windmill for shelter, where
they dismounted, Sir John holding the bridle of the
Prince's horse, till a boy appeared who took charge of
the two. When the storm had passed over, his
Royal Highness came out, and was about to remount,
when he observed that the lad had two thumbs
upon his right hand. This reminded him of a
prophecy of the famous witch, Mother Shipton, to
the effect that when the Prince's bridle should be held
by a miller's son with two thumbs on one hand the

72 TOWNSEND, THE BOW-STREET OFFICER.

kingdom should be disturbed by terrible convulsions. His Royal Highness appeared to be very much struck by this singular rencontre, but made immense fun at the expense of the prophetess, who was a sort of female Zadkiel. One of the old lady's vaticinations, however, that London would come to Highgate Hill, is nearly, if not completely, fulfilled.

It was at Brighton that I first saw the thief-taker, Townsend. He was a little rotund man. with a light yellow wig, and a big stick; in personal appearance, and I was told in pluck, quite unlike a man capable of dealing with a ruffian. Perhaps he was a good detective, and had other thews and sinews placed at his command. He was constantly in and about the Pavilion, and made much of, and familiarly talked to by the Prince, by my father, and by all the nobility at Brighton, peers and peeresses. I can just recollect a sort of beggars' feast at Brighton, or it might be, a dinner given to the poor of all classes, and I think it was in the open air. At all events, lords, ladies, and gentlemen, walked round the tables to see them at dinner, conducted in that circumambulation by the popular Bow Street runner; and holding somebody's hand, I made one of the party. Townsend knew, or seemed to know, every ragged person there, and to display his knowledge, he stopped occasionally and spoke to particular individuals. Thus, to one old woman he said, " Hullo, Nancy, how's this? What, not dressed in your best gown? Come, what are you up to now? I know you've got a better at home!"

Jackson, the prize-fighter, once the champion of the ring, having licked Mendoza in ten minutes, was often at the Pavilion sparring with the Prince, Lord Barrymore and others, and with the late Lord Fitzhardinge, then called Lord Dursley. He also taught me to use my then very small fists, placing me between his knees and holding up his huge palms for me to hit at. He subsequently married a lady with money, who espoused him on condition that he did not fight again, and a more quiet, better-mannered man never associated with gentlemen. In later years, long after he had retired into private life, the Prince Regent expressed a wish to see him and a more recent champion of the day set-to with the gloves on in his presence, that he might judge of the proficiency of the new school. . Jackson at once declared his readiness to obey what was to him a royal command, but the more modern fighter, though then in possession of that youth and freshness so necessary to gladiatorial success, declined, and his Royal Highness lost what would have been to him a very interesting exhibition.

Among the remarkable people who figure in the early period of my reminiscences was Watt Smith, another lively importation from the Emerald Isle. He was the brother of Mrs. Fitzherbert, and is said to have witnessed the marriage certificate of his sister; but that his attesting signature, for prudential reasons, was subsequently cut off. Watt Smith, particularly after his third bottle of claret, and under its genial influence, would have readily put his name to any document for the Prince, to whom he devoted himself heart and soul, and was a boon companion in the Pavilion jollifications; and so I think would his brother, Jack Smith. With him were associated the individuals I have already named—all well-known Brighton characters and confidential friends of the Prince of Wales. To these may be added a gentleman whose excessively kind manner, good-humour, and hearty, soldier-like bearing, which at times he would put on when in conversation, immensely interested me; this was Colonel, afterwards Sir Joseph, Whatley.

Prominent among the ladies was of course Mrs. Fitzherbert, with whom I was rather a favourite; more probably on account of the Prince being my godfather, than from any of my own juvenile merits. Then came Mrs. De Crespingny, afterwards Lady Whatley (mother of the present Lady Packington); Miss Vanneck, to whom I gave an unpleasant cause of remembrance by accidentally striking her with a ball while at play; Lady Nagle, and Mrs. Jones. There was also a young lady very often at the Pavilion, then a child of much my own age, Miss Seymour, afterwards Mrs. Dawson, a sister of the present Admiral Sir George Seymour, who used to play with me, and who considerably won my childish love. All these were very kind friends there and then, particularly during the races, when I was allowed to bet sixpences with them—always on the Prince's colours. In truth, it was to me a happy time; and though I was, later in my life, on terms of intimacy in London and elsewhere with most of them for the rest of their lives, it is to the Brighton period I always fall back for my pleasantest recollections of these early friends.

I have revisited the place but twice since. I have beheld the growth thus at long intervals, of its improvement, till it became the London *super mare* that now extends from Rottingdean to Hove; but no combination of modern attractions could make me forget the Brighton of my childhood. Almost all " the old familiar faces" have passed away, never to return; the very costume has become obsolete; most of the houses at which I visited have been pulled down; brilliant gas has consigned the light of other days (the link) to oblivion; and the well-remembered rendezvous of fashion, the renowned old Ship Tavern, is being looked down upon by a big, pretentious, joint-stock company hotel: nevertheless, old Brighton, with its limited accommodation, inconvenient houses, droll fashions, darkness, and sedans, is infinitely dearer to me than the nearly perfect Brighton of to-day: although I have still friends resident there whom I value very much.

I reconcile myself to the easy transit from town in a first-class railway carriage, in an hour and a half, in preference to a day's jolting over bad roads in an ugly postchaise; but I cannot so readily accept the change for the worse which has come over that scene of so many of my earliest and brightest enjoyments, the Pavilion. It ought either to be pulled down, or kept in a state of respectable repair. Noticing it in its present tumble-down aspect, while presented as a show for Cockney sight-seers at sixpence a head, no one could believe that it was for a long course of years the favourite residence of the most fastidious prince in Europe, and was often thronged by the cleverest as well as the gayest people his influence could bring together.

My first visit to Brighton as a man, after my residence there as a child, was during its races, when the late Lord Egremont used to keep a splendid table, open to any of his friends. I remember dining there on one occasion, when I was sent down by the present Lord Fitzhardinge to be his representative in keeping up his love for his first wife, the late Lady Charlotte Berkeley, a sister of the late Duke of Richmond, who for a time, and on account of some whim, the old Duchess of Richmond, her mother, had forbidden her to see. As a young man, I was always selected by my brothers to do kind actions for them, without reference to my own affections, which were then confined to the vicinity of Hampton Court. I instantly posted off on my delicate mission; and as I drove up to the hotel where Lady Charlotte was staying with the Duchess of Argyle and the Ladies Paget, I saw them on the balcony. I went to the races with them, and poured consolation into the ears of my future sister-in-law, who was one of the kindest and best-natured creatures in the world, and delivered to her a letter from my brother, receiving one for him in return.

Alas! "the course of true love," in regard to the return letter, did not "run smooth;" for in walking about the course my pocket was picked of it, as well as of my purse. Being unable again to see Lady Charlotte to tell her of my loss, and to obtain another communication, I had to return to Cranford to inform my brother that, though it was all wrong about the letter, it was all right about the love, for his intended sent by me every kind and wished-for assurance.

My love mission over, I put a fresh pair of posters to the carriage that afternoon, and trotted off to a *déjeûner* given at Dysart House, Petersham, where, as I knew I could securely cultivate my own affection, nothing was lost by my first trip to Brighton. But by serving my brother and his intended, whom I afterwards loved as a sister, I experienced the highest gratification. I am sorry to have to record that the aid I so readily afforded was forgotten by him in after years, when I needed consideration and kindness, and from conduct as well as position had a right to expect both.

CHAPTER IV.

BERKELEY HOUSE, SPRING GARDENS.

Power of the Berkeleys, Berkeley Square, Spring Gardens—
Berkeley House—Elopement of my aunt, Lady Georgiana, with
Lord Forbes — My aunt, the Margravine of Anspach and
Princess of Berkeley—Private theatricals—My father's friends
and contemporaries—Watt Smith, brother of Mrs. Fitzherbert
—Sir Philip Francis—The Duke of Clarence's account of Lord
Grantley—His practical joke at my expense—Mrs. Fitzherbert
—Enormous amount of jewellery presented to her by the
Prince of Wales—Gillray's caricatures, in which she is repre-
sented—Quarrel of the editor of the "Keepsake" with Count
D'Orsay—I make them friends—Bernal—His trick on Mansel
Reynolds—Insult offered to Lady Mary Berkeley—Demolition
of Berkeley House.

I COULD not help remarking the consultations constantly taking place among the seniors of my family
immediately after the death of my father, and before
my mother quitted Berkeley Castle, and I heard many
things that greatly affected me at that time, though
hardly conscious of their full meaning. Tears of
vexation and passionate exclamations were manifested
where there ought to have been nothing but sorrow
and a grateful affection. But I do not like to dwell
upon such scenes out of consideration for the dead,
though they forgot in their blind attempts to enrich
the elder born, the rights my legitimacy had given
me. I have since become only too well aware of what

BERKELEY HOUSE.

caused the angry discussion of a subject of the deepest interest to me, viz., the rightful succession to the ancient title.

Let it, then, suffice, in the present stage of my narrative, for me to say, that after hearing these angry discussions among my surviving seniors, in which some were blamed for not having done enough, and others for having done too much, and the probable course of events, which were assuredly looming in the distance, canvassed; Moreton, the present Earl of Berkeley, myself as the heir presumptive, my youngest brother Craven, now no more, and my three sisters, left the Castle and removed to Berkeley House, in London, which, with Cranford House, near Hounslow, were the jointure houses left to my mother.

Our town house was in Spring Gardens, but it was not the one historically connected with the family. In the reign of Charles I. this was in Berkeley Street, Clerkenwell, which took its name from our mansion there; but John, Lord Berkeley—who won for the King the brilliant contest with the Parliamentarians known as Stratton fight, being the first to dislodge the rebels from the hill—subsequently on his return from his viceroyship in Ireland, erected at an expense of upwards of £30,000—considered a large sum in those days—a house which Evelyn describes as a palace. It was built not only in the country, but where a rustic structure stood, called Hay Hill farm; nevertheless it was on the north side of Piccadilly, opposite the Green Park.

The estate of which it formed a part was afterwards

selected for building purposes by his widow, and a, square and two streets in a few years sprang up around it, much to the distaste of honest John Evelyn, who feelingly expressed his disapprobation at the overgrowth of London. This was entered in his Diary in the year 1684. Had he lived to reverse the two middle figures, when the builders have absorbed all the country westward to Hammersmith, and are making rapid advances upon Richmond, the worthy man might indeed have been astonished at "the mad intemperance of the age," as he calls it, for bricks and mortar.

Berkeley House, built by Hugh May, with porticos, in imitation of a design by Palladio, became subsequently the residence of the Princess Anne in the reign of her sister, Queen Mary, after whose death it was bought (1697), by the first Duke of Devonshire. It was burnt to the ground on the 16th of October, 1733, the conflagration attracting a large number of distinguished spectators, among whom were the then Prince of Wales and the Earl of Albemarle. This was the end of Berkeley House, for a new mansion was built on its site, since known as Devonshire House. Only the portico and marble staircase of my ancestor's "palace" have been preserved.

Berkeley Square, built in 1698, has ever since been a favourite and fashionable quarter. Here the great Lord Clive, the Earl of Orford (Horace Walpole), and Pope's Martha Blount died—here lived the Marquis of Lansdowne, and Lady Isabella Finch. About the year of my birth Walpole's niece, the

AN ELOPEMENT.

Countess of Waldegrave lived here, and it still contains the mansions of the Lansdowne, Jersey, and Powis families.

Spring Gardens was, during the reigns of the first Stuarts, a portion of the pleasure grounds attached to the royal palace, Whitehall, and was so called from a spring in the gardens which, by the pressure of a foot on the ground above it, sprinkled the person who made the experiment. It was a public place of recreation till after the Restoration, when it was built upon. Houses of the first class were erected, and in them lived Prince Rupert, Philip Earl of Chesterfield, Lord Crofts, Sir Edward Hungerford, Colley Cibber, and George Canning—the last resided here at the commencement of the century.

Berkeley House was among the best of them, and was the resort of the fashionable world from about the commencement of the reign of George the Second. The Countess, my grandmother, was Lady of the Bedchamber to the Princess of Wales. It was from here that, after her presentation at a drawing-room, my aunt, Lady Georgiana, one of the handsomest young ladies of that season, eloped with Lord Forbes, then considered about the ugliest man in town; he was afterwards Earl of Granard. At this period he is described as possessing "a very foolish sort of low Irish humour," was a widower, and had a son—by no means a desirable match, so the guardians, Lords Boston and Vere, thought, for they refused their consent. The result was the elopement of the lovers.

My aunt, Lady Elizabeth, after she had married

VOL. I.

Lord Craven, figured prominently in the fashionable world. She mingled in all the gay assemblies of the period, and among her most intimate friends were those eccentric people whose peculiarities afforded so many subjects for the humorous pencil of Gillray. There was Lord Cholmondeley, who was very fat, and was represented by him taking a dancing lesson of the celebrated Vestris. Lord Landaff, and his brothers Montague and George Mathews, who were leading dandies; Colonel Thornton, who imitated the personal appearance of the Duke of Hamilton. Boothby Clopton, commonly called Prince Boothby, and "Skiffy Skipton," Sir Lumley Skeffington, another beau of the old school. He did not succeed to his father's baronetcy till 1815. Though he figures in Gillray as "a natural," he laid claim to literary honours. He wrote several plays, and a considerable amount of verse. Byron, who was his contemporary, devotes several lines in his "English Bards and Scotch Reviewers," to his dramatic talent : the popularity of his "Sleeping Beauty" produced him this distinction. He outlived all his brother dandies, dying only a few years back, but it was difficult to identify the haggard face in a brown wig, and the figure nearly bent double, in a long-waisted coat, the skirts of which descended to his heels, who sunned himself in fine weather in some of the fashionable thoroughfares, with the erect, sprightly fop of half a century before.

Lady Archer was a celebrated amazon of that time. With her were associated Lady Mount Edgecombe, Miss Jeffries, Hon. Mrs. Hobart, afterwards Lady

BRANDENBURG HOUSE.

Buckinghamshire, and Lady Cecilia Johnston; their portraits may be seen in the print called "La Belle Assemblée." Mrs. Hobart has been separately delineated trying on the garters of the notorious empiric Van Butchell, a specific against barrenness; and Lady Cecilia he has represented as a Vestal, with "Ovid's Art of Love" in her pocket. In addition we have the Duchess of Rutland and her sisters Lady Gertrude Manners, Lady Coventry, who is introduced into the artist's "Lady Godiva's Rout," Mrs. Concannon, who, with two other fair votaries of play, Ladies Buckinghamshire and Archer, are made to appear as *Faro's* daughters.

Among other representative men were "Bubble and Squeak," Sir Watkyn Williams Wynn, and his brother Charles, and the hero of the following verse :—

> " What can Tommy Onslow do ?
> Why, drive a phaeton and two.
> Can Tommy Onslow do no more ?
> Yes—drive a phaeton and four !"

Mr. Onslow was afterwards Lord Cranley, a celebrated coachman. Lord Kirkcudbright, though a little man, was also a great buck about this time.

Lady Craven had opportunities of seeing and knowing these notorious persons before she went abroad. On her return to England, as the Margravine of Anspach, she became as well known as any of them. After the Margrave purchased Brandenburg House at Hammersmith for his residence, and very great improvements there had been completed under her direction, it became famous for its fashionable *réunions*, particularly for its private theatricals, for which the Mar-

G 2

gravine not only provided a theatre, and the necessary scenes, dresses, and decorations, but wrote the plays, some of which she published. Among her *corps dramatique* was Lord Cholmondeley, who, though remarkable for his portly appearance, chose to assume the character of Cupid, while Lady Albina, who was built on quite as large a scale, represented "Cowslip."

The Margravine, though now long past her *première jeunesse*, invariably selected the part of the youthful and interesting heroine. Sometimes, too, while giving this prominence to herself, she kept some of her aspiring assistants, as they thought, too much in the background. Angelo, then much in the gay world, was a good amateur actor, and finding himself cast for a part in which he had nothing to do and almost as little to say, observing too that the Margravine was absent, he seized upon the opportunity when he came before the audience to improvise a ridiculous speech: the roar of laughter it produced brought the imperious dramatist and actress to the wings, and the ambitious actor received a severe reprimand.

The Margravine was created, by the Emperor of Austria, Princess of Berkeley. She went abroad after the death of her husband, published her well-known Memoirs in the year 1826, and died in Italy a year or two afterwards. An account of her death will be found in the recently-published Diary of the Duke of Buckingham.

My father, who succeeded to the title when about two years old, whenever his mother and sisters were in London, remained with them till he went to Eton, and, subsequently to France and Italy. A portion of almost every year of his long minority was spent at Berkeley House, and his intimate associates of about his own age were the King's elder sons. With the Prince of Wales he was on the most confidential terms. Among the young nobility his principal associates were Lords Carlisle, Egremont, Cholmondeley, and Tyrconnel.

Narbonne Berkeley, afterwards created Lord Bottecourt, was a Lord of the Bedchamber, and brother to the Duchess of Beaufort. He was constantly at our house. In short, it became a place of general resort for courtiers, and the leaders of society of both sexes. I can only remember having heard the names of the Duke of Richmond, Lady Tavistock, the Duke and Duchess of Marlborough, Horace Walpole, Garrick, Dr. Johnson, George Colman, and Sir Joshua Reynolds; but there is little doubt that these *réunions* included every person in town whose acquaintance was worth having.

My father had for his contemporaries Beau Brummell in the zenith of his fame. I remember him only in its decay; George Selwyn and Horace Walpole when their social influence was on the wane; the Barrymores (Newgate, Cripplegate, Hellgate, and " Billingsgate," as their sister was ungallantly designated by the Prince of Wales)—Colonel Hanger, Lord Camelford, Sir John Lade, Calcraft, whom I can very well remember, and who committed suicide ; in short, all the fast men who flourished about the last quarter of the last century and the commencement of the present. With Fox, Sheridan, Burke, and other leaders of the Prince of Wales's political party, he was also very intimate, in consequence of being so much with the Prince; and of these I have heard him frequently converse.

Among our visitors at Berkeley House, I have a distinct recollection of Sir Philip Francis, because he used to speak to my brothers and myself in a rough, Hibernian accent, and was singularly thin in appearance. One day, on his coming into the dining-room, when my mother was giving us some wine and water, he exclaimed, on purpose to amuse us, "Oh, blood, Lady Berkeley, how those boys drink!" I know that he was supposed to have written the letters of Junius, which have been fathered upon so many of his eminent contemporaries.

As a boy, I remember that the Duke of Clarence was one day sitting at Berkeley House with one of my godfathers, the late Lord Grantley, whom he always facetiously called "old Nob Scobble." There were others in the room, whom I at this distance of time forget; so, by way of amusing us all, his Royal Highness told the following story. He said—"Old Nob Scobble there came up from 'Wanersh' to attend the levée, meaning to return to Guildford after it was over. He, therefore, had simply desired his Irish valet to bring his court dress for the occasion. His toilet finished, and those little white curls at his temples snowily powdered and primly arranged, bowing like a drake in a pond at his duck, as we all know he does

ROYAL JOKING.

whenever he is pleased, on having got himself up to his perfect satisfaction, he called for the finishing addition to his costume, his sword. Then he stood still, bowing and ducking before his looking-glass. What he waited for not being forthcoming, he called out angrily for his servant to make haste. The valet had become aware of that which he had forgotten to bring, but beginning to be frightened at the evident wrath of his lord, he at last came hastily into the room.

"'Sure, now!' he cried, 'I have not brought your lordship's sword, but,' stretching his hand out with the weapon in it, 'here's your lordship's double-barrel gun.'"

About the same time the Duke, calling at Berkeley House, began complaining to my mother that my brothers and myself had pelted him and the Duke of Cambridge from our garden walls, as they were proceeding out of the park by the well-known narrow passage of Spring Gardens.

"You young dogs!" his Royal Highness cried, as if in a tremendous passion, "if I had not ducked, you would have hit me. I escaped, but Cambridge got a terrible blow in the eye."

I stood aghast, and was about to speak. My mother, however, looking very angry, frowned me into silence; and I should perhaps have received a severe punishment, had not the Duke, observing my dismay, good-naturedly confessed that he was merely having a little fun at our expense. His Royal Highness was partial to such harmless practical jokes, but both himself and the Duke of Cambridge were too kind-hearted really to distress even a child.

Among our lady visitors was Mrs. Fitzherbert, who had been a frequent guest here in the zenith of her celebrity, when, with her royal lover, Devonshire House and the town mansions of the leaders of the Opposition were eagerly thrown open to her. She had a peculiar way of standing before the fire, that impressed itself strongly on my mind; but the stories circulated about her, and, more than all, the caricatures in which she was introduced, that were constantly exhibited in the print-shops, attracted me as much towards her as her amiability and her beauty.

Her alleged marriage with the Prince of Wales afforded more than one subject to the humorous pencil of Gillray. He ludicrously exaggerated the perils to the Commonwealth, arising out of the union of the heir-apparent with a Roman Catholic; but it does not appear that he entertained even the idea that a real marriage had taken place; indeed, after the public denial made by Fox in the House of Commons, with the express authority of the Prince, and the offer of his Royal Highness to give a similar denial in his place in the House of Lords, no one could regard the assumption seriously.

There was another feature in this transaction that attracted public attention: this was the enormous debt the Prince contracted for jewellery and plate for Mrs. Fitzherbert. It has been stated that this was never paid, and that the loss of so large a sum was the ruin of the tradesman who furnished the goods. The case excited much comment at the time. The writer of her "Memoirs" has passed over the circumstance; indeed,

GILLRAY'S CARICATURES. 89

seems to wish it to be understood that the lady never profited by the intimacy. However disinterested she may have been in other respects, there is no evidence that she refused these magnificent presents.

The caricatures in which Mrs. Fitzherbert was introduced, that were sure of collecting a crowd round the shop-window of the publisher, Mrs. Humphreys, of St. James's Street, were:—" Dido Forsaken," in which Fox, Lord North, and Burke are represented taking the Prince away from her, while Pitt and Dundas are blowing the royal crown from her head; " Wife or no Wife, or a Trip to the Continent;" and " The Morning after Marriage, or a Scene on the Continent." In the first, Fox is performing the cere-mony, and Burke, disguised as a Jesuit, is giving away the bride. "Bandalore," in which the Prince is idling with a fashionable toy for ladies, so called— apparently belonging to his *chère amie.* " The Lover's Dream :" this appeared about the period of his Royal Highness's real marriage (8th of April, 1795), and Mrs. Fitzherbert is represented, with other favourites, passing away like a vision. " The Funeral Procession of Miss Regency," where the lady is introduced as the chief mourner. It refers to the unexpected recovery of the king, and consequent failure of the Regency Bill. " Patent Bolsters," in which Mrs. Fitzherbert is introduced trying on a novelty in dress, that gave the wearer the appearance of *embonpoint,* or made her as " ladies wish to be who love their lords." As this pad, for it was nothing else, was worn by girls as well as by matrons who had no lords to love, the satirists attacked it vehemently. "Dillettanti Theatricals, or a Peep at the Green-Room :" this is a spirited quiz of the amateur actors and actresses, with whom are Mrs. Fitzherbert and the Prince, who flourished under the auspices of my aunt, the Margravine. "The Guardian Angel :" a late production, in which she is represented trying to convert the Princess Charlotte to Popery.

There were several others, but these are sufficient to show the light in which Mrs. Fitzherbert was regarded about this time, for such productions had a considerable circulation ; indeed, were an unrivalled source of amusement in great houses in town and country.

My stay at Berkeley House, after the trial respecting the peerage, was not long; but I was a frequent resident there a few years later. One of the incidents in which I was then made to figure, I will relate.

Mansel Reynolds, the editor of that fashionable annual the "Keepsake," announced to D'Orsay his intention of writing a book.

"Do, my dear fellow," replied the latter, "and call it ze 'Diary of a Dupe.'"

This was said just after Reynolds had been very much cheated as to a house he had taken on his marriage, I believe a happy one, with a wife educated by himself. He was always being done by somebody or other in the transaction of the commonest business. He took offence at the suggestion, being very sore on the subject. In fact, he suffered all the time I knew him from derangement of the whole nervous system, resulting, I have heard him say, from indigestion. If we read his works, particularly "Miserrimus" and

" The Parricide," it is evident that he wrote with " a mind diseased."

On the morning of his visit to me at Berkeley House, I never before saw a sane man in such violent agitation. As he stood the shivering of his frame shook the room, and his hands, arms, and lips trembled as if they had been withered leaves about to fall from the trunk of a tree. When he told me he must have an apology from D'Orsay, or a duel, and saw that I noticed the agitated state of his limbs, he held his arm across the table, exclaiming, as it shook violently, " Don't think this arises from fear,— it is a nervous excitement I cannot help. You give the word, and I will shoot and be shot at for a week if it be necessary to my honour."

" Quite right," I replied, " I am sure you will. Now, remember, that as you have told me your grievance, and I have taken your honour into my keeping, you must not say a word more about it, but be ready to fight à l'outrance if I tell you to do so."

On this we parted, and I immediately sought the offender, with whom I was also on terms of the most intimate friendship.

No other second was needed; D'Orsay, in the most kind manner, was really distressed at the way Reynolds felt himself, or fancied himself aggrieved at what he had said, and told me to return to him and say what I liked in the way of making up the quarrel.

On such slight causes of offence as these, often there used to arise the most serious differences when left in the hands of incapable seconds; we had also the further disadvantage of having to deal with the very mistaken course pursued at the time in regard to the duel, by the public press and dramatic performances. If two gentlemen met with pistols, and one received the other's fire, and on discharging his pistol in the air was immediately taken from the field by his second, the fact was seized on as a theme for public ridicule. Thus driving inefficient seconds who, as weak men always do, feared ridicule, to shun all amicable arrangement, unless blood had been shed. Whereas, the end of such personal appeals should be the maintenance of a chivalrous sense of honour, *not* the mean exhibition of blood-thirsty courage.

Mansel Reynolds was one day walking up the Haymarket when he was overtaken by my lamented friend, the late Mr. Bernal, at that time Chairman of the Committees of the House of Commons. Now, no one enjoyed a harmless joke more than Bernal, and no one delighted more than he did to get a rise out of Reynolds. To obtain this, he came gently behind him, and touching his arm while he kept out of sight, in the assumed voice of a female beggar, implored charity.

" Go away," growled Reynolds, " I've got nothing."

This refusal, however, did not do, and Bernal kept on imploring the whole way up the street, driving Reynolds into such a state of nervous distraction, that at last he faced about resentfully, and in a threatening attitude, when, to his astonishment, he only beheld at his shoulder the good-humoured countenance of one of the kindest friends he had, who had been indulging himself for the moment in a little too much of a practical joke.

After my mother's death, my sister, Lady Mary Berkeley, still clung to the old house in Spring Gardens, and asked Lord Fitzhardinge, as Colonel Berkeley was then styled, if she might go there to reside during the London season. To this he gave his consent. It soon came to my knowledge, that while his sister was there, enjoying the supposition that she was under his protection as well as at his mercy, he had a woman living with him, whom I shall have to mention more at length in the next volume, he occupying one wing of the building and my sister the other. As in all circumstances of difficulty I was consulted, and the duty of finding a remedy for evil, if that remedy ran counter to the wishes of Lord Fitzhardinge, was thrown on me; and Lady Mary asked me what she should do. As usual on every occasion where I had to give advice to others, I counselled a gentle but a firm line of conduct, and one which, in this instance, should meet my sister's wishes, as to the avoidance, if possible, of a rupture with Lord Fitzhardinge.

With my concurrence, therefore, she addressed to him a letter, simply asking him, " as long as she was under his roof, to give to every interest of hers due consideration, and if he could not do so, or if her presence in his house was in any way irksome to him, then she only needed his telling her so, and she would, as soon as possible, remove."

94   AN OBJECTIONABLE ASSOCIATE.

To this Lord Fitzhardinge replied by letter, "that he fully understood to whom she alluded, ánd it should not happen again," or words to that effect.

On this answer being shown to me, and as Lady Mary was very desirous of remaining in our old family house, and of not having any quarrel with Lord Fitzhardinge, I told her that so far she might be satisfied with it; that I was coming to occupy my old rooms in her wing of the house, and would see that proper respect was shown her; that if this were not done, she might rely on me to protect her, and take on myself the onus of advising her to go away.

For a few days Lord Fitzhardinge fulfilled his expressed intention; but shortly after I discovered that his mistress was again there. So to Lady Mary I repaired, and advised her instant departure, for she could in no way depend on such promises. She followed my advice, and took her departure. Of course it was very soon known by whose suggestion Lady Mary had acted, and the woman, to whose society she had objected, became furious against me. There were plenty of my male relations, brothers, and others, who knew what was going on, and who had heard, as I did afterwards, that Lady Mary's friends looked up from the gardens of the house on the other side of Spring Garden passage, while at a party there given by Lady Charlotte Guest, and kissed their hands to my sister in her balcony at one end of the house, while they observed the obnoxious person protruding her figure at the window of the sitting-room of Lord Fitzhardinge, at the other.

IMPROVEMENTS.

I shall here draw to a conclusion my recollections of this "old house at home," of which not a vestige now remains, it having been pulled down to make room for improvements; just as it had been built up two hundred years before, when the fashionable place of amusement, the Spring Garden, was removed to Vauxhall. This favourite place of recreation has within the last few years also been swallowed up by the builders, and it has obliged those who will not be content with such a substitute as "Cremorne" to go farther afield, to find every desire gratified in the beautiful gardens at Sydenham.

CHAPTER V.

CRANFORD HOUSE.

Ancient residence of the Berkeleys at Cranford—My ancestors—Colonel Berkeley after the trial—Arrival at my mother's dower house—My brother Moreton and the dancing-master—Our instructors and attendants—Sir Thomas Bell—An unexpected demonstration—Pugilism, how it came into fashion—Pierce Egan and "Tom and Jerry"—My brother Augustus—His idea of sport, and delight in a row—My tutor, Mr. Hughes—Riding—My first fall—Arrival of my brother Henry—His love of boxing—Charles Wyndham—My fistic combats—Lord Grantley—My affection for my brother Moreton—Lord Munster and the Fitzclarences—Departure of my favourite brother for college.

LORD BERKELEY of Stratton had a country residence at Twickenham Park, but he was a younger branch of the family, the elder branch, besides Berkeley Castle, were seated at Cranford House, in Middlesex, where originally there had been a preceptory of the Knights Templars; subsequently, in 1363, the manor of Cranford St. John became vested in the Knights Hospitallers of St. John of Jerusalem. For more than two centuries and a half the estate passed into different hands, but in the year 1618 Elizabeth, the Lady of Sir Thomas Berkeley, K.B., who died in the lifetime of his father, Henry, eleventh Baron Berkeley, purchased it of the co-heirs of Sir Roger Aston, for the sum of 7000*l.*. It has remained a residence of the

MY ANCESTORS.

Berkeleys ever since, and its parish church contains the monuments of many of the most eminent of them. Among these is the Lady Berkeley just mentioned, who was the daughter of George, Lord Hunsdon; she died in 1633. Her son George, Baron of Berkeley, Mowbray, Segrave, and Bruce, K.B., of whom his epitaph declares, " Besides the nobility of his birth, and the experience he acquired by foreign travels; he was very eminent for the great candour and ingenuity of his disposition, his singular bounty and affability to his inferiors, and his readiness (had it been in his power) to oblige all mankind." George, the first Earl of Berkeley, and Viscount Dursley, Privy Councillor to Charles II. and King James. This Lord Berkeley made a present of the library of his kinsman, Sir Robert Coke, to Sion College. There are many more of my ancestors buried in this church. Several of the family were baptized here; Lady Georgiana Berkeley, afterwards Countess of Granard, had for her sponsors George III. and the Princess Augusta.

James, Earl of Berkeley, Vice-Admiral of Great Britain, made extensive additions to the old mansion; these form the present building; the ancient house having been pulled down. But the place is otherwise deserving of veneration for the honourable asylum it afforded to several distinguished scholars and divines. In 1658 Lord Berkeley was the patron of Dr. Fuller, the eminent historian, and presented him with the rectory. He died in 1657-8, and was succeeded by Dr. Wilkins, subsequently Bishop of Chester, who though he had married Cromwell's sister, received

VOL. I.   H this preferment from so distinguished a royalist as Lord Berkeley. He was a member of the first council of the Royal Society. The portraits of Dr. Harvey, Dean Swift, and Sir William Temple, are among the family pictures, and to the best of my belief, the originals were frequent visitors at the old Manor House.

Cranford was one of the dower houses settled by my father, in his very remarkable will, on my mother. Lady Berkeley had, when the trial had terminated, for prudential reasons, taken a voyage to Madeira. Nor did Colonel Berkeley reside here any part of his time. He remained at Berkeley Castle, annoyed and baffled by the exposure he had brought upon himself, and too indignant at his own declared illegitimacy to trouble himself about the younger sons who had had the advantage of being born in wedlock. I have not the slightest doubt that this advantage in Moreton and myself was one of the exciting causes of his ill-will towards us, and he hated us the more for his failure in establishing his own birth.

However, he ought to have been able to reconcile himself to the bar sinister, as he had contrived to secure everything which legitimacy could have given him, while at the same time he had done his best to render insignificant those whom he could not prevent from having the title. He had gained all that was necessary for the thorough enjoyment of his position as head of the family, and having unbounded influence over his father's widow, he did not doubt his ability to keep his now helpless rivals in a state of such thorough dependence that any trouble from them on account of his ill-got gains, seemed totally out of the question. Confusion and mystery pervaded the elders of the family, when suddenly and unexpectedly my brother Moreton, myself, and my sisters were left at Cranford House in charge of Mrs. Purnell, the old lady mentioned in a preceding chapter, with the occasional assistance of an ancient city knight, one Sir Thomas Bell, who had a villa in Cranford village. We had to amuse ourselves as best we could under such untoward circumstances. The arrangements made for our education did not promise much—a very gentleman-like young man, a Mr. Benson, came to us from a school near Brentford three times a week, to hear us boys repeat our lessons; and an absurd, fat old fellow, named Second, possessing as little pretension to agility as to grace, arrived once a week to teach us dancing, always carrying a diminutive kit in his pocket.

With Moreton he made little progress, in consequence of his determined inattention; indeed, his brusqueness seemed incorrigible, and was a source of constant irritation to his would-be instructor in grace and deportment. One day, when I had nearly finished my lesson, and my somewhat ungainly *maître de danse* was assiduously scraping his kit as I was going on with what we called "the all round the room step," my brother very suddenly thrust nothing but his head into the room, and asked the dancing-master, "Do you want me?"

"Tut, tut, tut—horrible—horrible," exclaimed the

old man, accompanying his displeased exclamations by a hoarse scrape on the bass note of his fiddle. "Come in, sir—come in." On my brother complying, Second waddled to the door, and gaining the outside of it, thrust his great fat head in, making a hideous face with a protruding tongue. Addressing the offender, he exclaimed, "Is that the way, sir, to enter a room—head foremost, sir? There go out again, sir, and come in the other way."

The dancing-master now entered in what he supposed was a graceful manner, waistcoat first, evidently as a model for imitation, concluding, "There, sir; go, sir, shut yourself out, but come in again, and don't let me see your head first."

Moreton made his exit as desired, and without a word, or the slightest expression of disobedience, but at the same time giving a sly glance in my direction, which assured me that some fun was intended.

Myself and my instructor were waiting on the tip-toe of expectation, but with far different ideas, when suddenly, with a dull bump upon the panels, in flew the door, and my brother presented himself; certainly not head foremost—but exactly the reverse!

The dancing-master was speechless with rage when he beheld his pupil coming, as sailors might phrase it, "cutting the water with his taffrail;" but he contented himself with expressing his indignation on his instrument, as he strode furiously up and down the room. He had no one at hand to help him to inflict punishment, and did not seem to like attempting any-

INSTRUCTION.

thing of the kind unassisted. Perhaps he would have been less inclined to this course had he been aware that an alliance existed between his two pupils, defensive and offensive, by a secret article in which, if one were to be roughly handled by him, we were both to go, as we termed it, "bang into his waistcoat and fiddle."

We were not without other instructors; but the one who taught us most was a man engaged by Sir Thomas Bell to look after the game. His lessons we readily acquired, perhaps because we were not expected to learn them. Among other things he taught us to apply to a gun the sexual distinction of " she," and to drink beer at the Coach and Horses, a public-house that then stood on the verge of Harlington Common. We also had a footman named Reece to take charge of us, but both he and the gamekeeper shared our libations. They certainly took care that we should not drink too much, knowing that in such an event, discovery would take place, and their discharge follow as a matter of course; but that was the only restraint they exercised on our inclinations.

All day we were together fishing, shooting, setting traps for vermin, rat-hunting—in short, seeking sport wherever it was attainable. We very fortunately got into no scrapes, and enjoyed ourselves immensely. " Bring up a child in the way he should go, and when he is old he will not depart from it." I cannot say that my bringing up was exactly the one here suggested; but I know it laid the foundation of my after success as a sportsman.

Such was my daily life at Cranford; my mornings and evenings being passed under the strict surveillance of my nurse, my dear Mary Oldacre, who, as the daughter of the famous old huntsman, Tom Oldacre, was probably not averse to a liberal amount of indulgence in my sporting predilections, at least with hounds.

It so happened that Sir Thomas Bell discovered in the cellar a bin of particularly fine old port, and growing proud of his position as our temporary guardian, began to invite his city friends to dine with him at his villa in the village. My brother and myself had the privilege of coming in with the dessert, and had immense fun afterwards in mimicking the manners of some of the east-end guests—civic functionaries of great capacity, at least for eating and drinking. But at one of these heavy banquets a scene occurred that never was erased from my mind.

I must premise that though I had often felt myself neglected, I loved my nearest relatives most sincerely, and was deeply affected with whatever caused them pain or distress. I was ready to endorse the opinions of my seniors, and fight in their quarrels, if need be. I had been taught to regard the House of Lords as a lot of muddle-headed fools or designing villains, and to look on every one as a personal enemy who ventured to call my brother Moreton " My Lord." The reader will therefore readily imagine the excitement of my feelings when I beheld our appointed guardian, for whose good offices we had been taught to be so anxious, rise in his chair at the head of the table,

DUPES.

and propose the healths of my brother and myself as the Earl and heir-presumptive. Then the fourteen sleek aldermen and common-councilmen rose, and drank the healths of " the Earl of Berkeley and the Honourable Grantley Berkeley." Thereupon followed thumpings of the table and jingling of glasses, as if they had all been enjoying a corporation feed.

My brother and myself with difficulty restrained our indignation; but next day, when we were alone, he said to me : " I say, I only wish daddy could have come back to have heard those fellows. Wouldn't he have sent them flying !"

So strongly had we imbibed the lessons of those whose opinions had always been to us the law, that this demonstration of our city knight and his friends only excited in us a more powerful determination to stand by our seniors, whose " rights," in our benighted minds, had thus been questioned. As regards myself, so strict were my notions of obedience, that everything I was required to do or say, or even to think, was done without question. I could not form the most remote conception how much I was becoming my own enemy, by permitting myself to be the dupe of my affections. In the sequel it will be seen how, in my brother Moreton, this devotion to others was attempted to be made the means of destroying my prospects.

I met with two rather serious accidents about this time. The first was while following Sir Thomas Bell's carriage, my pony, Hermione, fell down, and broke my collar-bone. The second occurred when throwing a casting-net from the side of the Chinese bridge into

PRIZE-FIGHTING.

seven or eight feet of water below, it caught to a button on my wrist, and striving to disengage my arm, I dislocated my shoulder. Had I gone in hampered with the net, I must have been drowned. These evils, however, were soon remedied. The only inconvenience they occasioned was a temporary cessation of instructions from the gamekeeper, and the rigidly enforced rule of keeping away from the Coach and Horses, and from my out-door recreations.

I soon grew accustomed to rougher usage; for much of my bringing up, as the reader will see presently, was impressed upon me in a singularly Spartan fashion.

Long before my father's time or mine, prize-fighters found aristocratic patrons. The fights between Figg and Slack, and between Slack and Broughton, were attended by several noblemen and gentlemen, who betted large sums on the result. It was a public exhibition, and a place called the amphitheatre in Oxford. Street was where such contests were decided. The price of tickets, about the middle of the century, was five shillings.

Figg, whose portrait has been preserved by Hogarth in the second plate of the "Rake's Progress," was a celebrated prize-fighter, and exhibited his skill in a house erected for the purpose in Marylebone, where Broughton subsequently displayed his skill as a pugilist, or bruiser, as the prize-fighter was then designated. Such places were frequented by the fast young gentlemen of the time, and the exhibition became such an attraction that the Government tried to put down boxing by Act of Parliament. The fact

PUGILISM. 105

is, much rascality was practised by the fighting-men. They readily sold the fight if sufficient inducement was forthcoming, and sham battles were promoted, simply for the purpose of getting gentlemen to bet.

Frederick, Prince of Wales, father of George III., was one of the early patrons of "the noble art," and Paul Whitehead, "the champion and bard of Leicester House," as his biographer, Captain Thompson, styles him, wrote a poem in its honour called "The Gymnasiad or Boxing-match," which will be found in his collected works, 1777.

Pugilism was much more patronized in the last quarter of the last century and the first quarter of the present than it has been since. It was not unusual then for noble lords and gentlemen not only to entertain prize-fighters at their table, but to make up contests and back them to large amounts. In point of fact, though nothing then was said of "muscular Christianity," the art of self-defence was considered to be as necessary to the education of a gentleman as dancing a minuet or speaking French. It was a rough time, when, if a dispute arose, a word and a blow became a matter of course—the last not unfrequently coming first — and men of rank who could rely on their "science," as it was termed, did not shrink from displaying it at the expense of their inferiors, when the latter were insolently aggressive. It was to secure this superiority that they frequented the Fives Court, where sparring exhibitions were frequent— were often seen at Cribb's, an ex-champion's public-house at Covent Garden, where fights were arranged, and opened their town and country houses to the most celebrated boxers of their time. Woe be to the pugnacious snob who sought the honour of a turn-up with "a swell." Notwithstanding the dictum of the author of "Tom Brown at Oxford," the rustic bargee, butcher, or tinker invariably got a thrashing. The sense of superiority thus acquired frequently led gentlemen, particularly after dinner, first into unseemly rows, then into fights with any number of watchmen, and subsequently into the watchhouse—the night's entertainment ending in the morning before a magistrate, when the roughly-used "Charleys," as the night police were called, preferred charges of assault supported by black eyes and a few loose teeth carefully preserved for the purpose, and the offenders thought themselves lucky if they got off with only a moderate fine.

The fighting-men were generally a low lot, but of a more respectable grade than they are at the present day. They could produce such men as Jackson, whose tomb in Brompton Cemetery, with its carved caryatidæ, is a tolerably enduring testimony of the esteem in which he was held. Then there was Gully, long Member for Pontefract, who, as a representative man of the class from which he sprang will contrast most favourably with later heroes of the ring. Even the worst of them were not without good qualities, which, however, like the honesty proverbially said to be found among thieves, took some trouble to discover, and not unfrequently a little expense. If a patron had the misfortune to lose his

PIERCE EGAN. 107

watch amongst them—by no means an uncommon
occurrence—he might rely on its being restored—for
a handsome consideration—provided no questions were
asked.

Within the last year or two there has been something like a revival of pugilism, but this was owing
rather to the nationality mixed up in the last two
fights for the championship than from any regard for
"the noble art" as illustrated by the combatants. Much
the same spirit was excited when Cribb fought Moly-
neux, the black, and decided the physical superiority
of the white man over the negro, as conclusively as
Tom King, in his memorable contest with Heenan,
settled the pretensions of the Yankee.

I followed, or rather my elder brothers made me
follow, the example set me, and having through the
best available channel acquired a certain degree of
proficiency, have found it do me yeoman's service in
occasional instances in which, without such knowledge, I might have had the worst of it. But I am
not sorry to see a better taste and a better sense pre-
vail, than were displayed in the "Tom and Jerry"
absurdities that were so prominent in my earlier days.

These, in a great measure, were brought into vogue
by rather a low-caste Irishman known as Pierce Egan,
sometimes a newspaper reporter, and sometimes a low
comedian in third-rate Dublin and London theatres.
His "Life in London" was very popular, and he
dramatized it at the Adelphi with marked success.
He brought out a similar play in the Irish capital
called "Life in Dublin," and a third in the flourishing

108 BELL'S LIFE.

commercial port on the Mersey, called "Life in Liverpool." His "Boxiana" was considered a text-book on fights and fighting men; and his elaborate and exaggerated descriptions of a "mill," as prize fights were designated, stuffed as they were full of slang, were the delight of a large circle of male readers. He assisted in starting a sporting news-paper, now the still flourishing *Bell's Life in London*, the best sporting paper we now have; and subse-quently an opposition one, with a similar title. It failed, and he long outlived his reputation as an author, for he was totally destitute of literary inven-tion, the characters in his stories were thoroughly conventional, and his style never rose above that of an ordinary penny-a-liner.

He was a coarse-looking man, who seemed only to have associated with the very lowest society in England and Ireland. Indeed, he used to make a boast of his familiarity with the riffraff of both capitals. The intense vulgarity in his writings grew distasteful; and though he produced several works of imagination, all have sunk into oblivion. Indeed, they pre-deceased their author by a good many years. He died totally forgotten by his once innumerable patrons, and the literature of the ring died with him.

During this our continuous sojourn at Cranford, my brother Augustus paid us a visit, accompanied by a splendid Newfoundland dog, called "Lion," and a bull and mastiff fighting dog, rejoicing in the name of "Bull," whose full-length portrait, by an excellent master, I have now. He stayed but a few days with

AUGUSTUS BERKELEY. 109

us, and, by way of amusing himself, led us into every conceivable mischief.

After breakfast each morning he took us to the farms, and had a horse, cow, or bull bait every day; "Bull" caring very little what nose it was, so long as, in a row, he fastened his hold on something. When he seized an ox or a cow, Augustus would encourage him to keep his hold, from a purchase gained by himself on the animal's tail; but more than once he suffered considerably by his rearward position. Bull killed all the cats at farms and cottages, and when detected in the onslaught by their owners, my brother's willingness to box, and our position at the great house, put aside all ideas of opposition. Although, under such auspices, we essayed to do much mischief to every living thing around the park, as luck would have it, very little was achieved, when, to our great good fortune, our "fore-elder," as Mr. Pig, the huntsman to Mr. Jorrocks, would have called him, tired of the fun, prepared to take his departure.

His fraternal visit to us thus being over, we accompanied him one evening after dark upon our ponies, Hermione and Yellowbelly, across Hounslow Heath, to take leave of him, when we came to the then village of Hounslow. As we proceeded along the high road, nearing the spot of our separation, we were overtaken by a respectable tradesman, as he appeared, driving his wife towards the neighbouring town in a buggey. It was Augustus's last chance of inducting us into a row, and not to be lost; so he made some most insulting remark upon these unoffending passengers, which so provoked the female that she unfortunately took up the *casus belli*, and, with other abuse, called her assailant a "barber's clerk." He replied "I know I am a barber, and I have shaved you." When the man heard this wordy war, he joined in it. On this my brother told him "that if it was not for his woman, he would pull him out of his rattletrap and tread on him."

Here was a circumstance that caused my boyish mind considerable speculation. Hard names and some swearing seemed not much to insult the man in the buggey; but on hearing the female at his side called his "woman," his wrath knew no bounds. With the exclamation, "My woman, you rascal! she is my wife!" he set to work lashing my brother with his gig whip, commencing a sort of artillery duel at long practice, not in accordance with the cavalry arm of my brother, nor with his way of fighting. A charge upon the buggey was therefore made by him, keeping his right side open for mischief; and in the obscure darkness I could hear the crown of the hat of the driver get ten blows for one, for his long weapon was useless at close quarters. The female, wife or woman, whichever she was, very quickly saw that the combat was all one way, for with a very much damaged crown her king crouched down on the cushion at her side; so she awakened up the heath with shrieks of "Murder!"

"Be off, as hard as you can split!" was then the order to us from the offender. We obeyed, as we heard the heels of his horse speed on far in advance of the buggey.

UNGENTLEMANLY PURSUITS. 111

Fearing pursuit, as there were horse-patrols on the roads in those days, at the first turnpike he pulled up his horse on the shady side of a carriage and four, that had stopped while paying the toll; and to his great comfort, as he afterwards told us, on looking at the panels he saw the crest, and knew that it was Colonel Berkeley, on his way to London from Berkeley Castle.

This vulgar initiation into mischief, and the picking of wanton quarrels for the mere pleasure of a row, affected me not in the way they were no doubt intended to do; nor had they, as far as I could observe, any such effect on my brother Moreton; but I only speak for myself. I must, however, in candour assert that such ungentlemanly encounters were then far from uncommon. Nothing could be in worse taste, but taste was a quality very imperfectly understood. The law of the fist was with the young and strong much too frequently the law of the road; and they had recourse to it on the very slightest provocation—often on none at all. It formed a part of "The Life in London" system of education, and several years elapsed before it disappeared. As to the bating of unoffending cows and horses, such scenes only disgusted me; while insulting an underbred man, merely for an opportunity to establish my own muscular superiority, offered no attraction; the shrieks of a terrified woman, no matter whence arising, being horrible to my ear. This, though one of the first instances of bad example, had no more injurious effect on me than those which were to follow.

AN UNEXPECTED ARRIVAL.

Months, more than a year, I think, passed thus in our home at Cranford, when, one day, as we were bursting out like boys with a superabundance of hop and jump, to join the keeper Milton on his way to feed the pheasants, we were struck by the downcast, sorrowful look 'of that faithful functionary. Before we could ask him the cause of his grief, with a melancholy shake of his head he said, " Young gentlemen, I fear it's all up with me. Don't you know my lady and your tutor, Mr. Hughes, came home last night, so I shall get the sack, and you'll have to learn your lessons."

Had a thunderbolt burst at our feet it could not have taken us more by surprise. We doubted the fact, as we had heard nothing of it, when the finger of the keeper (we were then walking on the west front of the house, by the statue of the dying gladiator) pointed to the windows at the balcony of my mother's room, and to one belonging to the upper story at the other end of the house, of chambers known as Mr. Hughes' room, adjoining our double-bedded apartment. The keeper said, "Look there; those windows are still closed and the curtains undrawn; they arrived last night when you were a-bed and asleep."

It is impossible to describe what my feelings were. They were an admixture of regret and affection; I hated my lessons almost as much as my brother did, and I disliked my tutor only because he was the medium through which our lessons came. To have to sit at home and study books instead of roving the

LADY BERKELEY'S RETURN. 113

woods and fields from dawn till dark, there was the rub'; and so severe was the blow on my liberty, and so painful a drawback was it to my love of sport, that I must admit the joy of seeing my mother, on her return from abroad, was considerably lessened by the contingencies that accompanied her arrival.

However, we were forced to make the best of it—a day's grace only being given to us before our return to our schoolroom. Then once more the curb was put upon us, though the keeper did not lose his situation.

Things went on in this way for some time. At first there was some dread which I did not then understand as to certain officers of justice, and a curious mode of escape from the house was constructed, descending, I think, from the nursery or floor on which my mother's room was situated, to the pantry, and then to the open lawn; but as time wore on all apprehension of danger vanished, and she walked and drove about the park, and went to church as usual.

Subsequently to my mother's return, I observed that my brother Moreton, after school hours, was left to do as he pleased, and very particularly encouraged to preserve the game, and indeed to adopt the habits of a keeper. He was permitted also to retain and increase some harriers in the old foxhound kennel, for we had a few while Lady Berkeley was abroad; and on his wonderful jumping pony, Yellowbelly, to whip-in to a pack of harriers, kept at Heston by a Mr. Westbrook. At that time, on this pony or Galloway, for she was more of the latter, Moreton rode very hard, and harder still when a full-sized, clever bay mare was

VOL. I.   I

given him, famous for going over the new inclosures of the period, and at the double post and rails.

My Galloway, old Hermione, died, and was succeeded by a pony called Punch. By my side in those days, but on a smaller pony, rode my excellent friend, Mr. Charles Pugh, now of Marlborough-place, St. John's-wood, and at present sporting over the fields at Lincoln's Inn and Stone Buildings, and whipper-in to a Vice-Chancellor. He has had many a good day; his little charger emulated, but was not always so successful in clearing stiles, as my better-educated Punch.

It was from the latter that I had my first fall in attempting to take a fence, out of the road leading from Harlington to Dawley Wall. He did not jump far enough on to the bank to gain a footing, and fell backwards into the ditch. I don't know whether it was so or not, but my brothers, Moreton and Henry, teazed me very much with the assertion that I scuttled all fours up the ditch like a water-rat, much farther than I had need to go, under the impression that I was not sufficiently out of the way of my falling steed.

My brother Henry had come to reside at Cranford after a severe illness he had had, while doing duty with Colonel Berkeley as a subaltern in the South Gloucester militia. I shall never forget the consternation and annoyance his arrival occasioned to Moreton and myself. He, though barely approaching the threshold of manhood, was very much a man in his own estimation, while, in his eyes, Moreton and myself were very little boys. As to our keeping hounds, he laughed, and declared that such a thing ought not to be allowed ; while a very good shooting, old-fashioned, brass-mounted single gun, that Moreton was very fond of, and with which he shot remarkably well, he took away ; and putting on it a label upon which was written the word "unsafe," it was locked up with other guns in a closet. Our hounds, too, were sent away. We were terribly discontented, but had no power successfully to rebel.

As time wore on, he found that it was pleasanter to be friends with us than foes, and that, in sport, we could instruct him, though he was a first-rate shot, and probably before his severe illness, of his weight, the best amateur boxer in the kingdom. At sixteen years of age he went to the Fives Court, under the special introduction of the late Mr. Berkeley Craven and Colonel Berkeley ; and with the "trial gloves" on, set to, and had a great deal the best of it, with one of the well-known pugilists of the day, Caleb Baldwin. I remember in our earlier days, he never went to bed without suspending the clothes-bag full of linen to a nail, and hitting at it left and right, by way of practice, for half-an-hour together. It was then also, as boys, that Moreton and Charles Wyndham, the son of the then Lord Egremont, used to set to, in our house in Spring Gardens, till their faces were as red as fire, and their eyes full of water, scarce able to determine which had the best of it. When the good offices of Charlie Wyndham were not to be had, my elder brothers found a substitute in a well-set, hardy ruffian, Jack the postillion, at whose head they launched the two

116   YOUNG MILTON.

hands of Moreton, as if it was the chief object in life to punch and be punched again. Jack was older and more set than my brother, but with Jack Moreton had a good deal the best of it.

Fortunately for my comfort, in London there was nothing small enough for me to combat, until a boy, the son of old Carrington, the Vicar of Berkeley, whose evidence figured before the House of Lords, came to our house on a visit. The instant Henry saw him he resolved to make a match. The poor lad consented rather unwillingly to put on the gloves; he knew nothing about them, and the obvious consequence was, as I was ordered to go at him, the back of his head was hit against the edge of a doorpost, raising not only a sufficient bump upon it, but such an outcry as very nearly reached my mother's ears in the adjoining drawing-room.

The keeper Milton, whom I have previously mentioned, had a little, hard-faced, white-headed son, older than I was, and in figure much more set, of the name of Charles. He was hired to look after our -ponies, and to clean boots and shoes. This boy, under his father, who was a resolute old fellow, and famed in clumsy country boxing matches for his round hitting and his game, had had plenty of rough practice among his fellows, moreover was just the sort of lad to please my brother and to try me. I had never set to with any boy save giving a blow to the young gentleman I have mentioned, so the whole thing was new to me, and in its first contingencies very unpleasant.

A NASTY MOUTHFUL.

The first time we met, I shall never forget it—it was in an empty room over the stables at Cranford. I stood up, my hands well before me, as Jackson had taught me to hold them, when, before I could hit or see where they came from, for I had expected the fists to come straight at me, such a shower of round, rough blows was rained on either side of my head, and such a nasty mouthful did I get of his head, as the round, hard hitting of my foe brought him forward and full upon me, that, let alone the stunned sensation to my senses, the smell of this dirty fellow nearly made me sick. Giddy, with a feeling of faintness, without scarcely giving a blow in return, I went, or rather reeled away, in disgust, rather than in fear, and said I would not have the gloves on any more. Then came loud taunts from my brother that I was beaten and afraid, and this gave me exactly what I wanted, a cause for enmity, and *a reason* for combating with the dirty thing they had set up before me.

We faced each other again, and taking the initiative of blows to myself, without an attempt to parry, by the straight quick hitting, left and right, that Jackson had taught me, at his head, I hit the sturdy young countryman away; then we went on, round after round, till my brother saw that I had the best of it, and that both of us were tired.

Alas, for my comfort as a boy, and my personal foes as I grew up, whenever Henry desired amusement, he used to invite me to the stable with the gloves to fight this boy, and the battle always ended by my knocking the head of my opponent into the manger. I remember that for months, during these, to my brother, amusing combats, my lips were sometimes so cut against my teeth, that I could not eat any salad with vinegar, the acid occasioned so much smarting. I could lick my antagonist as far as the fight with the gloves was permitted to go, but in a few days at the word of command the lad was ready for another licking, so that week after week I had no peace and had to lick him again; nor had I resolution enough to withstand the taunts of being vanquished, if I refused to set to, although my superior proficiency had been a hundred times asserted.

All things must have an end; every day strengthened my tall and growing limbs, and every day my power over my antagonist increased, when, for some ill conduct, he lost his service, and these, to him, not very agreeable encounters.

My brother then for a time lost his amusement; " Othello's occupation was gone," for nothing came into service at Cranford that approached the age of a boy. A new footman was, however, inducted, a grown man and not a little one, but a cross-grown lout of a fellow; and mere boy as I was, we were ordered to the stable, in front of my brother's usual throne, the corn bin, and there desired to do battle. By this time I had got into such habits of pugnacious obedience that if a bear had been introduced, and I had been told that the beast was to vanquish me, I should at once have boxed with him. The combat I am now alluding to was not unlike one of a boy and bear. I stepped back, put in, and then gave way successfully, for a short time,

LORD GRANTLEY.

but at last the man met me with a half round blow, and hit me clean down on the rough stones of the stable. Henry did not seem to care much, but Moreton, who was present, spoke out loudly against the shame of putting such a boy to fight with a grown man; and I believe feeling slightly annoyed at the way he had overmatched me, our elder brother stopped any further assault on my part, and suggested that Peter should put the gloves on with his own servant, a well-built, active little fellow, whom he had daily thrashed into one of the most expert boxers of his size. Peter, all agreeable, set to with Shadrach, when the former caught such a right-hander in the face as sent him as if he was shot upon the stable stones. He arose crying, and deprived of all wish for another blow— my fall very sufficiently avenged.

I have often wondered why I was not cowed by all this brutality, or why I ever took to those more gentle, accomplishments in life, that used to get me the name of a "dandy," among some of my rougher compeers; however, time wore on, I fought through the stable boys and men servants, and had sense enough not to acquire any rudeness of manner, nor dislike to more refined occupations.

One day, the late Lord Grantley called at Cranford, in company with his nephew, the present Lord Grantley, and, as my godfather, made me a present of a guinea and my first single gun, made by Ronalds.

Not to dwell too long on these slight incidents, I must pass on to the selection of a few that tended to create in me, and I believe for a time in my brother, now Earl of Berkeley, as great, but not on his part as lasting, an affection, as ever long, fraternal association engendered. He and I, then, got up, for the acreage, an immense head of game, and, as game-keepers, we killed the vermin, watched at night at the head of our men, and devoted ourselves to such occupation; indeed, out of school hours, when not with our private tutor, it was our sole employment.

I was not so much encouraged in this as was my brother. On the contrary, I heard, to me, the most dreadful rumour, of the Duke of Kent's having advised my being sent to the Royal Military College of Sandhurst; but affectionately bound together as my brother Moreton and myself were, while at home it was impossible to keep us from each other. We slept in the same large room; we went out at nights to guard the game together; and before I was entrusted with a gun I followed him like his shadow.

The last time I walked in the well-remembered old place, I stood beneath the few holly trees that used to shelter us from "the great ash tree" at the top of the "Holly Cover," where the first woodpigeons and the first magpies used to alight when coming in of an evening to their roost. The old ash tree was gone; but my brother showed me a stout cudgel he had had cut and polished as a memorial of a large tree that had figured so prominently in our first impressions and affections. There were the hedges in which poachers setting snares had been captured, and the fields where we had taken egg-stealers; every spot was graven with some rustic and boyish remembrance. I came to

DUKE OF KENT. 121

Cranford on a visit to Lord Berkeley on this occasion, and we walked up from his little cottage to the park and woods.

Still suffering from the persecutions that the late Lord Fitzhardinge had put on foot against me, and therefore at enmity with him; in spite of him, however, I came to see my brother, whom I still loved, and together we talked of old scenes, and spoke of the impressions made on us as boys, that up to that time had never been effaced or changed. But to return to earlier days.

His Royal Highness, the late Duke of Kent, used to ride over to see my mother, either from Hampton Court or from Bushey Park, the seat of the Duke of Clarence; and I remember the former giving her a horse—alas! it was one day to carry me as a cadet to the College of Sandhurst. George Fitzclarence, the late Lord Munster, also came over to see us. In their earlier life, George, Henry, Frederick, and Adolphus Fitzclarence were a great deal with us at Cranford and in town. Frederick Fitzclarence, being much about my size, my brother Henry got up a quarrel between us on the lawn at Cranford; or rather, fomented a personal dispute while we were measuring which was the taller of the two. I remember hitting poor dear Fred with my fist at the fraternal suggestion, saying at the same time, "Why, that's the taller;" and his replying to the blow with a raised cricket-bat, with the intention of striking me in return; but his brothers and mine got between us, and we were made friends. They, my companions in those days, the Fitzclarences, are all dead now; but, until death, our intimacy and friendship existed. I have already, in the " Reminiscences of a Huntsman," published by Longman, written many of the sporting incidents at Cranford that occurred to me and my brother Moreton; and often and often, after some successful act against poachers and poaching dogs, we have pledged eternal affection to each other, and said that nothing ought ever to separate us. We are severed now.

Well, time in those days, which never stands still, went on. Moreton was called away perpetually from the loved pursuit of polecats, stoats, and weasels, to affix his signature to certain " beastly papers and musty parchments," as he termed them, though he never took the trouble to ask what they were, and therefore could not describe their meaning to me. I found out something about them, however, by asking our tutor, Mr. Hughes, what they were. I received from him an evasive answer, or else was simply told " that Moreton was called on to sign his name to things belonging to my eldest brother, Colonel Berkeley, only just for a time, or while Colonel Berkeley was setting aside an unjust decision of the House of Lords, and recovering his lost rights—a thing he was perfectly certain of doing." Brought up and educated to believe this, I should at that time have signed anything to which they had said my signature was required in right of my elder brother; for up to the period I was, like my brother Moreton, the victim of a most craftily-contrived deceit, planned and perfected

MR. FONBLANQUE. 123

by education—an education continued to us ever since the decision in the House of Lords, before whom Colonel Berkeley failed in proving his legitimacy. The signing of these papers keeping Moreton at times at the house at Cranford, at others taking him up to London—a journey he always detested, indeed was so hateful to him, that he often refused obedience simply from impatience at having to transact such affairs —he complained to me about the mere fact of being obliged to write his name—of the matters placed before him he knew no more than the man in the moon.

The hour of severance, however, came at last. It was after many consultations between my mother and my brother Henry, as to which I could only catch disjointed sentences. So far as I could learn, some suggestions had been thrown out by, I think, the late Counsellor Fonblanque, who was my mother's adviser. The purport of them was that it would be better, for public appearance, so I understood, if Moreton were not kept so much at home, or tied to his mother's apron-string, but sent, under the care of my brother Henry, who was then at Christchurch College, Oxford, to take a degree. The pros and cons of this I very well remember to have been quietly dis-- cussed by my mother, our tutor, Mr. Hughes, Mr. Fonblanque, and by my brother Henry. The pros had it on account of their thinking it possible to put Moreton at Christchurch, where Henry could look after him. In that they were deceived. If my impression is correct, Colonel Berkeley was at this time in anything but an amiable humour. I know he was very cross to my mother, and he seemed to be violent against her and her brother, Mr. Tudor, who had also fled the country after the evidence he had given in the House of Lords. In short, it seemed to me as. if Colonel Berkeley had said, "I will take no part in your machinations, because, swear as you all have, you have never carried them to success."

Christchurch College was full, and therefore could not receive Moreton, circumstances obliged him to go to Corpus, and I shall never forget my sorrow at his departure. We were then to be severed for the first time in our lives: at arms'-length I had held the miserable idea of it, and regarded it almost as an impossibility; but now that the time had actually come, my boyish desolation was beyond description.

The day before he was to leave Cranford we had been round to the traps together, and he had given me full instructions as to what I was to do till the vacation, at which he was to return. While he was with me I could bear the threatened loss, but when the post-chaise took him from our door, it seemed as if the light of my existence had left me, the companion from infancy of my sports and pastimes was gone, and with him the only brother who ever had shown to me one-hundredth part of the love I bore them all. Our dispositions were widely different, apart from our sporting habits. His mind was slower than mine in comprehension, and in action instantaneously called for by the course of events; and he was more easily imposed on than I was, and therefore prone to listen to his inferiors as well as to his elders and his equals.

OUR FIRST PARTING.

One strong attachment he had, and that was to his father and to his father's memory; I think he loved his father better than he loved me his brother, and I am sure he loved me better than any other of his brothers, and the only reason for this filial affection that I could ever call to mind was the fact that it was his father who first took him out shooting. This fact may seem a trivial one, but we often see a very slight circumstance in earlier days assume an importance over the future life of a man, particularly when there are those on the watch to discover and use the key to a casket, the contents of which they desire to share. It was on this childish love for his father's memory, that some of his seniors relied for the successful accomplishment of their scheme.

With a saddened heart I went the rounds of the traps, and did all that Moreton had left me to do with a minuteness as if I thought he could see me; and I was left by my mother to follow out the bent of my inclinations. One day, dull enough at heart as heaven knows, I was coming in from a field called Maidenmead to the beech walk, when, on the path before me, I saw the well-known impression of my brother's foot, left, as I remembered, on the day before, when we together came home that way. I had borne my boyish bereavement in sadness, and in silence until this minute; but now at this remembrance thus unexpectedly presented to me, I burst into tears, and sat for a long, long time crying bitterly under a lime-tree that then grew on the edge of that wide old walk.

Having recovered from these bursts of grief, I went home; but at dinner my mother saw that my eyes were red, and asked me "if I had been crying, and what for?" My reply was, "It is nothing," but I very nearly went off again when I looked towards the vacant place at the table. On that evening, on the plea of a headache, I got off to bed at an earlier hour than usual.

This severance was the first specimen of what my heart would have to feel in later years; but even now, when I have seen those whom I had loved from infancy vieing with each other how to do me the greatest unkindness, and when death has snatched a part of my family from me, I know not if any subsequent grief affected me more than my first parting from my favourite brother.

CHAPTER VI.

SANDHURST AND THE COLDSTREAM GUARDS.

My brothers at college—Moreton plucked—Returns to the university and passes his examination—I am sent to Sandhurst—State of that establishment — Wanting a piano — Bullying — Rough sports—Sir Alexander Hope and Colonel Butler—Teasing the French master—An unlucky shot—The Duke of Kent—My unexpected answer to his inquiry—Sergeant Hutton—A boy's affections—Love of poetry—I leave Sandhurst—Wear the Prince of Wales's uniform—My devotion to Colonel Berkeley—The Prince presents me with a commission in the Guards—Doing duty at Carlton Palace—The lost drummer—Dinner to the Duke of Gloucester—Battersea Red House—Tricks of my brother officers—George Bentinck—Taking leave of absence—Riding races—Beau Brummell and the Prince of Wales.

FROM my brothers, Henry and Moreton, being at separate colleges, the latter was less under the other's sway than my mother desired. He was no tufthunter, and sought not the "swells" of the colleges. He formed an intimacy with a Mr. Salkeld, and instead of reading, established a pack of hounds, and hunted as much as ever. In spring he kept a gun in his room, and with small charges dropped the old rooks on the heads of contemplative Dons, as they walked unsuspiciously beneath the trees of Corpus. He never was caught practising these tricks, nor do I think that, in his college life, he incurred any serious blame, but the upshot of it all was, that he was "plucked" on his first examination.

This was a serious blow to my mother, for had he passed he was to have come home upon his laurels, and not to have returned to college. It was the same to Henry, and to our tutor, Mr. Hughes, as well as to me, but for very different reasons. It added to the rumour in the world that Moreton's education had been peculiarly dealt with, neglected, or purposely retarded, by putting and keeping him in a position, over the obscurity of which no new lights as to his real state and station should penetrate.

Henry cared not a bit for any disgrace which might attach to Moreton for his failure, he evidently only thought of what Colonel Berkeley would say. My distress arose on two accounts, both very different from theirs. The one, because I always wished my brother to succeed in anything he undertook, and the other, because on account of his failure he was again to be sent to college, and taken away from me. He returned there and then, on the second attempt passed his examination, returning home with the same propensities as when he left it, and perfectly isolated from all the rest of the world.

My turn to leave him came next, and from my poor mother's apron-string I was sent to Sandhurst. Then I first learnt the difference between a comfortable home and its many amusements, and a dirty college, for in those days the establishment was not really a school for gentlemen. There were the sons of non-commissioned officers, boys who had to work their

SCHOOL TORMENTS.

way to promotion and to commissions—an excellent institution so far—while there were also a lot of us taunted with having been born with silver spoons in our mouths, and therefore more favoured than the preceding.

I remember that before I joined for my first half year, I had been very unwell, and to add to my difficulties my mother asked the captain of my company, Captain Wright, if I might have a pianoforte in my room, to keep up my practice on what had begun to be my favourite instrument. She little knew there were four or five boys in one room, or the annoyance to me the application would occasion. Captain Wright, a strict martinet, who commanded the B. company, said, " that if she sent a pianoforte, it should be in the room, and he would answer for it that it should not be broken." Luckily for me, his Royal Highness the Duke of Kent threw cold water on the idea, and I had only to struggle against the impression of my effeminacy among the boys, which the desire for a pianoforte had created.

I was bullied then by a big boy who had been thrust into the room over the regulated number, and had to undergo the usual torments of being "launched," that is, having my bed reversed while I was asleep; of being thrown on the floor on my face, with the mattress on my back, and all my friends or foes dancing on my prostrate body. Another plan was to noose my toe with sharp, strong whipcord, and tie the other end to the toe of the occupant of the next bed; one victim or the other awoke

VOL. I.   K

with a punch in the ribs; the snatching up of either leg, and the tracing of the string, of course occasioning a fight between the owners of the fettered toes, each charging the other with being the aggressor.

To be fast asleep with one's mouth open, attention to the fact being called by snoring, entailed the sudden libation of a jug of cold water poured down the throat, the fluid that escaped deluging the pillow. That was, perhaps, the most painful surprise of all.

The more hostile visitation from the boys of another room, armed with knotted and twisted-up towels or bolsters, I did not care about; it was an attempted surprise in the fair rules of war, and I thought it good fun with my companions to fight it out. The assailed always had the advantage of artillery, for they could, pour a volley of very heavy shoes into the assailing party, the assault being made of necessity, with no missiles of the kind.

My character in the first half-year, when that delightful time came of returning home, was, "Conduct good, but more application to study required." In fact, at Sandhurst the scholar could then do as much or as little as he liked. I hated arithmetic, detested the study of all foreign languages, but loved drawing, and in that and geography I succeeded. Sir Alexander Hope was the governor of our college, and Colonel Butler the lieutenant governor. My number in Wright's company was "B 16." Otter commanded the "C," and Erskine the "D" company, and in the

THE FRENCH MASTER.

two half years during which I was there, I never had a punishment. I was in French for part of the time under old Pellichet (I forget if so his name was spelt), and his eyes were not very good. I know not why, but all his pupils always came with a resolution to do nothing, and to tease him. "Keys" to lessons were brought in, from which everybody but myself copied what they chose to do, and at other times threw pellets of chewed paper from their pens over the edge of the table at their master.

I never joined them in this, for Pellichet was a good, kind soul, till one fatal day two good-humoured boys on either side of me asked me to try one shot, "only one shot with my more elastic pen," as it had not been used in that sort of work, at Pellichet. Alas, I complied, and shot so well, that the missile hit the Frenchman on the cheek, beside his nose, with a sharp smack that resounded all over the study, and made him jump a foot or two from his stool. Oh, what a hit he gave his desk with one furious hand, while with the other he rang the bell for the orderly sergeant!

When the official came in, he reported the whole study for insubordination, concluding thus, "All the boys bote vun;" and then turning to me he said, "You gentilhomme—you born of noble parents, you do no such thing, you good boy, I sal ponish all bote you;" and he forbad the sergeant to put me down on the list for punishment.

Never shall I forget my remorse! At once addressing my companions on either side, I said I would not let the whole study be punished for what I had really

K 2

132   AN EXAMINATION.

done, and was about to give myself up, when they said, "Don't be such a d—d fool, we shan't get much, and we don't care," and they held me down upon my stool.

I never shot paper at poor old Pellichet again, but ever after did all I could to atone for my fault and gain his approbation.

When the examination of the cadets was taking place, his Royal Highness the Duke of Kent being present, with the kind goodnature ever predominant in the heart of that august prince, he sent for me to his presence, and I came before him, while he was surrounded by all the Sandhurst officials. Taking me kindly by the hand, he said, "Well, Grantley, my little man, how do you like the college? have they treated you pretty well?"

Now, between the time that I had been warned that his Royal Highness wished to see me, and my presentation to him, I had been conning over my grievances, and thinking what a beautiful chance I should have to tell them all to so good and great a friend; leaving out, of course, any annoyance I might have received at the hands of my comrades, for any allusion to that I deemed would have been beneath me.

"Sir," I blurted out, "they don't give us good food: the meat is tough, the potatoes all eyes, the swipes (College name for the very bad beer,) double us up; when we drink water, tadpoles in the pots come up to look at our nose, the stickjaw fastens——"

"Sir, sir," broke in Colonel Butler, "your Royal Highness must not mind what this lad says; it's all nonsense; he has been tied to his mother's apron-string, and had never previously been at a public school. There, go back to your company, my man," he added, pushing me on one side.

Off I went, leaving his Royal Highness, and, as I thought, everybody but the Lieutenant-Governor, intensely amused with my attempt to gain a hearing. I am perfectly certain that the Duke laughed more at Butler's haste to send me away, than he did at my malapropos declaration.

Among other reminiscences of Sandhurst College, I often think of the refinement in cruelty practised by the sergeant of my company, Sergeant Nutton. I do not think that he was fully aware of the agony he administered, and yet he must to some extent have known what my feelings were, or he would not so have amused himself at my expense. When our dinner was nearly concluded, it was his duty to warn us all individually if there were any letters at the Post-office. I had always some, as at home I had left my mother, my three sisters, my favourite brother, and others, and Nutton had seen how my appetite paused, while, with the expressive eyes of a boy not yet used to school his longings, I fixed my expectant glance on him. My number entitled me to an early warning, and for some time I had it in just rotation; but at last this cruel practitioner on keen feelings would occasionally pass me over, till he had got long beyond my numerical position. More than once he has shut up his book and gone back the whole length of the apartment; and then, when I thought all chance of a letter was gone, turned round and said—"Sixteen, three letters."

Those loved communications, thus jested with, spoke to me of home, and of all I held dear in the world; they were to me the only solace of my Sandhurst life; and if I now look back at the sorrow which the loss of that affection has caused, I only see in those scenes at Sandhurst what Shelley saw, and so sweetly referred to in the dedication of the "Revolt of Islam," when—

"There rose
From the near school-room voices, that, alas!
Were but one echo from a world of woes—
The harsh and grating strife of tyrants and of foes."

Never can I forget the intense pain my mother caused me, I am sure in utter thoughtlessness, within a very few days after my joining the College for the first half-year. My first impulse during my wretchedness was to write home to her, to my favourite brother, and to my sisters, according to the dictates of what then almost amounted to a broken heart, in words that I have since thought were more like those of a distracted lover, than the verbiage of a sorrowing boy. My letters failed in their spelling, a fault which should have been previously remedied at home. My teachers, not myself, were to blame; *and sure am I that the language which the eloquence of grief taught me to use for the expression of love and sorrow, was not such as ever came in a lesson from my prosy tutors, or that I had ever previously

seen put to paper. In fact, I knew not what I wrote;
and my pen dipped in tears would run on, and might
have left the commonest monosyllable shorn of its
complement of letters.

My mother's communication was, at that stage of
my malleable life, a cruel one. She severely blamed
the errors of my pen, and sneered at and essayed to
crush the warmth of my feelings. Indeed, partly
from the use of that, towards a child, the sharpest of
all weapons, ridicule, she struck me down and made
me afraid to write, lest, by some trivial fault or warmth
of expression, I should again excite her reprehension.
With Moreton, however, I feared not to correspond.
We had, or in those days I thought we had, so many
little interests in common, that I was sure he would
not show me up, nor let those who did not understand
the warmth of my disposition comment on my letters;
and thus, with him and with my sisters, my communication with Cranford was retained.

I have often thought that I would some day visit
that Sandhurst scene again, were it but to look at a
ditch beneath a belt of fir-trees, over which at that
time went a flight of rails. On the top bar of these,
on the first day of my arrival, I cut a notch for every
miserable day that must elapse before the arrival of
the vacation, and every succeeding day I repaired to
that spot with my knife to obliterate what at first
appeared to be but an atom of the lengthened time.
The result at last disclosed to my longing eyes but a
speck between me and my deliverance.

This is a strong description of the feelings of a boy,

and since the times of which I speak I have grown up in the world's ways, and have become a keen observer of character in woman and in man, looking also within at what I am, and what I might have been. All—all my experience tends to show that it is the earliest wrongs which, in ninety-nine cases out of a hundred, mar the coming man, and that in every character, as in the earth, there are the seeds of flowers and of weeds, and that, if the best are rightly cherished, and the worst judiciously repressed, Heaven has sent very few specimens into the world which are hopelessly rendered to the bad.

A "circumstance," may make, as a circumstance may mar, the coming hour. Spare the child; do not ridicule its best affections. Talk not before it, if you do not desire it to hear; and if of an age indistinctly to comprehend, then do not look on the mind as any longer barren, but regard it as an open fallow, on which whatever seed may fall will grow.

At the commencement of life, and in my earliest days, I was immensely attracted by poetry, and at home I was ridiculed for it, and reproachfully called the "little poet." One of my sisters, too, wrote beautifully. Were I to begin life again, and had I children to teach, and boys to rear to manhood, poetry in a boy would be one of the things I should most desire to see, as a true poet needs no other monitor than his own heart to keep him from a mean or an unworthy action. His chivalric and high-toned feeling depends not entirely on the opinions of other men; he must be heroic and good in his own estimation, or if

LEAVE SANDHURST. 137

he is not I would not give much for the favour shown
him by the muses. Poetry is not only one of the
charms of existence, but it is eminently useful in
refining and restraining mortal inclinations, the conduct and the heart of man.

No sooner, however, did my boyish muse exhibit
itself than it was for the time ridiculed and crushed
out of being. The attempt was silenced, but the love
of the art remained, and ere long Scott's "Lady of
the Lake," and other similar productions, and Byron's
and Shelley's works, were not only, some of them,
learnt by heart, but all of them were constantly in my
hands. As Shelley says—

"I then controll'd
My tears; my heart grew calm, and I was meek and bold."

At the end of the second half-year I left Sandhurst,
as I before stated, never having had a punishment.
My gracious godfather, the Prince of Wales, promised
me the gift of the first ensigncy that should be vacant
in the Coldstream Guards, and permitted me to wear
his uniform for evening dress—a blue coat lined with
buff, and G.P.R. on the button.

The excessive delight with which I cantered up the
dear old park at Cranford, having taken leave for ever
of the Royal Military College, it is impossible for me
to describe, although I can recall to my mind the innocent, the affectionate heartiness that revelled in my
breast at every well-known thing I saw, and the real,
the unalloyed pleasure I had in again meeting those I
loved so well.

138   THE COLDSTREAM GUARDS.

My mother's horse, given to her originally for her
pony carriage by the Duke of Kent, had been sent
over to Sandhurst to fetch me; and by having obtained
leave to travel thus from the heads of our College, and
by early rising, I won from the sluggish time a few
hours of additional joy. Towards my brothers and
sisters I felt that I could never change, nor deemed I
then that any of them could alter in regard to me.

It is impossible at this period of time to be exact
as to dates, but I remember that I went to Sandhurst
some little time after the battle of Waterloo and the
occupation of Paris; and having remained there a year,
I take it that when I returned from the College I
must have been about fifteen years of age. I was old
enough, therefore, to join in any field sports; and as
my strength increased, so did my devotion to all out-
door exercises. Of course my pattern in these was
in my eldest brother, Colonel Berkeley. Indeed, from
the devotion and love testified for him by my dear
mother, he was an example by which we all guided
ourselves.

At the age of sixteen, my gracious godfather, the
Prince, afterwards George the Fourth, presented me
with a commission in that splendid regiment the
Coldstream Guards, and I joined it in the Tower.
I was let loose from home at a time when London and
the locality to which I was sent were little likely
to make very favourable impressions on my mind. It
was in the winter, and when not on guard, I had
twenty-four or forty-eight hours at my disposal, and a
horse at my command. Though I had but three

CARLTON PALACE. 139

hundred a-year allowed me, I was advised to keep one and a private servant, instead of availing myself of the privilege to have a batsman from the ranks.

After I had been doing duty in London, in Windsor, and at Chatham with the regiment for some time, an order came out that, in addition to the Guards at St. James's Palace, Buckingham House, the Tiltyard, and the Horse Guards, a picket should be told off to march at a certain hour into Carlton House, remain there all night, and march out of it at or before daylight on the following morning. During winter, I was one night on this duty, and marched into Carlton House at the appointed time. Dinner was sent in to me from the mess at St. James's Palace, and I had to sleep upon a couch, no bed being assigned to the officer. Rather an inhospitably uncomfortable mode of passing the night under the roof of a palace, and in times of profound peace, when there was no need to have such a watch at all.

On the night on which I mounted this guard, a thick, frosty London fog set in; and when daylight died away, the brown, black, inky darkness seemed thick enough for me to have cut it in slices with my sword. The tardy hour at length came for me to go my rounds; so I started as usual with a sergeant, a drummer-boy with a lantern, and a file of men. The moment we emerged into the garden and the murky air, the light in the lantern looked like the small inflamed eye of a dancing fiend; for the drummer kept it waving up and down like a boat on a swell at sea, sometimes on a level with his own very

140   AN ADVENTURE.

low head, at others apparently on the ground. We could only guess at the position of the different sentries, or make them out by their stamp, in answer to the signal stamp of my advancing men.

All at once, as we were proceeding from one sentry in search of another, there sounded very near us such a crash as brought us to a dead halt. At that silent hour of the night, and in such a sacred place, where there should be nothing living or moving but ourselves, we were utterly perplexed while endeavouring to guess at the cause of this noise. We could distinctly hear the rush of a body or bodies through the shrubs and bushes, as if people, aware of our presence, were endeavouring to escape by flight. Here then was a dilemma, disagreeable to my ardent and active mind, anxious as I was for any opportunity of distinguishing myself in the cause of my godfather and of my country. As far as my ears served me, something was in the gardens at Carlton House at midnight; moreover, that something, or rather somebody, at that moment was in full flight and endeavouring to escape. At the first noise my sword was out of the scabbard, and I felt inclined to chase at double quick, but it was no use to order my men to charge, and as to any pursuit, we could see nothing but the little red spot in the dancing lantern. This served only to render night more hideous, and helped us not at all. I murmured to myself—it was not intended for a military command or question—" What the deuce is it!" then, as we had come to a halt, I gave the word " Forward," and on we went, our ears open in order to gain some explana-

A LOST DRUMMER. 141

tory intelligence, not only of the whereabout of the next sentry, but as to what conclusioh he had come to.

The rush of the fugitives died away in the distance, and first one sentry's challenge, then another, still more in the distance, reached my ear. "Who goes there? who goes there?" was repeated, but there was not so much as a syllable in reply.

As benighted civilians do in darkness with an insufficient lantern, my little drummer did. He lifted his light as high as he could hold it over his cap, and peered out beneath the bottom to see if he could see anything. Thus the light was about even with my breast, when, swift as a descending star, and about the size of it, only not so bright, down shot the red spot. I could not see him; and with a slight cry and then a vast deal of splashing I knew we had lost the drummer, lantern and all, in some water close before me.

In water! What water? Was it the Thames to which we had strayed, or the water in St. James's Park?

"Where the deuce are you got to, drummer?" was the question to which, with soldierlike brevity, I commanded an answer.

"Here, sir," was the somewhat shivering reply. "Here, sir; here!"

"Where?" cried the sergeant, probing the darkness and the depth in the unknown land before him with the butt of his halbert.

"Here!" cried the drummer, catching hold of the

halbert, and desiring his superior officer to "pull."
"Here, sir; down in the cistern."

Among the gold fish he might have added, but in the Coldstream, discipline forbids superfluous words.

Well, we fished out our little drenched and shivering drummer, the lantern alone was lost, and that, with such a candle in it, and in such an overpowering darkness, we could afford to spare. Again I gave the word "Forward," but added a caution "to take great care in the method of advance."

We had not proceeded far before down upon us, all among the shrubs, came the rushing, hustling noise again, and as it came directly at us, I gave the word to halt, to let it come closer still, that at all events we might by touch ascertain what it was.

This was not to be, however, for there was a dead halt of the enemy close to us in the bushes; and then, —ye gods! how the heroic feelings in my bosom fell, for I heard the distinct ba-a-a-a of a fat sheep, and the panting of four or five more.

The fact was, that one of those cur-dogs who so continuously mount guard with every relief that comes, no matter from what regiment, had entered into the gardens with us; and finding a few sheep penned on the lawn to fine the grass, he had crept through the hurdles, and in silence sought a kidney. The sheep, big and strong, made a desperate effort to escape, and in a panic charged the hurdles, broke through them, and then, chased by the dog, ran round and round the gardens, challenged by the sentries, for they, hearing no dog, the cur remaining silent, and expecting no sheep, like myself, could not discover the cause of the unwonted row, nor even guess at it.

The orders were to send in a report of your guard in the morning, so that any unusual transaction within the limit of the rounds should be mentioned. Having stated the fact of the temporary loss of the drummer in the gold-fish pond or cistern, instead of saying that I had simply gone my rounds, and that " *all* was well," I had my report returned to me with a suggestion "to be more serious," and send it back with the watery occurrence omitted.

The next amusing thing that I remember was at a dinner at the Thatched House in St. James's Street, given to his Royal Highness the Duke of Gloucester, I think; but it was certainly to the royal Duke who had one of the regiments of the Guards. At the banquet, among the young officers who had lately joined, was Dick Armit; when, on his being presented to his Royal Highness, the Duke remarked, when he heard his name—

" Oh, I know—son of Armit and Co.;" alluding to the well-known firm.

" No, sir," replied Dick; " of Armit only."

In those Guardsman's days we would breakfast on the best flounders in the world, at the well-known Battersea Red House; or go there to shoot pigeon-matches. Sometimes we had lady sitters; and I remember Princess Esterhazy on one occasion being taken with *sea*-sickness. It was there that I shot my first three pigeon-matches against the late George Anson, all of which I won. This got my name up as a shot; and after this, dining at the Guards' Club in St. James's Street with a good-looking, nice young officer—I think of the Grenadier Guards, L'Estrange—at the dinner, pigeon-shooting was talked of, and.I was alluded to as the best shot going.

L'Estrange was not known as a pigeon-shot in London, but *he knew himself* to be a first-rate game-shot, and perhaps he had elsewhere shot pigeons; so he declared his readiness to shoot me a match, if I would give him so many birds *in*. I forget now which it was, two or three. We made the match, and my backers regarded L'Estrange as a rash young man. On the match coming off, L'Estrange, however, shot quite as well as I did; and the birds I had given made him an easy winner.

Before I had grown in size and weight I used to ride races. The first races I rode were on the review-ground on Hounslow Heath, gentlemen riders; and that extraordinary man, Sheriff Parkins, was one of the competitors. I rode my own horses, the "Prince of Orange" and "Brutus;" but my brother Augustus in both instances on "Shrog" and some other horse proved the winner. I also rode my own horses twice at Egham, winning in each instance; and once at Moulsey Hurst I rode for another man, but then again I was beaten, and I walked over on my mare "Tippety Witchet" in Moulsey Hurst for a hunter's stake. Height, length, and muscular power then sent me up to six feet two, and thirteen stone, varying from twelve stone eight pounds to thirteen stone; so that even for the usual Welter weights I became incapacitated.

MY FIRST HORSES. 145

While writing this book, and not in my accustomed exercise, my weight has decreased to twelve stone seven pounds and a half; and I am lighter than I ever was before.

The first two horses that had been given to me were really quite enough to have ruined the nerves of a beginner. One was a well-bred, little, powerless bay mare, which my mother bought for me for 30*l.* of my father's old huntsman, the renowned "Tom Oldacre," at that time hunting the late "Mr. Hervey Combe's" hounds at Gerrard's Cross. When this quadruped, who never could jump, was stumped up, my brother Augustus for 50*l.* put into my stable a one-eyed well-bred bay horse, called "Hertford;" hot in his temper, and so furious at the sight of a fence, that, not being able to endure the sight, he turned his tail to it, and then wheeling with a rush—and I believe closing his one eye for fear of putting it out—in an insane scramble he blindly trampled it down, or tumbled through into the next field. A nice animal this on which to put a boy, to perfect himself in the art of going *well* across country !

While my battalion was at that horribly slow place, " Chatham," in the height of the London season, I was perpetually riding backwards and forwards to London on a beautiful fast hack mare, called "Tippety Witchet," my brother officers, who were content with the barracks, most good-naturedly taking my duty. By way of amusement, nearly every one of them doing duty kept a dog of some sort or another ; from my being away so much, they all barked when

VOL. I. L

146   GEORGE BENTINCK.

I appeared; and Colonel Sutton, then in command, said, " I was such a stranger that not a dog in the barracks knew me."

It was at Chatham that the trick, or practical joke, was played on George Bentinck, or, as he was afterwards called, George the Second, on account of his being second in a duel to the present Duke of Somerset, which amused his companions in arms very much. If ever an officer had the luck to be asked out to dinner at that dull place, those left in the barracks were sure to play him some trick. In this instance the mess waiter was dismissed to his bed at an earlier hour than usual, and the lamp within the entrance door extinguished. All the cur dogs about the barracks that would permit themselves to be caught by the offer of food, were then placed in Bentinck's bedroom, and along with them the great he-goat of the yard, and the barrack-master's fowls.

When the diner-out came home all was pitch dark, and the first thing that reached the listening ears in other rooms, was something very like a curse on the waiter for not seeing that the lamp would burn, and then a heavy anathema against the goat for sending his effluvium even into the officers' quarters.

Upstairs our friend then advanced, muttering vengeance against goat and waiter. As he came on the landing-place, and set his hand upon the lock of his door, there might be heard a gathering of many nails to the crack that promised speedy exit; for the sensible dogs had made up their minds, from the humour of their ascending deliverer, that " more kicks

INTRUDER.

147

than halfpence" would, in all probability, be their doom. The instant the door was opened, as the lock turned, there was an audible whine, and out poured, between Bentinck's legs, such an avalanche of rushing, yelling dogs, each screaming in the dark at kicks supposed to be intended for him, as was astonishing to hear. Down went the pack; then, as far as could be understood, the irate owner of that bedroom closed the door, and putting his back to it, thus ventriloquized his voice to all neighbouring chambers :—

"I wish I knew what blackguards have done this; all I can further say is that they are a set of cowards if they don't avow it."

Thus addressed, or at least in words of similar purport, the inmates of the various rooms had enough to do to suppress their laughter, the mirth still inclining to break forth because they thought of what was yet to come.

No sooner was the door opened and closed with angry vehemence by the diner-out, than a noise of hard horny hoofs was heard, accompanied by a savage "ba-ha-ha-ha," the well-known war-cry of old Billy. Butting to get out of the room, and cuffed for being in it, Bentinck with the goat closed in mortal strife for supremacy, when after much tugging the door again opened, and the wrathful goat was, by force of strong arms, hurled down stairs.

Again the angry diner-out addressed all doors severally, and no doubt thought, from the stillness of his room, that his annoyances had come to an end. He moved about in it for some time, chairs were occasionally

L 2

148   BILLY ROUSE.

encountered, and a boot-jack used, till the undressing
was complete, but then, as his tall frame and long
limbs were cast energetically down, the arms, and perhaps the head dislodged, in startled dismay, from the
head of the camp bed, just above the pillow, where they
had perched for roost, half a dozen hens, who, with a
loud and terrified cackle, fled about the room.

Feet were then heard to leap out of bed on the floor,
much groping about began, a hen screamed, the window was thrown up, and one by one the fowls were
sent flying into the midnight air, making night
hideous with the unwonted sounds of day, and drawing no doubt the notice of many a wondering and
startled sentry, posted within hearing of the scene of
the feathery encounter.

The next morning at breakfast one tall officer was
moody. He spoke to no one, but looked unutterable
things at all, while each save the moody man asked
questions of each other as to noises in the night.

Some time after this practical joke a foolish vow
having been registered against a figure over the
premises of an auctioneer, Billy Rouse, George Bentinck, and some others whose names I forget, essayed
one night to pull it down. They got a rope over the
arm, and, I think, pulled the limb off, when the door
opened and the auctioneer in person made a somewhat
belligerent appearance, though in extreme dishabille,
with a drawn sword in his hand. This, on being
seized by Billy Rouse, was immediately drawn through
the aggressive clutch, very nearly to the severance
of the fingers; while George Bentinck, hitting at a

COLONEL BOWATER.

watchman who came up amidst the springing of rattles, and missing that functionary's head, 'tumbled clean off the high footway into the road with the force of his own blow; but never hurt himself. The attacking party then retired.

There was a monstrous row about it, and some compromise effected. Alas, the pain it gave us, for I was at the march out of the town, though I was not in the row! We had to pass under the renovated figure, freshly and triumphantly painted, as we thought, and with a new arm, raised as if in triumph over his baffled foes. There was a consultation at our halt of that night, whether we should not return and do vengeance on the figure; but some sensible heads had power enough to stop us, and we abandoned the idea, leaving the offending effigy to the enjoyment of his paint and new position.

In my Guardsman's days we did duty at the West India Docks, and also at Woolwich; than the latter a more stupid quarter cannot be, unless it is Chatham. At Woolwich, when I was there, the Coldstreams and Grenadiers were brigaded for it together. Colonel Bowater then commanded the detachment, and the late Lord Harewood, Sir David Baird, myself, and I think Captain, now General Shaw, were also there. Having nothing to do, we went out shooting in the colonel's absence, and were warned off by somebody's bailiff, to whom we paid not the remotest attention, and when Bowater returned he was immensely amused at our having shot over, without leave, the ground he was specially invited to beat. I remember that Henry Lascelles, as he was then, had a horse he called Orelio. The duty at Woolwich was at this period of the free and easy sort. The colonel gave himself leave of absence, telling us to look at his letters, and if there were any from the War Office or from head-quarters, to send off to him immediately. The captains then gave themselves leave, and left the ensign and lieutenant in command; so of course I went away too, and a non-commissioned officer looked to all, and no doubt did the duty very well, for without any exception, I believe that at that time, and I have no doubt but that they are so now, the non-commissioned officers of the three regiments of the Guards were the best in the service.

In doing duty at the Deptford Docks, the most disagreeable hole of all, the three officers managed things very well, the seniors gave themselves leave of absence for a fortnight, leaving the ensign to do the duty, and then when one of them returned, the ensign went away for a week.

I remember my term of duty included that to me loved day, the 1st of September. That is to say, I was to go off duty on the September morning. This running the thing much too near for me to withstand temptation, I went off to Cranford on the evening of the last day of August.

I had gone out at daylight on the 1st of September to shoot over and drive in the outskirts of the Manor, when, on returning, hungry for my breakfast, at eight o'clock, my appetite was taken clean away by a beautifully drilled military apparition standing erect

WINDSOR BARRACKS. 151

in ,the old courtyard. It came to the salute as I entered the gates. Recognising my sergeant, whom I had left at Deptford, I went up and asked, "What is the matter?"

"You forgot the report, sir," was the concise and soldier-like reply.

"Oh, so I did," I replied. "Did you go the rounds, and *was* all right?"

"Yes, sir."

"Very well; go in and get your breakfast while I write."

This having been accomplished, I slipped a guinea into his hand, and ordered him back as quick as possible to his duty at the Deptford Docks.

It was a very wet day once when we marched into Windsor Barracks, so wet that we were kindly met at Datchet Bridge by a royal messenger to say the gates in the wall of the park were open for us to come the shorter way to the town. Colonel Sutton, who was in command, was riding by the side of Wedderburn, then the adjutant of my battalion, both having their great-coats on. Attracted by Wedderburn's taller figure, the messenger addressed him as the officer in command, on which the colonel doffed his great-coat instanter, and defied the rain, rather than risk any more mistakes.

There, while at Windsor, came off the race in the long walk, between Joe Tharpe of Chippenham on his chestnut horse, against a horse of mine, and he won easily, carrying his whip in his mouth, to the intense amusement of Sir Henry Bouverie and our brother officers. After this, and against the same chestnut horse, I made another match with him, owners up, in Cranford Park, and my one-eyed thorough-bred, bad jumping, rushing horse, Hertford, beat the chestnut easily, for pace was his only qualification.

All this time I did not neglect the Graces in my ardour for sport. The fame of Beau Brummell had still a certain influence, though his day may be said to have gone by since his estrangement from his royal patron. By the way, there is a well-known anecdote respecting them I am able to correct, given to me by a medical friend of mine, who had it from the late Henry Pierrepoint, brother to the late Lord Manners :—

"We of the Dandy Club issued invitations to a ball, from which Brummell had influence enough to get the Prince excluded. Some one told the Prince this, upon which his Royal Highness wrote to say he intended to have the pleasure of being at our ball. A number of us lined the entrance passage to receive the Prince, who, as he passed along, turned from side to side to shake hands with each of us ; but when he came to Brummell he passed him without the smallest notice, and turned to shake hands with the man opposite to Brummell. As the Prince turned from that man—I forget who it was—Brummell leaned forward across the passage, and said, in a loud voice, ' *Who is your fat friend ?*' We were dismayed ; but in those days Brummell could do no wrong.

"Henry Pierrepoint might be called the ' Last of the Dandies.' I believe that at the time he told me the above he was the only surviving member of the Club to which they gave their name."

CHAPTER VII.

HORSES AND HOUNDS.

Skeletons at Berkeley—My first shot—Scattering the pigeons—
Grumbo—Among the blossoms—My first poacher—Officers
from the cavalry barracks at Hounslow—Hammersley—A
retort discourteous—Value of a horsedealer's recommendation—
Filial affection—Mr. Frogley of Hounslow—My presentation
at Court—Getting leave of absence—My brother Moreton's
signature—Counsellor Fonblanque—Serjeant Vaughan—Legal
advice—Deer hunting—My horse Brutus—Lords Alvanley
and Rokeby—Remarkable jumps—Colonel Standon of the
Guards—Earl of Cardigan—Duke of St. Albans—Hon. Charles
Tollemache—Jack O'Lantern—Hampton Court Balls—Duke
of Clarence—Cricket Club—Lord George Seymour—Receiving
a Royal Duke.

THE first time I pulled a trigger and smelt powder of
my own exploding, was on the lawn beneath the battlements of Berkeley Castle, near where a summer-house
stood in the grove, and not very far from the spot
where, when my father was making a new ice-house,
I stood by and saw seventeen skeletons disinterred, in
the mere circumference necessary for the surrounding
walls of the ice-house. I heard my tutor, Mr. Hughes,
hold conference with a skeleton jaw still filled with
very white teeth, and ask, though, of course, he got no
answer, how many pieces of mutton it had masticated
before being consigned to its place of sepulture? It
was supposed that they were the remains of soldiers

killed in the defence of the castle, for they were found on the outer side of the moat, and from the positions of some of them, seemed to have been buried in a hurry.

My first shot was with a shot-gun loaded with ball, at some empty tin powder canisters set up the one upon the other. My brothers, Henry and Moreton, had been firing at them without effect, but at this my earliest attempt, I was lucky enough to hit the middle canister, and to knock them all down. I fired from a rest.

The next experiment was after my father's death, and we had been removed to Cranford. I was passing the farmyard then, in company with the same relatives, when they said they would give me a shot at an outside pigeon sitting on the roof of the dovecote among some dozens of his fellows. With a caution to be sure to take the single bird, they entrusted me with one barrel of a double gun; so, resting it on the wall of our farmyard, I took so very good an aim as to scatter into the thick of the flock, bringing down such a shower of dead and wounded birds as filled us all with dismay.

The last of these three early shots was with the single gun given me by Lord Grantley. It was a lovely summer afternoon, when in possession of this little but immensely loved fowling-piece, the first of my own I had ever had, I proceeded down the stately old beech walk in the woods of Cranford. It was in the afternoon—the blackbirds and thrushes had had their suppers, and were rejoicing their nesting hens with a serenade, such as may often be heard in woodlands, just before every feathered thing except the nightingale, owl; nightjar, and white-throat, enjoys its respective roost. The wood-pigeons had been to the bean and pea-fields for their food, and with pouting crops were now sitting by their nests in the yews and hawthorn trees, and softly cooing to their mates in praise of the bounties of nature; and the turtle-doves were murmuring to each other their mono-. tonous satisfaction.

Oh, those dear old white-heart cherry-trees that stood at the end of the great garden wall, at the top of the ash cover; sorry am I that they are now cut down ! Against the butt of one of these trees I sat till a couple of fine young rabbits came out in the ride to feed, when I fired at one, but killed both of them, and with my victims I returned rejoicing to the house to get some one to reload my gun, for as yet I was not trusted with the materials for that operation.

The first dog I could call my own was a black one, of a cross between the bull and mastiff, and with some other stain in the blood of his progenitors that I do not know, indicated by the appearance of the puppy. His name was " Grumbo," and he became attached to me with an affection that a dog only can exhibit. He was my constant companion—and was the brother of the much handsomer sort of large bull bitch so well known at Cheltenham as the pet of Colonel Berkeley.

Grumbo and myself very soon came to a most extraordinary understanding in all matters, whether of sport or war, and to a mutual understanding to back

156 A REASONING DOG.

each other up, let the impending danger be of any kind whatever. He was a capital retriever, and soon began to exert that gift which all dogs are more or less in possession of, a nose; and when objects intervened between me and the possession of anything I wanted, Grumbo would fetch it, or use his best exertions to do so, at once. If, while out shooting, there was no obstacle between me and the dead game, the dog displayed no predilection in the matter, but left me to pick it up myself. In short, Grumbo seemed to reason in all he did, and on that account became to me a most valuable companion. It mattered not to him what the understood duty was; if I threw a brick into the artificial water in the park at Cranford, where it was not too deep, and told him to recover it, he would with his paws feel where it lay at the bottom, and duck his head and neck after it till he brought it up. Bulls and cows he tried to bring to me by the nose, pigs by the ears, and men or boys by any part of their persons which seemed to him to be at the moment most convenient for his hold.

It was on one of those lovely days, about the middle of May, I was walking about the cover rides at Cranford, to places where, from within the high palings, I could command views of the common fields that lay between the park and the sweet cherry orchards of what was then the pretty little rural village of Harlington. In the orchard at home, then blooming, and in its richest promise of fruit, I had paused beneath each apple tree to study the interesting and beautiful ornithological and entomological lesson

WILLOW WREN.

afforded me by the mass of lovely blossom ornamenting every bough. Each tree was a hive for happy, busy bees of every kind, and for tinier insects attracted by the honied cells so liberally provided for them, that everywhere glowed under the brilliant sunshine, and were redolent of perfume. There was not a breath of air, and yet as I stood by the grateful bouquet spread above and around, the soft flakes fell to the grass, and snow-spotted the herbage. What makes these showers of bloom drop from the budding fruit and fall before their time, it would take too long to dwell on; my attention would be attracted by other objects, the graceful summer visitors, the willow wren, and lesser flycatchers. How smoothly and noiselessly they glide through that rich world of sweets, with sharp and graceful head and taper bill, scaring the bees, but not hurting them, for they seek their proper prey in a totally different insect! The rustic, if he glances up as the blossom falls, and observes the bird on its beneficial duty, in all probability would believe that it spoilt the promise of his apples. In that conviction he fires at, and probably destroys his friend, the enemy of the smaller grub, the pest of every fruit tree. The blooming orchard is a glorious place for study, or for the enjoyment of that *dolce far niente* which can be experienced only in the society of the one loved companion of our youth or manhood; but at boyhood's less discriminating age we are too restless to appreciate such pleasant indolence. In later life a new taste is acquired, a filled cup is presented to our lips, and very few can resist its temptation—more frequently it is drained to the dregs.

158   POACHERS.

On the day to which I refer, accompanied by my
faithful dog, I left the orchard for the more exciting
amusement of watching the preserve of game, or
catching, if I could, any of the poachers who were
known to commit depredations whenever they could
find a chance.

Grumbo and myself were standing within and
beneath the high palings at the bottom of the "Ash
cover;" I was extending my vigil over the open corn-
fields through a chink made for the purpose, when I
observed two men come along the headland towards
the park, searching the long grass, young nettles, and
scrubby bushes, evidently for pheasants' eggs. When
about a hundred yards from me, a hen pheasant, with
her peculiar cry, flew from beneath their feet, and I
saw them stoop and rob her nest. I had not the key
to unlock the gate, and a hundred yards was a long
start, particularly when I had to help a heavy dog
over the palings it was impossible for him to jump, and
the space to be accomplished not over three or four
times the distance, to the Cherry Orchards and village,
and the fellows, if they reached the latter, would
soon be screened from sight. So, waiting till the men
turned to retreat with their booty, in the hope of
their not becoming aware of pursuit, I made a sign to
Grumbo that he was wanted, and to try to jump the
pales. He comprehended that I would aid him.
When he had sprung as high as he could, I was
ready, and pushed him up from behind until he got
his paws over the top, then he climbed on, and fell
outside the park.

IN CHASE. 159

I was not long after him, and together we set off, but before we had gone ten yards, the egg stealers discovered us, and commenced running at full speed. Grumbo gathered from my manner that he was to catch and hold something, but whether it was a man, a horse, a dog, or cow, as yet he knew not, nor did he much care. I gave the well-known word and sign, pointing to the objects in advance, when he dashed on, and soon took up the running at the only thing he at first saw, the distant figures of two men. By this time they had reached and turned up the orchard hedge and headland by its side, on which was tethered with a rope a grazing cow. They passed the cow, and then I dreaded the interposition of her tempting nose as the dog came up upon her traces. We were now on that long headland in full sight of each other, and I had seen the men, as they ran, throw the pheasants' eggs away. At that moment Grumbo came up to the cow, and stopping close beneath her nose, with an ominous lick of his lip, looked back at me for confirmation of his idea. A wave of my hand, and a shout, "Go on," disclosed to him that it was a man and not a cow on whom I wished him to fix his hold, so to make up for this erroneous pause he dashed away on the now well-assured chase, more furiously than ever.

The vagabonds had had time to turn short to the right down a little grass lane leading at once to the cottages of the village, and were lost to my sight; but gaining on them fast, my dear companion turned that corner too, and I felt almost sure that before they

A PRISONER.

could reach the village, one or the other would be caught. It was in breathless anxiety that I turned the corner, and got into the last bit of straight running that yet remained, along which I had a full view. Never shall I forget my joy, when, about three parts of the way down the path, I saw the back of one of the men, his figure stationary, his hands held high above his head, and Grumbo, my faithful, sagacious dog, a yard in front of him, barring his path, couched like a lion in the act to spring, his eyes, not his teeth, fixed on the fellow's throat. The menace sufficed, he stood in terror of the result of any further attempt to run, and in this position I presently seized him by the collar.

There was a good deal of difference in our muscular proportions, though he was not a big man; I was only a boy, but he was aware that if a struggle between us began, I had a resolute assistant at hand, that would give me sufficient odds against him; so he at once surrendered, praying that I would call off my dog. I could see that Grumbo very much wanted a fight, but understanding at once the surrender and a sign from my hand, he calmed down to what was to the prisoner a horrible and close inspection of his leg, and walked back with us to the park, close at his heels, with his broad muzzle occasionally nudging the limb, as if to remind the man of the close approximation of teeth, ever ready, at a sign from me, to meet in some part of his person. It was with much boyish triumph that I led my prisoner into the great stone courtyard at Cranford House, and thence into the

SULTAN.

seryants' hall; and leaving him under the surveillance of the servants, went to call my brother to come and look at the first poacher I had caught.

When Moreton returned from College, he brought back with him an Oxford hack, about the cleverest and best mare I ever saw, which, added to a very nice steady mare he already possessed, put him well into the saddle. With these mares, in the earlier part of his life, there were very few who could beat him; but strange to say, at his age, when he lost these, his first two hunters, he also began to lose his nerve, and did not ride in his earlier and best form. It was lucky for me that my brother Henry possessed a fine old bay horse, called "Sultan," as great a slug, but as safe a horse as man could ride. He mounted me on him, and on him I first showed any symptoms of going well; for it seemed so strange to me and delightful to find myself on a horse that I was obliged to run away with, instead of being over pulled and violently carried I knew not how nor whither.

My first mount on Sultan made a man of me; and Henry, seeing this, good-naturedly let me be frequently on the old horse's back. As I have said, we kept a few couples of hounds in the old kennel at Cranford, and hunted hare, bag fox, or fallow deer, whichever we could get; and my pride was excessive when, for the first time, at one of our meets on the Uxbridge-road, near Hayes, or between Hayes and Southall, I saw come to join us three red coats from the cavalry regiment at Hounslow barracks. These three officers, if I remember rightly, were

VOL. I.   M

Hammersley, Bailey, and I think a brother of the present Sir William Jolliffe. We afterwards came to know all the officers of that regiment very well, and a jolly, good-natured set of fellows they were.

Hammersley had a wonderfully clever little horse called " Claret," and so had Burton, of the same regiment, a chestnut horse he called " Buffer;" and we had a good deal of fun together. My recollection of all the regiments that came to the barracks at Hounslow, the officers of which served as our companions for the chase, is somewhat confused at this distance of time, but I think, though I am not sure, Hammersley, Jolliffe, Burton, &c., were of the 12th or the 15th Hussars.

In these days there was a tall young farmer, named Passingham. He lived at Heston, near Cranford, and was always out with us. He was an insolent, pushing, but good-natured young fellow; but the officers disliked him on account of his familiar assurance. One day after we had had a very pretty burst, young Passingham, on his very good old chestnut mare, rode up to Captain Hammersley, and slapping him familiarly on the shoulder, exclaimed—

" Hammersley, old chap! a smart thing !"

Hammersley's Irish soul was up in a moment.

" By Jasus, sir !" he said, "I never allow anybody to speak so familiarly to me unless he has been properly introduced !"

So saying, he turned his back on Passingham in indignation.

The next week we had another good thing. " Claret" had carried Hammersley very well; his

A RETORT. 163

heart was in his mouth; and in elated ecstacy he came up to Passingham, and said—

"By my soul, Passingham, I never saw a finer thing!"

"My eye!"—a favourite expression of the young farmer's—"Passingham indeed! Ho! I never allow anybody to speak familiarly to me unless he has been properly introduced!"

Saying which, Passingham, in retort, turned his back on Hammersley; and sticking out his apparently jointless, long, thin legs in a curious attitude he could assume by bending a knee-joint the wrong way, the hearty disgust he assumed nearly made me fall off my horse with laughing.

About the earliest period of my hunting, old Tom Marsden, a dealer very well known and liked among the swells in London, kept his stables not far from Buckingham Gate, and told me I might have any horse in his stud I liked, for which I was to pay him *when I could.* Among them he particularly recommended a splendid-looking, steady chestnut, the very picture of an English hunter to carry weight; and at his recommendation, he telling me he was a trusted friend of Colonel Berkeley's, as I believe he was, I took him and rode him down gently to Cranford. He was perfectly safe on the road, and a capital hack; and he neither started nor seemed to look at anything. I had examined him all over; had seen that he had two, as I thought, good eyes in his head—at least, they were open and apparently clear—and having taken him quietly to the stable at home, I ordered him

M 2

for our meet in the "Harrow country" the next morning.

We threw off, and were trying for a hare near Horsendean Wood. There was a fair hedge and ditch in my way, and I rode my horse at them; the ditch was towards me, and when the poor dear horse felt his forelegs going into it, without the least knowing what the sort of fence was, he made the most sagacious struggle I ever felt beneath me to prevent a fall, and succeeded in getting me safe to the other side.

I called out to my brothers that my horse was blind; they doubted it, and said he would not jump, or that I had not put him at the fence properly. I soon tested the matter, for I led him back to the fence with the rein on my whip, and jumping over before him, he tumbled gently after me, instead of seeing the bank and ditch. They then knew his deficiency, and waited while I went all the way home and returned with another horse. · Tom Marsden took him back again without a word, as he very well knew that he was perfectly blind.

I have one more anecdote of young Passingham that is particularly quaint. His old father did not like his always being out hunting, and, as he thought, neglecting his large farm; but one day, as luck would have it, though we met at some distance, our hare or bag fox, whichever it was, ran straight to Passingham's farm. Now, the young farmer had left home with an assertion that he was going to Uxbridge market; but suddenly following the hounds, he appeared in some fields of his father's called the "Little Tenterlies."

FILIAL AFFECTION. 165

Between these, from Tenterly Lane, there ran a very narrow footpath, with a considerable ditch on either side; and about the middle of this path old Passingham had stationed himself to holloa out "war wheat," and perhaps to see if his son was really at the market town. Young hopeful caught sight of the old man before the latter perceived him, and with an artificial shriek to get out of the way, he dashed down the path at full gallop bang at his respected parent, who, to save his life, tumbled on his back among the briars in one of the ditches, while the son passed on at furious speed, and went straight out of sight. The run, after a check, commenced again, and before it was over young Passingham rejoined us.

"What a shame it was," I said to him, "to charge your governor in that way; you might have killed him!"

"Killed him? My eye! no fear of that. I knowed the old cove would cut into the ditch in such a funk he'd never know me; so I did it, and he hasn't found me out. My eye!"

In the Harrow country, where some men called farmers much more resembled pigs than Christians, and were the most morose set of illiberal agriculturists I ever knew, one of their labourers knocked down Passingham's chestnut mare on which he was riding with a dung-fork; and the young man never resented it, for which I gave him a good jobation. He was so insolent in return, that, I suppose with some brief recollection of the gloves in my boyish hours, I offered to thrash him if he would descend from his horse,

166   THE DOCTOR'S HORSE.

and give me a legal right to do so by holding up a
pugnacious hand; but the suggestion was declined.

Among our field, too, from its earliest establishment, was that since-eminent surgeon, Mr. R. A. Frogley,
of Hounslow, who I regret to say died in the spring of
1864. He had a bay mare who used to charge any sort
of fence without lifting up her legs, and in consequence
gave him falls sometimes in such wet places that, from
sundry trickling sensations down his face, he used to
ask us, to our intense amusement, "if he bled." I
once replied, "I supposed he did, but not then."

He also had a little horse who was perpetually
fretting, and, unless at full speed, invariably going tail
foremost. He was always hot in mind and body,
never still; I do not believe his temper ever permitted
him to lie down, and his coat was invariably curled and
damp, while behind the saddle one scarcely knew what
it was that kept his hind and fore quarters together.
He had a pretty little head, and no sort of vice, but
the active desire to be in perpetual motion, and to give
his tail a fair chance with his head at times to lead
the way. We christened his horse "Spitfire," a name
he really deserved in more ways than one.

Dear hounds and horses of those early days, you
are all down beneath the turf now; and so are hundreds of those riders who have shared so many brilliant
runs with me, felt the same glorious, sweet-scented
warmth from the soft south wind, the bright, the long-
desired thaw, and joyed in an existence that seemed
destined to last as long as mine. Farewell, my friends!
Were Indians right in their wild ideas, I am sure you

would all be in the happy hunting-grounds of the great Father, to be joined by me in some future time.

I have often surmised, but I never could be quite sure why, there should spring up at home, as soon as I had obtained my commission in the Guards, an evident desire that I should not soon come back again. My mother parted from me when I started to join my regiment in the Tower, the best of friends; assured me that I should attain the rank of Colonel in a few years, and asked Mr. Weston, at that day the fashionable tailor, what regimentals it would be necessary to start me with, and how they were to be put on, and when worn.

With no one to give me advice, or to tell me any military thing, before I joined the regiment, in which I soon found many friends, I was told that I must be presented at the levée on my appointment to the Coldstreams; and for that purpose I repaired to London. I forget who undertook to present me, or whether I had to hand my card to a lord-in-waiting; all I know is, that to the levée I went, all right in my stiff gold-lace armour, which our full-dress coat then was—all right as to shorts and silk stockings, buckles and shoes; but to my full-dress coat I superadded the gorget to my bosom (only worn on duty), and to my waist, the sash.

When boys enter large assemblies of their equals, among whom are some who in age and rank may be called their superiors, it is natural to have an immense desire to be correct and well got-up in dress;

168   OFFICERS OF THE COLDSTREAMS.

the more so, where an appearance is in a uniform
rigidly defined. I had scarce entered the crowd when
I perceived that two general officers were looking at
me, one of whom, in the most kind and considerate
way, approached and said—

"You ought not to have the gorget on, nor your
sash."

I thought I should have sunk through the floor,
and hastily taking both off, I put them in the pockets
of my swallow-tails. The emblem of duty slipped
in very nicely; but the sash being a large one, and
intended for the office for which sashes were made,
and capable of carrying a grenadier, it must have made
an outward observer think I carried an enormous
pocket-handkerchief! However, feeling reassured as
to my appearance, trusting to an oppressive crowd
behind me, and hoping I had lost sight of everybody
who had seen the errors in ·my dress when I first
entered, I thanked the kind strangers with much
gratitude, passed in review order, and was kindly
greeted by the Prince, who called me by my Christian
name, and told me he was glad to see me.

Soon after this I joined the 2nd Battalion of my
regiment at the Tower, of which Colonel Elrington
was at the time the Governor, and, if I remember
rightly, Woodford commanded the battalion. Bentinck was adjutant; and among my brother officers
with whom I first did duty were Wedderburn, White,
and Shaw, Baines, Loftus, Tom Duncombe, Cornwall,
Serjeantson, Murray, Clifton, and Joe Tharp, Morgan,
Jack Talbot, Barrow, Sowerby, and others. Sir Henry

A HARSH RECEPTION.

Bouverie, Sir Richard Jackson, Colonel Macdonnel, and Colonel Sutton also commanded the battalion at different times.

I then found that I could always have at least a day to myself at home at Cranford, between those on which I was on duty, either at the Bank, at the Tower, or at the West India Docks; and often more time than that, when I got my duties taken, and leave to absent myself granted.

On the first idle day after relief from duty, I mounted my horse and rode down to Cranford, charmed to see the loved home again, and thinking to give an agreeable surprise to my mother. I rushed into her room buoyant with joy. Never shall I forget the harsh deluge of cold water that was ruthlessly and recklessly again cast upon my warm heart when she beheld me.

" *You* here again!" she said, in evident anger; "I thought you were gone for some months. What in Heaven's name brings you back?"

At this rebuff I cannot describe how completely my spirits fell, or how much I suffered at the moment from a harshness I never expected, nor could account for.

I simply replied, "I have no duty to do till the day after to-morrow, so I would sooner be at home than at the east end of London."

She made no further remark, and I then went to see my sisters, and to seek my favourite brother, Moreton. I confess that this harsh reception from my mother set me thinking; and in thinking, I remembered that, at consultations between her, my brother Henry, and my former tutor, Mr. Hughes, at this time Rector of Cranford, I had noticed that there was a "hush" said by somebody if I came unexpectedly into the room, and that they had matters of business in which my brother Moreton was concerned, when my presence was no longer deemed desirable.

The time seemed to have passed then, when careful tutoring prevented me from too close an observation, and those who most wished to have diverted my attention, by this, their own overt act, roused it to some extent, yet not sufficiently so to induce me to break through the education of years.

The more I was with my brother officers, the kinder they were to me; and every week, or except when I was the officer on barrack duty for the week, I passed at least some days at home. Moreton had been installed as Master of the Game and Hunt at Cranford, the moment he returned on the second time from Oxford, having passed his examination; and there was no idea mooted as to sending him away; on the contrary, every inducement was given him to remain at Cranford, and to keep him from the world; and I believe my return home was tolerated only inasmuch as we were immensely attached to each other, and it might have set his back up to have driven me away.

I did not know that we were then approaching a time at which a favour was to be asked at his hands— a favour which he had been closely brought up to believe was a duty—with a sort of implied threat that if he did not do what was wanted of him, he should be deposed, and I should have to do it in his stead.

SIGNING PAPERS.

At different times in the conversations of my
mother, Mr. Hughes, and Henry, I have heard thus
much; but I little knew what the duty was to which
they were alluding. I was not yet fully enlightened,
nor had I sufficiently shaken off the trammels of
implicit obedience, to make a bold step to thwart the
mysteries then enacted. Moreton, as I have previously said, much to his disgust and mine, had been
constantly in the habit of being taken away from our
sports, to sign papers at Cranford or in London—the
occurrence being to him of the greatest possible
annoyance. One day, some months after he had
come of age, Mr. Hughes came to him, and in my
hearing, spoke much to the following effect :—

"Morety, there are quantities more papers for you
to sign, but as I know you have always hated the
trouble, I have so arranged it that if you will sign all
those papers at once, *and one in particular*, we shall
not have occasion to trouble you again."

Moreton jumped at this proposition, as the greatest
relief to him, and I remember his saying, "Oh, oh! I
shall never have to go up to smutty London any
more; so now we can always be together every day as
we please."

Where he went to sign the papers I do not quite
remember, I think it was at Cranford, but certainly
not in my presence. I was either purposely prevented,
or by some curious accident I never saw him put
his name to deed or paper in my life that I know had
to do with the peerage. As to lawyers, at this period
he never employed one.

172   A PENAL CLAUSE.

The conversations I heard held with legal advisers
at different times as a child, as a boy, and latterly
as a young man, recur to my mind now by fits and
starts, but in an unconnected manner, and, indeed,
as referring to nothing that I knew at the time
they were spoken; they have lain fallow on my
mind, to bear only when things connected with their
import worked their way out, and then they illustrated
the meaning of the advice given years ago, both by
lawyers and other people.   Thus I can well remember
old " Counsellor Fonblanque " standing before the
fire in the dining-room at Cranford, dressed in a
suit of rusty black, with shorts and silk stockings,
and a crumpled frill to his shirt, which came out very
much after dinner—that suit did duty also for a
morning as well as an evening dress—one hand thrust
into his waistcoat, and the other in his breeches
pocket, or under his coat tail, and speaking to my
mother to the following effect :—

"It is questionable whether that penal clause in
Lord Berkeley's will has not obviated rather than
strengthened the intention of the testator to bind
Moreton and Grantley to a particular course, because
it is restrictive, or what may be regarded as a penal
clause, and leaves Moreton *not a free agent* in his own
affairs.   It is a ' penal clause ' which may be found
to be in antagonism with all your ladyship's desires.
With the *know*ledge of the law which I possess (he
always gave the first syllable of the word knowledge
without any abbreviation), I am bound to express my
belief that that ' penal clause ' is an illegal act, and

DEEDS. 173

that it will be found not to promote the object for which it seems to have been inserted."

At this moment, while thus writing, a vision of the old counsellor seems to stand before me as it did there one night after dining, his scanty white hair on his bald head combed back, his quick, restless, small, glancing eyes peeping on either side of his large and very aquiline nose and pallid cheeks, as they always did to see the effect of what he was saying upon his hearers, and my poor mother trying to combat the hostile view he was taking of the matter. This sort of furtive glance, even at dinner, used to seek the faces of attending servants, so prone was the counsellor to watch the effect of the very bad puns he was very fond of making.

With all the delight of a boy at being told he was not to go to school again, with the joy of a reprieved criminal whose execution was respited, my brother Moreton embraced the insidious offer I have alluded to, and to my certain knowledge he signed papers of the real meaning of which he was totally ignorant. On his return, I asked him "How he had avoided going to London again, and what he had been doing?"

He replied that "Hot Specks," a name he had given to our tutor, Mr. Hughes, knew all about it, and had got him out of any more musty parchments.

From that time, I am not aware that he was ever called on again to sign a deed that related to the birthright and fortune to which he was justly entitled, or that collaterally had anything to do with me.

174   HUNTING.

When this was done it was some months after his majority. My brother Moreton, as soon as he was of age, received a summons to his place as Earl of Berkeley, in the House of Peers, at the hand of the late Sir Robert Peel. On the reception of this document a letter was then written for him by Henry Berkeley, to be sent in reply; I have the copy of it now, and of others which were dictated to him, asking Sir Robert Peel if he intended to insult him by the summons, and suggesting (or words to the effect) a personal or hostile inference, if he ever should do so again.

During the occurrence of these more serious matters, our hunting increased in importance, much encouraged by Colonel Berkeley. He furnished us with red deer from the castle, as well as with hounds. But ere I resume the narrative of our sports, in passing, I must refer to a very important piece of news which reached my ears, at this distant period I cannot tell how, but which I very well remember caused to Moreton and myself some astonishment, though, considering the importance of it to him, it is impossible to account for the supineness displayed by both of us. It was this.

We in some way became aware of the penal clause in my father's will, by which either he or I, whichever of us might hereafter be in the possession of the earldom and baronies, if we took the seat in the Peers, assumed the title, or attempted to take possession of the castle and estates, upon that assumption, forfeited the younger brother's inheritance we possessed. The

A MONSTROUS WHIP. 175

mere fact of forfeiting a pittance on the accession
of a large fortune, at first sight, and as a *bonâ fide*
transaction, seems rational, but it conceals the penalty
of ruin to those against whom it was aimed. Moreton,
however, had been made to surrender his personal
right to the fortune of the earldom, for his life,
certainly—and if possible for ever. That fortune
having thus passed out of his hands, then, and not
till then, did he or I know that there was a penal
clause in the will of our father, by which Colonel
Berkeley could render him a beggar, if at any time,
or through any means, he should be induced to
attempt to recall what he had been made to do, or
to assert the rights of his birth.

It will at once be seen by this, that a monstrous
whip was in the hands of certain parties, for while
they made Moreton commit an act *as* Lord Berkeley,
at the same time they made him deny that he *was*
the peer, and then they held the " penal clause,"
in regard to depriving him of his younger brother's
fortune, after he had done their *deed*, over his head,
threatening him with the consequences of any attempt
at revocation.

Not content with this, their power over Moreton's
pittance of £700 a-year, the £5000 in cash, to which
we were all entitled on coming of age, Colonel Berkeley
also got possession of, continuing to Moreton the
interest, however, but without any deed that Moreton
knew of, or that I could discover, showing any warrant for the transaction.

During the passing of these circumstances, my

mother had a legal dispute with a neighbour at the park gate, as to the right of building or opening a gate out upon a piece of land. There was a trial at law, Serjeant Best was her counsel, and Serjeant Vaughan was for her opponent, the defendant being a solicitor of the name of Magnell. If I recollect right, my mother was beaten, or there was a new trial, and on the next occasion Serjeant Vaughan was her counsel, and she gained the case. This led to the presence of Serjeant Vaughan as a guest at Cranford; he used to shoot with us, and subsequently my mother took counsel with him on all matters, particularly on the future interests of the Berkeley peerage, the entire pros and cons from the commencement of which she laid before him. After he had shot with us, she often sent him to sleep with a narration well adapted to vex the dull ear of a drowsy man, drowsy from unusual exercise.

Serjeant Vaughan had a country house at Pinner, not far from Uxbridge, and as we became the greatest of friends, I used to go over to him in his leisure hours, to look for a supposed woodcock, and to help him shoot the few hares and rabbits his wood afforded. In those quiet evenings of very good living—for the serjeant, though I never saw him exceed, liked a good glass or two of wine—he used to caution me on peerage affairs, *to keep my hand from paper*, and not to be induced to sign anything that was put before me, *unless I thoroughly knew its purport.* So far only, in those days, did his kindly intended advice extend. He had a farm in his own hands, which he always

HUNTING.

lost by, and while giving this caution, he used laughingly, in his hearty way, to say, "I speak to you as Serjeant Vaughan, not as Farmer Vaughan, ha, ha! Serjeant Vaughan is a devilish deal better than Farmer Vaughan—I would not give much for the worth of the latter !"

We continued our intimacy after he became Baron Vaughan, and till the hour of his death; and shortly before, the last time I saw him, he most impressively addressed me thus : "You remember, Grantley, the caution I gave you long ago about putting your hand to paper on family affairs. *Keep your hand from signing anything;* in no way whatever consent that your rights to the peerage should be tampered with; what they have done against Moreton and yourself *will not hold water,* and you and your sons must come into your just inheritance."

I never saw my kind old friend again.

Our hunt was now becoming famous : Henry went abroad, and Moreton and myself, assisted by the late Harry Wombwell, the brother of the late Sir George Wombwell, who took the place of second whipper-in, did all the extra service with the hounds, in one respect because we liked it, and in the other, because we could not afford to keep any more servants than we were obliged to have. We housed our deer in barns and stables, and fed them with our own hands; a boiler, or kennel man, and a deer-cart driver, being the only servants we required other than those in the stables.

It was about this time that I purchased, for 140 guineas, the bay horse, "Brutus," of Elmore, whose

VOL. I.

178   BRUTUS.

stables were then in Duke Street, Manchester Square.
He was not a very fast horse, but his extraordinary
jumping and powers of endurance made up for it. He
was as perfect at a brook as he was at timber, or
hedge and ditch, double or single, and I rode him
over all the timber divisions of the Home Park at
Windsor Castle, the stag and the hounds gaining an
entrance over the river near Datchet, at which place
a portion of the park wall had fallen down. Running
round the park, after a very sharp run, I secured the
stag with my whip under the walls of the Castle, the
Prince Regent or his Majesty, I forget the exact date
of this transaction, witnessing the conclusion of the
run from the Castle windows. One of my field, a
horse dealer whose name I forget, attempted the
timber, but in his first effort caught a most severe
fall, and gave up any further competition.

   The late Lord Alvanley, and Edward Montague,
afterwards Lord Rokeby, were out that day, and a
great many more, but no other horse essayed the rails
besides those I have mentioned, not only because they
were so stiff and high, but, I am willing to suppose
also, because the run virtually was over, the pack
racing to pull down their deer, while it was my duty
as well as pleasure to ride to prevent their tearing him
to pieces.

   Brutus had more than once set the field over park
pales, and once by jumping the Brent, on the other
side of which I stopped the hounds while the field
went round, feeling no pleasure in riding to the
hounds alone. Another remarkable jump made by

him was over a gravel pit, on the powder mill stream. It was the first day of the season, before advertising the meets, and I had a good many young hounds out, one of which hesitated to swim the stream. Knowing the fact that there ought to be nothing before me but a little bank and young quick, after I had ascended the bank of the river, I had therefore turned my head round to cheer the hound across, when, after his little spring over the young quick, I felt my horse make a momentary pause and an immense effort between my knees to get himself together. Turning to see the cause of this, I found a large gravel pit with two men at work in it immediately beneath Brutus's fore feet. There was no power of stopping and no room to turn, so with a touch of the spur and a lift I stimulated the amount of exertion to which the dear horse had already made up his mind, when, with a bound that I shall never cease to be thankful for, we flew over the danger and landed safe on the other side with several feet to spare.

In those beautiful days, when the heart and soul were in the chase, and the mind prepared for anything and dreading nothing, and ever looking on, I knew that I had jumped a "yawner," but should have thought no more of it, if on my return home I had not found the two men, whose heads I had gone over, waiting in the servants' hall with the string with which they of themselves had measured the leap. The pit, from brink to brink, was twenty-three feet wide, and standing, with no vantage ground in his favour, my clever horse had cleared it considerably even with his hinder feet.

He never gave me but one bad fall, and that would have been an easy one over a hedge and ditch, but for his accidentally striking me on the forehead with his fore-foot. The blow did not knock my hunting cap off, but it drove its substance in above the peak so forcibly with the edge of the shoe, that it cut my forehead to the bone, severing a large vein, stunning me a little, and filling my cap with blood. I was whipping in then, and my brother Moreton was on with the leading hounds, and did not see the fall, but some of those who had observed it, rode on to him, and when they could catch him reported that I was killed; one foolishly affirming that he saw my cap taken off and some of my brains were in it. The man who said this was inclined to the idea, because the cap had been driven on so tight that no blood or very little had escaped, and a congealment of a good deal of clotted blood fell out when the cap was removed from its position. I could not resume my place in the field for a week or ten days, but by the termination of that period I was perfectly recovered.

Out of the many years I rode this loved horse, this was the only time that in my falls, which were very few, not one in a season, I ever received the slightest damage. Alas! a painful circumstance will sometimes arise in every phase of man and horse's existence, and I was suddenly deprived of my best hunter from the contraction of one of his fore-feet. In spite of the counsels of my father's old coachman,

A CURE. 181

Ben Beadlestone, who in the best years of his box in London, had been known as "Flying Ben," and who urged upon me a consultation with the cow doctor, who was virtually the village blacksmith, instead of what he termed the Witney College Doctor, I called in the excellent science of "Sewel," who at once assured me that the only chance of cure was in a seton passed completely through the frog of the foot. I gave permission for the operation, and saw, with tears in my eyes, the magnificent form of Brutus cast with ropes upon some straw, and never shall I forget the shriek of agony he gave when the instrument passed right through the centre of frog at foot. He rose at last, with the operation thoroughly and well performed, and as he limped to his loose box and again fed from my hand, I kissed his sweet face over and over again, and hoped that he would once more put me in the saddle.

My hopes were granted, the next season my horse became sound, the King's stag hounds ran by Cranford, and, to try if he would stand the work, I had him saddled and rode him for a few fields, and once more Brutus took his place as the best horse in my stables. During the time to which I now refer, I had married, purchased a house in the village of Cranford, and assumed the exclusive ownership of the hounds, my brother Moreton still whipping in. My horse Actæon was good, and so were Mason and Captain, both of whom I bought of Admiral Sir George Seymour, who paid me the compliment of saying " he always knew Mason was a good fencer, but that I had taught him to go fast."

GOOD RIDERS.

Lord Alvanley also purchased " Whisgig " of Sir George Seymour, a' horse under Lord Alvanley afterwards well known in Leicestershire.

Among the field, and the members of my hunt, there were my intimate friends, Colonel Standen of the Guards, who on Pilgrim nothing could beat; Henry Montague, the present Lord Rokeby, who, a splendid horseman, could on anything go as straight as a line; the late John Montague, not so hard nor so fine a horseman as Henry; the present Sir H. Peyton, at one time very good; Lord Brudenell, now Lord Cardigan, excellent across a country; Lord Alvanley, very hard; the Duke of St. Albans, very slow; and the late Hon. Charles Tollemache, very cunning and very jealous, but who on his magnificent brown horse " Radical," if he could by sly cuts keep his horse fresh while we were riding hard, would slip in at times when he saw that we were in for a good run, and with an advantage over us by having shirked a portion of the run, and made a " nick," he would then go excessively well.

On heavy land, Radical was the best goer I ever saw in my life. Tollemache one day, followed by my friend Colonel Parker of the Life Guards, then a young beginner, after making a nick at the Yeading brook, where the country was immensely deep and the brook a bumper, distinguished himself immensely. My horse Brutus and all the rest of the horses were done before we came to the water, and the hounds setting their heads for Harrow. Tollemache and Parker both cleared the brook, the former triumphantly pulling his hat off

JACK O'LANTERN.

183

to all of us, and then they had the hounds to themselves. Some others of the field on their blown horses went at the brook, but none got over; all went hopelessly in, and remained there some time. Those who held hard with me, and went round to the bridge, by a lucky lane, regained our wind, persevered, and by a turn in the run came up in time to share in a brilliant finish. There was no sort of doubt but that from the brook Tollemache and Parker had the very best of the best part of the run.

There was another run, in which I remember Colonel Standen and a Mr. Smith, who had a house at Hanwell, going best, each on a chestnut horse, over the Harrow country. I also well recollect finding a stag that we had lost some time before; he was one of those let out of his barn by some mischievous rascal at Harlington. We found him in the woods at Pinner, and brought him away close at him over the Harrow Vale for Hayes. I was on Brutus, and my friend Gaskill on, I think, a bay horse, and we went best in that brilliant burst and side by side till we stopped our horses, Brutus going the longest of the two.

About this time I purchased another perfect and, I believe, thoroughbred horse of Elmore, with one eye, whom I called "Jack O'Lantern." He was sixteen hands high, and shaped for going, in short had the steeple-chase been in fashion then, I do not believe that there was a horse foaled that could have beaten him. He was much faster than Brutus, good at everything, but not to my mind so good as Brutus at timber or at brooks. Brutus always would go slow at all sorts of fences; if you rode him fast at a brook, he would break into a trot when within a few strides of it. Jack liked to fly, though when he had shaken off the crowd, as he used to do so brilliantly, he would arch his neck, not pull an ounce, collect himself to an inch at his fences, and then to sit on him so within himself, was to me the most exquisite piece of horsemanship imaginable.

Both Brutus and Jack would always heave a long sigh to catch their wind, when they saw a large fence coming, and both of them, when in the air and over some unexpected width that they had not counted on in their spring, could expand and stretch out their shoulders to such an extent for the purpose of clearing it, as to tear out the "Ds" that held their breastplates to the saddle. In other cases they would drop their hinder legs and gain a fresh purchase on bank or stake-bound hedge, and I have known Brutus strike a stiff rail to send himself farther on. In double post and rails, when he saw he could not clear both rails and ditch in one spring, and that there was not room cleverly to go in and out, I have known him clear the first rail and ditch, and landing his fore-feet under the lower rail of the second flight, by preconceived intention, start the top bar by catching it on his fore arms right out into the next field, and then his hinder legs striking into the side of the ditch or its bottom, clear the remaining two bars, without the semblance of a difficulty.

Jack, once, in a heavy ploughed field, fell at full

HORSE DEALERS. 185

speed, and came down on his head, but we righted together without a fall, one of his fore legs through the reins, the latter still on his neck. Of the London dealers that used constantly to hunt with me in those happy days, were the Elmores, since dead—at least I know that my good friend is dead of whom I bought my horses—the Andersons, and Bean, and Robinson. Anderson said of Jack O'Lantern, that it was "more like flying than riding," and Robinson asserted in a tremendous run we had had nearly to Guildford, at the end of which Jack fell lame, that his fencing throughout was more like a posture master than the action of a horse. Lame as he was, he bid me three hundred guineas for him, which I then and there refused.

Our fields also were made up from the regiments of the Household Brigade, and the cavalry regiments quartered at Hounslow, and at last from all London, so that on the night before hunting, every stall in the inns at Cranford Bridge, at the Magpies, or in the village, was filled.

It is impossible for me thus to name all my friends, or all the men who hunted with me, or to remember all the amusing incidents that occurred during the time I took up my residence at Cranford Bridge Inn. Previously to my marriage I went to the inn, because the hours I kept in those hunting days were not at all compatible with the regularity of my mother's house. Balls at Hampton Court, dinner parties and dances in the neighbourhood, kept me out till midnight and till morning, whereas she always

186   HAMPTON COURT.

retired to bed at nine o'clock; the arrangement, therefore, suited us both, though much scolding was occasionally administered to me for the number of my
stud, and the extravagance of living at an expensive
inn.   The inn life was much too good fun to be lost.
There I could receive whomsoever I pleased, and no
questions were asked.   People used to come down over
night on hunting fixtures; and besides this, the quiet,
pretty inn at Cranford Bridge was in those days the
temporary resort of Londoners in no way connected
with the hunting field; there were occasional guests
who were also very agreeable, and if I chanced not to
go out on some invitation in the evening, there was
always something to be done at home.

Of all the most agreeable places in the world,
Hampton Court, its palace, gardens, and environs, was
perhaps, at least it *was* so to me, the most agreeable.
I belonged too to his Royal Highness the Duke of
Clarence's club; the club dined together at the dear
old Toy Inn, if I remember rightly, once a month.
I was also president of his Royal Highness's cricket
club, and for years the perpetual steward of the Moulsey Hurst Races.   But for me, at one time, they
would have gone down; however, by dint of great
exertion, I worked them up to such a state of progres-
sive prosperity, that then other men were desirous of
relieving me, and of taking my place.   This I had no
objection that they should do, thinking at the same
time that they might have proffered that assistance
when the game was all up hill.

At the club dinners the well-known faces that recur

THE DUKE OF CLARENCE. 187

·to me at this moment were those of Lord George
Seymour, Sir George, and Sir Horace Seymour, Colonel
Wheatly, Mr. Woolmore, and Mr. Campbell. The
dinner was always a very jolly one, for his Royal Highness liked it, and his extreme good humour, and even
boyish mirth, never let the spirits of his party flag for
a single moment. I recollect his Royal Highness
announcing his gracious intention to be present at
one of the race balls at which I was the sole steward.
There were races again on the following morning, the
programmes for which rested entirely with me; besides
which I had to preside at the ordinary dinner, held
that night on account of the ball at the Toy, at the
Red Lion. My time was, therefore, not at my command, nor could I entirely make it subservient to the
attention it was both my duty and happiness to dedi-
cate to his Royal Highness.

Colonel Wheatly, or some of the courtiers around
Bushey Park, ought to have known this; if they knew
it I suppose they forgot it; all I know is that I had
just hurried back from the ordinary to dress at the
Toy, when old Saunderson, the landlord, sent the
best of all waiters, Tom Besant, up to me to say
that the royal carriage was at the door. Not only
could I not be in my place to receive his Royal Highness, but he had been permitted to come so early that
the ballroom was not lit up, and to my horror, on
hurrying down I found the Prince in a cold, dark
room, stripped of all its furniture for the dance, and
the candles in the act of their primary illumination.
I could only bow and express my contrition, and what-

LORD UXBRIDGE.

ever I might have thought and felt, it was impossible for me to lay the blame on those who had been guilty of what I am willing to suppose was an oversight. I could not tell them in that presence, that they had brought his Royal Highness at least an hour before the ball could begin. His Royal Highness was very kind to me, but I saw that he was nevertheless displeased.

. What spirited things those balls were, and how we used to "keep it up!" In a waltz the present Lord Anglesea, then Lord Uxbridge, fell, or rather stumbling, went through the window on to the little balcony, but for which he might have whisked into the river. Hunting all day and dancing all night was then immensely agreeable, and so were the walks in the garden, and by the Maze in the Wilderness. Alas, in the latter walled garden the secrets of a beautiful life were disclosed in the hearing of a concealed gardener, who, without an intention of hiding to overhear, kept himself in ambush for us to pass on; we unfortunately stopped for a moment close to him, when on detecting his presence, though I do not think my companion did, we moved on again.

Alas! that unintentional listener caused me the deepest sorrow, for I feared disclosure. However, on seeking him out thereafter, I offered him death on the one hand, and a handsome Christmas-box on the other, if he maintained a discreet silence. He promised silence and faithfully kept it, and for years received his Christmas-box.

In those days of romantic feeling, this adventure in

POEM.   189

the Wilderness was thus set down as an early attempt
at versification.   I give it, copied as it is from a
sheet of writing paper grown yellow with the years it
has lain in my desk :—

How wayward is the human mind,
    How varied life's fond chain ;
Now firm, then fickle as the wind,
    'Midst summer sun and rain.

No merry mood one morn was miné,
    The ball-room waxing thin,
While brighter beams began to shine,
    Than those that waned within.

I lean'd against the folding door,
    Saw there the lingering few,
Who still were loth to quit the floor,
    As waltzing round they flew.

Upon those boards I look'd again,
    Devised with chalkings rare,
And saw the dying rosebud stain,
    In ruin scatter'd there.

How small a thing will speak of grief,
    Of pleasures past away,
A trampled bud, a wither'd leaf,
    Are symbols of decay !

I turn'd to leave the sadd'ning place,
    But turning thence, descried
A lovely form, a beauteous face,
    Were pausing by my side.

I knew them not, those lovely things,
    Nor whence their owner came,
But softly as the warbler sings,
    I heard her breathe my name.

And lingering there her little foot,
    Advanced and touch'd a pin,
Which had confined some glossy curl,
    And kept its gambols in.

POEM.

Wrapp'd in her thoughts a little while,
　　She turn'd to go away,
But as she moved I saw the smile
　　Upon her lips at play.

I saw her eyes look up to mine,
　　And then I dared to speak,
" Dear girl, thy face is too divine,
　　To wish my heart to break !"

" To break," she whisper'd, with a start,
　　" Oh no ! for mercy sake,
To-morrow come to Hampton Court,
　　And there thy fortune take.

"' Its Wilderness in shadow lone,
　　Safe trysting place will be,
Then at the Maze, be there at one,
　　And see who comes to thee."

The ring-doves were cooing in Hampton's "Home Park,'
　　And the mavis and blackbird were singing,
Then loud on the road to the horse's foot—hark !
　　For a rider in haste he is bringing.

That rider leap'd down by the great iron gate,
　　And a love ditty too he is humming,
Nor does he for long by the Wilderness wait,
　　Ere he sees that a lady is coming !

A lady, alas ! not the one he had seen,
　　In the ball-room to whom he had spoken,
But one still more beautiful, oh ! and I ween,
　　From a sister she came with a token.

" Oh yes," then, she cried, " from my sister I come,
　　But to give you this lock of her hair ;
She cannot to-day get away from her home,
　　And her heart it is sad in despair."

" Dear girl," then I said, " let despair have no hold,
　　On those hearts that are willing to love,
Let not a fond wish ever die in the cold,
　　While the sun sheds his warmth from above.

WILLIAM LOCKE.

"How white is thy hand, and thy lips! oh, how sweet!
    While thy sister is thus kept away,
As Heaven *so* wills it, for us it is meet,
    In her absence at love thus to play!"

The warblers kept singing, the dove to the pine,
    In confidence murmur'd of pleasure;
Too swift flew the hour on wings so divine!
    The miser must part with his treasure.

Stern Time, wilt thou *never* of joy spare the flowers,
    Oh, could I have broken thy wing,
They ne'er should have come to an end—those sweet hours,
    Which now to my soul fondly cling.

Among my hunting field, and indeed among my many friends, was one whom I loved like a brother; and this was William Locke, the brother of Lady Wallscourt. He had been in the Life Guards, if my remembrance serves me rightly, but had left the service when we became so intimate. At one of the Moulsey Hurst racing meetings he was steward with me, and there had been some dispute and judgment given by us which was adverse to some person whose name I have forgotten, and he made use of very insulting language to both the stewards, but only in William Locke's presence. The judgment we had given in our united capacity was just; we were alike bound and very willing to defend it; and the right course would have been to have kept together, and so have put an end to personal cavil by saying such is *our* irrevocable resolution, and *we* stand by it. A man would scarcely have been so foolhardy as to have picked with us a double quarrel. However, William Locke hesitated not on any such consideration; he

192   GEORGE BYNG.

took all responsibility on himself, too happy, as I
believe, to think that he saved me from any personal
risk; and before I knew anything of the matter, Locke
had met this man and fought a duel with him, neither
shot taking effect. The quarrel ended there.

In returning home to Cranford from Hampton Court
one very dark night, my postboy upset my chaise between Hampton Court and Hampton, at the narrowest
part of the road between the pales of Bushey Park and
the Thames; and, after rolling over, the chaise stood
on its roof, close to the water's edge, and I made my
exit through the window.

"I shall get the sack now, sir," observed the lad;
"for 'twas but last week I served another of Mr.
Saunderson's customers. the same."

"Well," I replied, laughing at this confession,
"give me your riding horse, and I'll ride to
Cranford; and you must fetch your poster in the
morning."

One of my fingers was considerably cut by the-
glass.

Hampton Court in those days was filled by all that
was agreeable, and on both sides of the Thames, in
its vicinity, there was hospitality as well as grace and
loveliness.

At Twickenham, too, there was the ever hospitable
mansion of the Misses Byng, the sisters of old George
Byng, who in my parliamentary days was called "the
father of the House of Commons;" his dress a pigtail
and leather shorts and top-boots—a very uncomfortable attire, to my mind, in which to sit out a long

LORD BROUGHTON.

debate in the House of Commons. I remember when my good old friend came to one of her Majesty's balls in the reign of William the Fourth, if I am correct; and as I was at the head of the stairs, I saw him coming to the full-dress ball in plain clothes. The late Lord Fitzhardinge was standing near me at the same time. Mr. Byng was then almost blind, and as he was stopped before he entered the State apartments and told of his mistaken attire, he hid himself, or they hid him, in a corner, to wait till his coat was sent for, when he exclaimed—

"Tut, tut! how could Mrs. Byng have let me come? She never did a foolish thing before."

"Yes, she did," said the deep voice of Lord Fitzhardinge, as he passed by Byng—"she did when she married you."

The many happy hours I have passed at dinners, balls, and parties, at the Miss Byngs, at Twickenham, will never be forgotten; nor will I, nor can I, ever forget that good old hearty friend of mine, the late Sir Benjamin Hobhouse, as well as Lady Hobhouse and their daughters, at their ever open house at Whitton. Time has made sad changes there; but in Lord Broughton still I find the sincerest and the most agreeable friend, who in no one instance, when I have asked him to be kind to others to oblige me, has ever failed to show his ready generosity. To him I am indebted for cadetships to two young men, one of them an orphan, who but for us would scarcely have had the means of gentlemanlike existence. I am not so sure that in gratitude the

VOL. I.

orphan has kept pace with obligation; but gratitude is a myth, and the less we look for it, or expect to find it, the less shall we be disappointed.

Neither shall I ever forget the balls and dinner parties at Pope's Villa, given by Sir Wathen Waller; nor the grotto in his garden, near the river, whence originated the idea in one of my mottoes, published many years after in "The Reminiscences of a Huntsman," and which is inserted in my poem of "The Last of the New Forest Deer."* Our host of those days at Pope's Villa was most hospitable, but he always marred his wealth and lavish profusion by some excessively pompous vulgarity that set his guests rather mischievously against him; and hence the most reprehensible trick played by two friends of mine now no more, the perpetration of which was unknown to me at the time—of opening a lot of sandwiches on the refreshment table at one of his balls, and sticking the several and greasy contents of them between the valuable and illuminated leaves of a very handsomely-bound book, to its utter destruction. I never either sanctioned or indulged in such practical and ruinous jokes as these; and had I felt personally offended at anything my host had said to me, as one of his guests collectively or individually, I should simply have abstained from going to Pope's Villa again.

---

* " Then would it grieve thee if thy favourite's eyes,
    So deeply full of wild and lustrous love,
  Should still turn to thee as their mistress dies,
    Denied the hope of op'ning them above:
  Or hast thou loved a love so dear and rare,
    That pity for her only couldst thou spare?"

WEST DRAYTON.

Spitefully to destroy, under the cloak of jocularity, is to commit an act—to say the least of it—of excessively bad taste; and one of which, thank Heaven, in my most frivolous mood I have never been guilty.

West Drayton, too, the seat of Hubert De Burgh, is also remembered by me as one of those places where some of my happiest hours were passed; and as the railway carriage carries me by those scenes so deeply impressed on memory, I endeavour to recognise in trees and lanes, fields and woods, old friends who need no voice to vibrate on the ear to awaken sympathy; for the rustle of a leaf, or wave of the slightest bough, goes to my heart, and speaks of past affection, buried, but never once forgotten.

CHAPTER VIII.

HIGHWAYMEN AND GHOSTS.

Cranford conveniently situated for tales of terror—Heroes of the road—The flying highwayman and the Irishman—Bow Street runners performing an artful dodge—Captain Hawkes' celebrated mare—Honour among thieves—The last Lord Coleraine —The ghost I and my brother Moreton saw at Cranford—The ghost seen by my father—Hounslow Heath—My father kills a highwayman—His retort to Lord Chesterfield—Changes at Hounslow Heath—Sleep-walking—Lord Berkeley saved from shooting his sister, Lady Granard, by the intelligence of his dog—Ladies' pets—Admiral Prescott and my father's pointer— Captain Cracraft and the pheasants.

THE state of English society, at the period I am endeavouring to illustrate, may be better understood by a delineation of some of its prominent features that came under my observation. Cranford adjoined Hounslow Heath, and the incidents for which it long retained a terrible celebrity were often canvassed in my hearing. In these unadventurous times it is not easy to realize the spirit which influenced people, sometimes holding a respectable position, to imitate, on a small scale, the heroes who lived upon the plunder they could obtain from every one they met unable to resist them. The wide unenclosed waste lands in the neighbourhood of the great metropolis were the usual resort of those who desired to better their fortunes at the expense of whoever happened to be travelling that way; they became the haunt of mounted gentlemen who cried, "Stand and deliver!" with a loaded pistol and a black mask, at the window of every postchaise or stage-coach, the occupants of which were obliged to follow that direction. The mails were robbed with the utmost regularity and despatch; every public conveyance, and every equestrian not well armed, courageous, and circumspect, shared the same fate. Purses, rings, watches, snuff-boxes, passed from their owners to the attentive highwayman, almost as soon as the muzzle of his weapon obtruded through the window. Horace Walpole has recorded some adventures of this kind, in one of which he suffered, that took place in the neighbourhood of Chelsea; but the most lively account of them will be found in that grand collection of heroic adventures, "The Newgate Calendar."

It is not necessary to remind the reader of the alleged exploits of Dick Turpin; no good book ever had the circulation which the history of that worthy obtained; in truth, the colporteurs of the last generation could scarcely find enough copies to supply the demand. The fascination of the subject was put to profitable use by a modern novelist, who made a large literary capital out of his ride to York; a modern dramatist seized upon its capabilities for Astley's Amphitheatre; and even introduced with prodigious effect, not only the hero and the hero's favourite steed, but night after night, to delighted audiences, the fabulous scene of the horse swallowing a rumpsteak as a refresher, after miraculous exertions to save his master's neck from the gallows !

Jerry Abershaw was a hero of a similar stamp, whose adventures were almost entirely confined to the Surrey roads leading to Kingston and Wimbledon. He well deserved the distinction he gained among the equestrian order of scoundrels. For the full period of his career he might have been marked A 1, in the professional list of such craft that was studied by the Bow Street runners. Whether that once-celebrated personage danced the hornpipe in fetters, which by stage tradition is the last saltatory exhibition indulged in by such accomplished cavaliers, I cannot say; if he did, it must have been when he was vainly striving to find a flooring on which to perform that deeply-interesting *pas* with which he was forced to double " shuffle off this mortal coil."

There were heroes of the road talked of within my remembrance by people who knew them, who, though they have not had the honour of circulating library or Royal Academy fame, were great men in their time. They rode as good horses as Dick Turpin, though they did not, like that ruffian, broil an old woman to make her declare where she had hid her money; they treated their victims as cavalierly as Claude du Val, though they lacked the effrontery as much as the grace with which that model *chevalier d'industrie* insisted on having a dance, on the public road, with a beautiful woman, when he had rifled her protector's pockets. Among these I must name Hawkes, commonly called the "Flying Highwayman,"

CAPTAIN HAWKES. 199

from the rapidity of his movements. He was quite a representative man. Had he lived in the dark ages, he must have been a great leader of condottiori, or an Italian count whose ancestral walls harboured a band of thieves; or the captain of a Salee rover; or some other distinguished and powerful rascal, able to make might right, and grow rich at the expense of such of the community at large as were not in a position to hold their own.

Living, however, under the paternal rule of George the Third, in a quiet country like England, he was obliged to be content with the modest honours and limited emoluments of highway robbery as practised in those degenerate days. He created a great sensation in the neighbourhood he frequented, and the fame of his exploits struck fear into the hearts of the boldest travellers as they approached his alleged haunts.

A vapouring fellow, apparently from the sister island, who, according to his own account of his antecedents, had been too often in action with hosts of enemies to care for footpads and such scum, when his postchaise stopped at the last stage, a way-side inn called the Plough, near Salthill, alighted, carrying a pair of large horse-pistols, and walking into the barparlour, called loudly for brandy-and-water.

The room contained only a Quaker—in the usual drab suit and broad-brimmed hat—who, in a very sedate manner, was satisfying his appetite with a modest meal. The traveller came swaggering in, and laying down his weapons on the table in such close approximation to the edibles that they evidently startled the man of peace, he began to inveigh against the cowardice of people who were afraid of the "fellow Hawkes."

"If they went armed as I do, what had they to apprehend from a single man?" he demanded; and with an abundance of oaths protested that half-a-dozen highwaymen should not be able to deprive him of a sixpence.

The Quaker continued his humble refection, now and then looking off the bread-and-cheese to take a mild glance at his noisy companion when he was most vociferous and demonstrative; for the latter drank his beverage standing, or rather stalking up and down the room. Presently finding his eloquence thrown away upon friend Broadbrim—who he at once decided was so quiet because he had nothing to lose— he unceremoniously turned his back upon him, and sat down on a chair to examine his valuables. This having ascertained, he deposited every article carefully in certain safe places about his person.

The taciturn Quaker was finishing his repast with the same air of indifference he had worn all along, when the traveller, after gulping the remains of his brandy-and-water, snatched up his weapons, and strode with an impatient exclamation out of the room to the bar. He was paying for his liquor, and expressing his opinions to the burly landlord, with his usual confidence, on the absurd fears entertained by some travellers, when the man in the drab suit and broad-brimmed hat passed by him hastily, and went out into the road.

A HIGHWAYMAN. 201

The boisterous gentleman continued his conversation for about five minutes, then paid his reckoning and re-entered his chaise, telling the postboy to drive fast, and holloa when a suspicious person approached. He threw himself on the seat after he had closed the door, stretched his legs as far asunder as possible, and planting his feet firmly, cocked his pistols, which he held at arm's-length, the barrels resting on the open windows.

The horses went on at a tolerable pace for about a mile, when the chaise entered upon a heath—a very desolate-looking place, without a house visible in any direction; indeed, there was nothing to enliven the perspective, unless a gallows with a skeleton swinging in chains, about a quarter of a mile off, might so be considered. The traveller gazed with a grim satisfaction at this spectacle. It seemed to him as to the shipwrecked sailor in the old story—an assurance of civilization. As he was musing on the certain protection thus held out to him, the rapid though dull sounds of horses' hoofs over the turf were followed by the stopping of the chaise, as a black-masked face appeared at the window, holding a horse-pistol pointed inwards. Immediately followed the hoarse cry of— "Stand and deliver!"

The traveller pulled the trigger of the weapon he held in that direction, raising the muzzle to the head of the highwayman. It produced a snap and a few sparks from the flint. With a terrible execration in the strongest brogue, he quickly brought his other arm round to the same side, and again attempted to fire, after making sure of his aim. The result was exactly the same. The man in the mask laughed.

"No good, friend Bounce, trying that game," said he, coolly; "the powder was carefully blown out of each of thy pans, almost under thy nose. If thou doesn't want a bullet through thy head, just hand me over the repeater in thy boot, the purse in thy hat, the bank-notes in thy fob, the gold snuff-box in thy breast, and the diamond ring up thy sleeve. Out with 'em, in less time than thee took when I saw thee put 'em there, or I'll send thee to Davy Jones, and take 'em myself!"

The muzzle of the pistol which the traveller saw was at full cock, was thrust closer to his head, and the flashing eye directed on the barrel evidently belonged to a man not to be trifled with. The occupant of this postchaise at once dropped his useless weapons, and with considerable trepidation drew one by one from their places of security the valuables named by the highwayman. The latter took possession of them as they were handed to him, giving a slight examination of each before he put them in his pocket. He then drew half a crown out of the purse and threw it into his chaise.

"There," said he, leaving off the jargon of a Quaker, "is enough to pay your turnpikes. I strongly recommend you to proceed on your journey as fast as you can. And, heark'e!" he added in a more peremptory tone, "for the future don't brag quite so much." He then turned his horse's head, and rode across the

RUSTICS.

heath at a rapid pace, and the chaise proceeded along the high road in a different direction.

It was on the afternoon of the same day that a man in a heavy topcoat and well-splashed riding boots, looking as if just off a long journey, entered the tap-room of "The Rising Sun," at a village about twenty miles from the heath. With a quick glance he observed that in one compartment on each side of a painted table sat two ploughmen, or other farm labourers, in smock frocks, their shock heads resting on their arms, which were spread on the table near an empty quart pot, and they were snoring a by no means lively duet.

The new-comer having been served with a glass of gin-and-water and a long clay pipe, without taking any further notice of the sleepers, began to make himself comfortable, and was speedily emitting smoke with a rapidity that showed his familiarity with the process. In a few minutes one of the rustics awoke with a snort, and glancing vacantly about, scratching his carroty head, seized upon the empty vessel. He put it down again quickly. "Ye greedy chap!" he cried, giving his companion a nudge that nearly sent him off the bench, "blowed if ye aint been and drunk up all the beer while I were a-sleeping."

"Then ye shouldn't have been a-sleeping, ye fool," retorted the other derisively, with a broad red face grinning from ear to ear.

"I'll gi' ye a dowse o' the chaps, if ye grin at me," exclaimed the other angrily.

"Haw, haw!" shouted his friend across the table.

"'Twould take a better man nor ye be to do it. And if ye don't want a hiding ye'd better not try."

Up jumped the two chawbacons simultaneously, and rushed at each other with equal fury, moving their arms in a roundabout way, and then closing and wrestling with tremendous exertions, like fighting-dogs in a canine battle.

The stranger smoked his pipe placidly, somewhat amused with the encounter, but perfectly indifferent to the issue. Presently the combatants rolled on the sanded floor, and cuffed and kicked there with equal energy, the spectator sipping his steaming beverage, and still looking on as though on a very harmless amusement. Presently, however, his aspect and manner changed, he looked excited, he put down, first his glass and then his pipe, and rose hastily. A clasp knife had been opened, the bright blade was gleaming in the hand of one of the combatants, and descending towards the breast of the other. In a moment it was arrested by the stranger's powerful grasp.

Quicker than I can describe the act, his own wrists were grasped firmly, and he was thrown on the floor, both men fixed themselves about him with the tenacious grip of a Polar bear, and when he rose to his legs he was handcuffed.

"Neatly managed that!" cried one of the pretended rustics, throwing off his smock frock and disclosing the red waistcoat of a Bow Street runner. "You must acknowledge, Captain Hawkes, as how we've done you brown."

The constables appeared rather to have done him

THE FLYING HIGHWAYMAN.

white, for he was as pale as a sheet. The surprise of his capture, and the knowledge of his danger, seemed for a few minutes to have taken away his consciousness. This time was employed by his captors in searching his pockets—in those at his breast they found a pair of pistols loaded with ball, and in others sundry purses, pocket-books, rings, and other valuables, the produce of recent robberies.

"All's clear as daylight," said the other officer sententiously; "nothing could be more regular and proper. There's nothing about him but'll 'wash!' If you please, captain, we must beg the favour of your company to town. A postchaise is waiting for you. Have the kindness to come with us to the door. This way, captain; mind the step. There's no occasion to break your shins nor neck in an unregular way."

The manacled man knew he had no alternative. He saw it was a step from his pipe to the "deadly never green;" so, summoning his resolution, he trod on with a firm step, and an air of stolid indifference, between his captors, who were now entirely divested of their disguise. He was "had" through one of the good feelings of his heart—but for a circumstance the case might have been different.

When it became known that the famous "Flying Highwayman" was in Newgate, wonderful was the excitement the news created. The lions in the Tower were neglected for a more interesting one in a more interesting den. Parties were made to visit him, as parties were made for Vauxhall. He was the principal subject of conversation in those tattle-shops, the clubs; indeed, was talked about everywhere, including balls, routs, dinners, the Court drawing-room, and the servants' hall. His antecedents were discussed by the lady visitors at Devonshire House, quite as much as they were by their masculine contemporaries in Carlton Palace. In short, he was for a time "the rage."

Among others who visited him more through curiosity than interest was a person of very eccentric habits, who subsequently became a member of the Irish Peerage. He went to Newgate, and easily gained admission to the place in which the culprit was confined. The latter received him as courteously as his fetters would permit, and, the two being left together by the accommodating jailer, willingly gave him some details of his past career, not forgetting to describe how he had rendered the bounceable traveller's pistols harmless, and watched him in a mirror, when his back was turned, securing his valuables about his person to make assurance doubly sure, and how he had presently rode away, met the braggart on the heath, and made him deliver up everything he possessed.

His visitor laughed heartily as other visitors had done at hearing the same narrative, for the doomed man himself seemed oblivious of his terrible position, but presently intimated, somewhat mysteriously, that he had come on a particular errand. Circumstances he said had made it necessary that he should purchase a mare of a certain description, and hearing that Captain Hawkes possessed one of a superior kind, he had ventured to wait upon him, partly for the pleasure

HONESTY AMONG THIEVES.

of making the acquaintance of so remarkable a man, partly to offer him a good price for an animal that he knew had served him well.

The highwayman understood the case at once. His visitor was unquestionably a gentleman by birth and breeding, but he was well aware that such gentlemen occasionally found themselves so completely the victims of circumstances as to have their only resource in a game such as he, Captain Hawkes, had been playing. Gratified by the sympathy and consideration that had been exhibited towards him, the man spontaneously displayed the truth of a certain adage, that is much to the honour of such players.

"Sir," said he, warmly, "I am as much obliged to you for your proposal as for your visit. But," he added, in a tone and with a manner implying increased confidence, " the mare wont suit you perhaps if you want her for *the road*. It is not every man that can get her up to a carriage !"

Having ascertained that the culprit's only prospect of escape was shut out from him, in consequence of his having been left entirely without funds, his visitor, who was constantly doing in those eccentric days what no one else cared to do or dared attempt, advanced him fifty pounds ; but although such a sum had often effected the liberation of as great an offender, it was found powerless in his behalf; the captain therefore honourably returned the money as of no use, and submitted to his fate.

This visit was one of the last eccentricities of the eccentric Lord Coleraine.

It was before I left the Guards, if I remember rightly, when my brother Moreton and myself saw the ghost at Cranford. I have often since thought of that apparition, and have never been able to account for its presence nor to divine why or wherefore it appeared. Appear it *most assuredly did*, for we both beheld it, and our descriptions of what we saw coincided in every particular. The circumstances were these : it was expected that our preserves of game were to be attacked by a gang of poachers. The poachers had been to Richings Lodge, Mr. Sullivan's, near Colnbrook, and not only shot pheasants, but, in bravado, absolutely killed the keeper's fowls from their roost at the very door of his lodge.

Such an outrageous insult as this fired our hearts with the resolve that Cranford should never so succumb, so we organized keepers and assistants, and went out night after night at their head.

It was the rule of my mother's house that all servants should be in bed at ten o'clock, and on the night of the ghost we were not to go forth till midnight, when there would be enough of a moon to dispel the pitchy darkness induced by a partial fog, that at first was an ample protection to the game. My brother and myself were together, and well armed, in no mood to be nervously excited, and little inclined to be afraid of anything. We passed by the still-room, intending, by crossing the kitchen and going through the scullery, to reach the courtyard by the back way. The large old house was as still as death when my hand turned the handle of the kitchen door, which opening, partially admitted me to the room, at the bottom of the long table which, starting from between the entrance where I was and the door of exit to the scullery, ran up to my left in its full length to the great fireplace and tall and expansive kitchen screen. The screen stood to the right of the fireplace as I looked at it, so that a large body of glowing embers in the grate threw a steady distinct glare of red light throughout the entire of the large apartment, making the smallest thing distinctly visible, and falling full on the tall figure of a woman, divided from me only by the breadth of the bottom of the table.

She was dressed, or seemed to be dressed, as a maidservant, with a sort of poke bonnet on, and a dark shawl drawn or pinned tightly across her breast. On my entrance she slowly turned her head to look at me, and as she did so, every feature ought to have stood forth in the light of the fire, but I at once saw that there was beneath the bonnet an indistinctness of outline not to be accounted for.

Holding the door open with my left hand with the right against the post, I addressed to my brother, who was behind me, simply the word "Look." As I uttered this, the figure seemed to commence gliding rather than proceeding by steps, slowly on, up the kitchen towards the fireplace, while I lowered my right arm from the post, and turned to let my brother in, then closed the door, locked it, and put the key into my pocket.

In reply to me Moreton said, "I see her, there she goes."

VOL. I.

I had not told him what I had seen, and therefore could in no way have suggested the idea he seemed to entertain.

After I had thus locked the door, on turning round there was no woman to be seen, so I asked my brother whither she had gone. He instantly replied, " Up the kitchen towards the screen."

" Come on, then," I cried; " let's have some fun and catch her, to see who it is."

. Our impression was that it was one of the maid-servants sitting up long after the usual hours, and we at once proceeded, each taking a separate corner of the screen, and meeting on the side next the fire—but there was nothing there!

Astonished at this, we then commenced a most minute search of the kitchen, looked up the chimney and beneath the table, into the oven and into the drawers—in short, into every nook and corner that could have held a rat. But there was no living thing in the kitchen but ourselves. The windows were fast, and so high in the walls that, even with the aid of the dresser, no one could have reached them ; the door by which we entered was locked and the key in my custody, and the only other door into the scullery we found locked, and the key on the side with us.

We hear of hats that turn and of tables knocked by the knuckles of ghosts, of pictures etched, drawn, and even coloured by spiritual agency, of handkerchiefs floating in the air, of words written by unseen hands, but not always well spelt by their in-

ANOTHER GHOST.

visible heads, not one word of which do I believe; but here I offer to my readers a fact impossible to be accounted for, an apparition visible to two persons who, when they saw it, thought that it was a living body; each supposed it to be a woman, and fearless of spiritual agency, pursued it, but in vain.

The form certainly resembled no one we had ever known, it came to indicate no treasure, nor to point to any spot of perpetrated crime; it came we knew not why, and went we knew not whither; and the only rumour of a ghost we had ever heard, arose from an occurrence that happened many years before to my father.

He had come down from London to Cranford, as was his usual wont, on a Saturday to stay till Monday, and he had been out with his gun in the evening to shoot rabbits at feed. As he returned through the courtyard, and repaired with his rabbits in the direction of the larder, up a narrow court, one side of which is formed by the kitchen I have described, he saw on the cellar steps at the end of this court, whence there was no other outlet, the figure of a man. It was just nine, and nearly dark, but beneath the bright sky of the summer night the figure stood on the steps out from the sable hue of the descending arch behind it, which formed the background, as distinctly as it would have done in noonday.

My father had brought down no male domestic, and he at once saw that the form was strange to his eye, so he advanced upon it with the words, " Holloa, sir; who are you?"

P 2

HOUNSLOW HEATH.

The figure answered him not, but as he advanced, seemed slowly to recede down the steps into the cellar, and in the darkness was lost to view.

My father ordered the spirit up from the vasty deep—the cellars under the old house are immense, and this portion of them, not then in use for the custody of wine, was open. As usual, however, with spirits, the call was not obeyed, so my father remained at watch, till by calling aloud he attracted the attention of the maid-servants, and brought them to the spot. He then, leaving them clustered together at the entrance to the cellars, candle in hand, searched the place for the expected delinquent, but his search for the man was as fruitless as ours for the maid, there being no one in the cellars. Of course, in this instance, there was the possibility of the figure being a "follower," and on that account might have been passed off by the maids.

Being on the subject of ghosts, I will conclude this part of my narrative by relating one more circumstance that happened to my father in one of these weekly visits to Cranford when accompanied there by his sister the Lady Granard.

In these days Hounslow Heath was as celebrated for highwaymen as it was for its plovers' eggs. Its lonely commons, thick furze bushes, thorns, and wide extent, running as it did to Hatton, Harlington, and Hampton commons, and so on to Bagshot Heath; and its intersection by the Thames, the Mole, and other smaller streams, made the pursuit of a malefactor on a fast horse very difficult, the latter of course well

BISHOP TWYSDEN. 213

acquainted with all the galloping paths between the furze bushes, while his pursuers, if there were any mounted, would be riding at random, and in the dark blundering over every impediment.

The vicinity of Hounslow Heath to London also rendered it a convenient place for the nightly occupation of villains of all descriptions, who, either from necessity or a love of adventure, liked to "clip purses" and to resort to violence as a relief to the more peaceful and less exciting pursuits of the day. Nor was the occupation of these highwaymen confined to the lower classes, for even a dignitary of the Established Church was found on the heath collecting tithes in rather a promiscuous way. Thus, the archives of the British Museum tell us that the "Lord Bishop Twysden, of Raphoe," a member of the old Kentish family of that name, was found suspiciously out at night on Hounslow Heath, and was most unquestionably shot through the body. A correspondent of the "Gentleman's Magazine" asks the question—"Was this the bishop who was taken *ill* on Hounslow Heath, and carried back to his friend's house, where he died of an inflammation of the bowels?"

As a child, I remember this story being talked about in conjunction with the occurrence which happened to Lord Berkeley when he shot a highwayman. The Bishop's death occurring in 1752, that of the highwayman in 1774-75; the distance between the two was not wide enough to prevent my father being fully aware of all the circumstances of the first. It is shown by Haydn's "Book of Dates," that

214 LORD BERKELEY.

the particulars as to the death of this bishop are, or
have been, in print; but whether they were suppressed
at the time, or have since been lost, I am not able to
discover. He was the father of the celebrated Lady
Jersey, notorious for her friendship with the Prince
of Wales.

When a child, I often heard my father describe his
rencontre, so my recollection can be relied upon. In
the "Gentleman's Magazine," vol. xliv., p. 538, Friday,
November 11th, of that year, there is the following
narrative :—

"As Lord Berkeley was passing over Hounslow
Heath in the dark of the evening, in his postchaise,
the driver was called to stop by a young fellow gen-
teelly dressed and mounted; but the driver not readily
obeying the summons, the fellow discharged his pistol
at the chaise, which Lord Berkeley returned, and on
the instant a servant came up and shot the fellow dead.
By means of the horse which he had that morning
hired, he was traced to his lodgings in Mercer Street,
Long Acre, and discovered; where Sir John Fielding's
men were scarce entered, when a youth, booted and
spurred, came to inquire for the deceased under the
name of 'Cran Jones.' This youth, upon examination,
proved to be an accomplice; and he impeached two
other young men belonging to the same gang, one of
whom was clerk to a laceman in Bury Street, St.
James's; after whom an immediate search being made,
he was traced along the road to Portsmouth, and at
three in the morning was surprised in bed at Farnham,
and brought back to London by Mr. Bond and other

A HIGHWAYMAN. 215

assistants. The other accomplice was also apprehended, and all three carried before Sir John Fielding. It appeared that these three youths, all of good families, had lately committed a number of robberies in the neighbourhood of London; that their names were Peter Houltum, John Richard Lane, and William Sampson. Sampson, in particular, had fifty guineas due to him for wages when he was apprehended, and had frequently been entrusted with effects to the amount of 10,000l. An evening paper says there are no less than seven of these youths in custody, from eighteen to twenty years of age, some of whose parents are in easy, some in affluent circumstances; all of them now overwhelmed with sorrow by the vices of their unhappy sons."

This account as to the actual death of the highwayman is at variance with my father's version of the matter, when he handed down to my brother, the present Lord Berkeley, and myself, a little, short, double, smooth-bored gun, for use in travelling. To this he always pointed as the one that killed the robber. I am quite certain of the truth of what I state. Lord Berkeley's account was as follows :—

He had, previously to this last affair, been twice stopped and robbed on Hounslow Heath. On the last occasion the door of his travelling carriage was opened, and a footpad, dressed as a sailor, pointed a pistol full cocked at his body. The man's hand trembled very much, and while my respected parent was producing what money he had, the scoundrel pulled the trigger : but the pistol very luckily missed fire. The footpad instantly exclaimed—

"I beg pardon, my Lord," and recocked his pistol.

After this escape from accidental homicide, Lord Berkeley swore he would never be robbed again, and consequently always travelled at night with the short little carriage-gun before mentioned, and a brace of pistols.

When the highwayman whom he shot stopped his carriage, he had these weapons ready. He was going to dine that November evening with Justice Bulstrode, a magistrate, who then lived in an old house surrounded by a brick wall, about where the new church in Hounslow stands now, and who dealt out summary justice, much better than the uncertain way of its distribution at present, upon all local offenders.

As he was proceeding across the Heath, rather nearer to the old precincts of the village of Hounslow, or Houndslot—as was its original title—than to Cranford, a voice called on the postboy to halt, and a man rode up to the carriage window on the left-hand side. As he came, my father let it down. The robber thrust his hand in with a pistol, directing it at the breast of the only occupant of the carriage. With the left hand my father caught the weapon, and pushing it up out of the line, without putting the short double gun to his shoulder, he thrust it against the body of the highwayman, and discharged one of the barrels. It set the highwayman's clothes on fire; nevertheless, he rode away for about fifty yards, and then fell dead upon the road.

The servant who was riding behind the carriage

discharged his pistol, but without effect. When the robber fell, he was immediately joined by two accomplices, who kept close to him. Lord Berkeley now got out of his carriage, and with the one barrel of his gun still loaded, and his pistols, advanced upon them. On seeing his approach, the fellows fled, leaving the dead man on the road, his pistol firmly clenched in his hand. His horse was secured, I believe, by my father's servant. Thus the tale narrated in my presence by my father, tallies exactly with the number of highwaymen as described in the "Gentleman's Magazine," but in no other particular. It differs also materially from the account of the same occurrence published in the "Memoirs" of my aunt, the Margravine of Anspach.

Three years and a half later, Lord Chesterfield, nephew and successor to the famous Earl of that name, arraigned his son's tutor, Dr. Dodd, for forging his pupil's name, June, 1777, and the Doctor was hung. Lord Chesterfield's prosecution of the tutor to the death was universally condemned. Now, as naturally might be supposed from the taunts of society in regard to this matter, Lord Chesterfield disliked any allusion to the execution; but one day, on meeting my father, he accosted him in a bantering manner, with, "Well, Berkeley, how many highwaymen have you shot lately?"

"As many," was the reply, "as you have hung tutors, but with much better reason for doing so." This "shut up" Lord Chesterfield.

Mr. Mellish was shot through the back of his post-

218   CRANFORD HOUSE.

chaise near the little, in those days solitary, inn on
the confines of Hounslow Heath, or, more properly
speaking, on Harlington Common; and the maid-
servants travelling from London to Cranford House
were also stopped on the heath and robbed; but on
the thieves depriving Mary Oldacre, afterwards my
nurse, of her watch, by which she set immense store,
she cried so that they relented, and gave it her back.

The site of these nocturnal depredations has now
undergone a change. Enclosures have taken place;
corn-fields have sprung up in lieu of furze bushes;
villas have filled the swampy gravel-pits, where, as a
boy, I have shot snipes; and blooming gardens, full of
roses and other flowers, have banished the bullrushes.
There are no heaths now; and where the pewit fitfully
hovered and enticingly screamed away from her nest,
the land is drained and cultivation reigns supreme.

In those days, Cranford House, with its manors of
Cranford le Mote, Cranford St. John, Harlington, and
Harlington-cum-Shipeston, was as isolated and lonely
a place as it is possible to conceive; and it was my
father's custom to drive down from London with four
long-tailed black horses, that took two hours to get
over the twelve miles, on a Saturday night, and to
remain at Cranford till Monday morning. On one of
these occasions he was accompanied by his sister,
Lady Granard, and they arrived at Cranford on the
afternoon of Saturday, bringing with them no additional servants, but trusting simply to the maids in
charge of the house.

My father's favourite pointer—whose name, if I

A MIDNIGHT INTRUDER. 219

remember correctly, was Doll—accompanied them in the carriage. As she was a stranger to the servants at Cranford, she attached herself exclusively to her master. After enjoying the extreme quietude of the place, and rambling about the gardens, redolent of the perfume of shrubs and flowers, and musical with the voices of the singing birds that sheltered in the thickets and laurels, they retired for the night. The perfect silence when all the birds were hushed, contrasted strongly with the bustle and stir of the streets of the metropolis which had so recently greeted them. In the midst of this tranquillity Lord Berkeley had sunk to sleep, Doll lying on his bed, as was her invariable custom. Slumber had continued undisturbed for some time, when, on partially opening his eyes, he thought he heard some very slight bustle outside his door. On listening, the fact became more certain, for he distinctly heard the slow and cautious sliding of a hand on the panels, as if feeling for the handle of the lock, and then the hand, for such it seemed to be, struck on the lock, and paused there as if in cautious suspense. The pistols he always travelled with were lying loaded on a chair by his bed; so, reaching out his hand, he seized one and waited for what was to follow. He had no light in his room, which was as dark as pitch.

He could hear the handle of the door cautiously turn, then the door slowly rub over the carpet as it opened to admit the intruder. Light as the step was, he nevertheless was next aware of its stealing towards his bed. At that moment remembering that

Doll was the best and most watchful house-dog possible, and wondering at her silence, he stretched out his left hand, the right holding the pistol pointed at the advancing object, to feel if she were awake. Awake she was, and conscious too of the presence of the suspicious visitor, for her head was erect, her ears up, and her attention riveted. This puzzled her master, for he knew that she would have flown at any stranger.

Suddenly, while his hand was on her head, thump, thump, thump, went Doll's tail on the bedclothes, and her ears subsided into their recumbent position. There was no one in the house, besides my father and his sister, that Doll knew, so at once replacing the pistol upon the chair, but with his strong right hand, and it was a very powerful one, ready for any required action, he sat up in bed and awaited the result. The almost noiseless step came on, till the slight rustle that accompanied it proclaimed the object to be within reach. My father stretched out his hand, and in his grasp he seized his sister's arm. With a shriek she awoke to consciousness. Lady Granard had been walking in her sleep, and but for Doll, and my father's knowledge of the dog's fidelity and his cool presence of mind, he might have killed his sister. The faithful, watchful, sagacious pointer had saved him from committing a frightful act.

To pass from the serious to the comic, or, at least, to the occurrences of every-day life, how this beautiful legend of Doll bears me out in the lessons I give to my brother sportsmen, and vainly attempt to impress

PET DOGS.   221

on ladies who keep canine companions—never to keep
a babbler, either among hounds, spaniels, or terriers; for
if they tell lies they deceive their owners and mislead
and corrupt their fellows. A dog, if properly treated,
can be made to speak with the tongue nature has
assigned him, and to speak of different things in different tones, so that his master will know what is the
matter: my retriever, Brutus, does so to this day; and
by his intelligent tongue, in the Deserts of the Far
West, I could tell if he called my attention to a mule
that was cast on the tether or picket rope, or to an
Indian, or stranger of any sort.

Why is it, then, that ladies cannot teach their pet
dogs anything but scratching, snarling, and noise? If
a lady sneezes or coughs, gets up or sits down, they
explode in ecstacies of barking. If a visitor ascends
the stairs or enters the room, they yell insanely round
the apartment, or leap into the lap of their mistress to
snap at his fingers when he shakes hands. If instead
of being a friend he proved to be a burglar or murderer they could do no more; nevertheless, say what
I will, or do what I will, ladies' pet dogs, with very
few exceptions, are ever trained or permitted to be the
same intolerable nuisances. Friend or foe, they bark
at all, and every ordinary occasion elicits a succession
of insane yelps.

Had Doll barked in this way when she heard and
knew of Lady Granard's approach, the consequence
might have been too horrible for contemplation.

My father had another favourite old pointer dog,
but I think he must have been subsequent to Doll.

By his sagacity in showing contempt for bad shots he produced a temporary quarrel between her owner and his friend, Admiral Prescott, who was in those days a good deal at Cranford and Berkeley Castle. Prescott wanted to go out pheasant shooting at Cranford in October, when his host did not wish to go, so to get rid of the admiral, who was a touchy old chap, Lord Berkeley told him he might shoot, but there was no keeper at leisure to go with him. "Humph," cried Prescott snappishly, "how can I shoot without some one with a dog?"

"Take the gun," was the reply, "show it to my old dog, and he'll go with you."

This Prescott did, the pointer was delighted to go, and off they set very happily together. In those blightless days, the haulm of the potatoes flourished and flowered, even till the frosts of October if they were not lifted earlier, and Prescott having to select his own field at which to commence operations, was sharp enough to choose one under the covers. No sooner had he entered on his beat, than the old dog came to a steady point. Prescott kicked the pheasant up, fired, and missed it, the pointer stared after the bird till it reached the cover, and then seeing that Prescott had reloaded his gun, ranged on again, and came to another point.

Up went the Admiral's gun, up flew the pheasant, a similar result attending as at the first discharge, and the old dog again stared, but this time as much at the strange sportsman as he did at the flying pheasant. The gun reloaded, again came another point, and again a miss.

THE OLD POINTER. 223

The old dog now neither looked after the pheasant nor at Prescott, but threw himself down among the potatoes and rolled. The admiral had then to whistle him up, and the pointer very slowly answered to the call for his services, and found another pheasant. This time he did not wait for the admiral's foot to put up the bird, but on the sportsman approaching he made a spring first under the potatoe haulm, but missing to catch the flying pheasant, sprang up as far as he could at its tail, which unusual piece of activity took him a little further from his companion. While Prescott was again charging and muttering execrations, laying all the fault of his want of success on my father's gun, which he swore he had lent him on purpose • to miss with, old Ponto · came very leisurely up to his leg and expressed his contempt in a very offensive manner; he then crooked his stern and trotted coolly home. Prescott's rage knew no bounds; he trod the potatoes as if in a tread-mill, put up more pheasants and missed them all, muttered to himself on the shameless trick that had been played him in the house (it was really one of the best guns), and at last went home in a fury, and threw himself down in a chair in my father's study.

In the old chamber, as a child, I remember game-bags and guns to be hanging, and a paper kite to make the partridge lie; also a board with militia-men painted on it in all the attitudes and facings of drill and the manual and platoon exercises. Among these trophies of chase and of war there was a single

CAPTAIN CRAYCRAFT.

gun of French make, with which my brother Henry used to shoot very well.

· Prescott had not sat there long when my father came in accompanied. by old Ponto.. "Well," he exclaimed, "how came you and Ponto to get parted? You had lots of shots; what sort of a bag?"

"Bag, indeed!" cried the admiral, his sharp and rather small eyes glistening with fury. "Bag! D— ye. You sent me out to kill nothing. You are a miser of your d—d game. The gun's no use, and you taught your infernal dog to insult me and go home."

"You blundering old muff," retorted his host, "you can't shoot, and that's the reason Ponto cut you. What else did he do? Something more sensible, I'll answer for it."

· "E-e-e-e," grinned the admiral in a fury, shaking his fist as he rose and left the room. "You and your d—d dog know perfectly well."

My father's quarrels with Prescott never lasted long, nor did they with Captain Craycraft who commanded the Nymph, and in the Daphne was taken prisoner and confined in France. I remember on one occasion Craycraft being sent out at Berkeley Castle with my brother Henry on a particular beat, on which they were forbidden to shoot anything but woodcocks and rabbits. As they came back by the outer gate of the castle, my brother Moreton being on the watch for their return, the captain called him, and showing him a full gamebag with some pheasants' tails sticking out, told him to run in to Lord Berkeley and say they had been shooting pheasants. Moreton did so, Craycraft taking very good care to go first into the castle in order that he might ascend to a safe place, and from the Ladies' Tower over the inner gateway observe the effect of his practical joke.

Henry came into the outer court, and my father in a rage rushed from his gun-room or study, and seizing the bag, furiously turned out the contents, which consisted of nothing but rabbits with pheasants' tail feathers somewhat quaintly attached to them. It was long before Craycraft ceased laughing at the hoax he had so successfully played. His host said nothing as to the affair at dinner, and Craycraft erroneously imagined the thing had blown over.

The day of the captain's departure from the castle, however, came, many days after he had indulged in this joke; there had been a considerable amount of shooting, and a good deal of game was in the larder to be disposed of, so just before he went Craycraft asked for some to send away to his friends. The request was at once complied with as usual, and the guest repaired to the larder, and was permitted to select what freshly killed pheasants he chose.

Having parted from the rest of the game the pheasants he intended to send away, he left them with their addresses to be packed up by the servants, and sent to different friends. My father then privately interposed, and attaching the tails of pheasants only to a similar number of rabbits, and substituting the latter for the birds, away went the parcels to Craycraft's friends, heralded by letters from him, telling them that on such a day they were to

VOL. I.   Q

226   PRACTICAL JOKE.

expect each of them some splendid pheasants. The
tables were now turned on the gallant captain; his
friends, immensely insulted at the practical joke they
thought he had played upon them, at some cost for
carriage, returned him very angry letters, and one of
them sent to his lodgings in London a very considerable hamper of brickbats.

CHAPTER IX

SPORTING ADVENTURES.

My guests at Cranford—The Duke of St. Albans' arrangement for saving himself trouble—Duke of York—His skill in shooting—Lord Grantley's method of shooting partridges—Liston, the Comedian—Dowton, his stage directions—Private theatricals at Boscombe—A large love-lock—Sir Percy Shelley—Varley, the Astrologer—His predictions—His astonishment at beholding a hunting party—Cause of poaching—Woodland scenes—Catching a pike—Salmon fishing—The otter and water-rat—A midnight adventure—Stealing rushes—Practice of poachers.

WE were one day going to shoot at Cranford, and the party consisted of the late Duke of St. Albans (who was on a visit to me at a house I had in the village), Sir George Seymour, and the late Sir Horace Seymour. We were assembled in the vestibule of my mother's old house, when the Duke's servant came in, bearing in his hand a silver waiter, on which was narrowly folded up a black silk handkerchief. We at first regarded this simply as an additional neckcloth; but when, with the utmost gravity, and in the midst of a dead silence, his Grace took it, and solemnly proceeded to bind it round his head, so as to tie up the left eye, I could hold my peace no longer.

" What on earth are you doing?" I asked.

" Why," he replied, without relaxing a muscle of

his countenance, "I hear you have a lot of game; so I am blinding my eye, to avoid the trouble of having to shut it so often when I fire."

The roar of laughter into which we all exploded, induced the Duke to restore the bandage to his servant, and send it away.

On another occasion, his Royal Highness the late Duke of York came down to Cranford to shoot, dine, and sleep; and "Punch Greville" was to meet him, as also Sir George and Sir Horace Seymour. Greville came so late that he kept the Duke waiting, as his Royal Highness would not begin without him; and then, in shooting, he shot so near the Prince that, after some time vainly entertaining the hope that his Royal Highness would check him for his carelessness, the imminence of the danger forced me to ask Greville to let the pheasants rise, and shoot at ground game when the latter were not under his Royal Highness's legs and mine.

Although the Duke had two loaders and three guns, the shots came so thick and fast that I often had to hand him my John Manton gun before one of his own was charged. His Royal Highness on that day, but just over twelve miles from London, bagged to his own guns more game than he had ever bagged in the same time anywhere else. I saw him kill three hares at a shot.

Lord Grantley's method of shooting partridges was also remarkable. He would enter the field, and stationing himself under the first tree, umbrella as well as gun in hand, in case there should be no shelter from the sun or rain, there he kept his place till his pointers had beaten the ground. If there was game, he went up to the point; if not, he proceeded to the next field, and did the same thing.

Among the visitors at the Cranford Bridge Inn, whence I hunted the stag-hounds, was the late Mr. Liston, the celebrated comedian; and he often came into my room in his dressing-gown, and sat with me while at breakfast. Alone, and when enjoying his leisure, he was a most agreeable and amusing companion; but, like the elder Charles Mathews and the late Mr. Yates, he hated being laughed at unless upon the stage, and never could bear in private a set party made up to meet him.

Dowton, too, I knew very well; and in private conversation he taught me the error and folly of the present fashion of over-acting a part. He illustrated it one day at luncheon thus:—pointing to some cold plum-pudding, he said—

"Now, according to the natural course of things, if I wanted that, I should say to you, holding out my hand quietly, thus, 'I'll thank you for it.' The act would be naturally done, with no extravagance whatever. But according to the fashion of the stage of the present day, suppose two persons were at supper, and one of them needed the pudding, he would make a hideous face at his friend, and stealing his hand along the table, pausing at every clutch, he would exclaim, 'Give me—give me—ah, give me—that—that—that p-p-p-p-pudding!' seizing it as if he intended to murder all its plums."

230   PRIVATE. THEATRICALS.

These suggestions from this great master of his art were not lost upon me, and when, playing the "Wreck Ashore" at the beautiful little theatre belonging to Sir.Percy and Lady Shelley at Boscombe, they came into operation, though highly condemned by our professional stage-manager, Mr. Plunkett.

It was at rehearsal, and I had to leave the stage, turning round at the wing with a *loaded* fowling-piece in my hand, in a threatening way at Walter, for having given me a fall. I displayed the intention naturally, my finger on the trigger and my thumb on the cock, pointing the muzzle towards him as I retired. This brought Mr. Plunkett from his corner with a remonstrance and a lesson. Taking the *loaded* fowling-piece in both hands by the muzzle, he raised it over his head, in a most extravagant exaltation, to menace Walter; but the action, from the position of the gun, only threatened mischief to himself. Mr. Plunkett said that this was the correct method for stage effect, but I did not adopt his suggestion.

While playing this piece, an amusing accident happened between Alice and Walter, the latter played by Captain Rickford.

Alice is represented with a profusion of curls, according to the fashion of the day; and having to cut off and present Walter with one of these, a ringlet was purposely arranged. In putting up her hand to her back hair to obtain this, the entire artificial structure came off. Unaware of the circumstance, and imagining that she held the desired love-lock, she presented her astonished lover with a keepsake in the

SIR PERCY SHELLEY.

shape of a good-sized wig. Rickford, however, did not lose his presence of mind. Unexpected as was the bounteousness of the gift, clasping it in his hand and pressing it to his lips, he contrived to insert it into his pocketbook, without allowing the mistake to attract the notice of the audience.

I know no better amateur actor than my friend Sir Percy. He is, moreover, an accomplished musician; and among other proofs of his talent in this direction, I must instance his recent setting of a beautiful lyric, written by his father, the poet, Percy Bysshe Shelley, "Pan's Sweet Piping," which has been greatly admired.

In or about the years 1818-20, the late John Varley, so celebrated for being one of the founders, if not the founder, of the new school of water-colour painting, used to come down once a week to Cranford to teach my sisters drawing. Several of his landscapes are in my possession now. Varley was a most good-humoured, amusing companion, with very strange ideas on many subjects, but perfectly wild on astrology, which he practised as an art, casting nativities and predicting fortunes, some of which proved to be wonderfully correct. Thus, one man, to avoid a prediction of his, that an accident was to happen at a particular time, lay in bed all day; but in the evening, thinking that the dangerous hour had gone by, having risen to go downstairs, he tumbled over his own coalscuttle, and rolling to the first landing-place, strained his ankle very severely—fulfilling the prophecy to the letter.

VARLEY THE ASTROLOGER.

Varley's way up to the house from Cranford Bridge, where the coach used to set him down, lay through the park; but one day he arrived much excited, in a great heat, and considerably behind his time. He gave me this explanation:—"I was born under 'Taurus,' therefore must some day necessarily be tossed. Just as I entered the park-gate from the road, a flock of sheep drew up in front of me, in what I believed to be a fierce and threatening attitude; so, to escape my impending fate, I made a circuit, and reached here by the village road."

When walking with Mr. Hughes, he encountered my hounds running a red deer. He had not the least idea that men on horseback rode over fences, and was speechless with admiration at the collected way in which Brutus leaped a flight of rails by the inn, and then the hedge and ditch into the road where he was standing. The cry of the hounds, the cheer of the huntsman, which I gave the rather to astonish him than to excite the hounds, who were running hard, and the notes of the horn, roused him up and drove him wild with excitement; and I presently beheld him running in the wake of the hounds like a boy. He called the members of the hunt "the personifications of the Centaur."

Poor Varley! I do not think a better-hearted fellow ever existed. If a man casts nativities, and predicts the consequent fortune of individuals very often, it would be strange indeed if some of his guesses at the future did not occasionally prove true, precisely as is the case with dreams. Among the many millions of

POACHERS.   233

imaginings during sleep, it must happen that occasionally some of them should be realized.

My brother Moreton and myself, from our association at a boyish age with the gamekeeper at Cranford,
as well as from the example set us by our father, in
the strictest preservation of game, may be said to have
had such an education in such rural matters as seldom
fell to other gentlemen. Since those days of boyhood,
the former was encouraged to act, first for his own
amusement and to wean him from better society, as a
mere gamekeeper, and then latterly but as a servant,
entirely subservient to a master in the shape of
Colonel Berkeley. I grew up attached to the sports
of the field of all descriptions, and a game preserver
entirely for my own pleasure. A constant residence in
the country and among rustic labourers and game, as
well as being in later years an acting and an active
justice of the peace, have perfected my study in regard
to the cause of poaching and the habits of poachers,
and led me to very well-matured conclusions.

The places where such depredators most abound are
on manors where game is scarce and unprotected, but
where there is only just enough of pheasants, partridges, snipes, rabbits, and wildfowl to afford beer
money without the least risk of punishment under the
Game Laws. The statistics of the police illustrate
this in a very decided manner, for it was shown in
the evidence obtained on Mr. Bright's Game Law
Committee, in which, on the part of the landlords and
proprietors, I led against him, that in manors where
there was a large head of game strictly preserved,

there were fewer convictions for offences against the laws, for either poaching, theft, sheep-stealing, or incendiarism, than on lands where the little existing game was not preserved at all. In short, that the gamekeepers and their nightly watch, in themselves were a rural police for the prevention of all crime, and of great service to the safety of private property.

The glorious scenes of spring and summer which I have seen by loch and river, brook and more humble pond, are still fresh in my remembrance as their own sweet herbs, their water weeds and flowers, and all things, as the year comes round, speak to my heart as if with friendly voices.

Look on that little rippling shallow, the clearest water gliding o'er its yellow pebbly sand; minnows and gudgeons play there as if to tempt the childish line and worm. There, beneath its wooded banks, its bed perhaps made by former gravel-pits long used up, is a large pond, its surface covered with green weed on which the ducks are feeding and moorhens are calling to their black and callow young. That sipping, sucking sound, is the tench beneath the surface weed, protruding its lips into the air as it seeks its food. Break but a space amidst the thin and floating weed in which to drop the line and worm to deeper water, and the boy will hook the golden-coloured prey, and find himself amusement.

While engaged in calm though busy contemplation, the ear is sure to be charmed by feathered minstrelsy. From some deep blackthorn brambly shade, the nightingale, in his Quaker suit, pours forth the song

SONG BIRDS. 235

that has been the poet's theme from time immemorial;
while over his head, upon some topmost bough, the
thrush trills out, with the like defiance of rivalry,
his woodnotes wild. In rich, and mellow, and more
mournful notes, the blackbird in his sable livery
sings to his brooding mate, while watchful to pro-
claim with screech a passing hawk, the missel-thrush
sweetly asserts her presence. The softer cushat and
the turtle-dove are cooing too. Down in the willows
breathes a warbling choir, amidst their bright green
shoots; there sing the whitethroat and the willow
wrens, the reed sparrow, and in the flags chirps that
beautiful and rarer bird, the blithe and bearded titmouse. From the high firs, as fluttering, pendant,
clinging on, the golden-crested wrens, the titmouse,
the colemouse, the blue and larger tomtit, keep the
air alive with chirping eloquence; while, low down
in that thorn, the long-tailed tits make for themselves
a home that, in ingenuity, surpasses man's architectural skill.

On yonder sunny spot of water among the weeds,
see congregated a shoal of tiny roach. They shoot
together like a "school" of mackerel at sea, the por-
poise or the bass beneath. Scared now by something
from above, they dart for shelter down below. The
"peep—peep—peep," a short, sharp whistle, comes
from their enemy the fisher-king. His bright blue jacket
and his brick-dust breast betray him as he skims away.

From the pond we will go to the river, with the
can filled with bright dace, and longer living, hardier
gudgeons. Behold that nook among the bull-

CATCHING PIKE.

rushes; there is a shallow, at the bottom of which, something, with wide-stretched eyes, matches the serpent in a death-like stillness. It looks long in its length and dark, and yet it is bravely mottled; it is a pike of more than twenty pounds' weight. No dead bait will take him, nor can the snap be used, in the cramped, sun-lit, shallow, weedy spot. Light must be the line, and lively, too, the living bait. Then, on the water, close beyond his cover, let fall the line, with its shotted hook, and pause to watch the result. The long, dark object scarcely moves his ready fins, yet turns and points his nose directly towards the bait. He quickly glides this way, and as he comes, the tall spears slightly move from the swell that laves their roots. Suddenly he makes a dash, and, see!—the gudgeon's gone! Pay out the line, so as to prevent a check being felt: now slowly the monster glides beneath the larger water-lilies; and there he lies, his moving gills proclaiming that the bait is gorged. Now strike, you have him; strong will be his run, but short, for, like all cruel tyrants when they are struck, an effort and he yields. Not so either the salmon, the trout, or the grayling; they are game to the very dorsal fin, and fight to the last.

Now swing that graceful, pliant rod with both your hands, and let the large fly fall on the edge of yonder current, just where it doubles back to enter a swift and circling eddy. There, ply the taper top joint wavingly, and play your fly down, across, and up the stream; now whisk it out, and take another cast.

SALMON.

What a glorious rise! As the fly left the water, a broad and glittering breadth of scales flashed up against the sun, and darting away, disappeared. It is useless attempting another cast there at present. Walk on to the next pool, and in twenty minutes try him once more. At the first cast he makes no sign; at the second, the easy line and scarcely bending rod show at once that they hold on to something heavy that has widely ringed the wave. The top joint doubles down, and out roars the whirling reel. Now show the butt, and take heed of the running line, or your hand will be sharply cut. The fish is hooked, and you must mind your tackle.

He runs for every pool he knows, then he lies quietly in the deeps with head to stream, as if to make you imagine that you had lost him; and, except by the waving of the line, you would think that you had caught the bottom. No such thing—he's sulking. Have patience, wear him this way, that way, if you can, but " tuck " him not at all. No snatches; all must be steady, and on no account for a moment slack your hold. If he goes not of himself we will scare him with a pole—that aid, however, is dangerous.

He's off more violently than ever, for he knows and feels that he is hooked! Hold the rod lightly; up he goes, flinging himself quite six feet out of water, striking violently with his tail, with the intention of breaking the line. As he flings and lashes out, drop your point, the slacked line thus evades his blow, and down on the flashing water he goes again, to repeat that desperate effort twice or thrice. He finds it will

238   SALMON FISHING.

not do, but still makes a noble fight! Deep down he
dashes, out he runs, now here now there, but equally
in vain. Beware, however; he evidently finds the
amusement to us is increasingly painful to him, and
means a run for rocky ground. Twice has he reached
the end of yonder shoal below the pool, which
leads to shallow rapids. If over that he goes in safety
he is lost, for there are rocks as sharp as knives, and
weeds and sticks innumerable. But his strength is
failing, lead him hither to the side, the gaff is ready,
and now we land him if we can.

I see his shoulders and his back! He is a fish of
thirty pounds! Draw him a foot nearer. Ah! he's
off again. Away he runs, the pool is passed, he's
down the rapid. Head him for your life, hold on
with all the strength your line will bear. Go into
the water; it does not reach your knees. Bravo!
Now you've gaffed him. There on the turf he lies,
made senseless by a blow, for instant crimping.

Let us sit down. Your arms are weary, for you
have had him on an hour; and let me ask, is not this
a pleasant life? These meadows green and gold—
how bright they look up to the sun, decked with
myriads of their yellow cups! How pretty are these
Forget-me-nots that seem to kiss the brink of the
water. Breasting the sweet gale, the lark ascends, apparently fluttering half way to heaven, while the swift
snipe drums in his downward shoots, and makes a
noise as if a kid were bleating. The green-hued, red-
finned, greedy perch shows good sport, and decks the
table well. The Hercules of the Scottish loch, the

"salmo ferox," there outdoes the salmon in his strength, and struggles to the death.

Put up the rod, the day is over; take home the fish for dressing, and as we tread the lonely river side mark then the rising fish to know their favourite pools. What dark thing is that above the stream, thrust up and now gone down behind the willow? Let us watch and see. There it is again, and hark how hard it blows stale air from out the lungs, and then, with a fresh inspiration, down goes the head again. It is an otter fishing. There is his head, and in his mouth a little eel, with that he does not swim to shore, but masticates it as he passes in mid stream.

Come on! Observe yonder brown lump upon the willow root. It is a water-rat. He dives, though he has not seen us; he seems alarmed. There is the reason. Stealing through the grass is a longer, larger, lighter, leaner rat who kills the other when he can; he at this season takes to water-holes as men to sea-shore places. There he rusticâtes, eats frogs and ducklings too, and when the lamperns throng the sides of weirs, he revels in fun and food, landing far more than he can eat, and hiding them away.

Summer snipe and water ousel, those graceful, flitting birds, are here; landrail and water-rail, gallinule and lesser gallinule, dabchick, coot, and moorhen, all show us God's vast bounty, and His store of graceful, sinless life.

I must here introduce an adventure I had, though it took place some years later in my career. It occurred on the night after a lovely day, on the approach of autumn. I had dined rather earlier than usual, to enable me to go out on the river to watch in the dusk for the otter, when, having failed to meet with that depredator, I continued my supervision of the lands and the River Avon, in order to feel quite sure that my rights were well watched, and that there was no theft of either fish or fowl.

I had said nothing to my men that I was going out, for two reasons. I have a fancy for this sort of solitary vigil when the whim strikes me; besides this, it is a favourite maxim of mine suddenly to find myself where I am the least expected.

It grew very late, and the night became excessively dark, although it was perfectly still and fine. A low fog had to some slight extent arisen from the marsh-lands, while at the same time a high mist had crept gradually in from the sea, throwing a cloak over the face of the heavens, and excluding the light of the stars. It was therefore a time of inky darkness, and I could not see my hand if I stretched it out before me: a capital time in which to hear the rumble of an illicit oar or pole, from boat or punt, upon the water; so I took up a position about midway in the over-three miles of the river to which my rights extended.

Nothing stirred; and having waited without any result, I was returning home, when suddenly a noise met my ear out among the marshy meadows by the river, at the side on which I was; which noise was not in the water, nor was it the sound of fowl or otter; still it was something that I knew had no business to be there, and it certainly seemed to come from land in my sporting occupation. At first it was like a horse or cow moving among high flags or rushes, but then I remembered that there was neither horse nor beast of any kind there; so I listened for further information.

At last I made out that it was a reap-hook at work, and immediately surmised that somebody was stealing the flags. Among all the wide deep reens or ditches that intersect these marshy meadows, running in various directions—water carrying sound so peculiarly as it always does on a still night—it is, almost as impossible to fix a spot whence a slight noise may come, as it is to define exactly the "craik" or cry of the landrail, when he is in the same cornfield or grassfield with you, and uttering his breeding call. There was, however, at my heels a creature blacker than even the night, whose sagacity had been my unerring guide in many dangers and difficulties. To my companion and retriever dog Brutus, then, I addressed myself; and kneeling down to where I knew I should find him, I put my hand lightly on his neck, and whispered in his ear, "Where is it, old man?"

His ears were up and listening, and his head pointed in one only direction, and that was up into the marshy meadows away from the river. You can't see those low unindicated reens, parallel with the land's surface, covered with weed, and without a hedge, even in a starlit night: on a pitch-dark night they can only be felt with the foot, so I had to proceed with the utmost caution, or I might have got a ducking, and alarmed the thief or thieves.

VOL. I.

242   REAPING RUSHES.

Making my way by passes known to me, twice I found that a deep reen was still between me and the dull, rustling scrape, scrape of the reap-hook; but while by the side of the last obstacle that intervened between me and the spot at which I desired to arrive, I kicked my foot under the tough root of a willow, stumbling slightly, and made a little noise; a rough voice immediately cried, "Jack, is that you?" I made no reply, while at the same time I knew that the depredators, whoever they were, could not be far off, and that the way out of where they were was at the top of the reen between us, by a gateway at the command of each of us : I therefore stood still.

The cutting of the reap-hook continued for some little time. longer, then it ceased, and I heard noises as if of tying up something, and then a heavy footfall come tramping towards me, to gain the gateway; so I proceeded up my side of the reen to give the fellows a meeting. As I suspected, there were two to one—no great odds, as Brutus was with me : in order to assure myself of it, I laid down in the gateway, to bring whatever was coming between me and the horizon—the only method by which you can distinguish such objects in a dark night. I immediately saw that the bulk of whatever it was, shut out the horizon from post to post.

On it came, and I stood up to let it come to me, well knowing that close at my heel there stood a creature who on occasions of this sort never stays behind and never roams in front, never begins a row, but for ever takes his guide from the word of his master or friend, and will fight for him as long as jaw

A CULPRIT.

and tooth will hold together. A sort of hayrick, then, on two legs—for the stuff being over and round every part of the figure excepting that which carried it— blocked up the gateway, and ran almost against me, when I said to it—

"Halloa, what have you been doing?"

"Cutting a few flags for my pig," replied a hoarse voice.

"'Tis an odd time of night to do it in," I rejoined; "and who gave you leave?"

"Oh, some on 'em," answered the voice.

"Some on 'em?" I repeated; "but *which* on 'em? I must know *who* gave you leave."

"No, you wont," said the culprit, "for they be so many, I can't remember who they be."

"You've a bad recollection, my man; I'll give you an easier task: tell me what's *your* name?"

"Oh, my name; I never was pertickler in having a name. I haven't got one," replied the hoarse voice among the stuff, to which I listened attentively, that I might learn a direction for my hand.

"No name," I replied; "and you never had one. Oh, you're just the curiosity I want; you must come home with me to the candle-light; you're worth a case in my collection of stuffed birds."

Saying which, I seized him by the collar, and as I did so I felt the side of Brutus brush by my leg, half his length in advance.

"Oh, sir, forgive I this once," cried the prisoner, and down went the little rick of flags, pitchfork and all; "forgive I this once; I'll never do so no more."

R 2

"I don't know that I will," I said; "you've got no name."

"Oh, yes, I has, sir; it's so and so, and I lives in a cottage so and so (telling me his correct address); and I have a large family, and I be very poor, and did but cut a few flags for my pigs to sleep on; do'ee forgive I, sir, and don't 'ee tell the farmer, or I shall never get from him another stroke of work."

"Bad work; you've been robbing your employer; and, besides, I know you to be a poacher, but at that you'd better never let me catch you. There," I continued, letting go his collar, "pick up your flags, take them to your pig, you've got enough to last him half through the winter; I *must* tell the farmer that I have caught you, for I can't compound theft; but mind, this once I will request him as a favour to me not to ask me to tell him who stole his flags, and I am sure he will grant it. So go home, but never be guilty in this way again.

"And hark you," I added, "tell your fellows that you and they have been in the habit, under some supposed right of common, of doing the tenant farmers mischief by breaking down their fences and gates. While I hold the sporting rights of this estate, I am the friend of the farmer, and I look on all his interests as mine; so mind what I say, and don't let me be down on any one of you so offending."

I then bade him good night, and the man went away, thanking me with many words. The gates were put up by the farmers, and were never, in my time,

HIS HABITS.

broken down again. What became of his companion "Jack," to whom he had called, I never knew.

I have invariably made it my rule to order my keepers to take as much care of the tenant farmers' gates, folds, fences, crops, cattle, and sheep, as if they were my own, as long as the tenant conducted himself properly by me; if he chose to make himself disagreeable, then only my keepers ceased to watch over his interests. As to the labouring population, my rule has ever been, to be severe with them when taken red-handed in any revolt against the law; but at the same time, while I was just, always to be even overliberal when they were well conducted, and respected my rights. Thus, if they took care of some little leveret they found, of which they could have made nothing in the market, or of a nest of game, no matter how few the eggs, I always gave them more for the pleasure they tried to give me than they could have got by being dishonest. I never found that plan fail in doing good to the game preserve.

Poachers, or thieves of game, never apply the money they acquire in their illicit practices to the maintenance of their wives and children. In all my experience as country gentleman and magistrate, I never knew an instance of their doing so. They invariably regard it as pocket-money, to be spent in beer and gambling, riot and debauchery; and in the whole course of my practice, I have not known a man take to poaching, or the theft of game, through want. The poacher is always grown up in and educated in evil, and, by long practice, a clever villain in a difficult craft, which no man can learn on the mere spur of a difficulty, nor follow out with success unless possessed of great local knowledge as to where he is to set his cunning devices, or use the noisy gun.

CHAPTER X.

TOWN TALK.

Forced marriages—Advantages of a young Guardsman—A man to be avoided—" Beware! she is fooling you!"—" Kitty" and her traducer—A party at the Star and Garter, Richmond—An imaginary elopement—Almacks as it used to be—Education of a beauty—Danger from male teachers—A desirable marriage —Lady —— and the loose prints—The royal guest and his awkward question—Extravagance and dissipation—Difference between Lord Augustus and Tomkins—" O, 'tis Love!"

A MAN, when he attains my age, may be thought qualified to preach against errors known to his experience. He may tell younger men what to do, and women what to avoid: but even the preaching of seniors, and the good seed they might sow in the most favourable soils, are not always to be relied on. In spite of the most careful cultivation, a plentiful crop of wild oats is too often the only one that is reaped. This knowledge, however, will not deter me from inculcating better husbandry.

Adopting the character, then, for a time, of a Mentor, and addressing the fairer portion of society, whence so large a moiety of the bliss, with some of the ills of existence emanate, I strongly condemn the custom of forcing girls to enter into marriages repugnant to their feelings. How many times have I known mothers to drive their reluctant daughters to accept men whom they disliked, and whose habits, long confirmed, showed the impossibility of their ever conforming to a course of life in any way likely to induce domestic felicity. How many times have I known such matrons acknowledge in such proposed *parti* the grave faults of drunkenness, gambling, and debauchery, and then, in overcoming their daughter's dislike to such a partner for life, to assure her, that, *after marriage*, she would be able to wean him from his vicious course, when not even the hope of securing a virtuous wife, or the ambition of possessing a very beautiful and accomplished woman, had the power to withdraw him from such ruinous habits. Alas, how often I have seen such miserably made-up matches entirely fail—in short, have no other result than to consign gentle and delicate creatures to a life-long misery, or an early grave!

Mammas have often an immense deal to answer for; and some daughters are quite as blameable, when, against the advice of their wiser relatives and friends, they accept as their lovers vulgar men or notorious libertines, under the idea that their charms have power to work a perfect reformation—placing reliance on the proverb that " A reformed rake makes the best husband."

A young Guardsman, at sixteen, on first joining his regiment in London, may be said to stand on the very verge of life, and see it in its brightest aspect, from the most favourable position. The impressions then made upon him are rarely forgotten. Thus,

FASHIONABLE BEAUTIES.   249

I was seated in an opera-box, my attention absorbed by,
and, as I thought at the time, with a heart full of love
for one of the fashionable beauties of the day; when I
say fashionable, it was the fashion for all young men
to be seen in her train. She was in society too; for
in those days a low adventuress was not permitted to
flaunt in the full-dress circles. She gave me my first
lesson as to what a *preux chevalier* was to do and *not*
to do. On the other side of the house the late Sir
George —— entered a box. Looking at him through
her opera-glass, she drew my attention to his advent,
and asked me, "Do you know him?"

I replied in the affirmative.

She removed the lorgnettes from her handsome face,
and setting her bright eyes full on mine, added,
"Then don't be like him."

"In what way?" I asked; "he is a most agreeable
companion; and if not a man I should select as
a friend in need, everybody appears to be partial to
him, and he is the life of every party, and much sought
after."

"Don't be like him," she rejoined, "at least in one
way. Listen. He would sooner be seen coming out
of a lady's bedchamber than going in."

Nothing could be more severe than this remark, or
perhaps more correct. It charmed me, for in my
young and ardent mind I took it as evidence of her
approbation, as well as of her confidence.

Another lady, a fashionable beauty—or, I should
rather say, fine woman—run after by all young men
of the day, also gave me a very good insight as to

what fools young men can be made of when gregariously inclined, pursuing not a face and figure with which they are really in love, but a thing set up for real or unreal intrigue, that, failing to inspire a *bonâ fide* affair of the heart, likes to make the world think she retains a host of devoted admirers.

We were riding in the Park one afternoon, and in rather a large party, for she was very agreeable, and was also an authoress, whose society men of all ages and understandings sought—some for an imaginary love and others for amusement—and were joined first by one of her most youthful followers, and then by another. She never allowed one of her *suite* to remain by her side too long, because when there he kept others away. It may be very well in a room to make in and cut out a by-standing admirer; but in riding in the Park, a horse on either side the lady, the manœuvre is next to impossible, unless she makes an opportunity on the next turn of her horse. So amatory youths were sent away to make room for others.

No. 1 had not been long in the blissful enjoyment, when she said, *sotto voce*, " Leave me, now; do go."

" I *can't*," was the devoted reply; " if I leave you I leave all."

" Yes, but do go—for *my sake* go—the world has its eyes on *us*, and *you* must not be too much with me."

" Her sake," and the " world's eyes!" *these* were flattering assurances the credulous listener could not withstand. The youth sat more erect in his saddle,

FLIRTING.

he looked unutterable things at her, and riding proudly and thankfully off, I saw him glance in contempt at a rival whose approach Mrs. —— had observed.

Well, the second was similarly favoured for a short. time, but another suitor looming in the distance, he too was dismissed with a sweet but delusive assurance that he was *the* one, regarded by *the world* with jealous suspicion. He too rode off triumphantly glancing at others of her admirers, who had purposely thrown themselves in her way to watch for their atom of evanescent excitement. Each lover, no doubt, exclaiming to himself as successive rivals came up to succeed him, "Fools! to think that *they* have any chance—*I* am *the favoured lover*."

An observer of events from childhood, such things were sure not to escape me, but among the many lessons I learnt at the onset of life, one was the most useful of all. It was to keep inviolable the confidence of woman. Never to betray it whatever might be the provocation.

The conversation at times arising among young men, and men much older than myself, often shocked me, for, fond of female society as I always was, I had often to sit as a silent auditor of verbal outrages which generally had no foundation in fact, but which I had not the means of contradicting. Among the most remarkable of these was one which referred to an excellent lady who had never given the slightest cause for slander. As a vocalist she ranked as high in her profession as her amiable qualities have elevated her in society, which she still continues to adorn. She joined a picnic at Dulwich, of which party I formed one. It was given by Mrs. Hammersley. Of course our charming companion entranced us all with her beautiful voice, and hushed the listening nightingale in the adjoining grove. She gave one of her songs, "Home, sweet home," for the performance of which she was unrivalled. She had to play that evening at Covent Garden or Drury Lane, I forget which, therefore it was of the utmost consequence to her that at the appointed moment her carriage should be on the spot to convey her to town : but her friends seemed to think only of their own enjoyment, and had ignored their fair friend's engagement and public position. She looked at her watch, and in answer to her inquiries was told that her carriage had not come. She was implored not to hurry her departure, but she assumed a look of anxiety, and evidently became distressed. The expression of her face was enough for me, so I at once set off, found, and brought up her carriage, and perhaps to this day she does not know to whom she was indebted for that timely service.

It subsequently reached my ears that she arrived late at the theatre, and received some slight rebuke from the public for having kept them waiting. It will be seen by this that it was in my power to account for her whereabouts all the afternoon, as well as in the early part of the evening.

On the next morning I was sitting in Colonel Berkeley's room, in Berkeley House, while he was dressing—he always arose very late—and a certain

SCANDAL. 253

noble lord who had then just come to the first of his
Irish titles, and who before that advent was, among
my seniors, known by the name of Dick ——, also
came in to talk to my brother. Their conversation
turned upon the theatres.

"What were you doing last night, Dick?" asked
my brother.

"Oh, I gave up all the evening," he replied, "to a
tête-à-tête with Kitty."

He suddenly stopped in his narration—as if he
had made some imprudent admission that alarmed
him. "Oh! what have I told you? Don't say I
spoke of her so familiarly by her Christian name,
don't. You'll promise me, I'm sure you will."

"Who the devil is 'Kitty?'" demanded Colonel
Berkeley.

"Oh, 'Kitty,'" rejoined her would-be traducer; "as
I have let you in to so much, I may as well tell you—
she is Miss ——."

I could not bear to hear this vile assumption. I
knew that nothing could be more false. I had heard
her songs, and her sweet expression of features was
still fresh on my mind, so I said, from the arm-chair
by the fireplace on which I was sitting, "That is not
true, Lord ——. You were not passing a *tête-à-tête*
with that lady during last night. I can account for
her presence from three in the afternoon till midnight,
so you must tell that to the marines, the blue-jackets
wont have it."

I shall not easily forget the stare of anger which
the Irish lord bestowed on me, a boy as I looked to be

and was, by contrast of our respective ages, nor the astonished glance my brother threw at me, as if deprecating the flat contradiction I had given to his friend. Neither said a word, however, and I arose and quitted the room.

This braggart some time later succeeded to his earldom, and though we met in society many years after this occurrence, we never spoke again.

On another memorable occasion I joined a large party at the Star and Garter at Richmond, with the intention after dinner of returning in time for Almacks, the ball at that time in great request. We were to go from town in a steamer, and Collinet's band was engaged in order that we might dance on deck as we returned. We were a large party, and the two daughters of our hostess were handsome and agreeable.

After dinner, while the people were getting together, the two young ladies, accompanied by, if I remember, an excellent chaperone, their aunt, walked down the garden of the hotel with me to the steamer, and then we got into a boat. I told Captain Ploughman, of the steamer, the son of a man who used to be our gardener at Cranford, and therefore knew me very well, he was to tell the lady who had given the party that we were pulling quietly on, and that the vessel must look out for us to take us on board; and then we rowed quietly down the river.

On our way it seemed to me as if there was some little delay in the embarkation of our friends, but at last I saw the smoke of the funnel coming on; suddenly, instead of proceeding after us, I became aware

IMAGINARY ELOPEMENT. 255

that the boat headed short back and returned to the landing-place.

We thought it odd, but still kept on, rather lazily floating upon the "silvery Thames" on that beautiful night, instead of pulling. Presently I observed that, after returning to Richmond, the steamer once more started towards London, and, to judge by the volume of smoke emitted from her funnel, unusual must have been the pressure put on the steam. Hand over hand she came down on us—nobody was dancing, no music playing, and a crowd of guests had gathered together at the gangway by which we were to be taken on board, and had their eyes staringly fixed on our little boat.

In silence dread we were picked up, and in silence dire were we received on board. People looked displeased, some of them very foolish, some seemed disappointed, and some quietly laughed and turned away, but much restraint apparently influenced every one. I at once made out that something had, or must have been supposed to have gone very wrong.

Suddenly word was passed to the deck for one only of the two young ladies to descend into the cabin to her mamma, as she had been taken very unwell.

The meaning of this was, that on the party re-embarking for home, two persons, two only, were missed—myself and one of the young ladies. This so bewildered the mamma, she jumped to the conclusion that we had eloped—in her confusion entirely overlooking the fact of the other daughter, as well as a most efficient aunt, being also missing.

256   A DUCKING.

She peremptorily ordered the boat back, with the view of commencing a search for, or of trying to gain tidings of the supposed runaways. On reaching Richmond, it being dark before the vessel had touched the bank, a gallant officer of the royal navy, and a most active dancer, was so excited, as well as anxious to gain the desired intelligence, that he sprang from the deck on to what he hoped was the green and grassy margin of the shore; it was, however, only water, covered with vegetation or vegetable refuse; he fell short, plunged up to his middle, and got a ducking.

The true story began to circulate, that I had most innocently gone a short distance with two young ladies and a chaperone, and that I was not in the least to blame. The change created in many countenances that had a few minutes before either shrunk from my inquiring look, or turned away in grim displeasure, would have formed a study for the pencil of that cleverest of all humorous artists, my friend Mr. John Leech.

In the delay and confusion which occurred on the return of the steam-boat, little Collinet saw all his hopes depart of reaching London by water in time for the ball at Willis's Rooms; so he, too, like the naval captain, launched in a hurry, and, with all his band, seized on the first conveyance they could get. The gallant naval officer either had to purchase ready-made garments, or to borrow clothes of one of the hotel waiters, or else he risked his life with his pockets full of old Father Thames, and thus went hurriedly to town.

ALMACKS.

Aboard the steamer there was, therefore, no dancing, consequently I was favoured with no end of frowns and discontented faces, for though I was *not* really to blame, and had run off with no one, still the loss of the band, as well as the absence of the agreeable naval officer, the hysterics of the mamma, and the consequent consumption of reviving salts and eau de Cologne, were all laid at my door; therefore, though among some of us there was a vast deal of suppressed mirth, the voyage back to London was far from agreeable.

One of the matrimonial marts in my time was an institution that seemed as expressly designed as the slave market at Aleppo for the appreciation and transfer of female attractions. It was known far and wide as "Almacks," the ball of the day, held at Willis's Rooms, and was presided over by a feminine oligarchy less in number but equal in power to the Venetian Council of Ten. They were of the highest rank and fashion, some of them relations of mine, and knew thoroughly what was due to them: they were mothers or daughters, and therefore fully sensible of the peculiar exigencies of either. With the title of Ladies Patronesses, they issued tickets for a series of balls for the gratification of the *crême de la crême* of society, with a jealous watchfulness to prevent the intrusion of plebeian rich or untitled vulgar; and they drew up a code of laws for the select who received invitations, which they, at least, meant to be as unalterable as those of the Medes and Persians.

I have often watched the passing of events at

VOL. I.

Almacks in its best days with much edification; the evident care taken by the superintendents of the entertainment that the supply of *débutantes* should not exceed the demand, and the business-like way in which they endeavoured to arrange all transactions.

The game here very closely resembles that known to old card-players as the " Earl of Coventry," with a certain variation, and is thus played :—

First Mother (accosting desirable partner).—"I have a very good bride for thee."

Second Mother (to the same *parti*).—"I have another as good as thee."

Third Mother (more · impressively).—" I have the best of all the three."

Fourth Mother (with exultation).—" And I've the Earl of Coventry."

What love had to do in such a place, it seems difficult to state with a proper approach to exactness; nevertheless, the strains of Collinet's band, and the opportunities presented by the quadrille and the waltz, joined hearts as well as hands, and a fair harvest of happiness was reaped, even in that unpromising field. That the crop was sometimes thistles, was no more than might have been expected when people marry for money; but for all that, there were some marriages which turned out well.

To prevent the slightest deviation from the course rigidly marked out for the beauty of the family, the strictest surveillance is maintained from the cradle to the altar. She is not suffered to go anywhere alone —nurse, maid, governess, footman, groom, father,

FASHIONABLE EDUCATION. 259

mother, elder brother, are always on guard. Her drawing lesson, dancing lesson, music lesson, languages, " ologies," if taught by a male professor, are given in the presence of a female Argus ; and very properly too.

It is within my certain knowledge, that particularly with Italian singing-masters (if the teacher be a distressed Pole he is at once regarded by his pupil as a hero), advantages have been taken when opportunity offered. In fact, no teacher—whether he be music-master, dancing-master, a riding-master, or a master of any sort—ought to be permitted to give lessons to a girl unless in the presence of an efficient chaperone. Look at the many instances of riding-masters riding off with their pupils at Cheltenham and other places, and the affairs we have heard of, and those which have been hushed up, that spring out of other educational lessons ; they make one wonder that there are yet many mammas who remain with their eyes unopened.

When all this jealous care is taken, and everything prepared for conquest, rank, and fortune, how often I have seen that the anxious and apparently affectionate mother has been ready to cast her living treasure at the head of Mammon, the moment a good match, in the shape of a rich young man, is cast up on the frothy waves of fashion.

To render the fair object attractive in the eyes expected to select her for transplantation from the parental hothouse to the matrimonial *parterre*, is the one object, aim, and end. Infinite pains are taken that the tender plant shall grow up straight, and those

s 2

famous floriculturists, Dr. Locock and Sir James Clarke, are referred to with the deepest anxiety as every bud begins to bloom. Later in its growth, when girths, dancing-masters, and reclining-boards have done their duty, dumb-bells and the Indian sceptre exercise are brought into requisition to make the plant strong.

She is made thoroughly to appreciate the cardinal virtues, but morality is not quite her all in all. She is taught every accomplishment that happens to be in favour with the circle she is expected to grace. Neither are accomplishments considered the one thing needful. She goes through a course of mental instruction that is expected to enable her to understand —as far as it is necessary to one in her position—the wisdom which has been created and written; but intelligence is not the aim of her existence.

Every ordinary girl is, to some extent, pious, virtuous, accomplished, and intelligent. The family of Lady This or That merely regard such qualifications in her as means to an end. The object of all this culture, the aim of all this training, the purport of all this care, is, in general, but *a desirable marriage*.

Even the best intentions will sometimes lead the sagacious matron into awkward mistakes. Lady —— had come up to London very early in the season, before the town mansion was put into its usual order, and his Royal Highness the Duke of —— being then in town, he was invited to an evening party; a select few were of course asked to meet him. Chairs and sofas that were stationary in the drawing-

ENGRAVINGS. 261

room could in a few moments be uncovered, and after the guests had retired, their chintz covering could easily be restored. The ornaments of vertù, however, had been carefully consigned to cupboards, and so had the beautifully-bound books and well-stored portfolios; and her ladyship intending to go out of town the next day, they were not to be disturbed. Still it could not be permitted that the tables should have nothing upon them. Ladies versed in the mode of producing pleasant réunions always like to give all their guests something to do. Collections of engravings, well selected, are generally amusing; they are often amiably serviceable to two pairs of eyes, that, pretending to look at pictured figures or landscapes, are really only gazing at each other behind an impenetrable screen, trying perhaps to reach the thoughts of each heart, while the ears are open to whispered words that sometimes convey a good deal of meaning.

Lady —— was in a fix as to how to amuse her coming guests, whether they were idle or whether they were in love: having determined to cover her tables at least with something to look at, she hastily ordered her carriage, and drove up Bond-street.

My lady's establishment was " up" for the London season. Her jolly coachman displayed his ample, gold-invested stomach, and had on his new wig and his three-cornered cocked hat. The tall footmen had on their gorgeous liveries, and in their appointed posts held their gold-headed canes projecting over my lady's head. The splendid pair of bays were stepping out, scattering the snow-flakes of foam from their bits among the populace, when the check-string was suddenly pulled, and almost on their haunches the perfect carriage-horses stopped at the kerb. The door having been opened, the steps let down with the usual emphasis, from between her liveried grenadiers her ladyship crossed the pavement and stepped within the shop door of a certain printseller. The rattling sound caused by her arrival, the stopping of errand-boys and others to gaze on the aristocratic turn-out, and the advanced age of the exquisitely-attired customer, made a powerful impression on the shopman. Bowing at every step, he advanced timidly, and asked my lady what she wanted.

"I come to look at some loose prints," was the reply.

Had a bomb exploded beneath the young man's feet, he could not have looked more surprised. The serious aspect of his customer, however, reassured him, and with faltering "Beg pardon, my Lady," he repeated his question.

"Some loose prints, sir; I wish to look at some immediately."

His embarrassment increased; for a moment he stared silently with his mouth open, then hearing the step of his master, he sprang from the spot, and met him at the entrance of his little parlour. A few words having been exchanged between master and man, the former, giving him a push to get out of the way, approached with a succession of bows.

A SURPRISE. 263

"What can I procure for your Ladyship?" he asked civilly.

Surprised at the order apparently not being understood, my lady somewhat sharply repeated it.

He too . became astonished, bewildered, flustered, and embarrassed, took two steps to stare at the equipage at his door, seemed to disbelieve the blazoned coronets he saw, then intently and curiously regarded his distinguished customer.

"I beg your Ladyship's pardon," he said, hesitatingly, "I think—that is, I believe—your carriage is at the door."

"Yes, sir," she replied, looking very angry, "it is, sir, and I want to take away with me a large assortment of prints, but they must be loose. Have you any to dispose of?"

On a sudden the printseller seemed no longer to discredit his senses. Laying a finger on his lips, he begged my lady to step this way, and introduced her into an inner apartment, inclosed in ground glass, carefully shutting the door behind him. Having set a chair for her and a table, he pulled from a shelf an immense portfolio, and opening it at random, he set it down close under her eyes, and retired respectfully to the further end of the room.

After a look that did *not* linger, my lady sprang from her chair as if she had received a galvanic shock ; another spring took her into the outer shop, a third into her open carriage door. So suddenly and unexpectedly did she make her exit, that the admiring crowd on the pavement heard only the monosyllable "home," and the carriage rolled rapidly out of sight.

The hour of the evening party arrived, previous to which my lady had seen several of her female friends, to whom she had told her adventure, and some of them repeated it to their friends, and of course it circulated far and wide.

His Royal Highness was punctual, and the guests who had assembled to meet him were sitting or standing in a semicircle. The moment the royal duke stood up with his back to the fire, there chanced to be a lull in the general conversation, when, to the intense amusement of her confidential friends, his Royal Highness abruptly said to his hostess,

"What's all this I hear, ma'am, about your loose prints?"

With a tact and self-possession which are a part of good breeding, her ladyship evaded a direct reply, and turned the conversation; but her friends who were in the secret had considerable difficulty in governing their risible muscles.

We are assured that love levels all distinctions, laughs at locksmiths, and performs an endless variety of other strange feats; but we ought to discriminate as clearly between Eros and Anteros, as we do between Oberon and Puck, and Ariel and Caliban. The universal moralist has stated that,

> "The evil that men do lives after them.
> The good is oft interrèd with their bones."

EFFECTS OF BAD EXAMPLE. 265

In the game of life, as much too frequently played, when hearts are the prevailing suit, the evil dogs the progress of the unprincipled player, and follows him as a shadow does a substance in the sunshine. Added to which are the consequences of bad example.

What the heir of a peerage with a liberal allowance is enabled to do, the banker's clerk with a small salary sometimes thinks it necessary to imitate. Tomkins is so extremely gentlemanlike in his ideas, that he aspires to be a man of fashion, and, under some hallucination that he is so, apes the habits of those who, by something more than courtesy it is to be hoped, are called his betters. But a couple of hundreds a year cannot be made to run a fair race with more than as many thousands, including a perpetual watch-movement in transactions with tradesmen, vulgarly called "unlimited tick;" and Tomkins, finding he cannot rival Lord Augustus comfortably out of his own resources, helps himself to those of his employer. The villa at Sydenham cannot be kept up in any other way. Mademoiselle Pauline's extravagance cannot be kept down, and his own private expenditure can neither be kept up nor down. The result is, that he saves the firm the trouble of writing its name in connexion with transactions of which it has no knowledge.

Gentility is all very well, and fashion is not a bad thing, under appropriate circumstances; but as a well-known fable assures us frogs cannot swell to the dimensions of oxen, so small people cannot attempt to be great without running a similar risk. That the line

266 A CONTRAST.

must be drawn somewhere, everyone must admit, and Tomkins may thank his stars that it isn't drawn round his neck.

The end of the race is, that while Lord Augustus merely outruns the Constable, a detective outruns Tomkins; the former, after a sufficient disgrace and rustication, gets his debts paid; the latter comes to a settlement—goes, I should say, certainly—but it is to a penal one. Lord Augustus may, in the fullness of time, marry, take a religious turn, or be converted to Popery, and become a pillar of idolatry, extremely steady, from plinth to capital. Unfortunate Tomkins! he can only hope to become a ticket-of-leave, which means to have leave to rob, cheat, or swindle again, and must submit to be ignominiously a marked man for the remainder of his discreditable existence. Love, as usual, incurs the responsibility of this misadventure; but, as the old song assures us,—

"O! 'tis Love, 'tis Love, 'tis Love,
   That makes the world go round;
Ev'ry day, beneath his sway,
   Fools old and young abound!"

CHAPTER XI.

RECREATIONS IN HIGH LIFE.

Imitations of stage-coachmen—Members of the old Four-in-hand Club—Lord Rokeby—Count D'Orsay at "The Ship" at Greenwich—His character and fate—Returning with an omnibus—An attempted extortion foiled—Colonel M'Kinnon and the hackney coachmen—His novel way of entering a convent—Changes in St. James's Park—Lord Malmesbury—Beau Brummel in an asylum—Defence of the Prince of Wales—Kindness of the Royal Dukes—Brummel's flunkeyism—The Kembles not knowing the difference between Shakspeare and Bernard M'Nally—Duke of Norfolk in a cockpit—Patrons of cock-fighting—Conduct of Count de Salis—Police interference—I am summoned to appear before a magistrate—My public declaration against Count de Salis—A ludicrous arrest—Committed to the treadmill—Judge Talfourd.

THERE existed long previous to my time, and there still exists to some extent, among some men, a sort of mania for driving four-in-hand. This never affected me, nor did I ever feel inclined, in the old public coach days, when by my finances I was reluctantly compelled to be a passenger on one of them, to "hold the ribbons," as the reins of the horses are termed, or become the bosom friend of the driver on the box, simply because he drove a four-horse coach, winked at the pretty barmaids at all the inns or public-houses on the road, wore a low-crowned broad-brimmed hat, and suddenly pulled off his thick gloves, and turning up the back of his hand in an uncomfortable-looking position, for some minutes curiously examined his nails, for no earthly reason that the passenger on the box-seat by his side could possibly discover.

The class whence these coachmen came was not one famed for its position or education, although a decayed gentleman, or a young man whose extravagance had outrun the constable, or who was addicted to low company and slang, might occasionally win his bread by driving one of those public vehicles, and touching his hat on the gift of a shilling : still no gentleman in his senses ever would have dreamed, save from such a strange fact being forced on him, that this class of low-bred, uneducated men were capable of setting a fashion (a very bad one) to some of the rising generation of the best families in the United Kingdom. Nevertheless, such was the fact. The heirs to dukedoms, lords, baronets, and esquires, not only were driving their fours-in-hand, dressed as the servants of the public, but they imitated their manners and conversation, and with their own private carriages mimicked the duty of the public ones, absolutely pulling up at the White Horse Cellar, and pretending to deliver parcels.

" The Four-in-hand Club " before my time was considerably the rage ; but in those days I believe gentlemen, though they were lavishly sedulous to turn out a splendid team and a good drag, did not so much imitate their coaching inferiors in dress and manner as they have done since. There were Sir John Lade, at one time the oldest amateur coachman in London ; Lord Hawke, considerably his junior ; Sir C. Bamfylde,

ON TO RICHMOND. 269

Sir John Rogers, Sir Wedderburne Webster, Captain
Felix Agar, and Captain Morgan. When these cele-
brities of the whip used to meet together for their club
drive, they were dressed in a sort of uniform, con-
sisting of dark green frock-coat and brass or gilt
buttons, leather breeches, and top-boots, and broad-
brimmed beavers—at least so I always understood them
to be—and this dress continued till I was about ten
years old, when a lower ambition made itself manifest.
It was said in the world, that the enthusiasm of
gentlemen for driving had arrived at such a height,
that the more they could make themselves look like
common stage-coachmen the better were they pleased
with their appearance.

"On to Richmond" then, as "On to Richmond"
now, the Four-in-Hand Club used to go; and in those
hard-drinking days I wonder that more accidents did
not happen. By degrees, the desire to imitate their
inferiors in appearance left the young men of the day;
and they got into the more sensible plan of simply
studying how to put themselves well on the box, and
how to drive; and we may now see our friends and
relations amusing themselves by driving their fours-
in-hand in a thoroughly gentleman-like turn-out, without being made to laugh at an awkward burlesque.

I once went down to Newbury, to take some red deer
for hunting in the park at Lord Craven's at Hamp-
stead, and at the request of my poor friend the late
Henry Wombwell, we journeyed together by one of
the coaches, and had the hind seat all to ourselves.
Instead of sitting by my side as easy as he could

make himself, and like a gentleman, Harry sat in a sort of one-side position, both hands stuffed into his great-coat pockets, and his hip resting on the rail or arm of the seat.

"Why the deuce, Harry!" I exclaimed, after regarding him for a time with some curiosity, "do you sit in that agonized way, like a cock on a too narrow perch? Here's lots of room for you!"

"Beg pardon, sir," he replied, throwing up a first finger to his hat, "but it's my pleasure to make the passengers as comfortable as I can. If you've room enough, sir, I'm satisfied."

"Don't be such an infernal ass!" I exclaimed. "You're not the guard."

"As you please, sir," again throwing a finger to his hat.

I have been to many most agreeable parties with these handsome turn-outs, sometimes with the Club, at others with fours-in-hand not belonging to the Club, and have seen some amusing occurrences; and at the Old Ship Hotel at Greenwich, and at the Star and Garter at Richmond, I have made one at many most agreeable dinners. Sometimes we went in drags behind four horses, sometimes in carriages open or close, and occasionally by water.

On two occasions I remember that the late Lord Rokeby went to Greenwich behind a pair of posters; and that in coming back the postboy, excessively drunk, upset him on the road. He was much too good-natured to insist on the man's discharge, and, perhaps because he liked a glass of wine himself, he was inclined to forgive a lad overcome by porter ; so the carriage was righted, and no notice taken of the matter. It so happened that some time after Lord Rokeby had again to go to Greenwich, and when his carriage and pair of posters came to the door, he saw in the saddle the same postboy who had brought him to grief.

"Oh, you're there, are you ?" he said, in that dear, good-natured way he had of speaking. "Now mind, my good fellow, you had your jollification last time; it's my turn now, so I shall get drunk, and you must keep sober."

The postboy touched his hat in acquiescence with this reasonable proposition; he brought back my friend in safety, at all events, and, I dare say, in a very happy state of mind.

I remember a dinner at the Ship, where there were a good many ladies, and when D'Orsay was of the party, during which his attention was directed to a centre pane of glass in the bay-window over the Thames, where some one had written, in large letters, with a diamond, D'Orsay's name in improper conjunction with a celebrated German *danseuse* then fulfilling an engagement at the opera. With characteristic readiness and *sangfroid,* he took an orange from a dish near him; and, making some trifling remark on the excellence of the fruit, tossed it up once or twice, catching it in his hand again. Presently, as if by accident, he gave it a wider cant, and sent it through the window, knocking the offensive words out of sight into the Thames.

D'Orsay was as clever and agreeable a companion as

any in the world, and perhaps as inventive and extravagant in dress as Beau Brummel, though not so original nor so varied in the grades of costume through which his imagination carried him. There were all sorts of hats and garments named after him by their makers, more or less like those he wore, and a good many men copied him to some extent in his attire. He and I adopted the tight wristbands, turned back upon the sleeve of the coat upon the wrist, in which fashion we were not followed by others, I am happy to say, and which I retain to the present day.

Among the peculiarities and accomplishments for which D'Orsay desired to be famous was that of great muscular strength, as well as a knowledge of all weapons, and when he shook hands with his friends it was with the whole palm, with such an impressive clutch of the fingers as drove the blood from the limb he held, and sent every ring on the hand almost to the bone. The apparent frankness of manner and kind expression in his good-looking face, when he met you with the exclamation of *"Ah, ha, mon ami !"* and grasped you by the hand, were charming; and we, who rather prided ourselves on being able to do strong things, used to be ready for this grasp, and exhibit our muscular powers in return. There is no man who can so well imitate D'Orsay's method of greeting in this particular as my excellent friend Dr. Quin.

Poor, dear D'Orsay! He was a very accomplished, kind-hearted, and graceful fellow, and much in request in what may be called the fashionable world. I knew him well in his happier hours, I knew him when he was in difficulties, and I knew him in distress; and when, in France, I heard from Frenchmen that those in his native country to whom he looked for high lucrative employment and patronage, and from whom D'Orsay thought he had some claim to expect them, rather slighted his pretensions; and when in his last lingering, painful illness, left him to die too much neglected and alone.

That D'Orsay was unwisely extravagant as well as not over-scrupulous in morality, we know; but that is a man's own affair, not that of his friends. His faults, whatever they were, were covered, or at least glossed over by real kindness of heart, great generosity, and prompt good nature, grace in manner, accomplishments, and high courage; therefore, place him side by side with many of the men with whom he lived in England, D'Orsay, by comparison, would have the advantage in many things. He certainly retained my friendship to the last, and induced in me very great regret for the circumstances which, in the end, disappointed him, and to a very great extent, I fear, embittered his last moments.

On one occasion I had dined at the Ship with a party of ladies and gentlemen, and we all went there and back in an omnibus which I had hired for the purpose. We were much amused on our way down by being called on to stop and take up people, and by their fury when we, the insides, laughed, and the coachman paid no attention to the hail, though he had room on the top of the omnibus for any number. As I had the management of the affair, on our return to

VOL. I.   T town I set down everybody, and then on being set down myself, I was to settle with the omnibus men. Halting to do this by the cab-stand near Hyde Park Corner, on alighting I gave the men the sum agreed upon; but they insisted that they had a right to more, because they had been "off the stones," viz., into Grosvenor Place. On refusing the attempted extortion, words rose between me and the two men, which at once drew around us a ring of cabmen, who, detesting the omnibus, all took my side of the question.

The two fellows swore that they would have more money, and that I should not leave the spot without paying them. I replied that they should have no more, and that I would knock the first man down who attempted to stop me. I moved on, the two men moved on too, thwarting my steps, but manœuvring out of distance, while a ring of wild and rough-looking cabmen danced around us, and shouted to me, "Go it, my lord, and knock the 'busses heads off." I believe they took me for Lord Waterford.

I laughed then, and I have laughed since, at this ridiculous scene, in the dawn of a summer's morning; but all pleasant sights must come to an end, and on the men from the 'bus seeing that fighting was fully intended on my part, with a large bevy of backers to pick me up, they danced out of my way. I went on, and the cabmen, disappointed of their fun, sang or said a sort of chorus, of "God bless'e, my lord," and I proceeded to Berkeley House.

Among the amusing stories which are told of Colonel McKinnon—and from his known extraordinary personal activity, I believe them to be true—was that of his ordering seven or eight of the old slow toddling hackney-coaches, with their ancient muffled-up drivers, to take him to a given door in London. As the old roomy vehicle progressed at the rate of two miles an hour, Dan McKinnon slipped through the window of the first, and so on out of the others, till the whole string of "jarvies" were bumping in procession to the destination, having no one in them. As they arrived at the appointed door one after another, the amusement of the bystanders or the people of the house must have been immense when seven well-caped, wooden-soled old fellows opened as many doors, and stared into as many empty coaches in search of a passenger whom they each had shut in, but who was not to be found.

While in Spain, I believe, and serving under the Duke of Wellington, the turnstile in the walls of some of the nunneries abroad was so tempting to Dan's partiality for active experiment, as to be irresistible. The custom is, when there is anything for the convent in shape of fish, flesh, fowl, or any other gift, to ring a little bell in the wall, and to deposit the parcel in a sort of box or basket, which, revolving, delivers it to an attendant nun inside. Having seen one of these contrivances rather larger than usual, by an extraordinary power which Dan possessed of twisting his pliant limbs into almost any compass, he contrived to pack himself up into the turnstile box; he then rang the bell.

The consternation of the portress, when she received

as a donation, inside those rigidly exclusive walls, a living officer of the Guards, must have been most amusing; but what the treatment of the intruder was when he had thus become a voluntary prisoner in the hands of the scandalized recluses, I never heard. I have been told, however, that on the adventure reaching the ears of the Duke of Wellington, the active experimentalist received considerable "goose."

When we look at the houses in London and in Brighton, once the joyous residences of the witty, prosperous, and gay, once loud with mirth, radiant with light, and joyous with wine, and rendered brilliant by the smiles and presence of the fair and beautiful; and see them now, cold and tenantless, black and sad, the soul of gaiety gone, their sites disregarded by every passer-by, whether belonging to fashion or to trade, we cannot but regard them with melancholy reflection. I sometimes stand in St. James's Park, at the foot of Spring Gardens passage, and look for "the old house at home." There, to the right, is the gate whence used to issue in his spencer for his daily walk, the grandfather of the present Lord Malmesbury, familiar to me as a child, because my nurse pointed him out as a great man. There are the two cows in St. James's Park still, pretending to produce as much milk as nature supplies to as many droves. There is a tall poplar or two that once looked over Carlton House, or the King's stables. But where is my old home now? that loved old home where I was born, where royalty attended my baptism, and where I commenced life

BEAU BRUMMEL. 277

with an affectionate heart for every relation I had,
and thought that as I loved them, they must as much,
then and for ever, love me?

Where is the balcony at my mother's windows, where
she used to give me the earliest strawberries; where
the old circular drive in the garden, by the entrance
door into which the cart from that worshipped land of
birdnests and of flowers, our estate and park at Cranford, used heavily to rumble with its loads of rose-
trees, and of fresh-smelling country things; and though
last, not least, the thrush or blackbird's nest, sent to
me as a treasured gift from the housekeeper? Where
are they? where are all these things? where are those
who brought me into the world, and those who loved
and cared for me in it?

Gone, all gone; or those who are not gone, are
severed from me and lost to me as completely as
death has taken from me the others. Not a stone of
Berkeley House stands the one on the other now; yet
still the wind blows by, the sparrows chirp as usual, and
no living thing but myself seems to heed the change.
This is the fate of all things. Let us once more look
back on the Beau Brummel, formerly the gayest of the
gay, and, to some extent, the life and soul of a particular circle, and revelling the best part of his life in
royal favour, wealth, and the height of fashion; how
wretched was his end—how terrible the fall he met
with! The last I heard of him was, that he went to
Calais, and there, the ruling passion not yet quenched,
he seized on a poor French tailor, nor did he leave
him till he had taught him the proper cut; and out

278   BRUMMEL'S END.

of a very indifferent ninth part of a man, he
made a rich one. From Calais he crept to Caen,
his fortune fallen, his senses failing, and his reason
gone. At Caen, a lady whom he had known in his
happier hours went to see him, and found him at an
asylum, seated alone in a room, brooding over the fire,
his elbows on his knees and his chin upon his hands,
with a large blue cloak. enveloping his person. He
rose as she entered, and with the wonted courtesy of
old, held out his hand, and at once exclaimed, "My
dear Miss Blake, how are you?"

He then conversed with her in a perfectly connected
manner, complained of ill-usage, and talked of the old
scenes in which they used to meet, with a degree of
self-possession perfectly astonishing. Yet poor Beau
Brummel was then a madman, and mad in the
asylum at Caen he died. If the complaints of his
friends which he made to Miss Blake included his
former patron, the Prince of Wales, I do not believe
there was the shadow of truth in them.

I never knew a man ruined in fortune by his own
extravagance who did not invariably assign his fall to
ungrateful friends, and even accuse those who at first
took him by the hand, raised his standard in life, and
gave him an opportunity to make his fortune, of
having deserted him and become his enemies. No one
took Brummel so much by the hand, or was so
generous to him, or so considerate, as was the Prince of
Wales. There ever was a kindness of heart about the
Prince, the Dukes of York, Clarence, Sussex, and
Cambridge, that prompted them to do generous and

THE ROYAL PRINCES. 279

humane things. As a child I was often in their presence, and as a child, boy, and man, they were ever most kind to me. I never preferred a request of my own that was not granted. To be sure, I did not ask much, but what I did ask was never refused; and to the last hour of his life the Duke of Cambridge showed me the most kind consideration.

During the life of his Royal Highness the Duke of Kent, in him I always found a friend, from before, as well as in my Sandhurst days, at the Military College; and after that his friendship and condescension never abated.

When I dined at St. James's Palace, soon after William the Fourth came to the throne, the King was precisely the same to me as the Duke of Clarence had been; while in regard to my godfather, George the Fourth, he spoke as jocularly and kindly to me when I was an officer in the Coldstream Guards as he used to do when he took me as a child upon his knee. I am, therefore, quite sure that no one of the late Royal Family would causelessly desert any one he had once taken by the hand. If the *protégé* had not regarded his own interests, and in any way had misconducted or forgotten himself, then, if neglected, he had no one to thank but himself.

If the well-known anecdote be true, that Brummel once desired the Prince of Wales, as "George," to ring the bell, his Royal Highness but requited such snobbish presumption properly by quietly fulfilling the request, and ordering the Beau's carriage to take him away, never to return to his presence. There is a characteristic flunkeyism about Brummel's presumption in this alleged impertinence, which suggests that however much he had been tolerated in the best society, all the gilding he had got was insufficient to refine the internal man, or permanently to cover the dross of his inferior nature.

The most prudent and peaceable men sometimes very unexpectedly find themselves in a position of considerable difficulty, menacing them even with danger. The late Charles Kemble told me that he and his brother John went one night to the pit of Drury Lane or Covent Garden, I forget which, but I think the former, in order to see one of Shakspeare's plays put on the stage in a new form. They were intent on the performance and in admiration of the scene, when Charles remarked to his brother, " I really think this the very best play for representation, Shakspeare ever wrote."

No sooner had he made this remark, than a huge, red-headed, broad-shouldered Irishman, who sat immediately behind him, leant forward and tapped him on the shoulder to secure his attention.

" I think, sir," he observed, with a strong brogue, " ye said it was one Shakspeare what wraught that play. It was *not* Shakspeare, sir, but me friend, Linnard McNally, what wraught that play."

" Oh, sir," replied Charles Kemble, coolly, " very well."

A short time after this, the Irishman tapped him on the shoulder again.

" Do ye belave, sir," he demanded, " that it was

me friend Linnard McNally what wraught that play?"

"Oh, yes, certainly, sir—if you say so," was the peaceable answer.

For a little time he remained unmolested, but at last he felt the heavy finger once more upon him.

"Your friend what sits on your left hand," exclaimed the Irishman, "don't *look* as if he belaved it *was* me friend Linnard McNally what wraught that play!"

This was too much for the brothers; they rose together and left the house, not deeming it either pleasant or safe to stay in such belligerent society.

Who the man was they never knew, but the friend whom he was so determined to pass off as the greatest dramatic genius of every age and country, was an obscure song-writer and playwright. In the former line he deserves remembrance only as the author of " The Lass of Richmond Hill ;" in the latter, he made one or two experiments on the stage both in Dublin and in London, but they are totally forgotten. Probably this lively appeal to the two great actors whose persons must have been well known, was intended by his zealous admirer and countryman as an introduction—*more Hibernico.*

Leonard McNally was a Dublin barrister. He was employed as counsel for the rebels in the trials that succeeded the rebellion in Ireland about the close of the last century, and obtained a reward from the Government for betraying his clients.

Cock-fighting in these days was still in existence,

though nearly all gentlemen, as well as the late Lord Derby, had given it up, and Germain was dead, who was supposed to possess the best breed in England. I can remember when this much-abused entertainment was honoured with the same patronage as the theatres, and when, as well as the Royal Opera House and theatres, there was an ancient building in Tufton Street, Westminster, called the "Cockpit Royal," and the royal arms had once been emblazoned over the door. It was in this building I first witnessed a main of cocks, and there that the grandfather of the present Duke of Norfolk—notorious for his extraordinary appearance—attired in that sky-blue dress which, when I was a boy, I had often seen, with large ruffles at his wrists, with which, in shooting, he would at times wipe out the pan of his gun—went to see one of the great "mains" of the day.

While a very severe battle was in progress, the large odds often changing from side to side, his Grace remarked to a friend seated by him—

"Well, I don't understand why they should offer those odds on the red; if I betted, I should say two to one on the yellow."

"Done with you, butcher," roared an eager voice from a costermonger behind him, while a huge dirty hand gave him a knock on the back to obtain his attention; "I'll take it."

Cock-fighting has been proscribed by a law, which absolutely appears to make it penal for any man in the street to stop and watch two cock-sparrows fighting in the gutter, if by his voice he aided,

COCK-FIGHTING. 283.

encouraged, or abetted either of the antagonists. A. good many of us, however, still like to see all fair combats, when a free option to surrender is accorded, and among them the fairest of all is the battle between game cocks; the most spirited and the most varying in the opportunities it affords for betting. Lord Sefton, Sir George Dashwood, Lord Waterford, the present Lord Sefton, and myself, were the last who kept up the sport. It had, however, become so contraband an amusement, that we could only enjoy it under secret and carefully-arranged circumstances. These were always left to me, and then every one of our "mains" was sure to be attended by a good many members of both Houses of Parliament; also by a few of the clergy.

I was once in search of some quiet place in which to fight a main, near Cranford, when the Count De Salis, who resided in the neighbourhood, offered me his premises for the purpose, assuring me that he had often fought cocks on his billiard-table.

I went to his house, inspected his premises, selected a large barn, and received from him the assurance that for the day of the main he would surrender the keys of his gardens, yards, and premises to me, that *I might have the whole place at my command* into which to admit my friends.

Upon this understanding a very large party came from town. Several four-in-hands brought down many of my guests, and everything was arranged with privacy and apparently under my direction.

The first thing that excited my suspicions was the

POLICE SURVEILLANCE.

presence of a policeman outside the premises. I therefore demanded his business. He replied, "Information has been received that a cock-fight is to be held here, and I am come to prevent it."

I asked him if a warrant had been granted against anybody, or for the entrance of the private buildings by the police, and he civilly assured me that he knew of none. Content with this information I told my assembled guests that they had nothing to fear, and shutting ourselves up in the ample barn within the walls of the grounds and the house, we awaited the battle. The main was fought, and when it was over, as we were leaving the barn several policemen stopped us, demanding our names—mine among the rest—for being present, aiding, and abetting in a cock-fight.

I shall never forget the terror this occasioned to some of the members of the House of Commons, to my brother the member for Bristol among them, and all apprehension at the prospect of being myself shown up was for the time banished from my mind by the grotesque shifts and hiding-places the selected of the People adopted in trying to escape the books and looks of the constables. To one thing I instantly turned my serious attention, and that was, to learn how the police came there—for the keys of all entrances were in my possession. They had no warrant, and they had forced no door. There was an evident disinclination among them to account for their mode of ingress, as if they desired to shield some person who had assisted them. This induced me to be very close in my investigation, for I had observed that though the Count had boasted

BEFORE THE MAGISTRATES. 285

to me how fond he was of the sport, he never once
came into the barn to see it. Known as I had been
all my life in that close vicinity to Cranford, there
was not a man, or boy, or labourer of any sort under
the Count but who was my friend, so it was not long
before the intelligence was covertly conveyed to me,
that as soon as the main began, and we were all safe
inside the barn, the Count with his own hand fetched
a ladder from the garden, and by a preconcerted arrangement with the police outside, assisted them over
the wall, and brought them up to certain holes in the
boarding of the barn which he himself had cut for
them to peep through to take the names down of all
present, he himself prompting them when their knowledge failed.

Before this news reached me the Count had left the
scene—and it was very lucky for him he had.

The consequence of this *amiable* conduct on his
part was, that I was summoned to the bench at Uxbridge, where the late Sir William Wiseman presided,
and there accused with others in "having aided and
abetted a cock-fight." It was very odd, but they
seemed to have selected me particularly, and a few of
the poorer classes, against whom to proceed. Not
another gentleman, that I recollect, nor anybody else
of any note was summoned.

I attended in person, with a clerk from the office of
Messrs. Clarke, Fynmore, and Fladgate. No doubt
the Count at first thought that I should simply appear
by my solicitor and pay the fine, for on my arrival in
Uxbridge I found the whole town in a state of

excitement. People came running to meet me, to say "he was in the town." I looked for him, but by this time he was *non est inventus.*

When the case against me was heard, having been informed that the late Sir William Wiseman was so impartial a justice that he committed himself much oftener than anybody else, I was prepared for something strange ; but on my taking a chair a little apart from the table, he objected to my sitting down, an objection of which I took not the slightest notice.

The evidence against me was now heard, and it having been shown that the proofs of my taking any part in the matter were very slight, on the conviction being decided against me, of five pounds, I gave "notice of appeal," and my solicitor proffered the required assurances. At the conclusion, the room being crammed with people, the staircase full, and a very large crowd reaching out into the street, I said, in so loud a voice that every one might hear me, "I have been betrayed into a trap; the Count De Salis is no gentleman, and a disgrace to any bench of magistrates."

Sir William Wiseman tried to stop me, but in vain, I got the sentence well out, when there arose three such cheers from the bystanders in the room, caught up by those on the stairs, and carried right out again and again into the street, that all the attempts of the bench in crying "order," were drowned in the vociferous cries.

In the rush to get out of the room with me, and the shaking of my hand by men and women who had

HIS UNPOPULARITY. 287

all known me years before, I was fairly carried into
the street, and then there were loud execrations, and
cries for my betrayer of "Where's the cock that wont
fight? he was here a little while ago."

I went back to town, and the next day was arrested,
on a warrant accusing me of "contemplating a breach
of the peace," and my appearance was demanded at
Uxbridge, to give the required assurances. Lord
Cranstoun and Major Cadogan passed their words for
my peaceful conduct, and in their company, as my
sureties, I posted down to Uxbridge.

When there, I was informed that the Count De Salis'
butler, and the adjutant of a small corps of yeomanry
he commanded, had, at his instance, given the information on which the warrant against me, and I
believe against himself, too, had been issued.

By this most extraordinary conduct, perfectly inexplicable to any gentleman, the Count so incensed all
classes in his vicinity against him, that he was obliged
to absent himself from home for some time, every man
and boy, from the corners of the streets and fields,
shouting out after him, in his rides or drives, "There
goes the cock that wont fight."

For myself, I cared but little for this aggression.
I had ever publicly declared that sports of the kind
would always be upheld by me, as long as the
battle was fair, and a surrender to either combatant
allowed; the baiting of animals alone I detested, therefore, being thus "pulled up" for a matter from the support of which I never pretended to have shrunk, affected
me but little. All that annoyed me was, the chance of

committing others who had depended on me for safety
in the enjoyment of an amusement. But the fun was
not over.

It was the height of the London season, and I was
resident at Cox's Hotel, in Jermyn-street, my favourite
old white charger, Beacon, had come to the door, and
I was about to ride him to the Park. My foot was
in the stirrup, when a countrified-looking man, appearing as if ashamed of what he was doing, very
respectfully pulled off his hat, and said he wished to
speak to me.

Having some sort of idea that his appearance was
familiar to me, I asked him whence he came, and what
he wanted.

He replied, "I come from Uxbridge, and have
something particular to communicate."

"Well, what is it?" I demanded; "out with it,
for I am in a hurry."

He then came close to my horse, as I had reached
the saddle, and looking at the porters at the door, he
said he wished to speak to me in private.

On this I dismounted, and took him into a vacant
room. The upshot of his communication was, that
he was a local constable, and the bearer of my com-
mitment to the treadmill for one month, signed by
Sir William Wiseman, in default of payment of the
fine of five pounds inflicted on me for being present
at the cockfight. The poor fellow looked like a
ghost when he showed me this document, but seemed
excessively relieved when I burst out laughing, and
said, "You don't suppose I'm going to the treadmill,

A TAME CONSTABLE. 289

do you?" I added, "Go and get yourself something to eat, I have no time to stop now, and when I come back from my ride in the Park, I will give you further directions."

The man with alacrity obeyed, when, having written a sharp jobation to the Messrs. Clark & Co., in Craven Street, as to their culpable neglect in not appealing in time against the conviction, or at least taking care that the penalty was paid, I went into the Park, and explained my position to the first lot of friends I met. It soon got all over the Park, for we rode there more collectively than we do now on the green by the water, and we had immense fun about it. I can see now one beautiful face that like many others of the fairest flowers, has since been gathered by the rude hand of Death, looking at me with serio-comic wonder, and saying, "They tell me you are condemned to prison, but that you have tamed the constable, and got him shut up in your hotel; shall I ask mamma to let us ride down and look at him?"

Many funny things were said to me on that day, and the applications to look at my constable were so numerous that I assured some of my fair friends I thought of killing him and having him stuffed, so that he could be perpetually seen at leisure.

The ride in the Park being over, I found that my solicitor had sent down the fine, acknowledging his forgetfulness, and the constable only tarried my return to thank me for a good dinner. Now, one would have supposed that any gentleman acting in the commission of the peace in such a case as this,

VOL. I.   U

290   JUDGE TALFOURD.

would, either himself, or through the clerk to the
Bench, have addressed a line to me or to my solicitor, calling attention to our omission; but Sir W.
Wiseman granted the warrant without any hesitation,
and, without doing me any harm, afforded to society
an immense fund of amusement.

It was about this period that a most ridiculous prize
essay appeared from the pen of a Dr. Styles, on the
"Relative Humanity of Man to Animal," or something
of the kind; the prize awarded to him by my late friend
Judge Talfourd, and I think by the late Lord Carnar-
von. The Humane Society having shown themselves
foolishly officious about our cock-fighting, I published a
review of this essay, exposing the ignorance of natural
history and other errors it contained, and wrote a note
privately to Talfourd, asking him what he was thinking of when he assigned any reward for such a pack
of nonsense. His reply was, "That the only difficulty
the judges of the essays had, was to find one that was
less ridiculous than the others, and after much difficulty the opinion he had come to was, that perhaps
the effusion of Dr. Styles bore that character."

CHAPTER XII.

HUNTING THE HARROW COUNTRY.

I determine to leave the Coldstream—Colonel McKinnon offers himself as a friend—His shabby conduct—Military laws—I keep a pack of hounds at Cranford—Yates the comedian at a dinner-party—My deer—Lord Alvanley and Gunter the pastry-cook—Sir George Wombwell and the farmer—Mr. Fermor pursued for trespassing—My fracas with the farmer's men—The trial for assault and trespass—Brougham my counsel—Scarlett's remark on Cauty the auctioneer—Jeames in a difficulty—The seat of honour—Excessive demands for damages—Lord Tavistock and the Oakley Club—Negotiations for my hunting the Oakley country—Adieu to Cranford—My deer attacked by Eton bargemen—The scholars come to my rescue—Taking a prisoner—Stag-hunting in Montague Place—A deer in a boudoir—Pugnacious turnpike man—He catches a Tartar.

THE time having arrived when I determined to leave the Coldstream Guards, and to go on half-pay, I looked about for a half-pay commission, and found one in the 82nd Regiment of Foot. In those days it was the custom of the retiring or exchanging officer to find some one wanting to purchase a commission on full pay, or by purchase to obtain a step in rank; and the fact was patent to, all men in the army, that the former always stipulated for and received a bonus above the regulation price of his commission from the purchaser; but the negotiation, for form's sake, was carried on *sub rosá*, and was not to be known at the Horse Guards.

Mr. Knox, a relative, I believe, of the Bishop of Derry, was then very anxious to join the Guards, and he assured me that he had received from his Royal Highness the Duke of York the promise of the first vacancy that should arise in the Coldstream; if therefore I would create that vacancy, he would give me the sum I named for the exchange.

My intention to retire on half-pay somehow or other got talked about; and one day on parade at the Tower, the late Colonel McKinnon, then in charge of the battalion, whom I had known only from regimental report, or from the conversation of my elder brothers, introduced himself to me in the double capacity of my commanding officer and the intimate friend of Colonel and Captain Berkeley. I remembered hearing their stories of his playing as a monkey at a masquerade, and walking round the wainscoting of the room, standing on his head on the battlements of Thorpe's Tower at Berkeley Castle, and other pranks I have already narrated; so I accepted him as *the friend* he assured me he was, and the following conversation then at that first interview passed between us :—

"I hear," he said, "that you are going to leave us. My advice may be useful to you in the private capacity of a friend, as well as the fact that everything that you do will have to pass through me as your commanding officer. Who are you going to exchange

SHABBY CONDUCT. 293

with? and have you taken care to get the worth of the bargain?"

I told him I had found Mr. Knox willing to give me what I asked, and that he had secured the promise of the first vacancy in the regiment from the Duke of York, so I had nothing to do but to retire.

"Very good," he replied; "you are all right, then; but are you sure you have asked enough money?"

I informed him that Mr. Knox was to give me several hundreds, at this time I forget how much, above the regulation price, and we parted. On the full understanding from Mr. Knox as to his money being ready, and his nomination to my commission certain, I retired; but the Horse Guards declined to receive him, accepting my retirement, of course, but only allowing me the regulation price, and *the brother-in-law of my commanding officer, Mr. Dent, came in in the place of Mr. Knox!* I had never told anybody what money was to pass between us, *except Colonel McKinnon.* I afterwards discovered that in an explanation, I believe with the friends of Mr. Knox, the Duke of York had said that the sum I was to get in the exchange had reached his ears, *therefore* Mr. Knox, with whom the bargain was made, could not receive the appointment he had promised.

This so angered me that I at once determined to call out Colonel Daniel McKinnon for the share he *must* have had in the transaction; but the second I sought overruled the warlike appeal, and I, very much against my will, was forced to put up with it. I had the satisfaction, however, of turning my back on my late commanding officer the first time I met him.

Surely there wanted then, as in some things there wants now, a better arrangement in military matters, governed under a *bonâ fide* rule, and acted on without distinction. There should be nothing winked at, and no uncertainty as to what may or may not be done.

Knowing as I do the great capacity for duty as well as rule of the present Commander-in-Chief, the Duke of Cambridge, I wonder that the putting up with personal insult, and prohibition of the duel, have not come under his consideration and induced him to take some step to prevent the consequences attending on the fear of being cashiered. A gallant soldier received a personal insult, I think at his Club—but no matter where—and because he did not call out the insulter, his brother officers signified to him that he had better leave the regiment. Thus, for not transgressing a military rule, an act that would have cost him his commission, he was to be deprived of it by a private combination originating at mess. An officer, therefore, if grossly insulted, as the military law now stands; must either put up with an insult, or sell his commission to place himself in a position to resent it. If he does not sell and fight, he must resign; so that, either way, a gallant man *may be put* in not only a senseless, but, in a pecuniary point of view, a ruinous fix, and under present circumstances I do not see how he is to get out of the scrape.

Having retired on the half-pay of the 82nd in the year 1823, I assisted my brother Moreton in keeping hounds until I married, when I bought a house in the village of Cranford, of a Mr. Ashlin, and took the entire pack and kennel into my own hands; the hounds still occupying their quarters in the old kennel at my mother's, and Moreton taking on himself the position of whipper-in instead of huntsman. I hunted the hounds myself.

Among the dinner-parties I used to give to my friends, usually the day before hunting, there was one that I shall never forget. Many of the cheerful spirits who that night surrounded me can laugh no more, and I hardly know if there is one person alive who then helped to form the social circle. Suddenly and unexpectedly on that day, the comedian Yates, who had been introduced at Cheltenham to me by my brothers, came down to see me, and I invited him to stay for dinner, well knowing that he was a gentlemanlike fellow, and that, *when he chose*, he could be the most entertaining companion I ever met. I forget now who were of the dinner-party, though I know that many who composed it are dead; but as Yates knew (he was, like Mathews and Liston, very sensitive on that subject), that he had not been asked purposely to amuse a private party, after dinner he broke out in songs and imitations to such an extent, that it was midnight even before the ladies retired. We all of us nearly killed ourselves with laughing.

The consequence was, that every lady and gentleman who dined with me on that occasion, begged of me in the following week to give a similar entertainment, and to ask Yates to be of the party. I complied. They came, and Yates came down from London; but on seeing that all the guests were those he had met before, and that it was a "set scene," he shut up, and every attempt I made to draw him out was abortive. Throughout the dinner, and the party in the evening, he was as dumb as the stupidest guest in the room.

My hunting fields at that time were very large, larger than those that attended the Royal Hunt, on account of the wild running of the Berkeley Castle deer, which I managed on a better plan than those selected for hunting from the royal park. My deer, about twenty-three in number, came up; and all that survived the hunting season were sent down again to the Castle, and turned out in the ample park with their wild fellows. By this means the same deer seldom came up in two successive years for hunting, and those that had been hunted, when they did return, had lost all their artificial education, and become as wild as ever. The royal deer, in those days, once up for hunting, were kept in a paddock, and consequently very soon got tame.

On these hunting days some very amusing things happened with my hunt which I have since seen attributed to various other persons. The Gunters, the renowned pastrycooks of Berkeley Square, were all fond of hunting, were frequently out with my hounds, and subscribed to the hunt.

"Mr. Gunter," remarked Alvanley, "that's a fine horse you are on."

LORD ALVANLEY. 297

"Yes, he is, my lord," replied Gunter; "but he is so hot I can't hold him."

"Why the devil don't you ice him, then?" rejoined his lordship.

Gunter looked as if he did not like the suggestion.

The same noble lord was out with me when the stag took an unfortunate line by Hounslow, Twickenham, and Teddington, and got into the Thames. The whole run, or nearly all of it, had been through nursery and market gardens, and the stag was so mobbed that he refused to leave the river. Alvanley, seeing the sport was over, went on early to town, and when, in the bay window at White's, some of his friends asked him—

"What sport?"

"Oh," he replied, "the melon and asparagus-beds were devilish heavy—up to our hocks in glass all day; and all Berkeley wanted was a landing-net to get his deer out of the water."

It was with me also that in the Harrow country the late Sir George Wombwell, having missed his second horse, spoke to one of the surly cultivators of that stiff vale, thus—

"I say, farmer, d—— it! have you seen my fellow?"

The man, with his hands in his breeches' pockets, eyed his questioner in silence for a minute, and then exclaimed—

"No, upon my soul I never did!"

It was in the Harrow country, too, that a hostile

298   TRESPASSING.

agriculturalist tried to stop us in vain, until the late
excellent gentleman, Mr. Fermor, came into his field by
a pretty good gap in the fence, made by the numerous
horses that had gone before. The farmer and his
labourers recognised their customer, and knowing he
disliked to jump, some of them ran up to head him,
while their master cast some bushes—merely a few
thorns—into the gap by which Mr. Fermor had
entered. Heading back to the loophole he *thought* he
should be able to escape by, he came up to it, but in
its repaired state did not know it again. The consequence was that he rode round and round the field,
with the farmer and his men chasing him, till he did
double the damage made by the whole lot that had
preceded him. At length he surrendered to his
pursuers, and was on the spot heavily fined for the
trespass.

It was in the Harrow country, too, under Harrow-
on-the-Hill, that an ill-grained fellow named "Baker"
first served me with a notice not to trespass, and
then, when I accidentally ran over the Harrow Vale,
deer and hounds going together into his barn, he and
three of his men tried to fasten up the barn-doors, so
as to let the pack tear the splendid stag to pieces. I
had avoided this man's fields, but a green lane brought
me up to the gate of his farmyard before my companions. Seeing his servants attempting to lock
the barn-door, I jumped off my horse and got up just
in time to put my left hand into the staple before
they could introduce the lock. There were three
to one, and the men were big fellows, one of whom

hurt my left hand very much in trying to force in the lock.

I offered to pay them any damage if they would only let me save my deer, for I could now hear him bellowing from the pain the closed-in and tearing pack inflicted. This was refused; so, to save my hand, I struck my assailant over the wrist with the hammer of my whip. On this he drew back, and hit left and right at my head. I could not give much before the blow, because my back was close against the barn-door. I, however, drew my head out of distance of his left hand, but his right told on the peak of my hunting-cap, and knocking it off over my face, gave me a bloody nose. I then retaliated by a severe blow with the iron hammer of my whip across his forearm, and hit it useless to his side.

I was swinging my whip round me to keep off my assailants, when the whole field came up to the gate. On my calling out, "Gentlemen, will you stand by and see this?" a dozen or more legs flew over the saddles, and the first man at my side was an efficient one, for it was Mr. Gully, the member for Pontefract. With him came the late George Hawkins, Mr. Norton (a coal-merchant at Uxbridge), a Mr. White, Mr. Baring, and many more stout friends; and they took the pitchforks and shovels, with which the farmer's men had then armed themselves, from them, forced open the barn, and enabled me to save my deer.

The big fellow whose arm I had struck held on somehow or other to his pitchfork, and was dragged from the barn-door on his back into the wet dung-heaps, and not permitted to regain his feet till the deer was saved and the *mêlée* over.

The present Lord Brougham defended me in the action for assault and trespass brought by Baker, and Scarlett, the late Lord Abinger, was against me, and never did I see a greater farce, among all the farces of trial by jury that I have witnessed, than the one on this occasion.

Gunter, my hunting friend of Berkeley Square, was summoned on the jury, and prepared to do his duty, no doubt, for he wore a great coat, and all the pockets seemed to be full of confectionary. He was objected to, however, and, had the admirable pencil of Leech been there to have sketched the twelve thick heads that the jury presented, he would have given the clever author of "Soapy Sponge" a splendid illustration of the tenantry of Jawleyford, when that proprietor addressed them at his audit dinner.

When this round dozen of honest men, they were all rotund, settled in their box, and were addressed by Baker's counsel, they nodded a mute acquiescence to every word that the comfortable-looking, jolly-faced Scarlett said. But when Brougham addressed them, with smiles that expressed contempt of his words, if they expressed anything, there followed a sort of shake of balls, called heads, the orifices in which seemed to say, "Oh yes, you're a going to wile our wits out on us, aint you, but we aint going to be done by your eloquence," they really shut their ears against reason and truth, and decided to go against Brougham.

The court was filled with the *élite* of society to hear

HEAD OR HEELS.

the trial, and when the three great hulking rustics
got up into the witness-box, one after the other, to
swear to damage which never was done, Sir George
Seymour whispered to me "that I had got among a
race of giants."

The one whose arm I had struck afforded immense
amusement to the court by his confused answers, when
Brougham cross-examined him with his wonted skill,
concluding with these words, "You seem to know
nothing about it; can you undertake to swear, whether,
for the chief part of the time, you were on your head
or your heels?"

The man scratched his head for several seconds in
silence, with a puzzled look, and the longer he refrained
from answering, and the more he scratched, the louder
became the roars of laughter from all parts of the court.
At last, to the intense amusement of all he swore that
he could not say whether he was on his head or his
heels. Brougham asked him no more questions.

The great stupid fellow, though thus laughed at,
was perfectly right, and really so far endeavoured to
speak the truth, for, in the *mêlée* at the barn-door, he
had been thrown down, on his head first, and then
dragged about and trampled on, on his back, because
he clung tenaciously to the handle of his pitchfork;
and he really never had been on his heels until
I had captured the deer and taken him out of the
barn.

I remember, too, that Scarlett was rather severe on
Mr. Cauty, the auctioneer, who had been hunting with
me on that occasion, and who came to the court to

offer his testimony on hearing of the trial, his name
not being on the brief.

His evidence went merely to show the violence of
the complainants, and as to that he could say nothing
new; so Scarlett, in cross-examination, told him he did
not know why he came there, unless it was (waving
his hand to Mr. Cauty's very red head) to throw a
colour on the transaction.

The jury found for the plaintiff, damages one
hundred pounds—if I recollect rightly—when in
reality sixpence would have amply covered it all.

After this there was another row between me and a
man named "Brett," who lived on what used to be
Hillingdon Heath, near Hillingdon, on the Uxbridge
road. This person sent out a powdered footman to
shut the gate of his field in my face, hounds running
very hard, and their heads pointing for the best of the
Harrow Vale. The late Colonel John Lyster, of the
Guards, was behind me at the fence by the gate,
a bullfinch of tall quick, the ditch on the off side into
a green lane.

Baulked in my passage through the gate, I had to
pull round to send my splendid horse, Jack o' Lantern,
at the bullfinch, and in doing this John Lyster
passed me, and I called out to him to "put in powder
enough to send him through;" he did so, and as I
did the same on the other side the gate, and landed
well into the lane, the footman seized one rein of
Jack's bridle, and stopped me just at the moment
that I tried to get down the lane. The hounds,
checking for an instant, and Lyster pausing, he saw

DUSTING A FLUNKEY.   303

the man seize my bridle, and then my leg, in an endeavour to throw me out of the saddle.

If the rider is not down upon the dodge by which it is accomplished, it is very easy to lift a man up with a peculiar cant to his leg, at the same time to dislodge him; but in this instance the footman perhaps knew more of a table than he did of a saddle, and by his hold on my leg, and his head at my right knee, he himself came to considerable grief. I double thonged and doubly dusted all the powder out of his pate, and broke his head besides, when he let go my leg and ran away towards the house, shouting for his master. We had a splendid run, and the rencontre with Jeames occasioned some mirth.

Mr. Brett brought an action for his servant against me for the assault, and when I was preparing to defend it, I found that my only witness was John Lyster, and that instead of hunting with me on that occasion he ought to have been a hundred miles away with his recruiting party of the Guards. He therefore begged me not to call him, or he should get into a serious scrape. I complied with his request, and instead of attempting a defence in law, I sent the late George Hawkins, who then lived at Ickenham, in the Harrow Vale, with a message to Mr. Brett, that if he attempted to proceed against me in the matter of his servant, he must fight me, for I held him to act most culpably and unlike a gentleman in countenancing the violence of his menial.

Mr. Brett refused the challenge, but expressed himself willing to compromise, so that eventually I had to pay a bill of the doctor who had been called in to attend the man.

I remember also running by Uxbridge, and the stag taking some garden pales too high for the hounds to jump, so I got off my horse to break a bar to enable the pack to get through. While I was thus occupied, the sharp knuckles of the owner of the garden from behind, crooked and inserted themselves into my collar, and brought me to my feet with a slight sense of strangulation. I was going to hit my assailant with my fist, but on his loosing his hold and turning away to avoid retribution, I merely administered a kick behind, where, as Hudibras says,

> " It hurts one's honour more
> Than many wounds laid on before."

I then finished breaking the pale, and rode away.

I had a great many friends in Uxbridge, and among them the coal-merchant, the late Mr. Norton, and they did all they could to prevent this person from going to law. He was wilful at first, and terribly riled about the kick, saying if I had hit him he should not so much have cared, but to be kicked on the seat of honour as referred to by Hudibras, was not to be endured.

I told Norton to assure him that I was very sorry; his own act of violence had excited a desire for retaliation; but as it happened so it was. The upshot of it, thanks to Norton and other friends, was, that no more notice was taken of the matter.

From the immense increase in the numbers of those who hunted with me, and from the fact that whenever

HUNTING DAMAGES. 305

I enlarged a stag it was always with his head towards Harrow for the chance of going over its beautiful, but very deceitful vale, a great demand arose for damage. When I use the term "deceitful," I mean that often-times after a frost, the smooth-looking grass fields were heavier than ploughed land, and in wet weather after frost, there were very many fields' in which horses were reduced to a trot. On account of the cutting up of these lands, the farmers' demands for compensation for damages were more than I could afford, so the friends who hunted with me resolved to form a fund to meet this extra charge. It was kindly and liberally intended on their parts, but the act was met by such an avaricious resolve on the part of the Harrow farmers, as to give the death-blow to all our hopes of continuing our long-established amusement. While I galloped over the country with but a few friends, the people who remembered the fox-hounds of my father, hunted by George Moulton and afterwards by Tom Oldacre, when Scratchwood, close to Worm-wood Scrubs, now the review ground of the Horse Guards, was a favourite fixture, and a bad day's sport occasionally happening from the fox hanging about the rough grounds and cover adjoining Kensington Gardens, the name went a great way in inducing forbearance towards me.

When, however, a couple of hundred well mounted men, mostly strangers to the vicinity, charged the fences with me instead of ten or twelve, the case assumed another aspect, and a demand arose for compensation. To insure their power to enforce it, some of the farmers

VOL. I.   X

serred me with notice not to trespass, giving me to understand that they intended no hostile proceeding against me at law if their demands were satisfied; then growing apparently insatiable when they became aware that they could be made against a *public fund*, instead of my limited and private purse, their cupidity knew no bounds.

The result of this at once became evident, a mine of wealth would soon have been insufficient to cover the cost of a single run over the Harrow Vale, and reluctantly I saw that if I intended to keep hounds, I must go further from the metropolis, and seek a wilder scene in which to hunt the fox instead of stag, and thus take a higher degree in the art of hunting. In search of a vacant country, then, I went to London and met with one of my stag-hunting field, the present Lord.Clanwilliam, who told me that a serious quarrel had happened between the late Duke of Bedford, then Lord Tavistock, and the Oakley Club, who, when Lord Tavistock declined to hunt the country in Bedfordshire any more, had asserted that he had no right to sell his own hounds, but must hand the pack over to the Club, to be dealt with as they might elect. Upon this Lord Tavistock sold his hounds out of the county, as he had a just right to do, and the great landed proprietors within the limits of the hunt, his father the Duke of Bedford, the Duke of Manchester, Lord Ludlow, Lord St. John (then in his minority), "Orlebar," &c., &c., turned a deaf ear to any other master of hounds in connexion with the Oakley Club. Up to the eleventh hour of the spring it seemed as

SUBSCRIPTION.

if that fine old fox-hunting county, with its "stump-bred" native foxes, was to be without any hounds to make sport for the resident gentry, and that excellent race of kind-hearted, liberal men, the yeomanry and tillers of its acres.

Lord Clanwilliam and, I think, Lord Clanricarde too, proposed me to his Grace of Bedford and to Lord Tavistock, as willing to succeed ·the latter in the Oakley country upon the fullest leave and promise of future support from the landed proprietors, but so great was the schism then existing, that all the Duke of Bedford and Lord Tavistock could give me was "permission to draw their covers." On that hint I spoke, and made applications to the other proprietors without reference to the Oakley Club, receiving permission from them all, and going down to stay a day or two with Lord Ludlow at Cardington that I might see my way to other matters.

As a subscription was necessary to enable me to get together an efficient establishment, the fact got about, and Mr. Samuel Whitbread, then resident at Cardington, who had been and was acting as secretary to the Oakley Club, communicated with me, and on the knowledge that I was in possession of the woods and fields, offered, on the part of the Club, to support me with a subscription, limiting the subscription to 1000*l.*, and for *two years. The limit* rather surprised me, for on such occasions the subscriptions of gentlemen are never counted on beyond their immediate pleasure, and I had never reckoned on any man's support, should he wish to withdraw it, beyond the cur-

x 2

rent season. I afterwards found that in this stated sum Mr. Whitbread included the subscriptions of the Duke of Bedford, Lord Tavistock, and Lord Ludlow, with which he seemed to have made himself acquainted.

On my urging that a thousand pounds was too small a sum for four days a week, a great portion of the most needful work to be done in very heavy woodlands, and· the season always commencing the first week in July, and continuing under favourable circumstances to the death of a fox in May, he replied, " Oh, but you must consider that the Club take *all the cost of the earth-stopping on themselves*, and other incidental expenses."

This certainly, with the knowledge I had of the Cheltenham country and the hills above the Vale of Berkeley, then hunted by my eldest brother, seemed to me to be a heavy item in a four days a week country, and though I deprecated the earth-stopping being done by other than the huntsman's order, I ceased to advance any further objection, and agreed to the thousand a year. On taking possession of the country, *I found that there was but one established earth in it, and that I stopped up*, and that the " incidental expense " was a solitary dinner to the keepers, who were then but few. As to any outlay for poultry said to be taken by foxes, the yeomanry and farmers were all too much of sportsmen and too liberal to desire it: a few shillings to some old cottage woman paid it all.

The time arrived when I was to bid adieu to those

ADIEU TO CRANFORD.

Scenes in which, from the age of eleven years, I had grown to manhood;—to the fields where, as Shelley has sung, the Lark—

> " Like a rose embower'd
> In its own green leaves,
> By warm winds deflower'd,
> Till the scent it gives
> Makes faint with too much sweet
> Those heavy-winged thieves."

Yes, to those dear woods and fields at Cranford then a long, long farewell. To the woods where, beneath the shading and faithfully silent trees, the first vows of a boyish love reached the listening ear, and where the heart felt and expressed a spring that the summer of manhood has never since surpassed! Those woods where in summer, song-birds of every kind flocked from the more open and trodden fields to pour out their living melody in security. Where the last quiet notes of the cushat and the murmuring turtle-dove, were taken up by the nightingale, and from eve continued through the night. To the lawn, whence the childish mirth of my sisters ringing in the wintry air, used to reach me when I lay concealed in the woods to shoot the coming wood-pigeons. To the river through the willows and the park, where Miss. Kemble, afterwards Mrs. Sartoris, once entranced my soul by singing to me—as the boat floated down the sluggish stream with us—Scottish melodies of heroism and love. Adieu to all. The scene of my sport and of my love now lies afar; and with the most intense affection for all I left behind, and many a sigh to the

310   ETON.

past, I broke up my establishment at Cranford, sold
my house to Colonel Freemantle, and went to Bedford
to make new friends, to find a home, if I could, as
happy as the one I quitted, and to seek a new scene
of sporting adventure. Time had no effect on my
recollection of others, absence only made me wish
to see those I loved again; the wider the time the
more I longed, but a strange spirit was coming over
my dream, through the shadows of which I could
not see. My eldest brother, Colonel Berkeley, needed
my aid.

I cannot depart, however, from the scene of so
many pleasures without a recollection or two of the
neighbourhood. One day I was with my hounds,
when the stag having crossed the Thames near the
cavalry barracks, landed between Eton and Surley
Hall. He was instantly met and set upon by a whole
host of bargemen and Eton louts, aided by several
dogs; one of the latter, a bulldog, as he came out of
the water, pinned him by the nose, and bargemen,
bulldogs, curs, and hounds, all began to worry the
animal to the best of their ability. A boat happening
to be on my side of the river, I jumped off my horse,
and getting into it, pulled across quite alone and
unaided, for the field had made for the bridge. The
bright orange plush coat in which I hunted my
hounds, or the "tawny coat," as it was called in the
olden time, when the Lord Berkeley of that date
kept his hounds and "huntsmen in tawny coats, at
the village of Charing," was therefore soon in the
mêlée. By dint of bodily force I got up to the deer,

ETON BOYS.

and seizing the bulldog, who still held him by the nose, by the hinder leg, I began to make the iron hammer of my whip tell on his carcase. On the falling of the second blow a sort of sledge-hammer stroke smote me in the back and felled me to the ground. There was no one by to pick me up. Struggling vigorously through the forest of trampling legs, hob-nailed shoes, and fighting animals, into the midst of which the bargeman had sent me, I immediately hit the first rough face I saw, and sent the owner of it sprawling upon mother earth. Then there was a wild scuffle and a furious outcry, and all the bargemen for a moment seemed to hug me and themselves too; when, as there was no room to hit out, in the phraseology of the ring, I "fibbed" at half-a-dozen waistcoats and faces with all my might and main. Thus the wrestling and raging throng passed over the hounds, stag, and dogs, and by means of the teeth below and the fists above, blood was drawn in many places. We were too closely engaged to do each other serious harm, but the 20 to 1 were telling severely against me. *Floreat Etona!* The scholars at a distance beheld the unfair combat one gentleman was carrying on against a host of plebeian assailants, and down they came pell-mell. I saw them approach, little and big, and cried, "Ho! Eton to the rescue!" and not in vain. From the least boy able to kick a man's shin, up to the big youth willing and able to box, there was not a boy who did not right willingly lend me a hand.

There was evidently no love lost between the bargemen and the scholars; and when or how the fight

312

OLD BALDWIN.

would have ended I cannot say, but at the critical moment the field and my men came galloping up from the bridge, and riding into the throng, they turned the tide of affairs. The "roughs" shrank from the contest, pretending to assist us in saving the very animal they had sought to destroy—whose leg, by the way, had been broken by some of their hob-nailed shoes.

When the row was over, my deer-cart arrived, and the driver, old John Baldwin, noticing the suggestive signs of a bloody nose or two, and finding that a huge bargeman had got into his vehicle to assist in hauling up the dying deer, while the noise was going on, drove away.

My horse having been brought, I was proceeding home with the hounds, when on reaching a solitary place, under the Home Park wall, not far from Datchet, I observed old Baldwin waiting for me with the deer-cart. As I approached, to my utter astonishment I saw that he was not on the box, but on the roof, making strange pantomimic gestures at something beneath him. This unusual sight angered me rather, my orders invariably being that, after the stag was taken, and the hounds had become quiet, the scent of the deer that day should never reach their noses. I made signs to my servant, therefore, to proceed. They were unattended to. I shouted an imperative order with no more effect. Instead of showing obedience, old John began dancing on the cart, waving his cap, and flourishing his whip as a painted Indian might be disposed to do after scalping his foe.

A DEER IN MONTAGUE STREET. 313

At that time the old fellow lived, had long lived, and I believe still lives, on gin and beer, so I thought him drunk; but on reaching the cart, I heard a voice of supplication proceeding from within, accompanied by an occasional bumping, thumping sound.

"Here he is, Mr. Grantley," exultantly cried my man; "come on, master, and take yer revenge. I've heard they hit yer, and here's one on 'em as did it. The stag's been a butting on him terrible. I'll let 'im out, and now you whop 'im well."

As John said this, I could see the man's mouth at the air-hole in the cart, and hear him imploring for forgiveness and freedom from his dangerous prison. He was then uncarted, with the words, "Come, my fine feller, we'll hunt *you* now." Not being able to recognise him as one of those who had assaulted me, I permitted him to pass without further molestation, and proceeded on my way home.

On another occasion, we ran the stag up to No. 1, Montague-street, Russell-square, where two pretty young ladies were standing at the parlour window. A crowd had, of course, collected round me and the three or four hounds that had not been stopped on the verge of the streets. I had dismounted in my orange plush coat and hunting cap, and was standing on the pavement in front of the stag, keeping back the hounds, the deer having backed up the steps and set his haunches against the street-door. The girls were full of pity for the noble stag; and when I asked them, cap in hand, to open the door, they were rushing to do so, when a little, fat, red-faced man, in what looked like a suit of black sticking-plaister, shorts and stockings, thrust them rudely on one side. "Let him in, indeed!" he cried, shaking his fist at me; "open *my* door, indeed! I say, you sir (addressing me), take your animal away; you'll get nothing here; if you don't, I'll send for the beadle!" His rage, and the evident delusion he laboured under, in taking me for an itinerant showman, and the stag for an animal that would dance or play tricks at my bidding, was too much for several horsedealers and others who had followed me up to see the deer taken. They received his address with shouts of laughter, which made him more furious. At this moment a butcher's lad came up with an empty tray; so borrowing this, as a shield to keep the stag's horns on one side, with the help of the lad and some of the bystanders I ran in on the stag and safely secured him.

In another instance, one of my stags entered a gentleman's house by· the garden door, which the proprietor closed, to keep out the hounds. At first he was very civil, and admitted me. Much to my astonishment, when I asked where the stag was, he replied, that he had been in all the rooms on the ground floor, but was now gone upstairs. I requested permission to follow. "I must first go up and see," he replied. I represented that such a proceeding on his part would be rash, as meeting an infuriated stag on a narrow stair was dangerous, and suggested that he had better let me go. He, however, would go up, requesting me to stay on the landing-place; I soon after heard rumbling noises from above, as if the deer

AN ENRAGED GENTLEMAN.   315

and my host had come into collision. It ended by
the hitherto civil gentleman coming down to me in a
towering passion, and with a rather disordered dress.

"Damn me!" he roared, "sir, your beast is very
rude, he has butted me, he's been into 'all the bed-
rooms, and is now in my wife's boudoir; I can't stand
this—what do you mean by this insulting outrage?"

To this violent appeal I could only reply by quietly
assuring him that I was very sorry for the intrusion,
and was as anxious as he could be to take the deer
away. This, after some little further parley, with the
assistance of three or four of my field, he permitted
me to do.

From the period of my joining the Coldstream
Guards, up to that of my marriage, in 1824, and during the time I lived in my house in the village of
Cranford, after my marriage, I used in the summer
season to be frequently in London, though not so
much so as I had been before it; hence, in society,
I had made many friends, and it is not within my remembrance that up to 1829, I could name an enemy.

On repairing to Bedfordshire, the depreciation of
West India property, and the larger expenses contingent on taking a country in which to hunt a fox four
days a week, made me resolve to give up my seasons
in London, and to settle down quietly to a country
life; thus avoiding every unnecessary expenditure.

Perhaps, for the sake of chronicling sporting events,
it may be right to observe that, on my resigning the
stag-hounds at Cranford, Hubert de Burgh kept a
pack at West Drayton, and to speak a good word for

his success to all the local friends I had, around my father's or "the old Berkeley country," as it was called long before I was born, was to me the greatest possible pleasure. I think it was about this time, or not long before, that my last sporting act, as I suppose it must be called, in Middlesex; took place, between night and morning, at the old Tyburn turnpike gate, since taken down. It occurred with the last turnpike-man of the last gate, who dwelt there to take toll of the king's subjects, and therefore the thing can never occur to anyone again.

. I was going up from Cranford to London to dine, in Cumberland Street, to return the same night, our peculiar yellow chariot with the crimson lining being as well known to every turnpike-man on that road, as my tawny or orange plush hunting-coats were known in the field—and when we stopped at the turnpike, my guardsman servant, whose discharge I had purchased, prepared to pay the toll and take a ticket. The toll was taken, but no ticket given, as the toll-taker said, "All right, I know you," and touched his hat as the carriage went by.

In returning from dinner, the gate being open, I was first aware that we passed through, and then of a swerving of the carriage towards the right hand footway, a rough jolt, and the missing from view for a moment of the hand-poster's head, which brought the carriage to a full stop. Voices in altercation followed—on letting down the window, and looking out, I found that the turnpike-man was refusing to let us proceed without a ticket, and that having seized

INSOLENT TOLL-KEEPER. 317

the hand-horse by the bridle, he had caused him to stumble upon the footway. My order to my servant was, to get off the dickey and take the aggressor away, which, with true soldierlike obedience, he attempted to do, but in vain. The toll-keeper kept possession of the horses, and had us all prisoners.

It was very far from my wish to be violent, for Mrs. Berkeley was in the carriage, and our magnificent deer-hound and retriever Smoker—in those days very well known, and often asked out—had been of our party to dinner, so I told my servant to resume his seat on the dickey, and informed the turnpike-man that he knew it was not twelve o'clock, and that he himself had passed my carriage through without a ticket; that, moreover, I was through the gate, and that he might summon me for non-payment of the toll, if he wished it, but he *must* let go the horse's head.

This he most insolently refused, so, casting open the door, I had to jump out in the buff shorts of those days, and white waistcoat and silk stockings, into the muddy road, a costume not much fitted to the occasion. As he still held the horse, turning his back against its shoulder, and his face to me, I told him that if he did not loose the bridle, I would thrash him; at which he laughed scornfully. This defiance was instantly met by a blow in the face, which, though from the support of the horse's shoulder, it could not knock him down, induced him not to risk another in that posture. He at once, therefore, jumped on the path, putting himself into what seemed to me, by the lamplight, a very good position. I was the taller, being six feet two, but he was, to look at, the stronger, though not so tall. Somehow or other, as he came at me, I missed him with both hands, and counting on his strength, he succeeded in closing, but not in a scientific manner. The speedy upshot of it was, that his head got under my left arm, and I held it there till he was licked, never letting him go till all attempt at punishing me had left him, and he had begun to scream for the "watch."

Sounding rattles, and heavy old toddling shoes, then came approaching from above and below; so, casting him from me, and hitting him up against the wall, I stepped into my carriage and drove away. He had hit me once in the face, but when or how I did not feel; the blow, however, had cut to the bone, and I have the mark even now. No proceedings were taken against me, and old March, the post-boy, then living at Cranford bridge, teased this toll-keeper nearly to death whenever he drove that way, by *kind wonders* that his face had not got well yet, though nearly three weeks had passed since the occurrence, and asking him if he would like to see "Mr. Grantley again."

A severe fight took place then between my brother Moreton, armed with a policeman's staff, and a poacher with a long knife, in which my brother effected a safe capture, but not without administering severe punishment to the thief, who was subsequently consigned to prison. A quaker at Uxbridge—they are always more or less belligerent and litigious, as my parliamentary practice afterwards proved, when coming into more peaceful collision with Mr. Bright—took up the case of this ruffian, tried to get the sentence mitigated, and threatened proceedings against my brother, but Friend Broadbrim burnt his fingers, and dropped the matter as if it had been a burning coal.

CHAPTER XIII.

THE OAKLEY HUNT.

My residence at Harrold Hall—My pack and whips—Cub-hunting —Ill-feeling in the Club—My first season in Bedfordshire— Mr. S. Whitbread a leader of the malcontents—A hard run— My horse Ready—The round robin—Memorial in my favour —The second season—Mr. Whitbread's opposition—Hostile correspondence—Lord Clanricarde acts as my second—A reference to Mr. Fysche Palmer—A Jesuitical reply from a Bishop—Thesiger's retort—My whipper-in taken by the Duke of Grafton, but fails to secure the sport he had with my hounds.

ABOUT the year 1829, in the spring, I proceeded to the then pretty county town of Bedford to arrange for the hunting of the Oakley country, and to procure not only a house for myself but a kennel for my hounds.

At first I was attacked with the measles, which confined me to bed for several days, but after that house-hunting went on, and at last I found myself, as I thought, comfortably settled at Harrold Hall, upon the River Ouse, a near neighbour of a much-valued old hunting friend of mine when I kept stag-hounds, Mr. Magniac, who rented Colworth, near Sharnbrook, a place of which he has since by purchase become the possessor. With the house at Harrold I also took some splendid woods for the preservation of foxes and

FOXHOUNDS.

game, and some excellent partridge shooting, as well as some rough fishing. What with the building of sufficient kennels on the premises for seventy couples of hounds, and stabling for one or two-and-twenty hunters, and the recovering, and for a time keeping, litters of cubs, which I contrived to rescue from people's hands, who had taken them on the plea that the country was not going to be hunted—I had enough to do.

When the kennels were finished, and my hounds came from Cranford to Harrold, many farmers and inhabitants of the little town turned out to meet me; and I was received, surrounded by my pack, with the ringing of the church-bells and other gratulations.

My pack to begin the first season, consisted of sixteen couples of the pick of my foxhounds from Berkeley Castle, with which I had hunted stag, a few couples of old foxhounds too old to be kept by their former owners—and parted with only because they could not run up—from Sir R. Sutton's, and Sir John Cope's, and Colonel Wyndham's (Sussex) kennels. The rest were a screaming, tearing lot of unentered puppies, able, willing, and clever enough in shape to do anything; it was for me and a few old steady hounds to show them what to do, and to bring them to their right condition. Forty couples of young hounds being double the number with which most huntsmen have to deal.

I was prepared for difficulty; but a magnificently extensive and severe woodland, reaching from the Duke of Manchester's, Kimbolton Castle, across Bed-

VOL. I.   Y

fordshire, through Yardley Chase; Lord Northampton's, to Salsey Forest, and into Buckinghamshire ; independent of the open country running down to Lord Fitzwilliam's, and extending in another direction by Woburn Abbey up into Hertfordshire—gave me hope that, as the day of cub-hunting commenced there always in the first week in July, and the immense woodlands were well off for foxes, by the time my fixtures were given out for the regular season, I should at least be able to show some sport. The foxes were all stump-bred, and a cub in July knew as much of the woods as an earth-bred cub in other countries did in September.

To aid me as whips, in my first season I had, as first whip, Tom Skinner, from Mr. Hay ; and a man from the Salisbury kennel, whom I took as second whip, who could have done nothing more with the hounds he claimed to come from than ride after Lady Salisbury, for he was as ignorant of the sport as a babe unborn. Tom Skinner was a very good man : a splendid horseman, a good sportsman, and quick as lightning in his work with hounds, with but one fault attached to him, which, under me, he never let me observe in the field— he was addicted to liquor.

So possessed of hounds, and so handed, I began my first season. I had health and strength, and the will to work. I was as much lord of those wild woods as if they all had been my own. Mrs. Berkeley was charmed with her new residence and two splendid horses she used to ride—a beautiful brown mare I called Norna, purchased of Horace Seymour, and

LEADING HOUNDS. 323

a grey mare called Giantess, which I bought of
Venables at Henley; and I was as happy as the day
was long.

It was not long before I saw that the almost total
absence of riot in these severe and tangled copse-woods,
matted with blackthorn and briar, around Harrold,
Odell, and Lavendon, cut into very available rides, was
to prove a most favourable circumstance to my beginning; for if I could only get the puppies from my
horse's heels, if they of themselves spoke, it was a
thousand to one but they proclaimed the presence of
a fox, because there was nothing else save an occasional martin, cat, or badger, that could excite their
attention. Old Stamford's long-drawn, melodious,
French horn-like note—he bore Sir Richard Sutton's
mark, and was the best finder I ever saw—very soon
got the tearing youth to cry; and from his tongue
being so peculiar, and never wrong, after a time
the bushes used to crack again when, from the midst
of some thick quarter of the cover, he flung up his
dear, sagacious head, and called for clamorous aid.

I picked him out of a lot of hounds offered me for
sale, with another old hound called Proctor, on
account of their sagacious looks; both were branded
on the side as the property of the late Sir Richard
Sutton. I think Stamford, who had the appearance
of being very old, must have been hawked about as a
draft for some time, and rejected for that reason; for
when I first saw him he was drooping, downcast, and
dejected. The instant that I addressed to him that
sort of, to them engaging, dog-language, of which

Y 2

every huntsman and dog-owner *should* be master, the fine old hound was himself again; and when once more introduced to a clean and ample foxhound kennel, he went in with a proud step and his stern up, as if he felt reinstated in his due position, and in the possession of one to whom he could attach himself as the director of his future exertions.

Of course, with such an over-cry of active young hounds, it was difficult to achieve the death of an old fox, unless by some fortunate circumstance; but plenty of cubs and lots of old foxes, combined with the greatest personal exertion, and in the larger woodlands very little riot, very soon enabled me to go out with such a crashing pack as made the woodlands ring again, and sent out many a hitherto idle old fox to smaller and more quiet places in the open, against the meets of the regular season.

From the first week in July till October, as the French say of a wild boar, my head was always under cover; and never before or since, as I have been told, had the great cub-hunting woods been so rattled.

For the cub-hunting work I bought ponies, or young horses of three or four years old; the latter large enough to make harness-horses, if they did not turn out hunters, for my men; or, if one in three made a hunter, in value then that one reimbursed me for the others. For these young horses I never went beyond 30*l.*, and one of them I sold for 350*l.*, one for 90*l.*, and another for 70 guineas; the worst always fetched for harness the full amount of, or more than the original cost. The ponies, too, included some of

NASTY FEELING.

the most useful creatures I ever saw; and, unless with favourite exceptions, were all again sold at the conclusion of the cub-hunting time.

Old Dick Perkins, of Sharnbrook, was the dealer close at hand, who was always on the look-out for me for anything clever, and from him I bought in almost every instance.

I began, then, the hunting of the Oakley country with many natural difficulties to contend against, and under an assurance from the Duke of Bedford, Lord Tavistock, Lord Ludlow, and other proprietors, that I had their confidence and leave, and that they would have nothing whatever to do with the Oakley Club, with which, as I have explained, they had been at variance before my arrival. I took care to have this assurance very distinctly made to me, because I foresaw that there was a nasty feeling existing in the Club, who, under the direction of Mr. S. Whitbread, had met with a good deal of snubbing from the chief proprietors, about the sale of Lord Tavistock's hounds, and which feeling I felt sure would show itself in one way or other.

I came into Bedfordshire as the chosen man of the higher party, and the Club came into me because it was to be myself, or no one else, and they hoped to tolerate me for a time, and then get rid of me by a side wind as easily as they could. When I say "they," I by no means include several excellent gentlemen who belonged to the Club.

With many difficulties, then, I commenced my first season, and though I had not, of course, the sport that the county had had, under the late old establishment of Lord Tavistock, or that I attained to in succeeding years, nevertheless I had quite as much as I could reasonably expect, and the yeomanry and farmers of the county over whose land I hunted, and who the oftenest saw the exertions I was making, and the care I manifested to do as little mischief as possible, took to me with the greatest good-fellowship and kindness, and rendered me all the assistance in their power—no small step towards attaining the sport at which I aimed.

It was not long before the temper of the Oakley Club, under Mr. S. Whitbread, exhibited itself. Every failure in the field, whether caused by the atmosphere or the dash of my wild and tearing over-cry of puppies, was attributed to me, and though no one at first spoke out, I could hear snarling remarks pass among the secretary's disciples—they were but a small clique—and all to my disparagement. Occasionally some foolish man was pushed forth to give me advice, but I at once laid down a rule that I would admit of no sort of interference in kennel or field. I had taken on myself to hunt the country, and on me alone should any consequences rest.

The clique in the Club were getting more and more loud against me behind my back, when one day, if I remember rightly, from Mr. Higgins's gorse, near Turvey, or at all events from that side of the county, we fell in with a flying fox and a scent, though not first-rate, to which my young hounds could address themselves. The upshot of it was—such a hard day in the then deep state of the country, and all of it over the open—that not only were all the horses beaten, including my second horse, but one of the malcontents under Mr. Whitbread, who had been most bitter against me, and who was neither a good nor a hard rider, killed his best horse, while at the same time the horse of my second whipper-in died.

I remember the intense satisfaction it gave me to see these fellows blobbing along at a trot on regularly done-up horses, in the course of the day, thoroughly wishing themselves safe out of it and at home, but not daring to leave me, because I kept good-humouredly cheering them along, with the sly advice to them to over-ride my hounds, *if they could!*

I am certain on that day in some of the double hedges or spinnies that we changed foxes; the sport terminated only when everything except the hounds was run to a stand-still.

On learning the mischief that had been done to my own stable as well as to some of the horses of my field, I ordered my second horse, who was the freshest, to be jogged gently on, to a bootmaker at Harrold, named Allen, and at once to put into the spare stall occasioned by my horse's death, a bay horse for whom he had asked me thirty pounds. I feared that some one else should buy him. That horse, to whom I gave the name of Ready, was the one I rode for five years, and then when I had ceased to keep hounds, permitted the late Lord Fitzhardinge to tempt me out of him by the offer of three hundred and fifty guineas. I never regretted anything more than the fact of parting with a horse which no money ever replaced, and who was as perfect across the country as he was good-tempered and beautiful.

From the time of this severe run the sport improved. All things being taken into consideration, the clique in the Oakley Club soon saw that they had no *casus belli* to lay hold of, as to the establishment at Harrold Hall, for there were twenty hunters, and from sixty to seventy couples of hounds for four days a week—not a bit too many in that severe country, and with a view to litters of puppies. Failing, then, any legitimate ground of complaint, a quarrel was attempted with me in that, my first year, by a sort of round robin, put forward under the secretaryship of Mr. Whitbread, containing the threat, that if I did not cease to hunt my own hounds, and keep an additional servant in that capacity, the Club would discontinue its support, and at once open negotiations with my successor.

That in fact conveyed a resolution, or rather a threat, not only to cease subscribing to me a year short of their declared and bonded time, but also to deprive me of the country, and to gainsay the permission of the great landed proprietors which I had in the first instance obtained.

Thinking that I could rely on the promises of the great proprietors, and particularly on those made to me by the house of Bedford, which amounted to the independent assurance of their support, and that I must fight my own battle with this coterie, with whom the proprietors would have nothing to do, I felt no sort of hesitation in my reply, and it was as follows :—

I refused to keep an additional servant, or to abstain from the long-indulged and loved occupation of hunting my own hounds; and moreover assured the Club, that if I found any gentleman—I cared not who he might be—in treaty with the Club for my country while I chose to hunt it by leave of the landed proprietors, I should fix upon him a personal quarrel. In the meantime, if any gentleman in the Club who was really dissatisfied with me would come openly to assure me that he regretted the support he had bound himself to give for two years, and to which I could hold them all if I pleased, as bound to continue for the specified time, I would, on individual application, give each a cheque for the half-year they had paid up, and cancel their obligation for the future.

Not a man accepted these terms, but the Club, as to any open assault, shut up. They found means, however, to my utter astonishment, of moving the house of Bedford to take the very step against me from which it assured me it would abstain; and Lord Tavistock informed me in writing that, in deference to the Club, I had better give up the country, "on account of my unpopularity." This of course produced a sharp remonstrance from me, in which I pointed out that his lordship was not recognising the pledge I had in the first instance received; that I had the leave of the landed proprietors, and must *fight my own battle with the Club*. I begged no favour, but simply to be left to do so, as I well knew that the unpopularity existed only in regard to the wishes of a small

330   MEMORIAL IN MY FAVOUR.

and insignificant clique, whose hostility, if left alone, I could very easily dispose of. By way of proving to Lord Tavistock that by listening to false counsellors he had erroneously deserted me, and been wanting to himself, I then and there told the yeomen and farmers the step the Club had taken, and the unexpected line assumed by Lord Tavistock on the influence of that which I conceived to be misrepresentation.

My appeal to them was at once met by the instantaneous adoption of a memorial to the house of Bedford, certainly, to my mind, one of the handsomest things that a Master of Hounds, a foreigner to the soil, could by any possibility receive. It stated in the most firm but respectful terms, " that they had heard with regret of the charge of unpopularity made against me, and that they therefore wished to assure the house of Bedford, and all the proprietors within the limits of the hunt, that, instead of any unpopularity or complaints of any kind existing against me, they, in a body, as the persons with whom I naturally came the oftenest in contact, and whose interests as to the chase were always more or less in my keeping, were but too happy to continue that support to me they had hitherto given, and which they deemed me so well to deserve, and therefore they humbly hoped that I should not be deserted by their landlords, or by those who, like many of them, had landed possessions of their own." This memorial, worded to that effect, was signed by the tenantry of Woburn as well as by the leading yeomanry around me. It had its effect. Lord Tavistock wrote to me

CHANGES FOR THE BETTER. 331

to say it was a most satisfactory document, and all further opposition for the time subsided.

On the following season, my immense force of young able hounds began to come into very sanguinary play. I had much less trouble in obtaining blood; there were no litters of foxes stolen ; and my sport was far superior to that in the first year. I discharged my inefficient second whipper-in, had put Harry Skinner, Tom's brother, in his place, eventually having reason to find fault with the sobriety of my first man, Tom Skinner, and I think, at the close of the second season, on Lorraine Smith's recommendation, I took George Carter from my neighbour the Duke of Grafton, put him over Tom Skinner's head as first whipper-in, promoted Harry, if I remember rightly, to the second place at Berkeley Castle, and made Tom my second man. Then really came the most happy hunting days of my huntsman's life. My pack became perfect from the very fact of their earlier inefficiency. I had an immense body of vigorous, well-entered, and hard-working hounds, in their third season, backed again by two-year hunters, and aided. by such older hounds who had proved themselves well up to the mark, and had sprung out of those which I had first entered to Reddeer.

There was no trouble in finding, and not much difficulty in killing the stout foxes of Bedfordshire, and my men, thoroughly knowing and adapting themselves to my manner and method with hounds, understood their places and mine, not only in difficulties, but to guard against difficulties arising. When severed by the wide quarters of the heavy woodlands, a peculiar touch on our horns to each other, telegraphed any alteration in the run. We could speak by our horns, instead of only making a senseless tooting, as is but too often the case among masters and men ; and from end to end of run, hounds, master, and men understood and could assuredly rely upon each other's aid.

In ticklish or uncertain scents, the only thing to be kept in order was the field; and in restraining those who need only to be spoken to when the hounds were *not* running, I had served a good apprenticeship in Middlesex, so I contrived pretty well to enforce fair play.

At the end of the two years for which subscriptions were pledged, and in which my sport was increasing day by day, Mr. S. Whitbread, and the clique in the Club, again showed their teeth by announcing the end of their assistance. This demonstration was met by me with a counter one, that I should hunt the country without it, and trust for sufficient support to those who intended to make use of the establishment in my possession. The subscription fund immediately arose to a larger amount than the first two years afforded, and the enmity which existed in a smothered state from the very first moment of my arrival died, in relation to any collective capacity, the death which it so thoroughly deserved.

It then came to my ears, from an authority I could not doubt, that Mr. S. Whitbread was in the habit of going about to the houses of residents in my hunting

PERSONAL REFERENCES. 333

country in an endeavour to shake their reliance in
me by saying I had made some promise that I had
not fulfilled, and that " I had forfeited my word." A
lady who heard him assert this in presence of the late
Lord Ludlow, assured me of the fact, but under a
promise that I would not quote her as my authority,
in the event of my taking any steps to call the slan-
derer to account. Upon this I wrote at once to Mr.
S. Whitbread telling him of what I had been informed,
and warning him that if he repeated the assertion, or
words to that effect, I would at once hold him personally responsible.

In answer to this, a communication was returned to
the effect that if I repeated the threat, he should put
the affair into the hands of his second. So I of course
again sent him the notice to which he thus objected,
and the reply to that was a message conveyed to me
by a Mr. Duberley that unless I withdrew my last
announcement, I must name a second with whom he
could communicate. I instantly set about looking for
some friend to whom I could entrust the matter, and
who would take on himself such a responsibility.

In a post or two I heard from Lord Clanricarde,
who kindly informed me he was ready to act upon the
occasion; on the reception of this letter, I directly
sent the news to Mr. Duberley. Lord Clanricarde
then received anything but a handsome communication
from this Bedfordshire squire, inasmuch as in calling
his lordship's attention to the case, an endeavour was
made by him to insinuate that I had been longer than
was necessary in my reference; a most gratuitous and

334   LORD CLANRICARDE.

unfounded insinuation.   It made us laugh as we read
it; so, being resolved to maintain my position, I had
eventually to lose a day's hunting, and to appoint to
meet Lord Clanricarde and my opponents at the Swan
Inn at Bedford early on a given morning.

To be in time, I went over night to sleep at the
inn, and on the next morning was awakened by Clanricarde arriving, having ridden all the way from town,
and seating himself on the foot of my bed. Mr. S.
Whitbread and his friend were to present themselves at
an early hour.   The words were few between my
second and myself; I simply said I consigned myself
and my pair of John Manton duelling pistols which
accompanied me into his care, and was ready to fight
till all was blue if he so willed it.   His rejoinder was
similarly concise; he said that if I maintained my
position *à l'outrance*, I must give up the authority on
whose information I took my stand.   With the knowledge that Lord Ludlow was in no way friendly to
Mr. S. Whitbread in these hunting affairs, I wrote to
him at once, told him I knew that the slander of
which I had a right to complain, had been uttered in
his presence on such and such a day by Mr. S. Whitbread, and that I therefore begged of him to permit me
to quote him, as my first informant, for certain reasons
to which I was bound to submit, did not desire to
appear.

His lordship wrote in answer, that whatever had
been said in his presence, and under his roof, he looked
on as a private conversation, and not one as to which
he was bound to speak in the way of an authority for

MY SECOND.

serious proceedings. He therefore declined permitting himself to be quoted as the author of the information I had received, or similar words.

On receiving this communication, I urged on Clanricarde, that though the letter refused to let the writer be quoted as the absolute authority, still it in no way denied the hearing of the slander; and, therefore, I thought on the whole it proved that the intelligence given me by the lady was correct, as I really knew it to be, and on that we could hold our own.

The time wore on, and the opposite parties arrived, and had an interview with Lord Clanricarde; and at that interview the ground they took, as I recollect it, was, that they must call on me to withdraw my threat of holding Mr. S. Whitbread personally responsible for certain alleged conduct, or for something I imagined he had done, unless I gave up my grounds for charging him with conduct unbecoming to a gentleman; a charge against him which I had twice repeated.

Clanricarde, again urged upon me that I must withdraw the charge and threat, unless I could give him a tangible referee as to the slander I complained of.

Lord Ludlow having failed me, I then urged that it was enough that I very well knew that Mr. S. Whitbread *had said* this of me, and on that I proposed that my second should let us meet. Clanricarde hesitated for a short space, and then said, " Well, if you can lay your hand on any approved gentleman here on the spot who will take your view of your right to fight, on the premises such as they are, I will forego my own opinion in deference to his, but I will not sanction a meeting on my own responsibility alone."

On this, I immediately sent to my old friend, the late Mr. Fysche Palmer, then with Lady Madelina, who resided in Bedford, knowing, as I did, that he disliked Mr. S. Whitbread. He was therefore called in to consult with Clanricarde, but he sided in opinion with my second, and their decision ruled the matter.

Clanricarde then withdrew my letter and the threat objected to, and my opponents demanded a written apology and the right to print and publish it; but there Clanricarde at once pulled them up with a direct refusal, so they were forced to be contented as they were. Before we, Clanricarde, Palmer, and myself, separated, the former laughingly said, "that my opponents were either sure that my second would not bear me out, or that they did not feel in a position to insist on much, for they had brought no pistols."

I returned to Harrold to enjoy my hunting, and heard no repetition of the slander.

Among the reminiscences of my life I have read the inimitable sporting tale of "Soapy Sponge," and seen men exactly coming up to his description in manners, method, and attire. We have all heard and read of a reverend "Soapy Sam," and perhaps seen his likeness in the *dramatis personæ* of the world. Among the tales that have been current in my day of this latter personage, was one which consigned him to a first-class carriage, on a very full railway train, in which there was a deficiency of room. All the seats were full,

JESUITICAL REPLY. 337

except the one opposite to his reverence, and to that, for his better comfort, he had consigned his holy legs.

It so chanced that a gentleman, like a great many members of the House of Commons, in search of a place, looked in at the door of the carriage; and, addressing the bishop, asked him if the seat opposite to him was occupied. The divine replied that it was.

The seat-seeker closed the door, and had to travel in a second-class carriage, there being no room in those of the first-class. It seems that he entertained some suspicions as to the truth of the answer he had received, so when the train stopped he again came to the window and looked in. He beheld the ecclesiastic still maintaining his position.

"My Lord," he cried, in great indignation, "at least I expected the truth from you. You told me that the seat was taken!"

"I did not, sir," was the somewhat Jesuitical reply. "You asked me if that seat was *occupied,* and with much sincerity I replied in the affirmative. I regret if my adhering so strictly to facts should have caused you any discomfort."

"It *is* of no use to attempt to catch *him* out," grumbled the traveller as he retired; "if I had told him that once I had been surprised at seeing him playing at Aunt Sally near Reading, it being an occupation scarcely becoming to his holy profession, he would have replied that his health required muscular exercise; that it was but a constitutional sally, and that for the moment he went into training to better his condition

VOL. I.   z

338 LORDS CHELMSFORD AND JAMES FITZROY.

to do good. You can't get the better of him in any thing.".

Among perhaps the readiest wits of the day was Thesiger. Since he has become Lord Chelmsford, his wonderfully acute perception, powers of conversation, and readiness at repartee have not deserted him. Long may he enjoy the exercise of such gifts. He was one day walking down St. James's Street, so my informant told me, when, as he was passing a man, the stranger pulled up suddenly, and turning on Thesiger with a look of pleased recognition, exclaimed, " Mr. Birch, I believe?" " If you believe *that*, sir," he replied, " you'll believe anything !" They passed on.

It was about this time, or not very long after, that the late Lord James Fitzroy rode over to Harrold from his Grace of Grafton's, in Whittlebury Forest, to make an offer, unknown to me, to George Carter, the whipper-in his father had discharged, and whom I, at the recommendation of the late Lorraine Smith, had taken, to offer him the place of huntsman as successor to old Rose. Thus putting at the head of the hunting establishment the man who but a twelvemonth before they had looked on as the least efficient servant they had. When George came to tell me of this, I did not like parting with a useful servant not easily to be replaced, but a consideration for his interests prevailed.

" They think, sir," he said, "that if I take up the old service again, I shall bring back new sport, for no doubt they think I have something to do with the success we have been having; but I feel sure I can

LORD NORTHAMPTON'S WOODS AND GEORGE CARTER. 339

lo no such thing unless, sir, you and your hounds go along with me."

"Well, George," I replied, "I suppose there is a good deal of difference in the value of the Duke of Grafton's service as huntsman and that of mine as first whipper-in. What is it? for if I can make it up to you by an increase of wages of 40*l.* per annum, you shall have it."

He then explained to me that the wages and certain other advantages which were given to him, made a difference of over a hundred pounds as between the two situations; so I at once advised him, as his master and as his friend, to take the offer of Lord James, and for this extra reason, that I feared I should be forced, through unexpected circumstances, within a year or two to resign my hounds, whereas the service under the Duke of Grafton might last his life.

George did not like to leave me any more than I did to part with him, and it was with considerable regret on both sides, as well as dissatisfaction on mine, at this interference with a contented servant, that we settled he should go to the Duke of Grafton.

He went, but precisely as he said, my sport did *not* accompany him. It remained with me to the last hour of my hunting the country. When spring time came, and Lord Northampton's beautiful woods of Yardley Chase were resorted to by the Duke of Grafton and myself, as a neutral country in which to close the season, and perhaps kill a May fox, on our fixtures being given out, with a glance at the wind,

z 2

George Carter always prophesied whereabouts in these heavy covers I should begin "to draw," and in regard to him I could do the same thing. Many and many a time have I sat in the hollow of "Cowper's Oak," my horse walked about at a little distance, giving to the arrivals of my field a few minutes' grace, to play with my favourite hounds, and to talk to that quaint agriculturist, Longman, of the farm close by, as to his horror of rabbits and the way in which he said the keeper Longstaff used to "bamboozle the old lord" as to there not being one on the place.

Those much-loved times have never been forgotten by me, nor will they ever fade from my recollection, nor the brilliant sport of my last season there, when in Yardley Chase alone I found seventeen foxes and killed fourteen of them *with a run*.

CHAPTER XIV.

IN PARLIAMENT.

Colonel Berkeley resolves to be a peer—His secret arrangement with the Whig Government—Induces me to enter Parliament —I am returned for the Western Division of Gloucestershire— Faucit corrected in costume—Lord Edward Somerset—Absurdities of canvassing—Colonel Berkeley ennobled as Baron Segrave—Withholds my allowance—Lord William Lennox and his tricks—Lord Segrave—Letting a box—Miss Paton— Daniel O'Connell and his beagles—Mr. Disraeli—Mr. Charlton's maiden speech—Sir Robert Peel's effective elocution— Mr. Cobbett's futile attack on the statesman—My motion to admit ladies into the gallery—Mr. Maurice O'Connell kisses the Dowager Duchess of Richmond by mistake—Objections to ladies in the House—Piece of plate presented to me by them —A new idea to insure their admission into the gallery—How defeated—Mr. John Bright—His committee to inquire into the Game Laws—His Quaker witness confuted—Committee on slavery—Cobden's opinion of his friend Bright quoted by me in the House.

COLONEL BERKELEY having come to an age when the life of a strolling player and the exhibition of his fine figure in gorgeous attire upon the stage had no longer any attractions for him, by way of amusement, and, as he said, to astonish the Tories, resolved to work himself up to the creation of a peerage, his illegitimacy having been definitely settled. Towards the attainment of this object of ambition, he had no assistance to look to from any of the powerful houses, he having no friends in the higher ranks of society. He had so completely forfeited its esteem, that perhaps no would-be peer ever started in a race for rank under greater apparent disadvantages. His hopes were based on the cupidity of the Whig Government, on their thirst for the maintenance of place and power at any cost, and on his possession of immense but usurped wealth. His wealth, the influence of his wide possessions, and the sway attendant on the castle towers as they looked over the fertile acres of the rich vale of Berkeley, that had maintained them for so many centuries, from the Severn to the Hills, in all their ancient feudalism, and the willingness of the Whig Government to barter rank for support in Parliament, formed a strong foundation for success. Unless, however, these means were skilfully brought to bear, and carried out in a popular way, so that the political support that was afforded, seemed to come from the people, the Government would have been put in a difficulty as to the creation of rank, and the expenditure of money would go for nothing.

It was therefore Colonel Berkeley's object to select one of his brothers to take the first step in political arrangement, who was popular in and around the castle, and well received by all the best residents. It is true that Captain Berkeley, R.N., afterwards admiral, now created to the barony of Fitzhardinge, had, before this idea of aggrandizement entered Colonel Berkeley's head, represented the city of Gloucester, but he had made a good many enemies, was not popular, and was by no means considered likely to

A GOOD MASK.

be eligible for the representation of the Western Division. Besides this, in those .days Colonel Berkeley liked me better, or at least he seemed to do so, than any of his brothers,' and was fonder of having me with him at the castle, where, as I have already stated, I had won for myself some amount of personal popularity.

In those days of the great struggle for free trade, through Messrs. Cobden and Bright, and by them, and in that particular through my much ill-used friend, Mr. Villiers, there was a desire bruited for purity of election and extension of the suffrage, though those held up to enjoy the extension were always stigmatized by the free-trade clique as the "most ignorant" of all the civilized or half-civilized peoples of the earth, viz., the farming and the labouring classes. There was, therefore, at this time, an immense opportunity opened to the rich, by money, of raising themselves to almost any political favour they pleased—for obtaining rank for themselves, upon a certain understanding with what *par excellence* was termed the Liberal Government.

Occupied as I had been since my marriage with my quiet home and the sports of the field, and living away from my county and Berkeley Castle, and seldom going to London, I was for a time ignorant of the new, and perhaps in one phase, better ambition of Colonel Berkeley. His riches and theatrical taste had given him an entrance into the green-rooms of the great theatres in London, but he was not liked elsewhere.

Lady Charlotte Bury, in her once famous "Diary,"

says of him :—" I have written so much that I can find no room for Mrs. Dauson's masquerade, where it was said that the only good mask was Mr. Fitzhardinge in the character of Lord Berkeley."

I remember his telling me that he was in the greenroom when Faucit came in dressed for Sir Mark Chase, in the *Roland for an Oliver*, in his first appearance in that character, with his shot-belt put on hindbefore. In the belts used in those days, this was a defect that, among sportsmen, might have occasioned a laugh, so my brother went up, and taking it from Faucit's shoulders, placed it properly with his own hand, much to that inimitable actor's satisfaction.

From the life Colonel Berkeley led, he was coldly regarded, not only in society generally, but by all the county families; therefore, in his new ambition of purchasing a barony through political support to the Liberal Government, it became necessary that he should indeed adopt an acceptable local leader. He therefore put me forward to propose my friend Hanbury Tracy (the late Lord Sudeley) for Tewkesbury, and then Henry Moreton (the late Lord Ducie) for the County, prior to the passing of the Reform Bill. Tracy was rejected, but Moreton was accepted at my hands; I was not then aware that he did this intending that I should take a decided lead. My two first public speeches were from the respective hustings I have named.

It was in the year 1832, that a letter came to me at Harrold Hall, from Colonel Berkeley, in which he asked me to come forward at the next dissolution of

HIS PROPOSAL TO ME.

Parliament, for the Western Division of Gloucestershire, the county having been divided since the Reform Bill, for the passing of which measure, I had, as I said before, proposed Henry Moreton. To this proposition I had several objections. In the first place, it would break in on my home, its retirement, and my amusements; and in the second, occasion me such an increased expenditure as would at once force me to discontinue my hounds. True, Berkeley Castle and Berkeley House in London, could entertain me, but under Colonel Berkeley's domestic arrangements I could only go alone to the Castle, and as the London house was my mother's, who was then living, I could not bring Mrs. Berkeley there, with an establishment of my own; and of course I should have to saddle myself with the cost of a house, or apartments at some expensive hotel.

I did not at first state these objections: I contented myself with a desire that Colonel Berkeley would apply to one of my brothers, not situated like myself, or who might not object to entering on public life.

The answer to this from Colonel Berkeley was, that if I refused I should upset all his arrangements, and his chance of a peerage, promised him under certain circumstances by the Liberal Government, for the Western Division of the county would accept at his hands only myself; but that if I would come forward, success was perfectly certain. He coupled with his entreaties a desire to know more of my objections. He also induced my mother to write to me, to implore that I would no longer refuse.

My position, then, was a very painful one. I confess that I was charmed to see my eldest brother, to whom I was sincerely attached, thus turning from the life of a strolling player, and attempting to do better things, but at the same time I could not bear to think of an infraction of my quiet life, and a severance from a home I had found so happy.

Everybody Colonel Berkeley could move, urged me to consent to the change; at last, and on a guarantee being given me for the costs attendant on my election and public position, and for an annual allowance while I had a seat in Parliament, for the hire of a house in London to which I could bring Mrs. Berkeley, I consented, though with extreme reluctance, to come forward for the Western Division. He then sent me a list of persons for me to write to, for their political interest and support; and in full reliance on his written promise as to what he would do to enable me to bear the cost of my public position, having taken the thing in hand, I entered into it heart and soul. I not only looked to the interests of my own seat, but did all in my power to serve the interests of my younger brother, Mr. Craven Berkeley, for a seat for Cheltenham, and to secure the City of Gloucester to Captain Berkeley, which he had previously represented.

The first thing I did not much like occurred on the dissolution of Parliament, when it became necessary for me to be in the Division among the people. I received a letter from Colonel Berkeley, who was then in London, telling me that my presence was required on the spot, and directing me to take up my residence at the house of the late Mr. Ellis, then Coroner for the Division, at Wickselme, close to the castle and town of Berkeley, and to transact all business there. This I at once declined to do, and wrote back to say that the Castle was the proper place for me to direct all proceedings from, and that I should go there; accordingly, thither I went. It seems there had been a convenient understanding come to by both sides that there was to be no contest, and as far as I was concerned, I was very happy to have the gallant Lord Edward Somerset as my colleague; but this was soon put an end to, on my arrival at the Castle, by the late Augustus Moreton, the brother of Henry Moreton, who on the death of his father had become Lord Ducie. Without consulting anything but his own ambition, he proposed himself to join me in ousting Lord Edward Somerset. Augustus Moreton had some wild supporters who, having nothing to lose by a contest, and everything to get by a row, backed him on; so I at once declared that if any unobjectionable candidate came forward on my own principles, to be consistent, I could not do otherwise than assist him. I was no party to any private arrangement regarding the Division, and it was my public duty to do the best for the party to which I belonged.

I was perfectly resolved not to canvass; in the first place, because my family, owning such an acreage in the county, a request from me might be regarded by some as dictation; and in the second, as a boy, I had seen Captain Berkeley, the present Lord Fitzhardinge, in his contest with Mr. Cooper, canvassing in pot-houses in the suburbs of Gloucester, and drinking beer out of the same pot with a sweep, who had a vote, in order to win over the sooty politician, but who gave a plumper against him at last.

I shall never forget the consternation of my friends when I refused to canvass; but as I had made up my mind on the matter, I kept to the resolution. Augustus Moreton canvassed; and in the insane idea that kissing a man's wife secured the husband's good wishes, he pulled all the females about, and shook hands and drank with every fellow he met, as if acknowledging a perfect equality. I remember in the Forest of Dean being present, when he was literally canvassing a ragged pauper, pulling off his hat to him, calling him "Sir," and shaking him by the hand.

"Lord, zir," said the poor fellow, "d'ye put on thick hat a top o' the head on thee. There, Measter Moreton, it be all very well now a gammoning me in this way, time o' the election like and all; but if thee wor to meet I at any other time, thee'd ride over I, if I didn't git out o' the way."

"There, Moreton," I cried, "there's a sensible man for you, who is not to be cajoled! Leave off your nonsense, and come along."

Moreton, however, stuck to his canvass throughout; and as I turned over to him all second votes on their application for my advice, I came in considerably at the head of the poll, and brought him in second, to the defeat of the gallant Lord Edward Somerset.

Colonel Berkeley was much pleased with the success in the Western Division, though he did not relish the incoming of Augustus Moreton, and with the success in the city and largest town of the county, for which two of my brothers were returned.

On the understanding to which he had told me that he had come with the Liberal Government, he sounded me—for I cannot say that he put any direct questions—as to my feelings in regard to his being created to any one of the four baronies which were included in the Earldom of Berkeley. They were "Berkeley," "Segrave," "Mowbray," and "Braose of Gower." I asked which he desired. He replied, "Mowbray or Segrave;" but to me he never mentioned the other two.

Up to this time I had lived in such thoroughly true affection towards him, that from education as well as from heart I really had no other thought in the world but to serve him, and indeed all my brothers; and from my first appearance in the House of Commons it was often remarked, among the members, "how the Berkeleys stood together."

The answer I made to him then, to his indirect questions, was that, as far as I was concerned, I had no objection to make, but every wish that he should be created to one of the titles he had named. He regarded me intently while I made this reply, and, without further remark, let the subject drop.

This again set me thinking on matters touching the Earldom, to which I was the heir-presumptive. As I said before, education, perversion of facts, and systematic

350   A PUZZLING QUESTION.

delusion, aided by the intense affection entertained by
me for my father in his lifetime, and for my mother,
brothers, and sisters since his death, my conviction too
that all they did and said was true, and that they would
not mislead or seek to injure me, had brought me to
but one conclusion, and that was the one in which I
had been educated ; viz., that my elder brothers were
all legitimate, that time only was wanting to convince
the erring mind of the world to that effect, and to re-
instate the eldest in his just rank as Earl of Berkeley.

On this indirect application of Colonel Berkeley to
me as to his being *created* to a portion of that to
which I had been taught to think him justly entitled,
I thought deeply and long; and not many days afterwards, when we were *tête-à-tête* in the library at the
Castle, I suddenly asked him if being created to a
seat in the Peers was not a virtual abandonment of
his claim to be the legitimate head of the family,
and shut him out from further proceedings to maintain it.

He evidently did not like that question, as coming
from me. He made the excuse that it would not shut
him out from the earldom, as the barony being within
the great title, it would be only a step gained in
advance.

When the second year of my public position had
come nearly to an end, I found that the promised two
hundred and fifty pounds a year had not for this, the
second year, been paid into my bankers, so I wrote to
Lord Segrave to tell him that it was due. From him I
received a letter in reply, unintelligible in some respects

LORD SEGRAVE.

351

to me, saying, "If faith in regard to money matters has not been kept with you, I have no hesitation in saying that it is the greatest breach of honesty I ever knew. You distinctly declined to come forward into public life unless you had an increase of income, and I shall write to my mother to tell her so."

On receiving this strange letter, as I had never any communication with my mother on the matter, I at once wrote to Lord Segrave and told him so, adding, "that I came forward at his wish, and to get him made a peer, and that I distinctly stated my disinclination to public life, as well as the terms that were absolutely necessary to enable me to meet the increased expenses, so that I should hold him to the terms agreed upon in his letter."

Before I received his answer, a communication came to me from my mother at Cranford, saying, that she found she was to be forced to pay me two hundred and fifty pounds a year while I continued in Parliament, an exaction she could very ill afford, and that if she did not do so, Lord Segrave threatened to stop that sum out of an allowance he made to her brother, his uncle, Mr. Tudor, who, from the false evidence he had given before the Peers in endeavouring to prove Lord Segrave legitimate, had been obliged to fly the country and forfeit his employment under Government.

I confess that this letter from my poor mother disconcerted me a good deal, for I foresaw that my duty and affection to her would not permit me to let her be inconvenienced, while at the same time I doubted if I could force Lord Segrave to keep faith with me, as he, knowing that I was publicly hampered by position, a growing popularity, and an increasing number of friends, would come to the opinion that, for their sake, and the interests of party, I would not at once accept the Chiltern Hundreds.

On receiving this letter from my mother, and without waiting for his reply to my former note, I wrote to Lord Segrave expressing my astonishment at the treatment I had met with, and telling him that in this transaction I should look to no one but himself, as I declined to be indebted to my mother. I should therefore expect that he would pay me the whole of the arrears that might accrue while in Parliament, during my mother's life, when at her death her jointure reverted to his hands.

To this he merely answered, "Very well."

As I expected, the loss occasioned to me by so considerable a diminution of my income fell very heavy. My West India property, too, was failing me, under the tilt run against it by the would-be saints, and though the subscription raised for my hounds in the county, totally independent of the Oakley Club, was larger than in the first two years, I became painfully conscious of the necessity of curtailing my expenses.

Lord Segrave's honours did not bring with them the consideration he seemed to have expected.

Indeed, he was now almost cut for certain outrages upon the decencies of society to which I cannot further allude, and wherever his name had been subjected to the ballot in any Club, he had been black-balled. Few

LORD WILLIAM LENNOX. 353

came to see him, and these were chiefly persons from the country, very old friends, and men who had known him from a boy. Lord William Lennox was one of the select few who then visited at Berkeley House, and he was there almost every day. Their conversation was exclusively about theatrical ladies.

"Where do you dine to-night?" William Lennox used to ask, with a wink at me or at my brother Augustus, if he were in the room.

This used to put me into a fit of mirth, as in the event of Lord Segrave not having an engagement to dine out anywhere, which he seldom had, I knew what would be forthcoming, and so did the questioner.

"Where you like," was the answer.

"Shall I order dinner, then?"

"Yes."

Then turning to me, Lord Segrave used to say, "Will you come?"

If Augustus was not in the room, William Lennox, who had had, in all probability, some previous communication with him, put the question—

"Shall I ask Augustus?"

"Yes, if you like."

William Lennox now exultantly went forth to order dinner at the Clarendon, or elsewhere.

My friend Willox, as in these days we used to call him, as an abbreviation of his name, had an immense appreciation of fun, and for the sake of his joke used to do the oddest things imaginable. Thus, on one occasion at some dinner at a tavern, the money was

VOL. I.   A A

354   QUESTIONABLE JOKE.

given him to settle the bill and pay the waiters, when,
on rising to take his departure, Lord Segrave, to his
intense astonishment, instead of seeing the invariably
most liberally-paid waiters bowing him out obsequi-
ously, cloth in hand, became aware that they glanced
at him with discontented—indeed, rather terror-
stricken—countenances, for they were afraid to speak
to him.   He saw at once that there was something in
the wind.

"Well, what the devil's the matter with you?" he
cried to the head waiter; "ain't you satisfied?"

The latter silently held out his hand, and his lordship saw in it what would have been a reasonable gift
from any one else, but which amounted to very far
short of that he had intended to bestow.

"Hallo!" he cried, "Master Willox, here's some
mistake; lug out the money."

This was done.   The trick was solely intended for
our amusement, but it was a dangerous joke.   Nothing
could be more rash than such experiments on a
temper like that of Lord Segrave; and once Lord
William went on to such an extent that, as we did not
see him for some days, we feared that he had met
with some violent treatment.

Every season he took a box at Drury Lane and
Covent Garden, or at the Opera.   On one occasion
after he had come up to town, he was called back to
Berkeley Castle on business, which he calculated
might last, if I remember rightly, a fortnight or more.
On this he sent for Lord William Lennox, told him
he was about to leave London, as he thought for a

specified time, and during that space put his boxes at his service, to take anybody to them he liked.

He went into the country, but his business there having terminated earlier than he expected, he wrote up to Willox at once to say, "I am instantly coming back to town, so you must not put any of your friends into my boxes any more." Lord Segrave arrived, and that same evening proceeded to the theatre. He came to the private box-door, and, with his lady—I forget which of them—stared at the bowing boxkeeper, and stalked up the lobby on his wonted way. When nearing the door of what he thought was still his box, on perceiving that the boxkeeper did not fly at once to open the door, but stood as if not knowing exactly what to do, he, in a voice of thunder, exclaimed, "Well; my box, you fool!"

The man fumbled his list from top to bottom, and then stammered forth, "Your lordship has got no box; the one you had has been let by Lord William Lennox."

On hearing this, if the latter could have seen the effect of his joke in the expression of voice and feature of his irascible friend, he would have felt quite justified in keeping out of his way. I believe Lord Segrave then went to the Opera, where the same scene as to no box was enacted over again.

I used in those days to be a good deal at Wonerch with the present Lord Grantley, and Colonel Berkeley (it was before he was ennobled) resolved to come to the neighbouring town of Guildford to play at the theatre. In these strolling amusements of his he was

A A 2

usually accompanied by my brother Augustus, and occasionally by my old friend Mr. Dawkins, all of them excellent actors; and of course Colonel Berkeley was most desirous of playing to the best actresses of the day.

On this occasion at Guildford, I remember Colonel Berkeley telling me that Willox, as he called him, had offered to bring the celebrated Miss Paton down —afterwards known as Lady William Lennox, before she became Mrs. Wood—if he, Lord Segrave, would " do the thing handsome, and stand the money for the post-horses to the carriage." This suggestion was jumped at by the amateur, and a handsome sum, he did not tell me its amount, was given for the purpose. " He brought her down," growled my brother, " by the pair-horse coach, and put the posting money in his pocket."

In spite of this reckless determination to have his fun, there was no one whom Lord Segrave desired to have about him more than he did William Lennox; and I remember his telling me he should like to see him in Parliament, for he was sure he had the capabilities of a close debater. As to his fitness for finance he said nothing.

Among my Parliamentary acquaintances, one of the most kind and agreeable I had was the late " Liberator," as he was called, Daniel O'Connell. Many an hour have we sat in the lobby of the House of Commons during an uninteresting debate, in which he has amused me with tales of " ould Ireland ;" for in regard to his fatherland and its history—

MR. O'CONNELL. 357

legendary, romantic, or political—he was as a mighty book.

I had a very sincere regard for him. He was passionately fond of hunting with his harriers on his native mountains, starting for the trail of a hare by daybreak in the morning; and then it was, on taking the teetotal pledge, that he told me he missed his glass of whisky. He said, however, that he found a very strong cup of coffee an efficient substitute for the potheen, and that at last he never missed it.

His dislike to a greyhound, or to the death of a hare by any means except beagles, was amusing. In one of our conversations in the lobby, a member joined us just at the time O'Connell was assuring me he spoke French so fluently, that at times he even thought in French—the greatest proof of perfection in the acquirement of that language.

The member who had joined us observed rather flippantly, "Come, come, Mr. O'Connell, that wont do."

"Some people never think at all," retorted the Liberator.

The other felt the hit and walked away.

I was in the House when D'Israeli made his first speech and failed, not because he did not speak to the purpose, nor because his delivery was bad. He spoke in rather too flowery language for a dry matter-of-fact subject, and simply because he did so the idle part of his audience, who, in the House of Commons, are ever trying to ridicule all that is above them, laughed him down. He was the only man I ever heard who, while being jeered, told the House with even menacing action, "The time *shall* arrive when you will be *glad* to hear me." The prophecy was fulfilled.

The late Mr. L. Charlton tried to make a maiden speech, and rising in his place with a *very bald head*, known too as he was to everybody, as one of the oldest stagers in all the ways of the world, he began with great affectation of inexperience, and with an exceedingly mild voice—

"Mr. Speaker—I am but a young member."

On hearing this assertion from so well known and crafty a man, possessing so venerable a pate, the entire House roared with laughter. Twice he stopped, and three times he commenced with these words; but it was useless; the House would not listen, and he never to my knowledge essayed to speak again, or if he did, the sight of his bald head set his audience in a roar.

One of the speeches which, in my opinion, told more than any other, was that delivered by the late Sir Robert Peel, when he was describing an agrarian outrage in Ireland, and quoting from the evidence of a little child who, from the top of a bedstead beheld the murder of an entire family; the little one owed its escape to having been tossed up where it was by its parents on the approach of the murderers, to be out of the way.

I heard old Cobbett's very foolish attack on the late Sir R. Peel when he moved an address of the House to the Queen to "remove Sir Robert from the list of her counsellors," and I heard Peel's withering reply, and then assisted in an unanimous cheer to the late

Lord Spencer (then Lord Althorp), on his moving that
Mr. Cobbett's motion should be forthwith " expunged
from the minutes of the House."

. While serving in Parliament, I was a good deal
fettered by the urgent requests of Lord Segrave as to
my not taking any political line without consulting
him. Thus in many a debate, when a chance of joining in it was offered, the opportunity was let slip,
because I was uncertain of the view he would take.
All who are acquainted with the business of the House
are aware how very seldom a chance to make a hit
occurs, unless a member gives up his whole time and
attention to look for it. Fettered thus, I turned my
thoughts to sport and pleasure, and merely attended
to affairs of State when put on Committees, or called on
to record a vote on some great public measure.

I must not forget the attempt made by me to procure a better gallery, whence the ladies might listen
to the debates, nor the fun we had in the House
when some of the oldest members in it rose to oppose
the leave I asked for, and assured the Speaker that " if
ladies were permitted to sit undisguised in the gallery,
the feelings of these gallant old soldiers and gentlemen would be so excited and turned from political
affairs that they would not be able to do their duty to
their country."

To prevent my elders being thus led astray, I proposed a trellis-work, or partial screen, betwixt the collective gaze of the House and the assembled beauty, and
tenderly alluded to a certain incident that took place in
the old dark hole, or " lantern," when the late Maurice

360   A KISS IN THE DARK.

O'Connell expected his charming wife to be there to hear one of his first speeches. By some accident her arrival was delayed. The place being quite dark, and the affectionate husband expecting and thinking of but one female, was led by his ear to the flutter made by flowing drapery, when on offering a conjugal embrace, he had his arms much fuller than he expected with the then Dowager Duchess of Richmond.

In spite of all opposition, leave was obtained to appoint a Committee to consider the best way of carrying out the resolution of the House for an alteration in the gallery; having achieved this I mounted my horse and rode into the Park, where the news had spread before me. On entering on the grass by the water, several groups of ladies and gentlemen who were riding together, cheered me.

We had very good fun on the Committee, and one dear, gallant old soldier, now no more, who served on it, asked me " what I could be thinking of to propose a gallery for women; you're married," he continued, " and you ought to have remembered that when a man is in Parliament the business of the House is always an excellent excuse for not being at home. If you get a comfortable gallery, and make an attendance at the debates a fashion among women, we shall always have our wives looking us up."

" Then why don't you move for a skulking-room for men ?" I retorted. " But at all events you have got the library, where you can be supposed to be reading or writing, if your better half should be scanning the benches and not see you; so, old boy, you may do 'em yet."

We studied an alteration in the ladies' gallery and got it through, but when I moved its adoption in the House, Lord John Russell rose, and was dead against it, and on a division I was beaten on the question of supply. However, the attempt, though openly defeated, covertly worked some good, and improvements, though not to the extent I wanted, were made.

A subscription was then set on foot by the ladies for the presentation to me of a piece of plate, in token of their approbation; but certain of their lords and masters thought proper to put a veto against it, and the amount collected was much circumscribed. It did not prevent a fund being raised, however, nor many ladies who were forbidden to contribute to it, doing so, and I had several letters telling me to look at certain initial letters on the subscription list, explaining who they really represented.

A very pretty figure of one of the graces, bearing a basket of flowers, was then purchased and presented to me, with the following inscription :—

"Presented, A.D. 1841, to the Hon. Grantley Berkeley, M.P., by some ladies, in token of their approbation of his having advocated their claim to admission to hear the debates in the House of Commons, and obtained, by a majority of 153 to 104, a resolution that ladies should have access to a gallery, the carrying into effect of which resolution was afterwards opposed by Lord John Russell, and defeated by him on a question of supply."

It went much against my inclinations thus to have the measure defeated, as it were, by a side wind, so I set about looking into the real state of affairs, which, according to the express rules of the House prevented ladies from at any time taking their places in the strangers' gallery, and I found that no law of the House affected the sex of the "strangers" named for exclusion, but that "all strangers," "reporters" and all, were merely there on sufferance. Custom alone prevented ladies from applying for, or gaining admission to the "Strangers' Gallery." An idea struck me that would at least create some fun, and it was to get a large party of ladies together, who would put on long military cloaks, such as I used to wear when in the Guards, over their dresses, and men's hats, and in that attire ascend to the Strangers' Gallery, and passing the porters, which, mingled with gentlemen, they could easily have done, take their seats in the gallery, and then, by doffing their hats and cloaks, disclose their sex to the astonished eyes of the Speaker.

I would have been in my place, with plenty of supporters to have defended their position, and as the gallery, by any "standing rule of the House," could only have "been cleared of strangers," we could have insisted that if the ladies "must withdraw," so must all the men, and every one of the "reporters of the press." The ayes and noes thus in antagonism, would have made, as Sir Lucius O'Trigger says, "a very pretty quarrel" as they would have stood, and the matter for the time have been scarcely within any prospect of settlement. An enactment of the House could only have ended the business, by thereafter defining the sex of the strangers.

MR. JOHN BRIGHT.

At first I thought that this attempt would have been made, for very many women in society, amused with the idea, agreed to put themselves under my direction, but, alas! that old and terribly true saying that "anything known to more than two never is a secret," told against me in this instance. My female volunteers let the affair escape their camp before I had said a word of it to mortal man, and the rumour getting abroad, the supposed-to-be wiser heads prevailed, and the experiment was abandoned.

In those days all our sporting institutions had to stand the attack of the leading demagogues, who seemed to be sent to Parliament to assail everything that rendered the possession of landed estates and the life of a country gentleman agreeable. Among these assailants was the present Mr. John Bright, a man with a great flow of words, of some brains, but of a belligerent and fault-finding temper, so stormy, that rather than not dispute, he would create an error, no matter how slight the grounds on which it was erected, for the simple reason of running his head against it. Taking the institutions of America as his great model for the happy arrangement of all countries under the sun, but more particularly for the reconstruction of the time-honoured constitution of England— a prodigious mistake, as circumstances have since declared—he also set to work to obtain from the House of Commons a Committee to "inquire into the working of the Game Laws," with a view to procure sufficient evidence to enable him to move their abrogation.

364 COMMITTEE ON THE GAME LAWS.

He obtained leave to nominate this Committee. The members were named to serve on it, and I was appointed to lead against Mr. Bright, on the side of the game laws, and the interests of the landed proprietors.

The Committee consisted of the following members :—

SESSION 1845.

Mr. Bright.	Mr. Villiers.
Mr. Burroughs.	Mr. Banks.
Lord George Bentinck.	Mr. Etwall.
Mr. Milner Gibson.	Mr. Grantley Berkeley.
Mr. Bouverie.	Mr. Manners Sutton.
Mr. Cripps.	Mr. George Cavendish.
Viscount Clive.	Mr. Trelawney.
Mr. Forbes Mackenzie.	

Mr. Manners Sutton called to the Chair.

At starting, I foresaw that it would be necessary to gain an insight into the characters of certain persons who were almost sure of being brought forward by Mr. Bright—persons who most likely had been punished by the laws they would now endeavour to upset, and therefore could not be considered important or trustworthy. To secure this, it was agreed by the Committee that Mr. Bright and myself should give each other three clear days' notice of the addresses of any witnesses we were about to call. This arrangement to me was very agreeable, because I knew that I should call only the most respectable people, with one or two exceptions, when I could lay my hand on

A QUAKER WITNESS. 365

reclaimed trespassers and thieves of game. The large landed proprietors were well known to me, and on their testimony I could rely. Such would be the source whence I should derive my information, whereas Mr. Bright would have to accept evidence from men who offered themselves to his notice—who came revengefully to prevaricate, as they thought safely, because they were not examined upon oath.

This Committee, one of the longest I ever was on, sat continually for two sessions, during which Mr. Bright and myself very frequently came into sharp collision. One of his witnesses was a Quaker and a seedsman, who, as might be expected from a "friend," was very unfriendly to those neighbours who happened to differ with him in religious opinions. This man recounted many instances that came within his knowledge, when, in one season favourable to game, a large quantitiy of seed *that had been bought of him was sown* over preserved estates, every atom of which had been destroyed and eaten up by game, so that not a blade appeared in the spring. When I cross-examined him, from inquiries made around his residence, and among his unfortunate customers, I elicited that not only did *none of the seed he sold* that year ever come up on estates where there was game, but none of it had come up anywhere else. In fact, his customers had deserted him because the seed was found to be worthless, had no vitality in it, and refused to grow even in the most favoured situations.

Another witness on the same side—a Quaker, too, I believe—gave the Committee a glowing account of the commiseration and public sympathy that were universally exhibited towards offenders against the game laws; so, when it came to my turn to cross-examine, I asked him if he had not known misplaced commiseration and sympathy evinced by a mistaken public to other and much worse offenders against the law than poachers.

"I have not," he replied.

"Are you not aware," I then demanded, "that the public showed great sympathy for and memorialized the Home Office in favour of the remission of the sentence on a Quaker named Tawell, for the horrible and disgusting murder of a woman with whom he cohabited?"

He was obliged to admit that he had, at the same time stoutly denying that the murderer was a Quaker, because, since the murder, they had read him out.

The encounters of our wits and the failure of Mr. Bright's attempt on the game laws are very well known, so they need not be repeated here.

I was also on another very long and tedious Committee, in which I was appointed to lead against Mr., now Sir Benjamin Hawes. It was an inquiry into the state of slavery as existing in the British West India Colonies, and the interests of the Colonial proprietors, of whom I unfortunately was one. Mr. Bright, with his accustomed pugnacity and inclination to abuse all institutions that were of long standing, had been repeatedly on his legs talking of Colonial affairs and interests, of which he was really profoundly ignorant. He declared himself opposed to slavery, and for immediate abolition; but with that crotchet in his head, there seemed to be no idea of gradual improvement, and not the slightest care for the means by which what he called "the object of humanity" should be reached.

Thus it appeared from all he and his coadjutors urged, that they cared nothing for the unfortunate white proprietors, their homes and their children, so long as freedom, in its abstract sense, was given to the blacks. Whether the latter were in a condition at once to receive it, or whether it would not have been better for all to have approached the change gradually and with due care and justice, never seemed to be worth considering. England was therefore hurried into a most unjustly carried-out Act, the Government pledge of apprenticeship was broken, and when a mere pittance was given to the ruined proprietors of land, they were insultingly told that they had received ".compensation."

In addition to this, Parliament passed the same enactment for Island and Continental possessions, though their interests and capabilities differed as completely as the market-gardens around London and the Highlands of Scotland.

In a conversation one day in the lobby of the House of Commons with Mr. Cobden, then representing the West Riding of Yorkshire, I complained to him of the restless and fault-finding nature of his friend, Mr. Bright; and urged on his notice that he attacked everything that came in his way. He agreed with me.

"Yes, I have often told Bright," he replied,

"that so pugnacious were his inclinations, if he had not been a Quaker he would have been a prize-fighter."

It chanced a few days after this conversation that there was a debate on the question of Slavery and the interests of the West India proprietors, when Mr. Bright got up and made an attack as usual on the latter, perfectly wild and erroneous in all the points he urged, and, as usual, very unjust. My attendance on the Committee having put me well up in the matter, I replied to him, and took occasion to taunt him not only with erroneous views of a matter he did not understand, but with always being inclined to find fault when blame was not justly due.

The latter remark he cheered in a dissenting tone.

"Does the honourable member by his cheer mean to deny his invariable propensity to attack?" I asked.

"Yes."

"Well then," I continued, "let me ask the honourable member, if in this matter of his propensity to attack, as well as in all others, he has faith—implicit faith, in all that is advanced or uttered by his honourable friend sitting now near him, the member for the West Riding?"

"I have," he replied.

"Just so," I said; "I am very glad that you pledge yourself to the truth of all he says, for no longer ago than the day before yesterday that honourable member assured me he had often told his friend (Mr. Bright), that so pugnaciously inclined was he by natural disposition, if he had not been a Quaker he would have been a prize-fighter."

The House went into fits of laughter at this announcement, in which Messrs. Cobden and Bright could not help joining.

CHAPTER XV.

DOINGS AT BERKELEY CASTLE.

Lord Segrave's compact with the Whig Government—Returns four members for the county, and is created an Earl—My influence for him and with him—Miss Foote and Mrs. Bunn at Berkeley Castle—Lord Fitzhardinge at this period—Sir George Wombwell—Accident to a valuable horse—My successful interposition—My brother Admiral Berkeley's serious fall in the hunting field—Lady Charlotte sent for at my request—Reports about the goings on at the Castle—Paul Methuen's parting with his host—Lord Fitzhardinge and the Severn pilot—The Bristol mayor and his offensive speech—Sir Alexander Leith Hay cooking—He becomes my second and exacts an apology—Affairs of honour in which I acted as second—Lord Macdonald, Lord Albemarle, and Mr. Drax (member for Wareham)—Sir Alexander Hood—Captain Berkeley and Squire Osbaldeston.

ANOTHER general election was not far off, and before it took place I found that Lord Segrave had made a bargain with the Whig Government that if he returned four of his brothers to Parliament instead of three, all in support of what were termed the Liberal opinions, they were to promote him again, creating him earl. It was as much a matter of engagement or a case of barter as any mercantile transaction could be.

Lord Segrave did return four of his brothers for the Western Division of the county, the city of Bristol, the city of Gloucester, and the town of Chel-

COMPACT WITH THE WHIGS.

tenham, and was immediately created Earl Fitz-hardinge. He now had got all he wanted, and obtained it chiefly through me—my own position to assist him being so strong that, for upwards of fifteen years or thereabouts, I held my seat for the county without a contest, or costing him a shilling.

While he was gaining these distinctions, and before that time, I had apparently been his favourite brother. I was more with him than any of the others, came and went to the Castle when I liked, and his dependents in and around the old place used to tell me that his lordship was always in better spirits and less morose and violent to them when I was there. than when I was away.

At the time Miss Foote resided at the Castle, I was a good deal there, but still more frequently after her position had been filled by Mrs. Bunn. With the former of these ladies, who was always graceful, gentle, and lady-like, my relations were always agreeable, nor did I ever hear a complaint made of her by any of the household. As to Mrs. Bunn, she was plain, homely, and good-natured to all with whom she came in contact; she gave herself no airs, was retiring and meek in her behaviour, and except that we saw her at the right hand of the head of the table in a chair at dinner, she might have passed for a piece of furniture in the room, so little import-.ance did she assume.

After I had come into the political representation of the division, I was of course a great deal more at the Castle than before; and as year by year Lord Fitz-

B B 2

hardinge led a more retired life as his old male friends
of the county, who up to that time had visited him,
died off, we were a great deal alone together.
The only interval in the twenty-four hours that he
really seemed to be in an undisturbed state of nerve,
was when he retired to the library after dinner, just
before going to bed, to smoke his cigars. Then he was
always, as from his earliest days he had it in his
power to be, a most agreeable companion. He assured
me that those hours with his cigar were the only
happy ones of his existence. Often and often have I
wondered at that announcement, for then, though
growing old, he retained nearly all the health and
strength of manhood, and I could not comprehend
why he should be at any time unhappy or at a loss
for amusement, with unlimited wealth at his command, and with a magnificent stable full of horses and
a kennel of hounds, the latter most agreeable to my
fancy, unless he was dissatisfied in his conscience with
his position, and the sort of life he had been leading,
and under that influence could not rise to the enjoyment of things that money and his usurped position
put at his command.

He was well read in all the poets, of course immensely "up" in Shakespeare. He spoke French
fluently, knew Italian, and no one could converse
better of the transactions in the world. The thing
that during the day really made him a burthen to
himself and a wet blanket to all who shared with him
the sports of the field, was a kind of nervous irrita-
bility that, from breakfast time till dinner, rendered

ACCIDENT IN THE HUNTING FIELD. 373

him almost passionately insane. Many of us who had got used to this mood of his, were amused at it, or at the curious scenes it created, and it nearly killed with suppressed laughter the late Sir George Wombwell, who was one of the few frequently at the Castle, when any of those strange incidents ot causeless anger used to occur in or out of the Castle walls.

On all occasions regarding the household, in and out of doors, I was made the medium by which a more agreeable state of things was attained. By way of illustrating this, I will recur to an event that occurred in the hunting field. One of his men riding a second horse, an entire horse, and if I remember rightly, nearly or quite thoroughbred, and a magnificent animal, had not swung a gate sufficiently from him that the latter might get safely through, and closing too suddenly it drove his hind quarters against the post, forcing the iron fastening at the gate-post, or the gate, I forget which, into the thigh near the stifle, tearing a mass of sinews to the bone—in fact, rendering the destruction of the horse inevitable.

I was on with the hounds, when first one yeoman farmer came up and then another with dismay on their faces, each avoiding his lordship and seeking me, to tell me what had happened. All requested that I would return to see the poor fellow who had been the cause of this accident. At first I thought that he must be hurt, but as I turned to go back, another rider of a second horse rode up.

"My fellow-servant, sir," he said, "wants to

speak to you before the mishap reaches my lord's ears."

I went back, ascertained the hopeless state of the horse, and then acceded to the entreaties of the servant, who was with him, that I would be the first to tell his master.

I was the first to mention it, and to ask my brother not to be angry with the man who, I represented, had quite suffered enough from his own regrets. He did not lose his situation, he was not even scolded, though the horse died shortly afterwards.

It was the same with the tenantry: they used to come to me to put in a word for them as to the repairs of farm buildings, or other estate business, which I must say was the only part of estate transactions that, in my opinion, Lord Fitzhardinge neglected. In short, I was on such good terms with him, that I should as soon have dreamed of a quarrel with the man in the moon as one with Lord Fitzhardinge.

All that I accomplished at Berkeley Castle was without an idea of further service to myself. I acted as I did because it always gave me pleasure to do a goodnatured thing by others.

It was while I thus held a sort of lead at the Castle, that my brother Frederick, the present Lord Fitzhardinge, on a rushing beast of a horse he had, caught a terrible fall at a small blind place not far from Redwood. The hounds were not running hard. I saw him fall, and that the horse fell on him, and that he remained on the ground. Dismounting, it was at once apparent to me that he was so much hurt

INTERCESSION BETWEEN BROTHERS. 375

that a carriage must be sent for as well as a doctor ; so, leaving my quiet, steady hunter, one from the Castle stables, for him to ride as far as the nearest farm-house, I got on his horse and galloped off to the Castle to give the necessary orders for a carriage. Admiral Berkeley was then brought to the Castle, terribly shaken and bruised, and apparently with some damage to the ribs. He was confined to his bed, and suffered the most intense agony.

Some few days after this, on our return from hunting, Lord Fitzhardinge having gone, as was his usual custom before dressing for dinner, to tell the French cook at what hour it was to be served, I went up to see my brother Frederick, and found him in great pain, excessively depressed in mind and body, thinking badly of his hurt, and longing for the presence of his wife by his bedside to nurse him. He requested me to ask Lord Fitzhardinge if Lady Charlotte might come, adding, "If you can't do me this immense favour, no one else can."

I saw that he watched most anxiously the effect of this appeal to me, terribly low about himself as he was ; so, though I knew it was sure to be distasteful to Lord Fitzhardinge, I at once said, "Of course I will do as you wish ; she *must* come."

He sank back on his pillow with tears in his eyes, with a far different expression of countenance to that which his face wore when in uncertainty, and I hastened away after Lord Fitzhardinge. As I came into the inner courtyard from the donjon keep, I met him about to ascend the stairs towards his apartment, and at once preferred our brother Frederick's request. He was excessively wrath, attempting to cut me very short.

"You know it's impossible," he said.

"I know no such thing," I replied, firmly.

"Why, is not Mrs. Bunn here?"

"Yes; but with that you have nothing to do as a reason for your refusal; that is Lady Charlotte's business, not ours. The wish is expressed from what Frederick seems to regard as his sick-bed of danger, and, in common humanity, you cannot keep Lady Charlotte away if her husband desires her presence, and *she will come*."

"Humph!" he cried, in the greatest fury and disgust; "you know I dislike her—her presence is always hateful to me. But there, mind, it's your business, not mine; I'll have nothing to do with it; bring her here, *if you like;* I wash my hands of the whole concern."

He went up to dress for dinner, fuming with rage, while I wrote a few lines to ask Lady Charlotte to come. She was only at the short distance of Tortworth, staying with her brother, Lord Ducie, and I despatched it by a speedy messenger on horseback. To Frederick I imparted the favour, which, though he had hoped for, he had seemed little to expect, and then gave orders that a suite of rooms adjoining his should be instantly prepared, putting that keep-garden wing of the Castle entirely at their occupation, as perfectly to themselves, and as private as if they had had the apartments in some other

INGRATITUDE. 377

house. Lady Charlotte came at once, and remained in the Castle till my brother's convalescence.

It is with deep satisfaction now that I remember this *the last occasion* that I had it in my power to do a kind thing by the present Lord Fitzhardinge. I had previously tried to make up his temporary quarrels with both the late Lord Fitzhardinge and Mr. Henry Berkeley, with the former arising from a political difference, and with the latter about a railway bubble into which Henry had led the Admiral, to his very considerable embarrassment. It is a remembrance that dwells pleasantly on my mind, now that my brother's, the present Lord Fitzhardinge's, hand is raised against me. It is a comfort to me to know, whatever their conduct has been since, that, while opportunity offered, I never lost a chance in which I could prove my affectionate attention to my brothers, or do them service.

The most absurd reports had been set about in regard to the life Lord Fitzhardinge led while, as Colonel Berkeley, he resided at the Castle. Sir George Wombwell was staying with him, when Paul Methuen, afterwards Lord Methuen, came for a visit of a few days. My brother, as he did by everybody, entertained him with the greatest hospitality. In the morning on which Methuen was to take his leave, before he went, the host had come into the breakfast-room, where his friend had just finished his breakfast, and the following scene occurred :—

Colonel Berkeley had just commenced on a breakfast-cake, so Sir George Wombwell described it to

378 COLONEL BERKELEY AND LORD METHUEN.

me, when Methuen came up to him and in the following words wished him adieu.

"I have been delighted, Colonel Berkeley, with all I have seen here, and I shall now go back to my friends and relations, and tell them those improper stories we had all of us heard about what goes on in your Castle are a fabrication, and not worthy——"

Wombwell assured me that, during this speech, Colonel Berkeley continued stuffing huge pieces of cake into his mouth apparently to stop any rough rejoinder; and Sir George thought that, if the cake had only lasted out the speech, he would have let his departing guest go in peace. Unfortunately, the cake was swallowed before Methuen had done.

"Humph!" exclaimed the host, looking anything but pleased, "I shall always be happy to see you here, Paul Methuen, but as for your friends and relations, they may——"

Now, all who have the pleasure of Paul Methuen's acquaintance know that his fault, if he had one, was being rather pompous; so when he heard what his friends and relations were to do, he turned short round and rushed through the breakfast-room and the vestibule doors into his own carriage, which was in waiting, with such velocity, that the slam of the three doors made but one simultaneous noise, and the carriage itself rattled off under the gateway as if the horses shared the indignation of their owner.

I had sold, as already related, to Lord Fitzhardinge, my beautiful hunter, Ready, and he was very fond

LORD FITZHARDINGE AND THE SEVERN PILOT. 379

of him; but, as he did with all his horses, he kept him too fat for work. In fact, after the work he had under me, Lord Fitzhardinge's riding him gently after hounds was mere play to him, so, light-hearted as he was, he did nothing but playfully squeak and kick all day.

While the hounds were running, a fence—not a large one—interposed. A huge Severn pilot, named Pick, who was following on foot, jumped over the hedge and ditch; my brother called to him in a voice of thunder, " Here, you sir, catch my horse."

The man had never caught a horse in his life, whatever he might have done by a rope, but such was the terror in which Lord Fitzhardinge was held by all the people around him, had he ordered him to jump at the sun, and put his hat over it, I think he would have attempted to obey.

My brother dismounted, led Ready up to the ditch, and let him jump to the pilot, who apparently stood prepared to receive him, but when the horse landed on the top of the bank, he gave such a squeak and second spring into the air, right at the man, that the latter staggered back, and got out of the way of what he considered an infuriated animal, instead of catching at the reins. Off Ready went, squeaking, leaping, and kicking at the stirrups, following the hounds, while the pilot stood staring after him in a state of the greatest bewilderment.

Lord Fitzhardinge, his hunting-horn in one hand, and his whip in the other, then charged the fence on foot, and in silence, some brambles catching him by the legs, added to his fury; however, he surmounted the bank, and when there, stepped back a pace or two to time his impetus, and suddenly, with a series of swift steps, sent the toe of his boot with immense force against that portion of the pilot's frame which presented the best target. The "ancient mariner" bounded frantically forward, but luckily for him, looked behind, just in time to seé his lordship taking another aim at him with his other boot. Out of his wits with fear, the poor fellow went bang at a corner of the fence where the two hedges joined, right through the bushes, head foremost, as a harlequin takes a leap in a scene in a pantomime, and vanished from his enraged assailant for the rest of the day.

I remember too, when I first began my public life, men in my opponent's camp, who ought to have known better, used to let their tongues run on at political dinners, probably when they had to some extent "put an enemy into their mouths to steal away their brains," in a way that I felt very little inclined to tolerate, but which I used to think Colonel Berkeley was slack in noticing.

After he had been created Lord Segrave, a speech of this sort was made at a public dinner at Bristol, by a gentleman then known as the "Mayor of Brass-heels," from the very large and warlike spurs he used to clash about on the city pavements. The speech was insulting to us all, to my party and to me, but more particularly to Lord Segrave. As soon as this violent effusion was in print, it came to my hands, so, thinking that I had a very good opportunity of put-

THE MAYOR OF BRASSHEELS. 381

ting an end to such things, I walked that evening into the kitchen of the old House of Commons, and therein, among others of my friends, found Sir Alexander Leith Hay, cooking his own mutton-chop, for there were so many dining in the kitchen, as well as in the coffee-room, that the cooks had more than they could do.

He was the very friend I needed, for his coolness and courage were well known. In all such matters I would advise gentlemen to take care that there can be no doubt as to the courage, as well as the high principles of the individual to whom they implicitly entrust their honour.

I tapped him on the shoulder, amid a Babel of friendly and joyous voices, assuring me that I should get nothing to eat. Seeing who it was, he said, " I can't come now; wait a second till my chop is done."

When that important office was concluded, and he had sat down to his repast, I told him what I wanted him for, and showed him the speech. I watched his face as he read the objectionable sentences.

" Well," he cried, " we'll go down to Bristol, and haul this fellow over the coals."

" All right," I replied, " if you'll be ready after the debate is over, the conclusion of which will be early, I'll have my carriage and posters ready, and by travelling through the night, we'll breakfast at Bristol, and get the thing done at once."

We did this, and arrived at Bristol the next morning.

As soon as we had breakfasted, Leith Hay started

382   LORD MACDONALD AND BROADHEAD.

on his mission, saw the Mayor of Brassheels, was by him referred to his second, a gallant and accomplished old soldier, commanding the district, who at once admitted that the language I objected to must be withdrawn, and a written apology for it given, to be retained by us for publication through the press. With this in our pockets we posted back the same day to London, and were again that night in the House of Commons.

It was my lot also to be called in as his second, by a very dear, but now, alas! departed friend of mine, Lord Macdonald, in a quarrel he had with Broadhead, then of the Life Guards, at the supper-table at Crockford's, which I at once disposed of amicably, without giving Broadhead, who was also a friend of mine, the trouble of calling in a friend.

I was also the second of Colonel Keppel (Lord Albemarle), when we received from Mr. O'Kelly the *amende honorable* for an insult the latter had too hastily given. This occurred near Lymington, and from the local notoriety the circumstance acquired, we were obliged to publish the particulars through the press. I attended the member for Wareham, in the same capacity, when Sir Alexander Hood insisted on an apology, and the withdrawal of a letter published by Mr. Drax, commenting on a public speech made by Sir Alexander in reference to some proceedings of his in Dorsetshire.

The demand was untenable, and so I had to inform Sir Alexander that the letter dealt with the matter, not with the man, and as my friend was not present to reply to his allegations, on the spot, he had a perfect right to deal with them through the means by which the speech had obtained publicity, viz., the public press. We, therefore, I added, would not apologize, nor should we withdraw the letter, but should continue to publish it again and again, as often as we pleased.

Sir Alexander Hood informed me that he was under circumstances that would prevent his fighting in England, by which I inferred that he was bound over to keep the peace; so I assured him that I was prepared to start with Mr. Drax at once to Calais. There our conversation ended, and he referred me to his second, who at once admitted that my view of the circumstances could not be combatted, so we repeated the publication.

The most concise settlement of a quarrel I ever heard of, was that wherein the present Lord Fitzhardinge was called in by the "Squire," Osbaldeston, to be his friend in a personal affair that took place in the stand at Goodwood. The Squire had been too violent, and had struck a gentleman, if my remembrance serves me rightly, which necessitated an appeal to arms. Lord Fitzhardinge, at that time I think he was Captain Berkeley, on being asked to be the Squire's friend, replied, "Yes, on the condition that you obey me, as the conductor of the affair."

Osbaldeston agreed to these terms, my brother added, "Then go and beg the gentleman's pardon." The matter, I was told, terminated in an apology.

END OF VOL. I.

CPSIA information can be obtained
at www.ICGtesting.com
Printed in the USA
LVHW111955050422
715401LV00006B/227